The Blind Pool

A novel

Paul McHugh

The Blind Pool
Copyright © 2017 Paul McHugh

Disclaimer:

This book is a work of fiction. All characters, names, businesses, organizations, places, events, and incidents are created by the author's imagination or are used fictitiously. Any resemblance to actual persons, living or dead, events, or locales is total coincidence.

Contact ElkHeart at elkheartbooks@gmail.com
www.elkheartbooks.com

Book production by Cypress House
Cover image: Victor Habbick / Dreamstime.com
Cover design by Kiersten Hanna

ISBN 978-0-9987320-7-7
Library of Congress Control Number: 2017907725

Printed in the United States of America
2 4 6 8 9 7 5 3 1
First edition

No price is too great for the scalp of
the enemy king.

— *Alexander Kohlentz, chessmaster*

Dedicated to heroes of journalism, governance and justice —
all those who battle for truth and fair play.

Chapter 1

Florida's Overseas Highway is a gray band linking isles of the Keys via bridges that arch over channels of turquoise water. On this day, as Highway 1 leaps across a channel to connect Boca Chica with Key West, it bears glittering rows of stalled automobiles. A few cars display geysers spurting up from radiators while drivers jig around their front bumpers, ineffectually waving rags.

"Just 'nother day in paradise," drawls Dan Cowell. He drapes an arm out the window of his own car — a vintage red Miata — and flicks open a button on his rayon shirt with his other hand.

"We not movin', okay, not a centimeter, even!" his companion, Linda Parker marvels. "And so-o long."

"We're near peak of tourist season," Dan says. "Add a holiday. Stir in a traffic accident. There's your recipe for happiness, *beyb*."

Dan says the word "babe" using a long and strong vowel, in the Caribbean's Creole argot. Saying it this way is part of their code of intimacy.

She peers out from her side the car at the blue waters that ripple beneath the highway bridge. Tiny wavelets fling back sparks of sunlight.

"We are not so high up," she says. "Let us jump into water, make a swim 'round to our place. Serious!"

Dan smiles. Linda is a young, strong Moskita Indian woman, raised on an island off the coast of Honduras. She's fully able to act on her suggestion.

"Might's well. Our highway seems 'bout done being a street." He gives a languid shrug. "Guess we're in a park-and-lock lot now…"

Bass vibrations telegraph an approach of powerful machinery. Dan checks his mirrors and sees two lines of big motorcycles bearing down on them from the east. One line seeks to thread the gap between the lanes of stopped cars, the other rumbles along the bridge's narrow shoulder.

"Shit. Crank up your window." Dan gestures with his thumb. "We're about to get hammered by noise."

Large bikes leading the pack are fattened by saddlebags and chromium crash bars. A massive Honda Gold Wing FGB touring machine roars by on the right, while a purple Harley CVO Road King thumps past on their left. Dan sees that the rider on the Harley is as bulky as his bike. Thick shoulders thrust out through armholes of a black leather vest to strain the long sleeves of a white T-shirt. Curve of his belly and chest bulge over the motorcycle's gas tank. His neck seems wider than the Nazi-style helmet on his head.

"Ah-ha," Linda says. "Here now is American motorcycle gang, jus' like your movies, right?"

"No!" Dan speaks loudly to be heard. "Only wannabes! Don't have on cuts, patches or colors. Plus, real gangbangers straddle Harleys. Wouldn't be caught dead on anything else. I only see one."

A few cars beyond the Miata, the motorcycles try to squeeze by a broad Cadillac sedan. The Honda rider can't make it on the right, he stops and insistently beeps his horn. The Caddy driver tries to swing a yard to his left, almost hits the Harley. That rider lifts a foot and boots off the car's side mirror. The sedan backs up and makes a panicked lurch to the right, just in time to smack into a sleeker machine trying to follow the Honda — knocking the bike and its rider into the guardrail with a boom and a screech of metal.

Motorcycles dip over their front wheels as they brake to a halt. Riders swing legs off over the seats, lean their motorcycles on kickstands. The engines keep running. The Harley rider loosens his helmet and strides back to the motorcycle behind his — a BMW GTL with so many antennas sprouting from a case bolted onto its rear luggage rack, it looks like a highway patrol vehicle.

Dan now sees the big rider wears over his nose and mouth a bandana printed with the naked cheekbones and jaw of a skull. He points at the BMW rider, who hits switches mounted on his handlebars. The Harley guy nods, stomps over to the Caddy. He yanks his helmet off a shaven head. He punches it into the driver's side window, bashing the glass into a spray of green crumbs. Through a succession of other windshields in front of him, Dan sees a dim pair of white-haired people who cower on the Caddy's front seat.

"Oh fuck," he says, "Now that just ain't right."

He plucks a cell phone from the pocket of his shirt and passes it to Linda. "Dial up 911, *beyb*? Tell 'em what's goin' on out there."

He yanks open the door and exits his car. He walks toward the Caddy through a haze of percussion that beats from the tailpipes of idling motorcycles. He sees the big Harley guy lean into the sedan's busted window and start yelling. Dan walks faster. Other riders smirk as they step out of his path.

"Hey, check it! This lame-o wants to bump chests with Tank!" one rider exclaims.

"That's a show," another says. "Guar-ran-teed."

The old folks in the Caddy have slid across to the passenger door. They stare, bug-eyed with fear, at the man haranguing them.

"Hey," Dan says, closing in. "Quit that!"

The big man pulls back from the window. The skull-print cloth that had covered his mouth has fallen around his neck. Dan sees stubbly jowls, a broad nose, and intense, close-set eyes with irises so pale they seem nearly white. He never sees the arm swinging a fist up into his stomach. That mighty punch drives air from his lungs and sends him flying across the pavement to thump against the side of a minivan one lane over. He flops into a heap, and all his attention focuses on where his next breath might come from.

He hears a hoarse, faraway voice grind out, "Dammit, you ol' farts just crunched a prime ride. Worth a hundred K! To make us whole, you'll do what? Sell this joke of a car?"

Dan finds himself able to gasp in a pint of breath, another. He levers himself on an elbow, grips the door latch of the van, and pulls himself onto his feet. He sees the big man plus two other riders hoist the damaged motorcycle up into the air, then tumble it over the bridge's railing. He only vaguely comprehends what he sees, since it makes no sense, and barely registers the sound of a distant splash.

The riders come around the Caddy, kicking at it, smashing the taillights and booting dents into its fenders. The big one has his Nazi *Stahlhelm* back atop his boulder of a head, and the skull-print bandana tugged again over his nose. He sees Dan, and waves a hand.

"Hey, bros, look!" he says. "Our citizen shook off his chin-check."

He strides to Dan. He's at least six-foot-eight, has to weigh more than three hundred pounds. Pale eyes study Dan. He tilts his head. "Aw-w-w," he says. "Did I hurt lil' punk's feelings? Let's hug it out." Thick arms encompass Dan's chest and upper back. He's instantly crushed into the broad stiff plates of the giant's vest — he realizes it actually is body armor — and into a miasma of leather and rancid sweat. His ribs creak from the remorseless force. He feels the man's crotch gyrate obscenely against him.

"Feelin' any better *now*?" he croons. "I am! Wanna be my lil' bitch? After I turn you out, we'll pass you all 'round."

It sets off a bout of raucous laughter.

Dan squirms to escape, which makes the big rider shove him firmly back into the van and dry-hump his body. The others howl with glee. Dan twists hard and kicks the man in the lower leg with all his strength. His assailant merely grunts, and the white eyes narrow. He swings open his arms, cuffs Dan across the face as he falls, then snatches him with one hand by the nape of the neck and hoists him up so his feet barely drag on the pavement.

"Like it savage? Hey, me too! You won't sit for a week."

And suddenly, Linda is there.

"You! Let 'im go! Now, I say!"

As she rushes in, the other riders try to haul her back. She swats their hands aside then leaps like a wildcat, going for the leader's eyes with her nails. They grab her and yank her away. But the leader beckons.

"No. Lemme have her," he says.

They propel her forward. The big man catches her by the back of her neck with his free hand. Dan and Linda gape at each other, beat with their fists at the hideous power of the big man's grip, try to twist and kick themselves free.

"Hey," he says. "Your squeeze? Mud-bitch and her race betrayer! Hot for each other, huh? So... let's see some licks."

He brings them closer together. "Go, kissy-kissy," he growls.

Linda jerks up her chin and spits a gob of saliva just past his face.

He scowls. Dan sees knuckles on the huge hand whiten, also notices a strange detail, the end of one middle finger is emblazoned with dark lines of a tattoo of a letter "Y" that wavers like a rune. He feels his own body swing helplessly as the big man spreads his arms and pulls them apart... and then accelerates their faces directly at each other. Dan tries to duck, to turn or thrust out an elbow, to do anything that might soften the coming collision.

None of it reduces the impact. He smashes the heads of Dan and Linda together with a vicious *crack*, lets their limp bodies drop. As he steps over them, he wipes his sweaty palms on his vest. His crew laughs, applauds. His gaze wanders across windows of cars nearby. Occupants shrink back inside those vehicles, avert their faces, desperate to avoid drawing attention to themselves.

He gives a brief, amused snort.

"Let's be smart," the leader says. "Sanitize the crime scene."

"Wha'chu like, Big T?" another rider asks.

"One-eight-seven these fish." He gestures toward the bridge railing. "Put 'em over."

Through a dim red haze of lapsing consciousness, Dan feels his wrists and ankles seized by rough hands. A moment of weightlessness follows, next a hard smack of water against his upper back and shoulders. The tiny spot of awareness left to him takes in a procession of colors that swirl before his eyes, blue, green, indigo and back to blue again. He realizes that he's underwater, and spinning.

Linda, Linda… he thinks as he struggles to clear his brain, to make his limbs move. *They must have thrown her in too! Got to… revive. Find her.*

The big rider looks down at the channel, and a double trail of bubbles that rise from the dark, azure shapes of the sinking bodies.

"Yah, bros," he says. "Done 'bout best we can, I reckon. Deek? Let ol' Cranker warm your back, 'til we snatch another ride. High time for us to roll, 'case John Law gets his ass in gear and tries to crash our party. Right?"

Chapter 2

"Eggs. Didn't we have more?"

Dan yanks his head out of the fridge to look back at Linda. She sits on a canvas folding chair, beside a coffee table made from an old wooden cable spool. A copy of the *New Keys Weekly* lies unfolded in her lap.

"Only two," she says. "But I can go get us some."

"Nah, bag the omelet idea. I'll cook up pancakes."

"Really, I go," she says. "Not a problem."

She pitches her newspaper up onto the table. Its front page bears a large photo of Dan and Linda from five days earlier — a shot in which their heads are swaddled in so much white gauze they look like Q-tips with human faces. The photo had been snapped in a waiting room of Lower Keys Medical Center, where they were being questioned by Key West's chief of police.

"No, see," he says. "It is."

"How?"

He points at the newspaper. "We're famous for all the wrong reasons." He gestures at his own battered face, and at hers. "Ready to handle follow-up questions? 'So, how do you feel? Who do you think they were? Why haven't police caught 'em? Are you still mad? What charges will you bring if they're arrested?' Blah-blah-blah."

She scrutinizes him. "Why you guess they ask us for so much?"

"Went down *just* that way a minute ago. I went out to snag that paper, and I caught an earful from Dev Baker next door."

She tilts her head. "If a person asks a story about what happens to us, it makes you shame?"

"Oh, come on. We were friggin' humiliated! Who needs to be reminded? Those idiots showed me up in the worst way."

"No." She shakes her head emphatically. "Not true. To me, you are that man in the old photo at China. Who stands in the middle of the road to make all those tanks stop? You are hero, totally, 'nah mean? Many on one, yet still you go. And who else tries to stop the guy from scaring the old folk? Nobody."

"Hey. *You* stood up to that shaved gorilla, too."

She smiles. "You are fonny," she says. "And you say it ju-u-s' right! Yes, he is ape, but no hair."

He walks to her, reaches out a hand, pinches her chin gently, turns her face up.

"I mus' fight, y'know," she says. "When this giant monkey dare to hit my *beyb*."

"But if you just let me deal, you would not've gotten hurt. What pisses me the most is that he used my own fuckin' head to hurt you."

He looks rueful, sighs. Almost a week after the savage encounter on the bridge, their original turbans of gauze are reduced to plaster-doused bands worn across their cheekbones to stabilize their re-set noses. The eyes of both remain blackened and bloodshot, and they have purple, blue and ocher blotches of bruised facial tissue extending from forehead to chin.

"Oh well. Too bad we're near Thanksgiving," Dan says. "Could've made these rainbow raccoon masks really work for us on Halloween."

"Don't!" Linda warns. "My face hurts when you make me laugh."

"Okay. No jokes. Hey, looks like Mr. Coffee's done his job. Ready for a cup?"

"Yes. Is there milk?"

"No, sorry. How 'bout a glob of mayo, instead?"

"Ouch. Stop, you!"

~

They sit outside, on the back porch of their little rented bungalow, at the end of a narrow lane paved with crushed limestone. A tottering wooden fence topped with a cloud of bougainvillea blossoms casts a violet glow into the fanning rays of a morning sun.

"Well, grub wasn't bad. Such as it was, and what there was of it," Dan says, wiping his lips with a paper towel. Their pancakes were improved by finding pats of butter in the fridge, a quarter-bottle of Vermont maple syrup, and a small bag of wild blueberries in the freezer compartment.

"You make food out of nothin'," she says. "This is a great skill."

"Yeah. Learned how as a kid. Often had to feed myself breakfast, then pack my own lunch. Necessity can be a mother..."

"Yes, see? We live great without so much."

"I *do* know how to stretch a dollar. Bu-u-ut you still need something to stretch. Been meaning to say, our piggy bank's getting light. Couldn't bring much cash out of Honduras, since we didn't want to be grilled at Customs. More's being sent, but that takes major finagling, and I've not yet heard when it will arrive."

"And this means?"

"*Hate* to mention the 'j-word,' but we might need to go out and find us some jobs."

"That is not so..."

Linda is interrupted by the bass bellow of a motorcycle exhaust. They look at each other wide-eyed. The machine sounds as if it's coming rapidly down their lane.

"Shit!" Dan leaps to his feet. "Those jerks back after us? Run in and call the cops!"

"You..."

"Don't fuckin' worry about me. Go!"

He glances rapidly around the porch, looking for anything that might serve as a weapon. His eye settles on a small, classic anchor, warted with barnacles and corrosion. He'd found it on a recent dive and hauled it back ashore to use as a yard decoration. He wrenches the stock loose — a steel rod used as a crossbar — from the anchor's shank. Swinging the weighty bar by one end, he sprints around the corner of the house.

A motorcycle is pulling up, a huge red V-twin with wide handlebars, flared fenders, and fishtail exhaust pipes that spurt out sharp bass thuds. Its lanky rider wears a cut — a denim jacket with the sleeves sheared off — that bears a single rocker patch low on the back, with the word "nomad" stitched on it. Above that is a cartoon face with everything but its angry eyes concealed by a camo *keffiyeh*.

The rider himself wears a matte-black half-helmet, old-style aviator goggles, has a thin ginger beard running around the rim of his jaw to blend with a fringe of chestnut hair swinging below the helmet's edge. His arms show generous curves of sculpted muscle, bare of tattoos. He shuts down his machine, leans it over, and dismounts.

Dan runs up as the rider swings down his kickstand, and pokes the man hard in the middle of his back with the steel bar.

"Get back on your putt and ride the hell away. *Now!*" he demands. "If you know what's good for you."

The rider turns, faces him squarely. "Oh fer chrissakes," he says, "that any way to greet yer ol' pard?"

The vocal twang from rural Texas is disturbingly familiar. The rider loosens his helmet, tugs it and the goggles off his head. Dan finds himself gazing at a lantern-jawed man with intense gray eyes — he bears some resemblance to British action star Jason Statham, but he stands two inches taller and owns more hair.

"Shit. Carl!" Dan exclaims, in rueful recognition. He turns his head and shouts toward the house. "*Beyb*? Those cops? You got 'em on the line, tell 'em to cool their jets. Never mind!"

"Hey, all cool already," the rider says. "Made a courtesy call at the copshop, soon as I hit town. Also let it be known that I was comin' to see you."

~

The new visitor is Carl Blackadar, a USN veteran like Dan. They'd been adversaries and bitter competitors amid training days at Coronado, then went through a long period of separation in different branches of the Navy. They met by chance again in Honduras, where they were forced to ditch their enmity and become allies in order to extricate themselves from a battle with a drug cartel. At that time, Carl worked as chief-of-station for the CIA in the Honduran capital, while Dan was an ex-pat vet who hoped to build a diving resort on a remote island off the coast. Trouble erupted when the cartel chose to use that very same island as a base. Now, a year later, Carl has a discreet job with federal law enforcement in Washington, while Dan and his gal Linda have just been hanging out and loving life in Key West — burning through funds that Dan had scored through a variety of scams. Dan's morals have never been as unyielding as Carl's. It was one reason they'd initially been at odds.

Dan and Carl drag a pair of the veranda's wicker chairs around into the warm sunlight — which is shifting around to shine on the front of the house — and put them on a miserable patch of crabgrass that constitutes the cottage's lawn.

As they begin to talk, Linda interrupts to announce she won't let Dan delay or dissuade her, she insists on going out this instant to buy fresh groceries so she'll be able to assemble a proper lunch for their new guest. She pedals away on her rusty beach cruiser.

Dan admires the motorcycle Carl parked. "What is it, an Indian Chief, new model by Polaris? Power's humongous, right, with 111 cubes?"

Carl shakes his head. "That's a machine worth only twenty grand or so. Not swank enough to make your bad lads get hot and bothered. No, this un's the real deal. A restored 1950 Indian Black Hawk, buffed out and showroom ready. Worth maybe sixty, seventy. Feds confiscated it during a drug raid, and loaned it to me."

"To use as a bait for the cycle thugs?"

Carl nods. "They're still here on the Keys, might smoke 'em out. If just to kick the tires."

"Isn't making a collar on a pack of greasy road bums way-y-y below your pay grade?"

"Usually, yeah, it would be," Carl concedes. "But ain't no ordinary gang. That bike you saw get smashed on the bridge, then they just pitched it over the rail? Coast Guard hauled it out of the drink yesterday. It's a Vyrus 987 from Italy, state-of-the-art, supercharged, with a pricetag runnin' north of 90K. What's that tell you?"

"They're picky."

"Right. But they're also willin' to just toss it? *Boom.* Zero hesitation. As soon as an asset turns into a hazard, it's gone. Tells *me*, stealin' motorcycles is a thing they do with military discipline. If that don't clue you, let me try something else…"

"Yeah?"

"Man they stole this bike from was a millionaire in West Palm, and to get it they gunned him down. Right out in front of a roadside café on Southern Boulevard. Just a single round, put a .22 short right here." Carl taps the back of his neck at the base of the skull. "Pro-grade placement. Lets the lead rattle around in his head and deform, making it hard to trace. And they also used a revolver. No expended cartridge left lying about."

Dan whistles slowly. "So… what you're saying is, Linda and I got let off easy."

"So far." Carl raises an admonitory finger. "But I recommend you take further measures. Like, go to ground for a while, someplace distant."

"Hm." Dan frowns. "Actually, that's a notion we had already. Our plan was to be rolling stones over the next few months. But, tell me. How'd you pick up on this mob, and so goddam quick? I mean, you were up in Washington. How's this ever pop on *your* screen?"

"Popped on someone else's screen first," Carl admits. "But I got pinged 'cos of a detail that you mentioned to the cops. You saw some kind of wiggly 'Y' tattoo above the knuckle on the big bastard's middle finger."

"I did. And?"

"Let's spoon up some alphabet soup. The FBI, in 2007, launched the BCOE, its Biometric Center of Excellence. That devotes staff and equipment to facial recognition, iris scans and palm prints. Bolsters stuff they already had up, like IAFIS, the automated fingerprint system. Now there's NGI, Next Generation Identification, to study things like scars, hair patterns, body marks, tattoos.

"Just lately, an outfit drawin' our interest is a secret global ring. Some of their lead dudes wear tattoo squiggles like the one you described. Transactions monitored by the CIA suggest these guys are into top-drawer, international theft. No foolin'. Stealin' a few bikes and assaultin' citizens might be mild entertainment for 'em. We call 'em the 'Y's guys."

"*We*? The FBI? Aha! So, that's who you work for these days."

Carl's smiles, shakes his head. "Oh, I'm majorly damaged goods. Couldn't get me a job anywhere near that important."

"Uh-huh."

"No, really. 'Member that video shot of me at the drug compound with those Hondos? Well, it leaked. My cover is *kaput*, since anyone who wants to can easily find out what I look like. Plus, at a high government level, I've become a total laughin' stock."

"Hey, none of that crap was ever your fault. And you were not only tough enough to survive, you chased a drug sub and took it down."

"Oh, there's more. I also got convicted of solicitin' a bribe. Internal hearings discharged me from every form of federal service. With prejudice."

Dan studies him. "Horse-puckey," he says, after a moment. "What I bet? You've been sent off into some kind of double-deep undercover."

Carl throws back his head to laugh. "Haw! I'm not the only one 'round here with a hidden life," he says. "*You*, sir, roam about pretendin' to be just a dumb cowpoke who stumbled out of rural Wyoming. Am I right, Cow-bell?"

"Right. When actually, I'm the abandoned love-child of Albert Einstein and Tammy Wynette. My existence was hidden from a scandal-hungry media by stashing me away on a ranch near Laramie. I got raised by ravens and prairie dogs, all of whom were sworn to silence."

"See? Just *knew* it had to be a thing like that, all along. Means you and I are not so damn different, when you come right down to it."

"OK, 'nuff of the bull. Back to the so-called 'Y's guys. You make 'em sound like whizz-kids. But I can tell you, all of 'em talked and acted like a bunch of chuckle-headed morons. Furthest thing in the world from a criminal mastermind."

"Maybe some of 'em *were* boneheads," Carl concedes. "Maybe most. But the big dude runnin' the show could have a lil' more goin' on. All I'm sayin'."

Gravel under the fat tires of Linda's beach cruiser makes an audible crunch as she turns her bicycle down the lane. She pedals toward them, with a canvas bag of groceries swinging from the handlebars.

Dan waggles his fingertips at her in a small wave and looks back at Carl. "So. Those squiggles. The 'Y' tats. That got your attention. How'd you find out *we* were involved?"

"Started off just lookin' like a federal hate-crime in the assault on you and her…" he nods at Linda. "Due to the racist language. That's why your local blues passed a report onto the Bureau. The 'Y' tat deal put a ping on my screen. Then I checked the report, and scratched my head when I saw your name. How many Dan Cowell's could there be?"

"Nowhere near enough."

Carl grins. "Seein' Linda's name too kinda cinched it. Normally, a lower-level agent might have followed up, but I asked for the case to be given to my detail."

"Which is?"

"Need to know, *compadre*."

"Right. You hide behind a dumpster in an alley, back of FBI headquarters. Get rancid cases everybody else throws out. No standing whatsoever." Dan sighs heavily, shakes his head. "Might've grown your hair out, Jar-dar, but *inside* you've not changed a bit. You keep about as leakproof as a bullfrog's hiney."

Linda leans her bike against the wall, holds up her canvas bag. "I buy roast adobo chicken," she announces. "Cuban bread, mango-avocado salad from the deli, and Honduras coffee. So for our lunch, we go feast!"

"Perfect," Dan says. "Anyone in the store bother you about the assault?"

"They try to do," she affirms. "But then I say to them, you many times punch at me and I hit you back, serious, so I often look this way. And you too."

"Oh, great."

"Hey. They stop ask me questions." She shrugs.

"Well, if you don't mind, I'd still like to pitch you a few," Carl says.

Below the sprawl of her nose plaster, Linda's teeth gleam in a smile. But she flinches immediately and shuts the grin down. "Whatever, sure."

"On the bridge, when you tried to call for help, what happened?"

"I dial 911, as Dan asks. But I hear one ring, then, only buzz. And next, it shows no signal."

"Interestin'. No one else in a big radius all around you could make a call, either. We think they had a couple CTS signal jammers going. They're illegal, but a guy with the right — or wrong! — connections can find 'em. Or even fancier stuff. A driver nearby tried to make a video of the assault, but couldn't record. Our only images came from further up the road, where someone was idly shootin' a wide panorama of Florida Bay as that mob went by."

"So, at least you got license plate numbers?"

"Yep, saw some plates. But they're of no use."

"Stolen?"

"Uh-uh. Look just like genuine plates, but their numbers don't exist. I mean, as real vehicle registrations."

"Hm."

"Pickin' up some sense of how sharp these ol' boys might be?"

"I guess. But I was already wracking my brains over the way they vanished once they hit Key West. *How?* It's the end of the road, a cul-de-sac! Is that bunch holed up in some warehouse? Or did they manage to sneak out at night, one-by-one, back up the highway?"

"Dan." Carl looks at him. "Key West is a what, surrounded by what?"

"Ah-hah-h-h." He exhales, looking embarrassed. "Boats!"

Carl nods. "One suspect was the *Caribbean Marquess*, a cruise ship that was docked at the harbor's main pier and sailed the next mornin'.

Coast Guard held her up en route to Nassau and searched while her captain stomped around on the bridge, pissin' his shorts. But? *Nada.*

"Or they could have shipped out on a couple of fishin' boats, I suppose, or some kind of cargo vessel. Inter-island traders still chug through here. We're also interested in four large yachts that sailed out, just recent. We'll check 'em when they make another port-of-call."

Carl gives Dan a toothy grin and arches both eyebrows, achieving a look that goes about halfway to Jack Nicholson's appearance as he played The Joker.

"That's where *you* come in."

"Me?"

"Sure. You and Linda are the sole eyewitnesses who can make a positive ID on our lead baddie. Other than the elderly folks... but they're still so rattled they can barely talk. If we get you onsite in a foreign jurisdiction, officials there would be way-y more likely to let us make a bust."

"Got one e-ee-ntsy problem." Dan scowls. "Last time I scampered off with you? Wound up in a worse mess than I ever could've made on my own."

"See it 'zactly the other way, my man. You pulled me into a nasty, not vicey-versa. Anyhow, you're already in a hole."

"How so?"

"Think *only* guys from the law side have you tagged as an eyewitness? Your toss off the bridge looks like attempted murder. You weren't meant to survive. It was like they were throwin' away a couple bags of dirt. Didn't figure you to be rubber balls, bouncin' back onto the scene. Must be tougher than you look, hey? Maybe smarter, so more of a threat as well."

Carl eyes him.

"Since you didn't oblige those suckers by gettin' dead, they could take another swing. Caution is advised. In addition to blowin' town, you oughta mull over signin' onto our home team. More safety in numbers — know what I mean?"

Chapter 3

After lunch, Carl thumps away from the cottage on his vintage Indian motorcycle. And then, Dan and Linda chew over some revelations from the morning's conversation.

"I do not feel what Carl says to us about Mel is clear," Linda says — referring to their final group topic. "I am very suspicious that Carl holds us away."

Mel is Melanie Olson Symes, a prominent former journalist, and the divorced wife of a wealthy Seattle congressman, who had become deeply ensnared in the mayhem their quartet had endured down in Honduras.

"You mean, Carl's holding out on us? Well sometimes, you need to look at what he *can't* tell you as his only way of saying it." Dan says.

Linda stares at him. "Say this again, please?"

"Um, not sure I can. But listen to his silences. When Carl avoids giving a straight answer, could be 'cos your question's spot-on."

"But Melanie, she is a lover to him now. He should be so proud in what she does. Why will he not say? Is she still wishing to be a FBI?"

"She went into the FBI's Academy, we know that. Didn't try to join because she needed a job. More like, our lil' fracas down in Honduras got Mel addicted to excitement. Plus, she worked once as a reporter. If she becomes a Special Agent, she'll be able to not only ask questions, but also brandish her credentials and demand the truth! Bet you that notion has a lot of pull for her."

"You think she wishes to work like Carl?"

"Like he does? Sure. Maybe, more'n that. Could be hoping to work right beside him."

"Oh, on a team? Like your Scully and Mulder?" Linda seems intrigued.

"Sure," Dan grins. "Absolutely! That TV show and everything about it. Except for the UFOs."

Linda frowns. "Also, Melanie and Carl, I now be guessin' they argue too much more."

"Uh-huh, right, one glitch. They do both seem to love their tiffs, huh? But a still bigger prob' might be his status. Carl now operates at a level so high I get a nosebleed just trying to think about it. 'Member how competitive Mel is? Doubt she'd take joy in being anybody's junior partner, 'specially his."

"But she must be near to graduate, or finish already! Why does Carl not tell us how her agent work starts?"

"Well, gets back to what I was trying to say. Our man indicates he can't tell us diddly-squat. Could be a big sign they *might* start to work together."

"Aha! So. Our talk now about Mel makes me wish we can please see her again, soon."

"You 'n' me hittin' the road lets us make that happen, easy. What do you think, should we begin by just driving north? Make DC our first real stop?"

As Dan and Linda chat about Mel and plan their roadtrip, he continues to clean up the kitchen of their cottage. Linda bustles around packing their bags. Two side-zip duffles of green nylon lie open on the floor, and she kneels to shove items of their rolled-up clothing down into each. She turns her head, looks up at him thoughtfully.

"We drive away from the Keys this soon, because you wish to heed what Carl warns."

"Hell, yes."

Dan wipes an iron skillet with a wad of crumpled napkins, then shoves the pan into hot water to soak. It's a classic Les Crow pan, and he intends to re-cure it and bring it along to use over grills and fire pits. Even a Miata's cramped trunk will let them tote along the luxury of a great camp skillet.

"Carl comes all the way to Florida to warn us that we had a run-in with a major dickhead? We'd ignore that at our peril!" he says. "What I *don't* want to do is help him track the bastard down. Different order of business. I can ID that shaved gorilla if he's dragged back to the U.S. and even up the score that way. But chase him and his mob onto foreign turf? No good. You and me need to heal ourselves up. Let the real pros handle the tough stuff."

"That is most smart," Linda agrees.

"Besides, after visiting Mel, I want to show you some of my fave spots in Wyoming. They say you can't go home again. But still a kick for us to see how much is left of my boyhood scene, huh? Can't have it all fracked into oblivion. Hope not, anyhow."

He runs a copper scour lightly over the pan, drains and shakes it out, then sets it on a stove burner to heat and dry before oiling it.

A knock comes at the door. Linda peeks out a window. "Mailman," she said. "Um, or a mailwoman, I mean."

"Huh, again? Didn't know they did twice a day, anymore. But hey if it's special delivery, maybe a wad of our cash *did* arrive from Honduras! Great, we won't have to trace it through a bunch of forwards."

Dan sprinkles on fresh olive oil and rubs it around the inside of the pan with a napkin. Linda moves to open the door.

"I have a registered package here for a Daniel Cowell," the woman standing at the entry announces. "Is he home? I need a signature."

"Sure." He turns holding the pan, sees a thin face wearing big dark glasses under a blue, Postal Service pith helmet. Despite the warmth of November in the Keys, she also has on a gray jacket and gloves, as well as long slacks and black boots with three-inch heels. Instead of the fat envelope he expects, though, she holds up a medium-sized cardboard box. And she does it oddly, as though about to deliver a pizza.

As he sets down his pan, Dan sees her box fall and the woman's other hand emerge gripping a thick, short-barrelled pistol and time instantly begins to stretch and distort like hot plastic. All their movements — the woman's, Dan's, Linda's — seem to occur in nightmare slow-motion.

The phony postal worker cups the gun butt with her free hand as she raises the weapon and aims it through the doorway. He instinctively snatches the cast iron pan back and brings it to his chest, knowing as he does how absurd it is to try to use it as a shield. The gun jerks, the pan shatters in his hands, rough metal digs into his chest, he falls back against the sink.

Linda rams the door closed, pinning the woman's arms against its jamb and the pistol drops to the floor. Then the door crashes back against Linda and knocks her over, and the woman rushes inside, bent over, scrabbling on all fours across the floor to grab the gun.

Dan still grips the frying pan's handle, now reduced to a jagged shard. He flings it like a throwing knife at the intruder, the rough spike of iron pierces her shoulder and she emits a lusty screech, yet she still comes up holding the gun. Linda rolls and jumps at her, seizing her arm before she can fire. They tumble, wrestling over the weapon.

As Dan jumps to help her another shot booms in the small house and Linda falls back. But as she does, she lashes out with a foot and the gun once more goes sailing. The woman watches it bump against the low ceiling, fall, then skitter across the floor toward Dan. As he lunges to pick it up, she chooses to cut her losses and bolt. She slams the door shut and he hears running footsteps crunch on the gravel outside. He reaches the door, wrenches it open in time to see the assailant vanish out the driveway. He almost gives chase, but when he glances back to check on Linda he sees blood spreading out like a puddle of dark varnish on the floor.

He falls to his knees beside her.

"Oh fuck dammit goddamit. Please. No!"

Chapter 4

The pilot bestows a banality over the plane's intercom, first in Spanish, next in heavily accented English. "Good morning. I should like to be the very first to welcome you to our lovely mountain city of Quito, Ecuador..."

Dan grunts as he uncurls stiffly in his window seat. "No one could possibly beat you to it, pal," he mutters.

He shoves up the window's plastic shade to gaze out upon a dark green stretch of the Andes. A band of scarlet glowers above a white line of sawtoothed peaks — arrival of a new dawn looks about a minute away. He's been awake to see five more sunrises, he thinks, since the day Linda was shot. Or could it be six? He feels groggy. Over the last week, sleep has come to him in catnaps, if at all.

The plane hits the tarmac with a bounce and a lurch. He never ceases to marvel at the way the wings on modern airliners seemed to instantly disassemble themselves to disrupt air flow and provide braking. He guesses that in Quito's thin air, 9,200 feet up, every move that helps a plane brake upon landing must be crucial.

Soon he strides down a corridor of the new Mariscal Sucre International Airport with his black leather carry-on swinging from a hand. He has his passport stamped by a bored and sleepy immigration officer, slings his bag through one more x-ray machine to prove that he isn't sneaking in bombs or any heretical tomes of conservative political rhetoric. Then he exits into a long, bright, tiled lobby.

He immediately spots Carl leaning against a pillar, arms crossed, chewing on a colored toothpick. The nomad-biker look of a week before has been shed like a carapace. Shoulder-length hair is now tied neatly behind his neck, he wears khaki slacks and jacket over a white shirt. Wire-framed glasses and a straw fedora complete the ensemble. He looks like a nerd trying perhaps a bit too hard to enjoy a vacation in a country that makes him nervous.

"Hey," Carl says. "So, how was that?"

"I fella long. Kind of cramped. Not too bad."

"How's your gal?"

"Surgery went well. She's got new plates installed on the bones up and down her left arm, both radius and ulna. And she'll be in a cast and sling for weeks. But her attitude's good. Moving on. Ready to try something new after she gets to DC."

"Yeah?"

"First thing, she'll take up Muay Thai kickboxing. Says the next person who messes with her will get a boot up the poop-chute."

"Well, well. So I guess that won't be you."

"Duh, ya think? Learned my lesson about getting Linda mad, way-y-y back. It's somebody else's turn."

"And you got Mel to take care of her? I'd call that a most startlin' development."

"Hey, c'mon. They're pals."

"Hm. Sure. But nurture ain't 'zackly Mel's strong suit."

They exit through sliding glass doors and head for the airport parking lot. Dan inhales a deep breath and looks around at the rumpled, olive-drab landscape, its streets already beginning to writhe with traffic. *Every country has its own odor,* he thinks. *For urban*

Ecuador, especially Quito, seems like a reek of diesel smoke, with just a hint of trash fires…

"We've got a few hours to kill, 'til we fly on to Manta," Carl says, as he sticks Dan's bag in the trunk of a small Nissan sedan. "What's your pleasure?"

"Coffee, coffee and coffee, in that order."

"Let's do it."

"Don't drive too far into Quito. Rush-hour traffic might tie us up. You know, just remembered a great little inn and breakfast café on the outskirts, in Cumbayá. Before we bought our place up in Honduras, I'd hang out there. Want to see if it's still around?"

"Your wish is my command, *señor*."

"Now there's a switch."

"Joke."

"Nope, a contract. I'm gonna scribble it out on a napkin. And I *will* figure a way to make you sign it."

～

They sit within the maroon walls of *El Café Rojo*, having various installments of breakfast served to them by a barrel-chested Indian man who wears a fedora of shapeless felt and an embroidered shirt.

"Well, after recon on all the large yachts-of-interest, we've managed to whittle our fleet down to a single candidate," Carl says. "The envelope, please. And a drum roll…"

Dan obligingly taps out a rhythm on their table's edge with fork and spoon.

Carl shoves the remains of breakfast aside, slides a folder out of a leather attaché and flops it open. "Our target vessel is the *Dean Swift*." He shows Dan a photograph of a sleek blue hull with a sharply raked bow and a white superstructure with multiple decks.

"More ship than boat, eh?"

"Over four hundred feet at her waterline," Carl affirms. "Steel hull with all-aluminum topside, powered by CODAGs — combined diesel and gas turbines. Cruises at 20 knots, can hit 30 with the pedal down. Big custom job by Germany's Herholdt Shipyard."

"Custom for who?"

"Great question. Literal answer is — Upsilon Group, wholly owned subsidiary of Nephele Holdings, a consortium that's managed by its senior partner, Tenemos Ltd, based in the Cayman Islands. So, it's shells within shells. More than most hermit crabs would see in a lifetime. Ah, but who's our hermit, where's Waldo? My figure is, got to be the honcho glimpsed aboard her the most often. Which would be..." Carl tugs out another photo. "...him."

Dan sees a blocky head topped with a mane of gelled and combed silver hair, a tan forehead dotted with darker age spots, a pair of eyes hooded by lids that recede into deep fleshy folds under bristling eyebrows, a mouth with a firm and straight upper lip that bespeaks a formidable will, and a drooping bottom lip which hints at an indulgent sensuality. The man stares back at the camera with a predatory level of interest. He wears a sardonic smile that produces deep pits under broad cheekbones.

Dan lays down the photo and reaches over the stacked plates to grab the last remaining *humita*, a corn and cheese tamale that tops menus here as an all-day snack.

"Kinda sharp looking, for an ol' dude," Dan says. "As in, still plenty of action goin' on upstairs. Got a name?" He unwraps the roll and bites into it.

"Uh-huh. Leonid Andreyev. He was a Russian general who presided over the transformation of excess military gear into scrap metal after the fall of the Soviet Union. One helluva business opportunity. He focused on sellin' stuff that was *supposed* to have been dismantled or ground up, yet somehow hadn't q-u-i-t-e made it through that second stage. Paperwork said it was done, but that was all faked. So costs, minimal. Profits, extreme."

"You mean weapons."

"I mean weapons."

"Kalashnikovs, Dragunovs, Markovas…"

"And gear a few notches up. Tanks, ships, jets, helicopters. Remember that day up on the roof in Tegucigalpa, when I told you that Pablo Escobar tried to buy a titanium-hulled, fast-attack Russian sub? With crew and captain? Well, for that deal, Andreyev was the go-to guy."

"Yowza."

"That 'un didn't get to happen. But others did."

"And now he's into?"

"Oh, cruisin' hot spots of both hemispheres on that giant tub-toy of his. He renounced his Russian citizenship, and bought a Maltese passport for a cool two million after parkin' his boat there for a year. So, Putin's mob doesn't have much of a handle on him. Andreyev pioneered capital flight from the mother country well before the current trend. Word is that he feels he's got almost too much dough, and plans to just relax and enjoy it. Only play around with a few of his remainin' investments on the side."

"Like?"

"Well, one Tenemos firm enjoys a near monopoly on supplyin' goods and services to prisons in several former Soviet states. Plus, he runs all the joints now in Syria."

"Golly." Dan rubs his chin in mock consternation. "Wonder how the dude maximizes *that* income? Let me guess. Why feed those lousy jailbirds one cup of watery soup, when only half a cup might keep 'em tickin' along?"

Carl plucks up the photo print. "For a badass playboy, ol' Leonid's kind of shy. Shuns the social whirl. Likes to bring parties onto his boat, not go out for 'em. This photo's one of the few new shots of him that exist. Snapped by a CIA op through a 1600 mm lens when he spotted the *Dean Swift* anchored off the Quai du Large at Cannes, for the film festival there."

"Really? Yet the dude looks like he *knows* he's being photographed."

"Yep, he does, doesn't he."

"How?"

Carl turns both palms upward, lifts his arms and shoulders in a shrug.

As their waiter approaches, Carl slides the picture back in the folder and stuffs that in the attaché.

"*Mas café, señores?*"

"*Sí, por favor.*"

He pours hot milk in their cups, and offers a bowl of dark instant Colcafé Clásico powder. Carl and Dan each stir in two spoonfuls.

After the waiter departs, Dan says, "Okay, so you tell me good ol' Leonid finally is hitting port here, in Manta. And it's your theory that our attackers are still aboard the *Dean Swift*? And they're in league with Andreyev?"

"I'd imagine. Either that, or it's work-for-hire. On some sorta project."

"So what's our plan?"

"Happenin' already. The purser from the *Swift* went ashore in Manta, to take a huge pile of the ship's crew uniforms, sheets, towels and whatnot in to a commercial cleaner. Also, to re-victual the yacht. We assigned one of our most gorgeous Latina agents to set a honey trap. I'm told our man's just droolin' over the prospect of pollinatin' her, while she strings him along.

"With him distracted, we grabbed the boat's dirty laundry — not so much as to make anyone leery — and ten of those items are in flight to an FBI contract tech lab for analysis. Then we'll index 'em on a big DNA database. Any luck, we might be able to figure out more stuff about who they have aboard without, uh, rockin' their boat.

"Anyhow, soon as you and me fly into Manta, we connect with that purser. I'll try to close the sale and score intel. If we get the purser to squawk, and we know for sure that your bad lads and those stolen bikes are still onboard, we can mount a raid with the Ecuadorian harbor patrol. Make our bust."

"And, if they aren't?"

"We move to Plan 'B'."

"What about 'C'?"

"Let's not get ahead of ourselves."

Carl glances around to see if any onlookers have taken an untoward interest, but all other customers in the restaurant continue to steadfastly chat and chomp around their own breakfast tables. He pulls the folder back out to extract one more photo. "Here. Saved the best for last."

Dan sees an overhead view of the yacht's sundeck, one that looks as though it were taken from only about forty feet up. On a white deck, a lounge chair is set up by a swimming pool. A big man lies sprawled on it, his thick limbs overwhelming the chair's slender frame to drape loosely off both sides. He wears dark glasses, a broad-brimmed straw hat, and nothing else. Two trim women in bikinis seem to be rubbing a substance on his nude legs and belly.

"Shot from a drone or something? A satellite? Those lenses are getting damn good."

"Can even read a license plate. But a label on a bottle of sun lotion? Not *quite* yet."

"Hell, it's probably KY."

Carl snickers. "Right. So, that your boy?" he asks.

"'Maybe' is as far as I'll go. His face is shaded, so I can't really tell. But at least" — Dan flicks the photograph with a fingernail — "dude's got the shaved gorilla part down."

The more he stares at the black-and-white image, the more certain Dan becomes that this big lunk was indeed their attacker. Dan's heart begins to slam against his ribs. A jet of shame becomes rage, then a thirst for vengeance that astonishes him with its intensity. His fingers start to tremble and he lays the photograph carefully back onto the Formica table top.

"Could be your ape? Strong likelihood?" Carl asks, watching him carefully.

"Yep."

Dan takes a deep breath, and sweeps his eyes around the small restaurant as if to ascertain his real position in space and time. He wonders how he'll feel if he gets to physically lay eyes on that big bastard. Or better yet, his hands. Hopefully, he'll be gripping an ax handle or a steel pipe at that moment.

"Got anything else on the guy in this shot?" Dan asks.

"Just one thing."

"What?"

"Place he buys his clothes."

"Really?" Dan seems puzzled. "Where's that?"

"Rochester Big 'n' Ugly."

"Funny," Dan says flatly as he slides the photo back. He studies Carl.

"So, Linda understands why I had to come here," he says. "Do you?"

"Sure, I get it."

"But it's for one thing, and one only."

"Get that part, too."

"Don't hit me with any of your whacky add-ons."

"Not in the plan."

"Good. Needs to be a tidy operation. Fast and clean. Then I run on back home to Linda, so we can roam the U.S. and kick back some." Dan looks at him. "That's our plan, and I mean to stick to it. So, how about you and Mel? What's up? How're you guys doin', these days?"

Carl grabs his coffee mug and swigs from it. He offers a wry, bemused smile to Dan.

"Oh, heck. I'd say, us've been gettin''long like a house on fire."

"Yeah? One alarm, or two?" Dan asks.

Carl swallows, sets down his cup.

"Eight," he says.

Dan winces. "Well, you know, Melanie's a more intense package than most men would ever want to deal with. Way more. I mean, once they got past all those lovely layers of wrapping paper. My hat's off to you since you gave it a go. Maybe striving for top marks at the FBI Academy was a stress on Mel. Could be that things'll ease up, now she's aced it."

Carl is noncommittal. Dan eyes him.

"She did ace it, didn't she?"

After holding his gaze for a beat, Carl gently shakes his head. "No."

"Hm. You know, Linda and I were trying to figure that out, the other day. I mean, we knew Mel wasn't at the Academy. But we didn't know if that meant she quit, or she was so good they sent her right out to work. Like, by putting her into deep undercover with you. Last time we asked, seemed like your answer was that it was all secret. So that's what we thought."

Carl gives another head shake. "Uh-uh. Didn't answer Linda's question straight,'cos it's classified. My reason was, Mel's story is *hers* to tell. But since you're certain to keep bird-doggin' me on it, I might as well say it — she's outta there. Gone."

"Quit or flunked?"

He sighs. "In theory, if Camp Q kicked Mel to the curb, why would you guess that might be?"

"Insubordination?"

"Bingo."

"I see."

"*Massive* dose. She really brought it."

Carl raises a forefinger, and signals for the waiter to deliver their *cuenta*. It's time to head back to the airport.

"Oh. Sorry."

"Tough deal, all the way around. Especially for the Academy staff."

"I hear ya." Dan pauses. "She decide what to go for next?"

"Don't think she's chosen. 'Fore I left, she was yackin' 'bout tryin' to go back into the world of journalismo. Stuff she did before she married the congressman from Seattle, y'know. Mel was quite the muckraker at *The Post*, how she met and hooked up with the boy wonder."

"Ah. Charmed the pants right off her."

"Sure did," Carl agrees drily. "And she, him."

"But that's all over and done, though. Now it's you."

"Seems that way."

Dan clears his throat. "Well, it was great for Mel to agree to stick around DC for a while and let Linda move into her place. Linda needs somewhere peaceful to try and recoup."

"Uh-huh. And it should also be a great help to Mel to chill for a while with a gal pal. Doesn't have too many of those."

"Plus, maybe those two can keep each other out of trouble."

"Yep." Carl nods. "Always our hope, right?"

Chapter 5

*M*elanie. *Something big and new and most fantastic must happen for her,* Linda thinks. *Her look is so excited. Serious!*

She observes ruddy blossoms in Mel's cheeks, a sapphire gleam in her blue eyes, an elastic bound in her stride as they ascend the front steps of the stately old Hamilton Trust off K Street near Franklin Square. That classic bank had been transformed into Washington's new "It" destination, a see-and-be-seen bistro for power lunching called Mason's.

She's not feeling sad about getting thrown from the FBI school, as my beyb Dan says, when he calls me from Quito. Looks just the opposite way! Mel's into some brand-new game. And she will tell me this story over our lunch?

"Hullo Mrs. Symes, how lovely to see you heah again," the maitre d' says to Mel, in a southern drawl that falls just a skoch short of parody. His mint julep accent, white-tie get-up and show of deference are all design elements of the Mason's experience. The restaurant deploys high style to serve fat-rich portions of Southern cookery that are impressively priced and absurdly small.

"You know, Kent," she informs him, "mah divorce from thet wicked goofball who pinned his name on me was made final 'bout a month back."

Linda's knowledge of American dialects is scant. But she can still tell that Mel's tone imitates the maitre d' and also mocks him.

"Might's well go on back to jus' bein' plain ol' Mel Olson, now. What mah byline used to be. As jes' a few folk heah in this town might recall."

His response keeps studiously neutral — "Verruh good, ma'am" — as his eyes slide toward Linda. He struggles to categorize Linda, but makes scant progress.

Mel is an easier read for him, a soigné, urbane professional, slender and chic in fawn blazer and slacks, a smidge of eyeliner and lip gloss to emphasize her cool Nordic charms, lank blond hair in a jaw-line cut. Adding to creds, she became a regular when Mason's opened, companioned by those endowed with DC's *ne plus ultra* — a dose of political clout.

Beside her looms tall Linda in worn leather sandals, tight-fitting and artlessly ripped jeans, a low-cut, v-necked white blouse that promotes her remarkable bosom, a scuffed leather jacket with only one arm thrust through a sleeve — the jacket's other sleeve is draped over the cast and sling on her left arm. Gigantic silver hoop rings dangle from her ears, a long silk scarf printed in a clash of colors is wound carelessly around her throat. Lips painted a vivid shade of plum are bowed in a smile aimed at nothing in particular. A crowning touch is her pile of black hair, brushed out into a rippling pyramid.

Mason's doesn't have a dress code per se, but the maitre d' feels certain that this... er, ah... calypso gypsy isn't a great fit. 'Specially for his uptown lunch crowd! These guests are serious DC power brokers, at Mason's for a respite, a chance to relax with those of their breed. And maybe sniff out a deal or two on the side...

The maitre d' has brought to his station more than a syrupy dialect. He also bears nostalgia for rules in play decades ago. That part of him yearns to provide just Melanie with a seat in his tony bistro, and to suggest that Linda go dine in a different locale. Among others of her own kind, perhaps.

Mel observes the maitre d's agitation, intuits its cause, and beams a smile at him that is notable for its false warmth.

She slips her arm into Linda's. "This sweet lady right here is Linda Parker," she purrs. "And I can tell you, she's every *bit* as hot as she looks." She stands on her toes to buss Linda on one smooth, dark cheek. "Ain't you, hon'?"

The man's sallow face flushes slightly. "Would you care to sit at your regular table, Miss Olson?" he mutters.

"No, today, we want a private room upstairs," Mel says. "In fact, give us the most private room you have."

"Ex'lent," he responds, though his bonhomie now sounds a tad strangled. "Can do. Please follow me."

Mason's principal dining area is a warren of subdued lighting and dark furnishings, where scurrying, white-jacketed waiters balance wide trays that emit spicy aromas from loads of covered entrees. The place is packed with lobbyists, pols, operatives and hangers-on. A light shrewd kiss of judgment flickers between tables drowning in soft talk. This aural drone falters as Linda and Mel promenade down the room's central aisle. The buzz resumes, punctured by titters, a moment after they pass.

Linda does not precisely grasp why Mel clings to her arm so tightly, why she quivers with so much suppressed laughter. But her friend seems to find something terrifically amusing, and of this Linda always approves.

～

Their lunch occurs in a pine-paneled chamber, formerly a high executive's suite.

At their elbows, a canted stack of porcelain bowls and plates is dabbed with yellow smears of jambalaya, strewn with crumbs of hush puppies and breaded fish fillets, shreds of coleslaw, crawdad tails, chicken bones, gnawed ribs, bits of cornbread, melon rinds, shells of steamed mussels and crabs. The portions might be small, but by working down through the restaurant's menu, they've created a pile of debris.

Melanie yanks a green bottle of chenin blanc from an ice bucket, dribbles its last droplets of white jade into both of their glasses. A waiter approaches with a tray perched suavely on his fingertips, preparing to bus their table. Mel reaches into her purse, takes out a long tube, places it between her lips. When she sucks on it, the end glows. She blows a faint stream of pale mist out from pursed lips.

"Ma'am," the waiter reproves. "No smoking is allowed in Mason's, sorry. We do offer a deck outside where…"

"Not smoking," Mel tells him. "I'm va-a-aping," drawing out the long 'a.'

"Makes no difference," he says. "Other guests have some…"

"It's a private room, yes?" A vertical cleft appears between her tawny eyebrows. "We pay extra for it, true?" She looks at Linda. "Am I botherin' you?"

Linda shakes her head.

"So?" Mel grins. "Bugger off, sweetie."

Lips crimped, the waiter avoids any moment of further eye contact as he proceeds to clear the table.

He exits. Mel holds the e-cig out, regards it thoughtfully.

"Carl'd like it if I stopped even this crap. Rides my butt about smoking *all* the damn time, y'know. But… it's my next best thing to quitting."

"Why not just quit, okay?"

"Know what?" Mel takes a drag, blows out a puff of mist. "Hate being *told* what to do, by anyone. Really gets my back up. Always has."

Linda considers this. "So be minding your business, all you other folks," she announces. "Mel alone decides what to do! Others should just accept."

"Damn straight. Well, mostly." Mel caps the white tube of the e-cig, thrusts it back into her purse. "That's why getting my tail pitched out of the FBI Academy could be for the best. I prefer total independence. Going along with ol' boys to get along, puts a twist into my... never mind. In that outfit, they aim to control everything about you. No real fun in your private life, for example. I got to thinking. Last time I *really* enjoyed my work was back when I wrote a column for *The Post*. Could go after anybody. Harder I fought, the better my readers liked it. Me, too! Had my own logo, a drawing of Joan of Arc clutching a long pen like a lance."

She grabs her wine glass, drains it. "Want more of this stuff?"

Linda shakes her head.

"Best gig ever. As ol' Madonna once said, 'I think everyone's entitled to my opinion.' Pretty much like that." She sighs. "But I'm flush, after my split from the dishonorable congressman Asshat Symes. Didn't take him to the cleaners — no one could, not with lawyers like he's got — but I'll never grovel for a paycheck again. Still need to do stuff, since that's how I'm made. But *something* worthwhile. And with a big fun factor." She cocks a look at Linda. "Got an idea, what it will be. Want to talk to you about it. See if you might have some interest in signing on."

"Yes?" Linda smiles pleasantly, unsuspecting of the slippery slope Mel is about to shove them onto.

"See, investigations by news groups are *not* what they were. Yet I'd say, they don't really need to be. What with modern tech, apps and private drones and hirable hackers and whatnot, almost anybody can pull off a good investigation. Just be brave and bold, willing to snatch up any available tool."

Linda seems puzzled. "You mean, you wish to investigate like a news guy now? Or like a police?"

Mel grins. "Both! On a freelance basis, handling it however we like. And Linda, you're smart, you're strong. Be my partner! It'll be a kick. Maybe I can wind up proving something to Carl. Not to mention, all the dickheads at the Academy. Remember, it was you and me, working side by side, who found that drug base in Honduras and hauled everybody's nuts out of the fire. Well, let's have an adventure like that again!"

"What can you be thinkin'?" Linda wonders.

"Okay. Those biker thugs who attacked you and Dan? Got some fresh info on them."

"How?"

"Well-l-l," she peers at Linda. "I can let you in on my secret, but you don't tell anybody, *ever*. Understand?"

Linda spreads her hands out, as if to say, *hey, please slow down.* "Dan and me, we always tell each other about all that happens. That is our rule."

Mel's lips purse.

"Okay. What if you can tell him, but just not for a couple days? Our guys are all wrapped up down in Latin America. When they come back, we can blow their minds with all the cool stuff we find out. Move this case a *mile* further down the road. Dan will be impressed, guaranteed. And admire you all the more! So, how about it, girlfriend?"

Linda sucks in her lower lip, and ponders. Then she holds up three fingers. Her smile is slow, conspiratorial. "Just a few days. After that, we tell."

Mel's blue eyes glow with enthusiasm. She speaks quickly. "All right! Here's the deal. In Ecuador, some of Carl's operatives got hold of clothing, bed sheets and stuff that have some DNA on them from people in the gang. Well, that haul was overnighted to an FBI consulting lab right here in Washington, for fast testing. Just this morning they discovered a strong match for someone, a man who's already in the criminal database."

Linda puts a fingertip to her mouth. Her eyes are wide. "How do you know?"

Mel giggles. "Carl's laptop? He stashed it in my big safe in my condo."

Linda's forehead wrinkles. "And you can use?"

"Well… yeah."

"How?"

"Got my security cams. From my time with the dishonorable congressman. He insisted on having them put up all around our condo. Kept 'em switched on. So I know what his passwords are."

"Your husband?"

"Sure. He kind of forgot and slacked off on checking the feeds. But I never did. It's how I learned way-y too much about his wacko sex habits. But, no." She laughs. "I mean, I've got Carl's passwords, too."

Linda's face turns grave. "Me, I do not see Carl liking this much, 'nah mean?"

Mel waves a hand. "Oh, foo. Taxpayers bought his laptop, and paid for that DNA lab test, plus they financed their whole junket down south! Far as I'm concerned, *whatever* info they come up with is owned by all American citizens, including you and me. Well me, anyhow. But hey, I'll loan it to you. How's that?"

Linda weighs this line of reasoning. It feels specious. Even so, she finds herself feeling tempted. Mel's idea is an alluring blend of the righteous and the naughty.

"So…" She sips dregs from her wine glass. "Tell me, at least. The criminal who this test finds? He is who, okay?"

Mel glances around to make sure the waiter hasn't come back, leans forward. Her voice is low. "You know, darlin', that's where it all gets so ver-r-ry interesting. This guy, name of Ted James Burnett, is actually a serial murderer. Killed his dad, back when he was a teenager, then a few years later, did in his mom for good measure. Supposedly, now consigned to prison for life. Held in solitary, out in Texas." She leans back.

Linda presses a palm to her forehead. "But then, how does his DNA come to Ecuador last week?"

"Well, exactly!" Mel's eyes sparkle. "It's a huge thing we must figure out."

She grips her empty glass by the stem, waves it. "You know, we can order wine by the glass. Doesn't need to be a whole 'nother bottle."

Linda considers it. "A glass, but one we split. Just a swallow more, each. Then we drink more than plenty."

Chapter 6

Eloy Alfaro Aeropuerto — a tiny airport based in the fishing port of Manta, Ecuador — consists of two runways near a flat gray beach laced by rills of breaking surf. The plane carrying Dan and Carl flies in low, appears as if it's about to land right in the sea just before they feel a reassuring thump of wheels on solid pavement, then watch the white sides of terminal buildings flash past the plane windows.

They exit in the old-fashioned manner, via a set of aluminum stairs pushed up to the side of the aircraft. They stroll across the tarmac, pass a security gate and go through the airport lounge. It's a small building dominated by a huge painting, of an elderly man who wears a jutting white beard and a mournful expression.

"Guy right there is El Viejo Luchador — the Old Warrior," Carl says, pointing. "Named the airport for him."

"Yeah?"

"Eloy Alfaro. He was a liberal president, who got killed back in 1912 by a conservative mob in Quito. Was dragged to death, then tossed onto a bonfire. A signal of how seriously they take their politics."

"No shit."

"But the guy didn't stay buried. Correa, the current prez, had Alfaro's ashes dug up and reinterred with full honors during a convention in '08. That was when the airport was named and honored with his portrait."

"So, why didn't the painter put a smile on Eloy's face?"

"Dunno. But we weren't smilin' much, either. Same year, Correa displayed another burst of national pride by evicting us from our surveillance base. After we practically built this airport next door for 'em! Put seventy million bucks into it."

"Ingrates. So, what's Correa's take on the U.S. now?"

"He's not our pal." Carl shrugs. "Still spews out populist rhetoric, but his actual policies run full spectrum. He'll be termed out next year. But no matter who replaces him, dumpin' on Uncle Sam never really goes out of style."

"Which means what, as far as cooperation from local authorities?"

"The local cops?" Carl extends a hand, waggles his fingers. "*Comme ci, comme ça*," he says, pronouncing it "cum-see, cum-saw," with a Texas twang. "We still have some friends left from the good ol' days. They'll help us out, as long as we don't draw too much attention from honchos in Quito."

"So we'll fly under radar."

"You got it."

They emerge into a flood of sunshine, and a concierge on the sidewalk hails a taxi for them. At that moment, Carl's cell phone vibrates, and he takes a few steps away to answer the call.

He smiles as he settles back on the rear seat of the little yellow Hyundai.

"Stylin'," he says. "The purser from the *Dean Swift* has been *totally* sucked in. Our gal's enjoyin' a date right now with our man on the deck of the Hotel Balandra." He chuckles "What he doesn't know, cocktails for two is about to become cocktails for four."

~

"*Cabañas Balandra, de prisa por favor,*" Carl tells the driver. "*A calle veinte y avenida siete.*"

"Your Spanish has improved. A lot."

"Thanks."

"But, cocktails for four? Thought you didn't drink."

"Right. So, care to join me in a Shirley Temple? I'm buyin'."

"Blechh…"

"Sorry. That yes, or no?"

～

The cab hurtles down the town's main shoreline drag, the Malecón de Manta, past a giant, brightly colored fish sculpture atop a flagpole, and a roadside fountain where more fiberglass tuna frolic amid plashing jets of water. To the east rise blue and white administrative buildings of the port authority. To the west, all along a curve of the bay, large trawlers can be seen beached on the sand at low tide.

"Welcome to the tuna capital of the Western Hemisphere," Carl says.

"I *do* pick up something fishy about it."

"World's freshest sushi. Cheapest, too. But we *do* have bigger fish to fry. And by God, thar she blows." He points out the window.

Dan squints into a glitter of sunlight on the slate sea. He sees a long blue shape with a sharply raked bow anchored off the end of the port's crane-bedecked shipping pier. Its low superstructure is a modernistic mélange of tilted slopes and extreme angles.

"That's the *Dean Swift*?"

"Yep."

He shades his eyes with his hand. "Some yacht! Does look fast. And big. Even has a crane of its own, right on the back there, see?"

"Yeah. To pluck Leonid's float plane off his deck, then plonk it in the water for takeoff. A Pilatus Porter turbo. All-weather, all-terrain, STOL capable."

"Handy."

"You betcha. No better plane for landing on lakes, a jungle strip, or mountain meadow. Useful for all kinds of enterprises, includin' some that might be legal." Carl points again. "Over there's the *Swift's* dinghy, tied up at the Manta Yacht Club. Deep-vee, go-fast boat with three Mercury outboards. Custom job, called the *Liddle Putt*. That's how our guy zoomed into town. Yuri Tyraslo. He's a Ukrainian."

"The purser?"

"Uh-huh."

"Well. Let's go meet the gent."

"Hey, you brought any shades, put 'em on now. This dude ain't nothin' special, but our gal is a dazzler. I'm tellin' ya."

～

Carl has not exaggerated. Núwa Robles is a beauty to make a priest flick away his celibacy vow faster than he could snuff a votive candle. Long black hair hangs over Núwa's chair back like a sleek waterfall. When she turns her head at their approach, Dan sees golden-hued cheeks lit by roseate blushes, dark chocolate eyes framed by long natural lashes, Cupid's bow lips bent in a smile that seems both sweet and knowing.

The man across the table from her is short and pudgy, his thinning blond hair combed with a part that begins just above his left ear, and a fat, sunburned nose as pored as a grapefruit. He turns to see what his sexy companion is looking at. His eyes narrow down to slits when he sees two large and fit American men in dark glasses are approaching. He puts his hands on the table and pushes his chair back as if he's ready to bolt.

The woman stands up. She's quite tall, for someone whose coloring suggests indigenous blood, young, curvy — and, as her tight black slacks and white corset top reveal — firm-bodied. She holds out a slim hand to the purser of the *Dean Swift*.

"I thank you for these drinks and the lovely time we shared," she says, her voice gentle and musical. "I enjoy your stories. Yuri, I think you are a basically kind guy, but you've been forced into a bad position. So now, you must listen to what these good men have to say. I'm sure they can be of great help to you."

She smiles at Carl, nods at Dan. The veranda's still air gets tickled by a graceful wave of her fingertips, then she saunters off. The three men spontaneously and mutely join in a moment of reverence. They watch her go, admiring their view of a work of living art.

Carl then clears his throat and sits down.

"Hey Yuri, I mean, come on now, man. How lucky did you think you were gonna be?" He pokes the Ukrainian hard in the shoulder, as if to jolt him awake. "Got to keep it real, buddy."

The purser's eyes dart back and forth between them. He sucks in his cheeks, blows out a breath, tilts his chin up, and thumps the tabletop with a meaty fist. "And you are who?" he demands.

Carl removes his dark glasses. "We're the cops you always were going to meet some day, one way or t'other."

"Why?"

"Mainly, due to a cesspool of crime where your boss Andreyev swims laps."

He scoffs. "And you dream this is what? And your proof is…?"

Carl steeples his hands, taps his index fingers against each other. "Yuri, let's not waste time, huh? Now you can say you love your job and your skipper, claim you stand by him, and plunge straight down into hell on his ship. I'm usin' a figure of speech. But I can tell your English is good, so you know what I'm talking about. See, ol' Leonid's yacht is steamin' at a reef called international law enforcement. Your priority should be figurin' out what that means for you. Because the big wreck *will* happen, and soon."

A long silence.

"You are both Americans?"

Carl nods curtly.

"And you work directly for U.S. government? You can show IDs?"

He nods again.

Yuri hesitates. He raises a hand, gnaws on a knuckle, glares down at the table as if trying to assign it with all the blame for the jam he's in. He drops his hand and lifts his face. A single tear breaks away from his right eye, to glide around that pitted bulb of a nose. A narrow pink tongue flicks out in unconscious reflex, licking the tear away from a corner of his thick-lipped mouth. He looks at Dan, then Carl.

"Thank God." He breathes. "At last, finally, some real police come. Tell me a first thing, please, why did it take you so damn long to catch onto this terrible son-of-a-bitch?"

~

"Now, that was *awesome*," Dan says.

"Yuri's come-to-Jesus? You bet. Never had one go easier," Carl replies. "If our pricetag is just gettin' his family extracted from east Ukraine, then re settled? Easy! I can put our people on that. But I'm bummin' over the fact that your baddies and their bikes got yanked off the ship before it reached Manta. I was *so-o* lookin' forward to a bust."

"Okay, but we *did* learn how ol' Leonid works his magic — nighttime rendezvous with other blacked-out ships and yachts. Well out of range of land-based radar."

"Right. Now I just need to figure out what other damn boats met him, and where they're bound."

"Isn't crunching satellite data and other feeds what the NSA does best? Your Bureau buds too, for that matter."

"True. But I'm majorly old-school. Don't want the nerds to win it for us *all* the time. I want to follow a trail of clues, make a dramatic entrance, then collar the bad guys personally. That's how I define job satisfaction."

"Shit, Carl. You're doin' that! And, may I point out, you're using a nerd trick? When Yuri plugs your thumb drive into the *Dean Swift's* network, the ship's computers will upload content via a radio link, right? Satellites will pick up a core dump, and you'll probably score all you need. Isn't that what you told me? I mean, who knows what stuff you'll harvest, but I bet it'll be hot. And then, using that link in reverse, you can infect the boat with malware and fix Leonid's super-duper water-wagon but good. Or maybe, use his own computers' mikes and cams to spy on him some more."

"Depends."

"On what?"

"*His* techs. Russia has black-hat nerds that are at least as skilled as our white-hats, and often better. They trot out the freshest hacks, while we try to catch up."

"Naw, come on. Not too early to declare a modest victory! Should only be a matter of time, now." Dan pointedly seizes the pale, dew-frosted globe of his piña colada glass and takes a gulp. "Cheers."

"Don't jinx it."

"Oh, for crying out loud. Lighten up. Have a beer."

"No. Drugs and booze are reward without performance. Fake joy."

Dan rolls his eyes. "We just *did* perform. Anyway, that's your big reason? Why you abstain?"

"In a nutshell. But I've also seen where it gets most people — nowhere fast."

"People, like who?"

"Me."

"Oho! I'd pay a dollar to hear that story."

"No."

"Two dollars? Three-fifty? It's my top bid."

Carl pushes back his chair and gets to his feet. His brows are drawn low, while his bony face corrugates in a frown. "Okay, you've had lunch and you've had your drink and you've had some fun. Let's quit burnin' daylight. We need to head down to the waterfront and chat with the port captain. See if there's any reason they might find to hold the *Swift*, then have an inspection team board her. And see if one person on their team could be me."

"Ah, so. Big-shot Western detective, he lacks patience."

"Goddam straight. I'm like a cartoon buzzard, perched on a branch. 'Fuck waitin'. I wanna kill me somethin'.'"

"Who's jinxing it now?"

"Actually, more to the move than you might think. If we distract Leonid, less chance he'll notice the stuff we put Yuri up to."

As they depart from the outdoor patio of the Balandra, a chromium blob of white sun sags onto a misty horizon. The bartender waves a cheery farewell, and waits as they vanish down the stairs. Then he bends over and grabs a phone off a handset that sits on a low shelf behind the counter.

～

Dan recalls watching the port's offices go by earlier, as their cab whisked them along the waterfront en route to the Balandra. He saw a large white building on the west side of the main boulevard, emblazoned with the words, *Autoridad Portuaria*, and across the street a smaller structure labeled, *Capitania del Puerto de Manta, Fuerza Naval*. Its blue and white facade was further distinguished by a striking logo of a condor perched atop an anchor.

Wow, wonder how many times a real condor has perched like that? Dan thought, when he glimpsed it. *I'll bet — never.*

To walk back to that military office now, they need to go downhill and make their way past a row of ramshackle waterfront bars. These bistros aren't much more than open-air corrals, bordered by a low fence, filled with battered chairs and tables. As sunset draws closer, the bars grow jammed with disheveled men in T-shirts and ragged jeans who sing and shout and swear over thumping beats of Latin pop, pausing briefly to swill foamy beer out of huge plastic cups.

"Must be tuna boat crews, blowing off steam," Dan says.

"Man, I had to sweat like those guys, might let myself have a beer 'casionally," Carl concedes. "It's a hard life."

When they amble past the largest of the bars — one named *Sinaloa,* according to its carved wooden sign — a pair of men who sit close to the sidewalk lurch unsteadily onto their feet. One is thin and rodent-like, he has a long nose projecting above a slit of a mouth and underslung jaw. The other is rotund, with fat arms bulging from the sleeves of his jersey. The pair totter for a second. Suddenly the big one clutches at his mouth, doubles over, and pitches a yellow gout of vomit onto the concrete.

"Oh Jeeze! Look out!" Dan yelps. He jumps into the street to avoid the splatter. At the same instant he sees the smaller drunk stagger into Carl, clutching at him for support. Carl sends him reeling backward into the bar with a single mighty shove. The man's skinny butt hits the floor, and he vanishes under a table, sliding in between the men who sit at it, as they shout in laughter and yank up their legs.

In front of them, the bulky one props himself up, putting one hand on a knee while groping with the other for the rail of the fence. "*Lo siento... Siento...*" he mutters.

Screech of tires.

A glossy black, extended-cab pickup swerves to the curb, and Ecuadorian national policemen wielding batons spill out from its truckbed and doors before the vehicle stops moving. Two of the khaki-clad cops yell incomprehensible phrases as they point the dead zeros of handgun muzzles at them.

Even Carl looks dumbfounded.

They both are seized, frog-marched to the side of the truck, shoved forward into a lean, their hands slapped onto the cab roof, their feet unceremoniously booted out into a wide stance by kicks to their inner ankles.

Dan turns his head, sees Carl's eye, wide and white and gleaming. Carl gives a faint shake of his head, a message that Dan takes to mean, "Don't resist."

The cops quickly strip them of their cell phones, passports, wallets, watches, and keys. Then one of the friskers whoops in triumph. He hauls a fat roll of cash out of Carl's hip pocket. Made of purple and white bills, bound with a thick rubber band, it looks like it holds thousands in high-denom Euros. A policeman standing near him applauds. Clearly, it's the find they'd hoped for.

Dan and Carl have their arms yanked down and twisted up behind their backs, their wrists tightly cuffed. Next, they find themselves hurled into the back seat of the truck cab.

Dan peers out through a small, tinted window. This sudden turn of events looks like it has sobered up most of the boozy fishermen. A shocked silence now reigns as they gaze back out at the police — a stillness broken only by the thumping bar music.

And of that fat *pescador* and small, ratty companion who'd barreled into them just a few minutes before, Dan sees not a sign. They have vanished.

Chapter 7

"Damn! Every mile we go takes us deeper into a giant bunch of empty," Melanie says. She and Linda sit in the front seats of a rental SUV. They'd driven for most of a morning on a narrow highway leading west from Corpus Christi into the olive-drab sprawl of southern Texas.

Linda points at a ranch gate, one of the few they've seen over the past hour. A plate-steel arch above it has been cut by an acetylene torch into crude silhouettes of cattle, horses, and heavily antlered deer.

"Well, plenty of brush and cactus, sure, yet then sometimes these animal places, y'know," Linda says.

"Yes, I mean those too," Melanie mutters.

Linda looks amused. Pavement hums under their tires, and unbroken countryside again stretches away before the windshield like a great frozen sea of dull green.

"Not many towns," Mel comments. "Half of what's in them is either boarded up or falling down. Prospered with cotton, fell. Went up again with oil and gas, fell when the wells played out. Only a few are prospering again because new prisons were built in them. That's what we're looking for, one of those. Sojourn, Texas — kind of an odd name."

"Sojourn?" Linda inquires.

"Means having a nice long stay, like you're on vacation," Mel explains. "Probably a huge dose of soldiers' irony there, when they gave the place that tag. Sojourn's way out on the Rio Grande, near the Mexican border. Began as an outpost for Confederate militia back in the day, got used as a depot for supplies from Mexico, like rifles, gunpowder, and medicines. Then the locals fell on hard times, till they got their new jail. Only a hundred and fifty years later."

"How do you know all of these things?"

"Shit, girl, I was a reporter! Always study my topics to a fare-thee-well. Why I got paid the small bucks. I mean, at the start. Pay got better after they asked me to be a society columnist, but that gig bummed me out. Had to write too many blow jobs. One day I came to work nursing an epic hangover, and decided to pour on the snark. And I hit, big-time! Like, I finally got the joke. Great fun, while it lasted."

She absently gnaws her lower lip with her small, even teeth. She reaches into her purse, extracts the white tube of the e-cigarette, brings it up to her mouth and makes its green tip glow.

Linda studies her. "Maybe that is best," she says. "To do your work in this reporter guy way. Not to try to be police, or join the FBI."

"Ha!" Mel grins. "Right now, I *am* working that way. It's how we'll get into the private prison! The top editor at *Nation's Forum* mag is my pal, so I asked him for creds and cover. Appears as if I'm doing a story on the impacts of solitary confinement, which happens to be a huge issue now. So, we'll check up on that notorious homicidal maniac Ted James Burnett, see if he's turned into a better or a worse human being during his ten years in the hole."

"What are you thinking?"

"Honey. Only stuff I know gets better in tight confinement is wine in barrels."

"And you say, 'we,' yes? Am I reporter, too?"

"No, you are my photographer. Can you work a digital camera? Doesn't matter, they won't let us shoot. But please, act mad about the 'no pictures' deal, anyhow." She giggles. "At first, they didn't even want to let *me* in! But I worked 'em on what are you trying to hide, and you people will be part of my story no matter what, and there's the Texas Department of Criminal Justice monitors, let's see what those watchdogs have in their files on you — and finally they caved."

~

They leave the pavement between rural towns of Cinnabar Springs and Nopales. The last street sign reads, NO SERVICES, NEXT 40 MILES, and it's no joke. For the next hour their car churns up clouds of ocher dust on a road of crushed rock that arrows between hills swathed in dense brush.

"Look," Linda says at last, pointing out the windshield. Crowning a hill in the distance is an improbably large white shape. Poking up from that is a thick black line — probably a microwave tower — that thrusts a hundred yards into the sky.

Another sagging ranch gate appears on the left. A sheet of plywood, whitewashed to serve as a signboard, is wired to the fence. It shows a crude image of a large boar's head frozen in a slavering snarl as well as the legend HANK's HOG HUNTS painted in blue. For added decoration, a sun-bleached "Stars and Bars" — a Confederate battle flag — flops limply atop a staff bolted to one of the gateposts.

They next see a brown and white sign. SOJOURN TX, it reads. POP 1,894. EL. 603. The road flattens and broadens into a paved boulevard that travels between three blocks of buildings and ends abruptly at a barbed wire fence.

Mel slows the car and drives thoughtfully past the buildings. "Something's weird…" She snaps her fingers. "Got it. See? Everything looks nice. All spruced up and painted. No broken windows, no boarded shops." She points through the windshield. "Even the trucks and cars are good. Zero jalopies. Dirty, yeah, but new. We've finally reached a place with some cash."

They pass a lawyer's office, indicated by a chalk portrait of a Lady Justice on a brick wall near the door. A tattoo parlor announces itself with tall red gothic letters on the black-painted glass of its front window. A restaurant with rounded stucco walls meant to simulate adobe is spray-painted dull yellow to match the town's dust. "Fátima's Cantina," the bistro's neon sign reads, "Best Tex-Mex in the West. Breakfast, Lunch, Supper. Nightly Entertainment."

"Oh, breakfast!" Linda brightens. "The burrito we had the airport was small and too long ago. Let us do it again."

Mel glances at her watch. "Sorry, hon'. It's near our appointment and I think we ought to arrive on the dot. Don't want to give them any reason to say no." She eases the car to a halt at the end of the street. "But, shit. Where the hell is it?"

"The prison?" Linda points. "Up on the hill, white and big. We see it as we come in, okay."

"Sure. Right. But where's a road to it? I don't recall any sign pointing the way. Do you?"

Linda shakes her head. Mel sighs. "What's a visitor supposed to do, just drive till you stumble onto a route that goes up there?"

Frowning, she turns the car about, and probes down the side streets. There are pedestrians around, not many, a few men in cowboy hats, women in jeans and baseball caps, a Latino boy peddling furiously on a bicycle, another sitting on a bench, idly booting a soccer ball against a store front. Just as they cruise by the tattoo parlor again — the one with MARK'S MARQUES: CUSTOM TATTOOS AND PIERCINGS in red on the black glass — its door swings open and a man steps onto the sidewalk. He wears a black top hat with a sparse fringe of long brown hair drooping from the back, dark sunglasses with circular lenses, black leather gloves, a black frock coat with bone buttons, and glossy black boots that reach almost to his knees.

"Now I must say, he is a strange cowboy," Linda says. "One like him, I never see in a movie."

Whereas other townspeople gave them and their car only brief, sidelong looks, this man stares at them with a cool hauteur.

Mel awards the fellow a glance as Olympian as his own, drives on. "Steampunk," she says. "That's his style, not cowpoke. Guess in this town, it's whatever you can get away with. And he aims to come across as a wacky artist. Maybe helps him sell tats."

She takes another side street. It also appears to dead-end, but then makes a sharp right around a telephone pole, and forks into two roads, one arcing away up the hill. "Aha!" she says. She brakes and gets out, then shading her eyes with a hand, gazes up the hill. "Might be it," she tells Linda. Something makes her also look up at the phone pole. A bulbous structure projects from it, resembling a streetlamp. She points. "And I think *that* just might be a 360-degree security cam. If so, this is definitely it."

"But... why not just give people a sign?" she grumbles, as she yanks the SUV's shifter into drive. "Why's that so goddam tough?"

～

The white building looms ever larger. They check in at a front gate where uniformed men take their IDs and run them through a scanner. They make their way through a gantlet of tall fences garlanded with razor wire and punctuated by gun towers. After they park, they pass through sliding doors of thick ballistic glass, send their handbags down conveyor belts with metal detectors and watch them vanish into lockers. They have their bodies and clothing examined by drug-and-explosives-sniffing wands. They're forced to stand in body scanners themselves, arms raised over their heads.

A final straw is the notice Mel reads upon emerging from the scanner. "All visitors!" this sign declares. "A search may be conducted on or about your person and/or your property at any time while you are present on the complex, or when leaving. Persons refusing such a search will be escorted out of the complex immediately."

"Jesus!" She grouses to the last guard, a bulky specimen in a tan uniform and green bulletproof vest, with a five o'clock shadow in place on his square jaw — though it's not quite noon. "You bozos check us eight different ways from Sunday, and stuff everything we own into a locker? What's next? Want us to tug our butt cheeks apart and cough?"

He looks up from his chair, and gives her a cool stare. "Are you stating that as a request, ma'am?" he drawls.

"You wish!" Mel informs him. "Look. I'm down to a notebook and one pen. What in God's name you scared of now? I might draw a picture of a gun? Slip it to somebody so he can bust out?"

"Warden Sanders' office is that way," he says tersely. He points down the hall, then toward another guard, this one with a shaved head. Baldy strolls at them with thumbs hooked in his duty belt so that dangling hands frame his crotch. He smiles broadly. "Follow him," the seated guard orders.

After tapping on a blond oak door and receiving a grunt of reply, the bald guard turns the knob and ushers them into a carpeted room that glares with fluorescent light. Warden Tom Sanders has a moon-face adorned with tortoise shell glasses and a peevish expression. Dark hair is combed straight back from his wide forehead. His coat hangs on a tree at one end of his steel desk. He's clad in a white shirt, a pale blue tie and black alligator braces. Crescents of sweat darken the armpits of his shirt, despite a breeze of cool, conditioned air being pumped steadily into his office.

"So, you're the reporters," he says.

"Guilty!" Mel responds brightly.

His eyes narrow. "Why don'cha start out by tellin' me what makes you so all-fired interested in Ted Burnett."

"I'm Melanie Olson, here on assignment for *Nation's Forum*," she says, leaning on the desk with one hand, and extending the other to the warden. "We're very pleased to meet you too, Mister Sanders."

He squeezes the tips of her fingers reluctantly, releases them as soon as possible, then leans back in his chair and laces both hands over the swell of his belly.

"So why don't you be a nice Southern gentleman, and invite us to sit down?" Mel suggests.

Sanders grunts and nods. "Sure," he says, "y'all can go on ahead and do that."

Melanie glances meaningfully at a row of gray vinyl-padded chairs pushed up against the wall, then at the bald guard, who stands just inside the door with his thumbs hooked again in his belt. When the warden utters another grunt, the guard drags a pair of chairs across the carpet for them.

Mel sits and crosses her legs, which hikes her skirt up. Sanders quickly seems to warm to her presence. Linda sinks gracefully down on the other chair, turning both her knees demurely to one side, even though she's wearing slacks.

"Mister Burnett. He's spent ten years here in solitary…"

Sanders holds up a short, thick finger. "We call it disciplinary segregation on this complex, or D-Seg, for short. Solitary, strick'ly speakin', don't always apply. Secure confinement in that module can mean varyin' degrees of social contact, dependin' on the inmate."

She smiles and jots in her notebook. "Okay. But what we want to inquire about is how the system has affected Burnett, in particular."

"'Course! Made him a lot safer to deal with. Why we do it."

Mel scribbles some more, and draws a question mark. "Psychologically?" she asked. "How's that make him different? Could

he function now, going back into the prison population? Or even —
if you think about it — if he happens to return to society at large?"

Sanders jacks his jaw sideways. Beady eyes study her
condescendingly, as if he now realizes that he's speaking to an idiot.

"Tank Burnett slayed his dad, miss. Then a few years later, his mom.
Premeditation was involved, certainly. But also, a ton of torture.
Lyin'-in-wait. Sexual abuse of both their corpses. Lord a'mighty, that
scumbag ain't never getting out. You writin' this down? He 'scaped
the death penalty 'cos he was a minor when he did in his pop. And
then with his mom, 'cos he scored one of the few temp' insanity pleas
ever worked here in Texas. After he was made comp'tent to stand
trial, he got dropped to life without parole, 'stead of gettin' his sorry
tail strapped to a steel gurney. Still, add it up, he's in for 150 years.
The cons call it a day and a night. Get me? Lucky he ain't dead. But
free? Won't happen."

Mel holds her pen above the pad. "Tank?" she asks.

"What we call him. A nickname." The warden frowns. "Everyone
here, screws and cons both, tends to wind up with a monicker of
some kind. Tank got that 'un 'cos the man comes with a pretty good
size. Ain't had nothin' to do for the last long while 'cept his push-ups,
and whatnot."

"Well. Let's have a look at him, okay? And our scheduled interview.
Might have more questions for you, afterwards."

Sanders looks slightly bug-eyed. "Miss Olson. You're aware, are
you not, that you are in a highly secure facility? This place was
planned, designed, built, and is now run, to confine the worst of the
worst? Coahuila Corrections Institute has contracts with the state
and nation to protect our citizens from these predators — which is
not too strong a word! — 'cos it seems to me that you truly fail to
'preciate that. And I assure you, I'm just barely sketchin' the reality.
You're about to enter one of hell's deepest circles, and meet one of its

most awful bein's. Only CCI's excellent facilities, professional skills and trainin' can keep folks like that…"

"Ready," Mel says. She looks at Linda. "You?"

She nods, smiling.

~

They pass through more clashing steel doors, go down corridors that cradle a dank must of male sweat as well as hints of fecal vapor, stale urine and vomit, all laced by a turpentine reek of Pine-Sol. They are escorted into a visitation room where four metal chairs bolted to the floor face a long slab of ballistic glass so thick it bestows a green, aquarium cast on the quartet of small, whitewashed rooms behind it.

Mel sits while Linda stands behind her, resting hands on the back of Mel's chair.

A door opens in one of the small rooms. A man wearing a short-sleeved yellow jumpsuit, handcuffs and leg shackles — what prisoners dub a "four-piece" — shuffles inside. Mel hears a sharp intake of Linda's breath. The man is tall and bulky, with a shaved scalp and stubbly jowls. His forearms are ropy with muscle, and wreathed by crude tattoos of serpents that writhe down to end in a triangular snake's head on the back of each hand. These images are distorted and smudged, as though hurriedly drawn with Sharpie pens.

He leers at them through the glass, licks pendulous lips, and plops down in the chair. The convict picks up a phone handset that hangs from a bracket, and Mel does the same.

"You're Ted James Burnett," she says.

"Uh-huh. Thanks for comin'. Don't get me too many visits, not so much anymore."

"How are you doing?"

He rolls his massive shoulders in a shrug. "One day goes by awful much like 'nother."

"They treating you all right?"

He looks puzzled. "Compared to what?"

"How long have you been in solitary?"

"It's where I live."

"What do you have for stimulation?"

"Jackin' off, mostly."

A faint blush starts to bloom on Melanie's cheeks, but she fights it down. "I mean," she says firmly, "can you get books, television, or exercise? Do you have any legal work or appeals underway? Are you able to see a lawyer?"

He slowly shakes his head. "Don't much care to. Don't make no difference, so I don't bother myself any with it. See, my body might be jailed here, payin' off my debt to sassiety for all them evil things they say I done. But in my mind, I'm already free. In my head, that's where I perject real good shows, the only kind I want to see." He leans forward. "About wimmins, mostly," he confides. "Like you two. 'M tellin' ya, a man can grow real tired of scorin' only boar pussy in the joint…"

"Okay, got it. But, listen," Mel interrupts.

"Awesome kick to dream 'bout somethin' different, for a change," He continues. "You gals are purty tight buds, huh? You do each other? Love to see that. And even help out some! I heerd about them *menagerie a twats*, but never ever did get me a chance to try one. So after I get back to my cell, I'll be thinkin' real hard about you ladies, and in my head I'll have you both, in just 'bout ever' which way I can…"

The conversation plunges downhill from there. Mel gamely seeks to keep up her façade of reporting about solitary confinement and its effects, while the convict either ignores her questions or bends his every answer into vivid depictions of sex he's enjoyed in the past or forlornly wishes to have right now. By the time he begins to paw vigorously at his crotch with both cuffed hands, she's done. She jumps up, claps the phone into its bracket and goes to knock on the door to the visitation chamber.

Before she even reaches it, it swings open.

The bald guard stands there. "Well now, ma'am," he asks. "Did you get all the material you were hoping for?"

~

Linda starts to blurt something to Melanie as they leave the visitation chamber, but Mel stops her with a faint shake of her head and a warning look. Finally, only after they are in the car and riding away from the prison, it comes out.

"That's not him!" she says.

"Yeah, well," Mel replies. "I'm not surprised."

"They try to make him look so. But result not so very close, 'nah mean."

"Uh-huh. So, let's assume the DNA match is correct. Then this psycho killer Ted James Burnett, who should be locked up, instead gets out to travel. Doing what? Meanwhile, these asshole jailers act like they've still got him!"

"And why?"

"Two reasons, maybe. Either he's escaped, and they're desperate to cover their hineys 'til they can bring him back. Or, worst-case? Whatever the actual Burnett is up to, people in charge of this prison are into it, too. They intentionally let him go outside to do some piece of nasty work. *Exactly* how a few prisons are run down in Latin America. Parts of them are actually secret bases for total scumbags."

Linda sinks down in her seat. She rubs the cast on her left arm.

"All right," she says firmly. "Now, I think, it is time we must call to Dan and Carl, and say what we find out."

"Well-l-l…" Mel equivocates. Then she grins. "Not quite yet. Please? I'm starting to really love this, aren't you? I've not done an investigation for way too long. More fun than I even remembered!"

Linda looks dubious.

"Oh, come on. Let's poke around just a tad more. Then we'll call Dan and Carl."

At the fork in the road, Mel glances toward town, then at the alternate route that disappears out into the brush.

"For instance, what might we see if we go down that other road? Let's take a look."

～

This new gravel track cruises a half mile past feathery branches of mesquite that lift and sway in a faint breeze. It ends at a closed gate of galvanized bars, held upright by a pair of rock pillars. The crest above the gate bears cut-steel-plate outlines of various animals, similar to those they'd seen previously. However, these shapes are all smooth and artistic. They represent not only native buck deer, but other, more exotic-looking species, with long spiky horns that would look right at home on the African veldt. Below this crest in letters of gilded metal glow the words, XANADU PARK.

"What is it?" Linda inquires.

"I'd guess, a game ranch," Mel says. "Place where rich folks go to shoot all sorts of critters. Get to play bwana, without the mess of a real safari. Umbrella drinks on a tray, but no tsetse flies in the tent. I'll take a picture of that gate, so we can show it around and ask folks about it."

"You want the camera?"

"No, I'll just use my iPhone." She reaches into her purse, and frowns. "Now, that's weird," she says. "I keep my phone in a case. Don't want it to get scratched up. But it's out." She sucks in her lower lip. "Look in your bag," she tells Linda. "See anything messed up?"

Linda checks, shakes her head.

"Well I guess around here, your locker *really* belongs to the guy with the master key, right? They checked us out, all the time we thought we were researching them." She laughs. "Right. So it's game on! Or 'the game's afoot,' I guess, like Sherlock used to say. Now I'll just keep it off, and I will use that camera."

She jumps from the car and snaps photos of the gate. Then she becomes aware of the drone of an airplane's engines. Mel surveys the pale blue dome of sky until she locates a winged shape with a high, T-shaped tail gliding just above the horizon. It drops into the undulating green landscape as the engine hum fades into silence.

"Looks like a Beech'," Mel says. "Maybe, one of those new Kings."

Linda looks confused.

"A business airplane," Mel explains. "I got my pilot's license a few years back, though I haven't used it much. Liked to fly, just never had enough spare time to do it.

"Makes sense for a place like this to have its own airstrip, to serve all the high-rolling hunters," she says, as she re-enters the car. "What I can't figure *at all*, though, is why they'd put a game ranch next to a supermax jail. Freaking odd." She glances at Linda. "Still hungry? Let's drive back into town, grab some lunch."

～

They park in front of Fátima's Cantina, wedging their SUV into the last slot left by a row of pickups, plus one F-650 with a prisoner-transport van body. That hulking rig takes up two full spaces. It's just past noon, and the joint is jumping. Mel pushes open the door, and many male faces turn their way as they enter. Men who gaze at them the longest wear tan guard uniforms and sit at a cluster of tables shoved together. One guard makes a comment, and the whole group erupts into guffaws. Then their focus wanders back to the platters of food, mugs of coffee, and steins of beer that load the tables before them.

Linda and Mel ignore the men as they move through a ruckus of clattering plates and the buzz of conversation. When they spot an empty table over in a window niche, they head for it. A young Latina waitress trots over to slap down a pair of menus and plastic tumblers of water. She holds up a forefinger, mutely promising to come back, then scurries off.

The door opens again. In comes a man clad in black boots, frock coat and top hat — the steampunk artist whom they'd first glimpsed outside his tattoo parlor. Faces in the restaurant that glance at him turn away again quickly. Even the guards bent over their plates focus more intently on eating lunch.

He plucks off his round sunglasses, scans the restaurant lunch crowd, then struts over to Linda's and Melanie's table. Up close, he looks considerably older than he'd at first appeared. Skin on his narrow, aquiline face is networked by lines that fan out from the corners of his mouth and dark eyes.

"Ladies," he says. "Our newcomers, yes? Mind if I join you?" His diction is quiet but crisp. A theatrical use of hard consonants allows his voice to pierce through the café's din easily.

Mel looks at him. Their eyes lock for a moment, and some wisp of intuition makes her wrinkle her nose.

"I do mind," she says. "My friend and I are enjoying a private chat."

He smiles with scant warmth. He reaches behind him, grabs the back of an empty chair at the next table, swings it over between his legs and sits down facing them. He props both forearms atop the chairback.

"Thanks," he says. "So kind."

He dips two fingers into an upper pocket of his frock coat, extracts a business card, drops it on the table. He taps it with a black-gloved fingertip. "Mark Nader," he says. "At your service. Able to meet any and all of your inking needs." He crosses his forearms once again, leans forward and rests his chin on them.

The card's logo is a skeletal hand holding a red needle that squirts a pair of small lightning bolts out of its tip. Linda uses her fork to push it back toward him.

"A highly experienced artisan," he says, "innovating at the vanguard of personal imagery."

"No doubt," Mel says. "But since we've zero interest in you or your 'art,' why don't you trot off and, uh, service yourself?"

His mirthless smirk takes on a cast of actual glee. He tucks the card back into a pocket.

"Miz Melanie Olson, social commentator *par excellence*," he says. "You know, I'd expect you to be spirited — well, peppery is what we call it in West Texas."

Mel's eyes narrow. She glances at Linda, then back at him.

"How'd you know my name?"

He grins. His teeth are yellow and stained, perhaps by coffee and tobacco, and the incisors are slightly crossed. "Our town's small. Word spreads fast. 'Specially, if a celebrity pops up, a major news gal like you. Had your column for what, three or four years?"

"That's right," she says. "But it only ran in papers in New York and DC."

"Count me as a giant fan of your work," he says.

"How'd you ever see it?"

"Oh. What I mean is, I'm a fan, as of this morning. Heard you had come to our fair community, and went to check out your archives on the 'Web. Love it. Tough stuff. You can drop molten sarcasm on pols when the mood strikes. Incinerate 'em!"

"Want to hear how I'd write up meeting you?"

"Probably not." His grin fades back into a thin-lipped smile. "Now, I also know you haven't scribbled for a while, guess 'cos you married that ol' moneybags congressman. Then you divorce him. Sad to lose a link to so much clout. Not to mention, his cash. Suddenly, you're a freelancer once more. Radical change, huh? But a body does go through 'em right? Lots of big stuff comes down in Washington. HQ for all sorts of outfits, ain't it?

"You, though, are independent, can pick your own jobs. You take interest in a badass by name of Burnett, and trek all the way to Sojourn. Guess we should be flattered, getting a Brenda Starr like you. So, how'd the sorry tale of Ted James Burnett ever catch your eye?"

Mel waves a dismissive hand. "Oh there's what, about eighty thousand people in solitary in the U.S. now, right? I drew straws and picked a few. Why do you care?"

"Curiosity. Might kill cats, but it keeps a man entertained. On the *qui vive*, like the French say." He turns his eyes to Linda, who meets his gaze with a glare of her own. "And this delectable — *ahem!* — lady of color. Linda Parker-r-r. Could not find a thing on her. So, who *is* she?"

"Executive assistant," Mel says. "Screens all my calls and visitors. Which reminds me. Did you make an appointment?"

"Actually?" Linda says "I most like my work as Melanie's bodyguard. I learn now to clear space for her, with kickboxing. You like to see some?" Her gaze remains level as she arches her eyebrows in invitation.

"Not at the moment." He chuckles. "Well, such a formidable pair. I always like to interact with visitors. Broadens my horizons. Never know what I'll find! So how long do you plan to be in our…"

"About two more seconds," Mel tells him. She looks at Linda. "Feel like my appetite's shot. How's yours? Want to scoot? Let's."

She pushes back her chair and stands up.

~

"Could *not* believe that guy!" Mel says. "Seriously creeped me out. Worse, even, than that horndog con up in the supermax, our phony Burnett, whoever *he* really was…"

Their SUV barrels down the dirt road out of Sojourn, trailing a plume of ocher dust.

"Not just you," Linda asserts. "Other guards who sit there in restaurant? Your steampunk man, he scares them too. I see this, okay."

"Uh-huh-h," Mel says, nodding slowly. "Now you mention it, I think you're right."

"So, *now* we call Dan? And Carl?"

"Well-l-l…" She glances over, sees her companion's frown, laughs. "Hon', you probably want to kill me, but one more thing for us to take a look at, before we call them. Tiny, okay?" She holds up a pinky and crooks it, trying to summon her compliance. "See, this boots-up all my old reporter programs! Couple tricks I had, whenever I didn't *quite* get a picture. I want a chance to use them, please? One trick was to go interview ex-wives, ex-husbands, ex-girlfriends or whatever…"

"And the second?"

"Business competitors. Need to find us another tattoo parlor."

Linda's frown melts. She feels intrigued.

"Got an idea that weirdo Mark has left a string of people behind who all hate his guts, don't you? Now, many of those might not be easy to find. But a competitor? Bet you, any neighbor town out here boasts a tat shop." She smiles. "We can find out more about him, and more about Sojourn. Our flight back to DC doesn't take off until nine at night, so we've got a ton of time yet. Should use it best we can, right?"

Chapter 8

As the Ecuadorian police drive Dan and Carl down the boulevards of Manta, they act as though Carl's protests amount to less than the whine of a mosquito. Their truck lurches to a halt at a headquarters for the national police. Ultimately, a cop in the front seat turns around to poke Carl hard on the sternum with an end of his baton.

"*Cierra el boquino!*" he says, meaning, "Shut your deformed hole."

At the gate, a shadowy figure in a round guard station with reflective windows touches a control, and a broad steel portal jerks and begins to shudder open.

As they wait to enter, Dan sees a sign with peeling paint, COMANDO CANTONAL DE POLICÍA MANTA. By it is a wall decorated with many colorful drawings, crude stuff, barely more than primitive street art. One shows a long-haired captive, bound and hanging by a harness from the roof of a cell, with a square of tape stuck over his mouth. Next to it, a line of Spanish is scrawled: "Try to escape, and you will only get tired."

Another image champions a team of black-clad cops who level automatic weapons. Words near it read, SERVIR PROTEGER, or SERVE TO PROTECT.

The truck surges through the gate. Soon they get yanked from the vehicle and hustled down a corridor.

"Under questioning, we say that roll of Euros got planted on me!" Carl whispers to Dan fiercely. "Say, by the bastard who frisked us!"

"Sure, a set-up," Dan agrees, *sotto voce*. "But not by the cop. Those drunks did it. Pickpocket team at the bar. Fat puker was the 'stall,' that skinny dude was the 'dip.' Didn't try for your wallet, just wanted to shove in that wad. Soon as the cops saw it done, they pounced."

Carl blinks. "Okay. Let's back up. Cover story. We should agree…"

One of their escorts turns and bustles in between them, shoving them hard into opposite walls.

"*Cállate!*" he orders. "Shut up!"

At the next hall intersection they're separated and frog-marched in opposite directions.

～

Dan's interrogator is a natty officer whose stern face is decorated by gold-wire rim spectacles, and his slender body by a tailored uniform with sharp creases on the shirt sleeves and pant legs. The Ecuadorian detective kicks a polished black loafer out intermittently, as he perches on a corner of a metal desk.

Dan answers all of this officer's questions with boilerplate. "I am Daniel Cowell, a citizen of the United States. I demand that I be allowed to contact my embassy."

The officer shows no exasperation. He smiles at Dan, and asks a guard in the room, "Check on this guest's safety and comfort, *por favor*. See to *las esposas*."

Dan has been sitting atop a low metal stool, his cuffed arms hanging behind him. He hears sharp clicks as those steel bands are cinched tighter. Instantly nerves in his hands tingle as if from electric shocks. Seconds later, they grow numb. He has a daunting vision of his fingers turning into blood sausages.

The officer leans toward Dan, levels a hard stare.

"You gringos were the last people to see Yuri Tyraslo alive," he accuses.

Dan is startled. "Um, he's dead?"

"Yes! Found where you tossed out his body, like trash! Floating in the *bahia*! With his ID and all his things. But not the money he carried to buy supplies for his vessel. You *must* have known of it. At the Balandra, he flashes this bankroll for you, yes? What did you hope to buy with all his cash, after you stole it? Drugs? Weapons?"

"Hold on, whoa. We *can't* have been the last to see him," Dan says. "Only one chunk of that is right. Yes, Yuri was another traveler we met, and we had a drink with him. Foreigners meet in a port town all the time, right? Yes, we were at that bar. But he left, like, an hour before we did."

"Not true!" the officer yells. "You left at the exact same time! We have witnesses!"

Dan is quiet for a moment. "I am a citizen of the United States..." he begins.

"You are a thief and a murderer."

"... and I demand..."

The officer bounces up onto his feet, making as if to strike Dan in the face. But that blow does not land.

"*Ir a la mierda.*"

Dan shakes his head at this gross obscenity. "*Besa su madre con esta boca?*" He asks him. "You kiss your mom with that mouth?"

"After we finish with you," the officer grimly assures him, "your mouth will not be able to kiss anyone. Not even your ugly gringo boyfriend, *maricón.* You'll be lucky if you even know where your own head is located."

He glances at the guard. "*A la celda,*" he orders.

～

Dan sighs with relief when the guard unlocks and strips off the tight handcuffs. The dank cell where he's shoved is a cubicle with rusting steel slab walls. The steel door has a shuttered viewing slot up high, and another low, for delivering food trays. The cell's sole other feature is a hole in the floor that emits the stench and sluggish gurgle of sewage. He has a hard time deciding which is most nauseating, its sound or smell.

As circulation returns to his hands, they feel as if they are being sawn to pieces by serrated knives. He sits in a corner and gently massages each wrist. His mind whirls. *What next?*

An hour passes before the door clanks and creaks again, and Carl gets shoved inside to join him. "Well," he says calmly. "How'd you do?"

"*A cover story?* You bet, a good one on tap, that would've been great!" Dan snarls back. "You're the all-time pro, right?"

"Well…"

"It's under control though? Locals clued in? Everything on a master plan?"

"No," Carl admits. "But, it's not as bad as it looks."

"It's not? Hey, cheer me up."

"We've got a lawyer."

"Oh, snap. *Now* I feel better!"

"Not just anyone. It's Núwa."

"What? Is she for real?"

"Yep. Lawyerin's her day job."

"And they let you call her?"

"Not right away. Had to impress them."

"How?"

"With my cell phone, which is a highly secure module. No way to get at the SIM card or any of the innards without sparkin' off a booby-trap. They noticed it was odd, and asked me to switch it on.

So I did."

"And?"

"Set off the booby-trap, of course. It farts out a big dose of CS gas."

"Didn't they get pissed?"

"Heck yeah. But I pointed out, me ownin' such a nifty piece of gear could mean I'm hooked up in lotta 'portant ways. Want to charge me with a crime? Best not omit a step of legal protocol en route, or it'll come back to haunt 'em."

"What about me?"

"Told 'em you weren't cool at all. To you, they can do whatever they like."

"Thanks."

"Don't mention it."

"But… why screw around? Cut to the chase!"

"Meanin'?"

"Astound 'em, for example, by saying you're a U.S. intel officer of high rank, here on a mission of great importance."

"Um, no."

"Why the hell not?"

Carl looks uncomfortable. "No need, as of yet."

Dan studies him. "Okay, you're scaring me. What, we're out on a limb? A 'Mission Impossible' deal? Like, 'anyone killed or captured, a secretary of deep undercover gummint horseshit disavows all knowledge,' and blah-blah-blah?"

"Sort of."

"Jeeeezus. Christ."

Carl points at the walls of their cell. He touches a finger to his lips, to suggest silence.

Dan crosses eyes theatrically, leans back, and lets himself slide limply down to the floor.

~

After Núwa comes onto the scene, their situation improves rapidly. Dan sees the wisdom in having such a gorgeous operative on call. Sure, ugly or nondescript agents, the sort of folks who can blend in with wallpaper, they might have their uses. But a looker like Núwa? Who wins male attention the instant she sashays through a door, who can score favors simply by asking for them? *Mas mo' bettah*, he thinks. Now getting the trumped-up charges dropped and their freedom restored could be in the cards. Or so Dan dares to hope.

They're brought to a room with stained white walls, a folding table and wooden chairs. A tray of Styrofoam coffee cups is on the table, lifting coils of steam up into the humid air. And on the table's far side, appearing altogether cool and calm, sits lovely Núwa. Her long black hair is pinned up in a tidy bun, and a ruffled white blouse peeks out from the collar of a forest-green blazer. Her charms are dialed down a mite by that all-business garb. Nevertheless, any healthy male's first impulse would be to try to persuade her to please undo at least the top button on that blouse.

"Damn! Am I glad to see you," Dan says.

Carl shoots him a warning glance — *Don't act as if you know her.*

"Evenin', Miss Robles," Carl says. "Think I recall you once did a service for some friends of mine, a year or two back. Passport and visa issues, if I'm not mistaken. You worked as a paralegal in the office of your father, back then. Thank you for takin' my call."

"Correct," Núwa says. Corners of her mouth crinkle in a smile. "I must say, the situation you find yourself in tonight, Mister Carlos Black — and your friend Mister Cowell — is difficult. But I can recommend a solution."

"I'm all ears, Miss Robles."

"Let's describe your situation. The man who planted that roll of Euros on you is known as 'Rata.' He's a pickpocket, the most notorious in all of Manabí State."

Dan looks smug. He reaches for one of the cups of coffee.

"Your big stroke of luck is that some off-duty *Guardacostas* men were downing drinks in the next bar. They know who Rata is, and saw this entire event unfold. They have caused this to be described to certain key people."

"Hence, these cops have to admit that it *is* a tainted case?" Carl grabs a coffee for himself. "Can the port captain make 'em let us go?"

"No, unfortunately not." Núwa sketches a line with an exquisitely trimmed and lacquered fingernail. "Since it occurs on a wrong side of the road, you see, which presents a jurisdiction problem. If on the ocean side, the port captain has the authority to prevail, but in this case, the national police do. Plus, officials in Quito have begun to take a keen interest. Which complicates the matter."

"I see." Carl gulps coffee, rubs a brown rivulet off his chin.

"A point of leverage? That money," she says. "Ten thousand in Euros. Was it Rata's? Or not, after he gives it to you so kindly? One thing, surely, no links to a dead man, since it is planted on you by Rata. Not taken off that Ukrainian. So what happens to it, then, plus American dollars you carry? I suggested this total be sufficient for bail, especially since the murder and robbery charges they wished to bring on you now seem so fragile."

"You get to be voluptuous, pretty, and hella smart too?" Dan says. "Not very fair to other women, is it?"

Núwa awards him a luminous smile.

"So this idea ran up the flagpole. Did they salute?" Carl asks.

She nods. "You'll be released on bail at three o'clock this morning. But you must commit to stay right here in Manta, and not depart until all your legal difficulties are resolved."

"Cross my heart, and hope for pie," Carl says.

"If you try to skip bail, national police at any place in Ecuador can arrest you. That would be a separate and distinct crime, easy to prosecute."

"Right. So, who collects us on release? That's sort of important."

"I believe certain parties have assisted you before, in similar situations," Núwa says.

"I believe that also."

"Therefore, I should contact them."

"We'll see you-all at 0300."

~

They return to the steel-lined cell.

"Must be their maximum pit," Dan says.

Carl shrugs. "I've seen worse."

"We both have."

Carl grins. "No rabid bats! Major improvement. But you, you seem the same."

"If I could pick one person for my cellie, you wouldn't be it."

"Mutual. I asked the cops to exchange you for Núwa, but they wouldn't bite."

"Bet she wouldn't, either."

"Don't rub it in."

Dan smiles. "Okay! Sore point. Let's change the subject. A deal was just worked out for us, right?"

"Uh-huh."

"So why are we back in stir? I'm not feeling the love."

"It's because…"

Boots stomp up to their door. It clanks, swings wide. The cops who stand there now look more hardcase than any they've yet seen. They're clad in full riot armor, hats-and-bats. Helmets and black ski masks conceal everything except hard stares. And the two biggest guys standing in front clench in their thick fists the striped yellow plastic frames of M26 Tasers and aim these at Dan and Carl.

They jerk the Taser barrels in a universal gesture that says, move your butts.

"Ay muchachos, a donde queren conducirnos? Esta el tiempo exacto, todavía no." Dan asks. "Hey boys, where is it you want to take us? It's not the right time yet."

"Vengan!" A taser-wielding cop barks. "Come!"

Dan considers a double set of 50,000-volt barbed darts as persuasive, so he nods compliance. As he walks slowly from the cell he glances at Carl, and sees a "v" forming between his brows. At the same time, Carl's body relaxes, as if he might be seeking to collect some energy before an athletic contest… or, perhaps, as if he wants to suggest a bit of fake submission to a potential opponent.

They've really begun to piss him off, Dan thinks.

With the Taser cops striding at their backs, they are ushered with considerable force down a hall, through a series of metal-clad doors.

"Wrong direction," Carl mutters tonelessly. "Not taking us out to the main gate."

"Wrong time, too," Dan answers. "It's just midnight and change."

They reach a utility lot soaked by a dewy night. Black hulks of patrol vehicles are parked in lines on both sides. Before them is a concrete block wall inset by a steel slab door. One cop keys a massive padlock and slides back a bolt. They are shoved forward, into what looks like a schoolyard, complete with a soccer field and a basketball court.

The armored police have not handcuffed them, and do nothing to prevent them from talking. Obviously, the cops are confident.

"Dudes got a plan," Dan murmurs.

"Course," Carl replies. "You 'n' me are tryin' to escape. Do whatever they want to do to stop us."

"But, why break out?" Dan is puzzled. "Already got us a deal to go free."

"And who knows that?"

"Ah."

They're led to another steel slab door, this one set inside a welded wall of more steel slabs.

"Distract them," Carl says.

Dan hesitates. Then, "*Por favor, señores? Donde estan mis carteras, y relojes, y mi mobíl?*" he asks. "Please, gentlemen? Where are our passports and wristwatches, and my cell phone?"

One cop chuckles, none reply. Before them, the door is unlocked and pushed open.

Carl turns to one of the Taser cops. "*Un momento, qué hora es?*" He points at the man's left wrist. "One moment, what time is it?"

The man flicks a glance at his wrist. Carl pounces, snatching his striped M26, forcing it up and firing it into the neck of the other Taser cop, who leaps, quivers and topples. Carl swings an elbow into the nose of the cop whose weapon he'd grabbed. The man stumbles. Other policemen jostle each other as they try to swing batons or draw their pistols. Carl bends, picks up the unfired Taser from the fallen cop, gives Dan a sharp look, and jumps through the open door. Dan follows. They land in an alley, slam the door shut, brace their bodies against it. Immediately comes a thud of boots and shoulders crashing into it from the other side. The door lurches, but they are able to hold it.

Carl holds up a finger. "Let one through," he says, and steps back, aiming the Taser.

Dan straightens, backs away.

The door *bongs* open. A man hurtles through and Carl fires the Taser right into his face. Dan jumps forward and gives the door the mightiest shove he can. It thuds into whoever is trying to come through next, knocking him back.

The policeman Carl darted tumbles, skids, writhes, goes limp, and shudders. Carl sends him another jolt, takes away his automatic pistol, checks its chamber and safety, then aims it at the door.

"Hey, they're not shootin'," he says. "Keep it all mum, I guess. But I don't mind a hullaballoo. Sometimes it's a good thing."

He gestures for Dan to move away, then pops a fusillade of five shots right into the steel slab. Shouted commands are heard on the far side, next comes a frenzy of return fire. Dimpled by all the rounds banging into it from both sides, the steel door creaks and shudders. A silence falls. Nobody else tries to go through.

At one end of the alley, vehicle headlights switch on. Other bright lights ignite at the opposite end, and they stand washed in the combined glare.

"How's your eight hundred-yard dash?" Carl asks.

"Ready," Dan says. "Which way?"

He points.

~

They bolt across the pavement to a low iron fence, vault it, and — suddenly and incongruously — stand inside a parking lot for an upscale shopping center. "El Paseo," reads a sign on the mall façade. It's the wee hours, so only a few cars occupy the lot, the vehicles of employees who are mopping floors and restocking shelves.

"Search for a car with keys?"

"No," Carl says. "Better keep on initiatin'."

Roar of an engine and a tortured squeal of skittering rubber come from somewhere.

Dan and Carl sprint across the lot, plunge through brush. They cross a four-lane boulevard. Dan recognizes it as the *Avenida 4 de Noviembre*, the street on which the cops had taken them to jail. As they reach its far side, a pickup with headlights and fog lamps ablaze backs from an alley at full throttle, spins out and bashes into a street lamp that topples over amid a shower of sparks. Another SUV roars out, squeals around the corner and heads straight for them.

They run for a fence, pull themselves over it, jump into a lot, vault another fence, find themselves in a back yard with a staked-out dog lunging at the end of a chain, spinning in circles, and barking wildly. Inside the house, lights switch on.

"'K," Carl says, panting. "They'll hunt for two people. We split up, doubles a chance one of us gets free. If it's you, make it to Núwa's, at 1240 Calle Guerrero, south side of town. But if that looks compromised, double back to the port captain's office. Have him bring you to our embassy in Quito."

"Really?"

"Yeah. Difference is, with him, it can happen."

"But… is it best for your mission if we both stay on the lam?"

Carl blinks. "Sure," he says.

"How about this, then. I saw that this boulevard, Fourth of November, crosses the Rio Manta. If we lose our pursuit, meet you under that bridge. I think it's on the way to Núwa's."

Carl's mouth quirks. "Deal." He claps Dan on the shoulder. "Don't screw the pooch."

"Same."

They sprint for opposite fences when a door in the house opens. A burly man wearing a T-shirt and striped boxer shorts appears, silhouetted by the interior light. He brandishes an aluminum baseball bat and shouts, "*Quién está ahí?*"

~

Dan can hear the sounds of a pickup screeching around. He figures out which direction it's going and heads a different way. He reaches an alley behind a line of small shops. A stooped figure in a battered hat and poncho made out of a ragged swatch of plastic tarpaulin is bending over garbage cans. As he rushes by, the figure turns its head to look at him, and Dan notes a grizzled, sagging face, a sad and rheumy eye.

Un hombre del campo, Dan thinks, *old peasant displaced from the country, just struggling to survive in this harbor town.*

A few strides further on, a sudden idea strikes him. He stops and goes back.

"*Abuelo, necesito su ayuda para escapar de hombres malos. Puede cambiar la ropa conmigo?*" Dan says. "Grandfather, I need your help to escape from bad men. Can you swap clothes with me?"

The brim of the battered hat raises, and a weary face studies him while a toothless mouth works. When the old man speaks, his voice sounds thin, clogged with phlegm, like a faint breeze rattling through dry palms. "*Sí, señor... Y sus zapatos, también,*" he says. "Yes, sir... and your shoes, too."

Dan looks down at the man's sticky black flip flops, almost worn through at both heels. "Oh all right, you old goat!" He yanks off his relatively new boots.

The oldster wheezes out a chuckle as he doffs his hat and tattered poncho, hands them over.

A few minutes later, Dan shuffles down a sidewalk of the main boulevard in what he imagines is a decent mimicry of the beggar's limp. From his hand dangles a bag of garbage he'd plucked from the can.

A pickup screeches to a halt beside him. "*Viejo!*" someone shouts. "*Has visto a dos gringos?*"

Dan rotates slowly, points at his ear to indicate deafness, shakes his head to show utter incomprehension. The man curses, the truck roars off. After Dan reaches the bridge, he scouts around, shuffles down past the abutment to peer into shadows. Nothing. But then a whistle comes across the turgid green water. Carl must already be across the river. Despite the risk of losing his flip flops in the muck, Dan decides to wade over to him.

"Quite the fashion statement, there," Carl greets him.

"Yep, my look says I ain't worth bothering about."

"Works."

"Then you work it too." Dan dumps out his garbage bag, and offers Carl the dripping sack. "Here's your new shirt."

"Ugh."

"Just turn it inside out. Rip some holes for neck and arms, you're good to go."

"Shit. Oh, all right. Long as I can accessorize with this."

Carl holds up the pistol he had seized from the cop. Dan gets his first good look at it — a Taurus model 1911 chambered in nine millimeter.

"Heavy piece! Well, if the sucker jams, you can always use it as a club."

"'Zackly."

"So, what's the next big plan?"

"You mean, now that Manta cops are in full uproar?"

"Uh-huh."

"High time we hightailed it home, back to the good ol' USA."

"Fine. Do we stroll to the highway and stick out a thumb?"

"Well, boardin' a vehicle of some kind now would be good."

"How?"

"Now let's look for a car with keys, or an old rig we can hot-wire. Spot any decent option, jump on it."

"I'm game."

Carl snickers. "Perfect. 'Cos it j-u-s-t happens to be huntin' season."

~

Moving along backstreets and alleys, hopping a fence whenever they must, Dan and Carl make their way southward along the east side of Manta. They keep about a block apart, observe each other carefully, and give hand signals to indicate the approach of vehicles, or alternatively, to show when the way is clear. Pedestrians don't yet pose a problem. At least, not until they reach a residential one-way street near the Via Circunvalacion.

Dan sees Carl point at his eyes then point ahead, and beckon for him to come up. Together, they peer around a corner. Three young men in dark-colored hoodies are quietly unloading sawhorses and traffic cones from a flatbed, and using them to build some sort of traffic funnel and barricade.

"Checkpoint?" Dan whispers.

Carl shakes his head. "In a neighborhood? To what purpose?" he replies softly. "Plus, no uniforms on 'em. And who does a thing like that in the dead of night?"

Dan hears the mutter of an engine, and sees a tiny sedan turn a corner and start up the street. He taps Carl on the shoulder. They watch the car approach, then turn around to see how the hooded men will react. They've all mysteriously vanished.

The car slows as it nears the barricade, its driver acts confused by what he sees — there seems to be no obvious route through the obstacles. As the car pauses with its brake lights on, the three men leap from the nearby doorways. Two of them flank the car, pounding with their fists on its doors. One moves in front, and points a handgun through the windshield at the driver.

"Carjackin'!" Carl says. "Come on!"

He sprints up the block, keeping to the shadows. Dan kicks off his sorry flip flops and runs barefooted in his wake. As they get close, Dan can see the driver sitting with his hands raised, but making no other moves. The goons on the sides are apparently not armed. But they make no progress by shaking their fists and yanking on the door handles, since the driver keeps his car's windows up and doors locked.

Dan decides in a split-second to offer Carl an advantage. He runs out into the center of the street, waving his arms up over his head, and yells, "Hey!"

The goons turn and look at him. The one with the gun points it approximately at Dan, who quickly drops to the pavement.

Carl bursts out of the shadows, reaches the gunman in two strides, and whips him across the forehead with the steel barrel of his Taurus. He crumples. The other two men look at each other, decide they hate the fresh course this encounter is taking, and they bolt. One decides to sprint past Dan. It's a mistake.

Dan rises in a crouch, jumps, rolls, and takes the runner out with a leg sweep. The man is moving so fast that he seems to fly above the pavement horizontally for a second before his head and arms and chest slap down with a satisfying thump and he skids to a halt on his face.

Meanwhile, the driver has his own notion on how to escape the mess. He flings the car in reverse, backs up through a sawhorse and over some cones, over-accelerates, and crunches a taillight and rear fender against a building. He twists the wheel, shoots forward, and bashes a headlight and front fender into a brick stoop on the opposite side of the road. The crumpled front bumper hangs up on the bricks, and the wheels spins uselessly.

Lights come on in the windows of nearby homes.

Carl carries two guns now. He walks to the car and taps the barrel of one against the windshield. The driver throws his hands up again. Dan finally can see him clearly, a lanky young man with brown curly hair, black-framed Buddy Holly glasses, and a panicked expression. Carl sticks both guns down into his waistband, holds up his own empty hands, and gives a peace sign with two fingers. The driver looks puzzled, then swivels his head to take in Dan.

Dan removes the old *campesino's* greasy fedora to reveal his face, and smilingly gestures for the driver to roll down the window. He hesitates, then complies.

"*No tenga miedo, somos amigos, y queremos ayudarle,*" Dan tells him.

"Don't be afraid, we are friends, and we want to help you." He reaches inside and touches the button that unlocks the sedan's doors.

The driver looks skeptical. "You are Americans?" His English is both grammatical and fairly well pronounced.

"You bet," Dan says. "And we…"

"It's your turn to do something for us," Carl says curtly. "Let's *vamanos, comprendes?*"

The driver's eyes rove back and forth between them.

"First, let's get this car loose." Carl leads the way to the front. He kicks savagely at the snagged bumper.

"No, it's ridden up on the first step. Lift it off."

"Right."

They curl their forearms around the front of the vehicle.

"One, two…"

"Three!"

And heave. The small sedan rolls back a foot.

Carl goes to the window. "Can you drive?"

The young man yanks on the car's stick shift, engages the clutch, and promptly stalls the engine.

"Never mind," Carl says.

He opens the door, bunches up the driver's shirtfront in his fist, and — over his yelp of protest — hauls him out like a sack of wet laundry. He opens the rear door and pitches him on the back seat. Carl inserts himself behind the steering wheel, starts it up. Dan jumps in on the passenger side. Carl revs the engine, steers the vehicle, and they shoot away down the street. Residents emerge from doors to stare after the rapidly departing vehicle. Their gazes shift to the pair of limp bodies left behind on the pavement.

～

"Núwa," Carl says.

"We're late."

"That, I know."

The streets remain drenched in shadow, it's still at least two hours before sunrise. At Calle Guerrero, they slow to make a sharp left. They go by a parked SUV with pale vapor oozing from its tailpipe. They pass a small knot of young men and a few middle-aged men who stand bunched together on the sidewalk. All of them wear civilian clothes. A few smoke cigarettes, others flick ash from cigars. They seem to be waiting for something.

"Oh, fuck me," Carl says.

Dan tries to recon the group without being too obvious about it. But one of them stares directly back at him with squint-eyed intensity as their car passes.

On the back seat, the car's young owner sits tensely, his spine straight. His knobby hands are clasped tightly between his knees. He's also noticed the men on the sidewalk. As he speaks, his voice goes high and tight.

"You help me to escape from the attack on my street. Thank you. I help you flee off from what I don't know. You are welcome. Now I think the time is high that somebody says what the hell is going on."

Dan and Carl glance at each other.

"*No problema, compadre*," Carl says. "But hey, it's okay, we grab one more sec' of your time, here? You happen to be carrying a cell phone, or what?"

Patches of color burn in the young man's cheeks.

"Yes," he says primly. "But first, you will answer my question."

Carl grunts and ignores him.

"That's Núwa's place." Carl points at a six-story apartment building, flanked by two lower structures. Boasting a two-tone paint job and a swatch of landscaping, it looks to be decently upscale lodging for a young attorney with a practice in Manta. He drives by without slowing.

"No one's posted out front," Dan says.

"Probably set a wider perimeter," Carl says.

He continues uphill for four blocks, steers up a side street, finds a dead-end alley and parks. He turns around in his seat.

"Okay," he tells the youth. "Here's what's goin' down. I'm Carl, he's Dan. We're here in your country on a job for the U.S. government. One we hoped to do quietly, but it's turned noisy. Your police want us to move in with them for a stay — an invite we prefer to decline. My number-one goal is gettin' our tails safely out of Manta, and even better, your whole country. Next, I want to make sure that anyone who has helped us keeps safe. That does include you. All right. Short 'n' sweet, what's your story? Why'd those knuckleheads want to boost you, back there? Looked like a carjack. They just after your auto, or maybe somethin' else?"

The young man takes a deep breath and releases it slowly. "I am Bernardo Hitchens," he says. "I work for *El Satirico*, have you heard of it? A journal of opinions, that is very combative. We poke hard at, how you say, sacred bulls? It is our job to be in a small degree of trouble, all the time. However, lately, there has been much trouble, especially for me. People high up in our government hate my work, and I have threats. Not from them, directly, but anonymous. I was simply driving to my home after a late visit to… my girlfriend. What you just saw on my street was a threat coming true."

Carl's mouth quirks into a smile. "Well, well. Seems like we're turnin' into quite the lil' mob of outlaws. I hereby declare you an honorary member. Now, may I trouble you for that phone?"

Bernardo reaches into a cargo pocket on the thigh of his pants and takes out a Samsung. "I don't know who might be listening in on me," he warns.

"We never do, right?" Carl says. "But at least, in terms of our gal, a call from you comes straight out of the blue. That's got to confuse 'em, at least some." He keys in a number, lets it ring once, and ends the call. He repeats the process, and on his third call, quietly speaks into the mic. "Bravo, Oscar, Tango, Charlie, Hotel," he says. "Click once for 'copy,' twice for re-play…"

Satisfied, he gives Bernardo back his phone. "Now take out your battery and SIM card, please," he requests.

"Okay," he turns to Dan. "And as for you, I just want to borrow your hat. Then I'll go slink around a bit. Keep your eyes on the north wall of Núwa's building. Might spot something entertainin'. But if you see or hear a fight, or I'm not back in half an hour, go throw yourself on the mercy of the port captain, Rodrigo Sanchez." He jerks a thumb at Bernardo. "And take him with you. Unless he happens to think up a better bet for himself."

"Roger all," Dan says. "But jeez, man… got to say, you really put together one hell of a vacation package."

~

He can find no flaw in Carl's choice of parking spots. The mouth of the alley looks out above the roofs of low houses to afford a view of the upper floors of Núwa's building. As he studies it, Dan sees something like a roll of thread tumble down the wall facing him. It drops down by a dark corner shaded from street lamps. Something begins to glide down that line. Then he realizes the moving dot is a human being.

"She's on rappel!" He chuckles. "So, that's how she'll get past 'em."

He yearns for night vision or good low-light binocs so he can better track Núwa's progress. Looks like she's scooting along pretty good, though. That sight takes him back to the mountain-climbing days of his youth.

Probably using a Figure Eight 'binered to a swami belt. I remember that, those first giddy seconds as you lean out over a steep face, trust the pro', and off you go over the edge. If she's on a full-pitch rope, looks like she is, should have the length to reach ground, even if she's got it doubled through the Eight....

Sooner than he imagines it possible, he hears a rapid patter of footfalls approach the alley. He peers around a corner and spots Carl in the lead, recognizing him by the shapeless hat on his head.

He jumps back to the car — "Hey, here they come," he tells Bernardo — starts the vehicle up and backs from the alley. When Carl and Núwa reach the car, they yank open the doors and pile inside.

"Hell-Hound Limos," Dan welcomes them calmly. "What part of Hades you folks like to go to, t'night?"

"Good friggin' question," Carl says. "People? I think blowin' this popstand is a non-starter. There ain't that many roads out, and all are likely under scrutiny. We need a joint in town where we can lay low. On that, I'll take suggestions from the floor. Or even the back seat."

Bernardo and Núwa eye one other with an air of recognition, but also a jot of discomfort. They'd noted each other in passing, as they moved around in Manta society, but never happened to meet before. Doing so gracefully at this moment is complicated. This car's narrow back seat forces a pair of tall people like them to touch each other more than is proper for strangers.

Bernardo is grateful for being given something else to think about.

"My father's penthouse?" he suggests. "He owns a place on the rim of *El Murciélago*. And I have a key."

"Your pop, eh? Might he be home?"

"Most likely, not. Deep-sea fishing, that is now my father's big pursuit. He owns a Bertram boat that he uses to chase after tuna and swordfish, he likes to hunt for them out in the bluest water. That's where he probably is right now. Halfway out to the Galápagos."

"Fun guy. Owns a penthouse and a yacht. How'd he make his dough?" Carl asks.

"Oh, exports," Bernado says, waving a hand.

"Yeah? Like what?" Carl persists.

Bernardo gives him a blank look. "He does not talk much about that," he says, after a pause.

"O-o-kay. But he's also got this stylin' crib above the beach."

"Yes."

"Where does he live mostly?"

"On the boat."

"Convenient," Carl says. "Núwa? Your opinion?"

"I know of no better spot," she says. "What he describes, it is out among the very wealthy, it overlooks a boardwalk and Manta's public beach. The police have no way to guess we might go there."

"Cool beans, then. Let's roll."

～

Carl pads outdoors through thin, billowing curtains, out into morning air, walking on a tiled balcony that feels cool and slick under his bare feet. He's just emerged from a shower, and wears only a bath towel tucked around his waist. His bare back is lean and well-muscled, but in many places his skin is ridged with dots and lines of pale tissue. This topography of scars is the souvenir from a covert mission in an unnamed country, where he was ambushed by a radio-controlled IED and peppered with a shrapnel burst. Under one arm is a dark, puckered divot — what's left of a sutured bullet hole, a memento from the previous year's soirée in Honduras.

The morning air is starched by a light smell of sea. He stands at the balcony railing, uses it as a prop to steady himself during a series of stretches meant to retain his spine's flexibility. As he performs these moves, his eyes sweep back and forth along the shoreline, studying the contours of land, water and piers, the moored vessels. The *Dean Swift*, of course, is not among them. He wonders which direction she sailed, north or south? Or west, even? Leonid Andreyev apparently can go wherever he wants, whenever he wants, with full official cooperation — no matter whose officials they happen to be.

He hears a faint sound, turns.

Out onto the balcony comes Núwa, swathed in a white terrycloth bathrobe. Her long hair is loose and tousled, and her makeup has been swabbed off, but her natural coloring is more than sufficient to render her luminous.

"A beautiful day," she murmurs.

"Any day out of the slammer is a good day…"

"How are you?"

"Wringin' out my noodle, as I try to figure a next move."

"See any good possibilities?"

"Well, I'm inspired by Bernardo's dad and his long fishin' trips. See some pretty stylin' boats tied up, down there."

He points at the blue-water fishing yachts moored in a row next to the Manta Yacht Club, then ticks off a few of their charms on his fingers. "Seaworthy. Fast. Radar. Strong radios."

"Maybe a hot tub?"

"Nah. Bet I could find one with a live bait well, though. Water's sorta cool, but at least you'd get some bubbles. Might have to share it with a fish."

Núwa makes a face. "No thank you. So… is your thought, we wait here for Bernardo's daddy to sail in, then convince him to take a new voyage?"

"Nope. Why waste any time? Let's just grab a rig we like. I'm a do-it-yourself guy."

She nods. "Hitchens senior would likely not help, anyhow. He does not want to put his relations with the authorities at risk. He was in the National Assembly, and later worked as a Minister of Natural Resources. Now that he's retired, his export business consists of sending illegal cargoes of dried shark fins to China."

"Shock me."

"I'll try. His son's a cartoonist."

"Say what? At that satire magazine?"

"Yes. He is highly respected by many people for that. Except by his dad, of course."

"And he irritates the government too?"

Núwa smiles. "Yes, his specialty is making fun of officials, even the president. You see, lately Correa insists he should say who gets to run all the media outlets. He even wants journalists to be licensed, so everything they say can be controlled. These days, if he gets mad at a reporter, he challenges him to a fistfight, or even a duel. Bernardo has mocked all this. He draws the president many times wearing a foolish *lucha libre* outfit, bouncing around in a ring. And about this, they get so-o-o upset. Or 'pissed' is a better word. Correct?"

"Uh-huh." Carl looks amused. "Well, it was a stroke of luck, runnin' into Bernardo the way we did," he says. "It's great that he's lettin' us hide out at his dad's. But I think we'll have to make our own luck from here on out." He looks at Núwa speculatively. Her hourglass figure remains in evidence, despite her robe's enveloping folds.

"So, why don't you go in and wake Bernardo up in your own sweet way, and lure him out here. Let's have him use his skills to draw us a lil' picture that shows us all the ways his daddy's yacht club works. Layout and so forth."

Chapter 9

Mel and Linda wink at each other as their rental SUV finally glides onto smooth pavement. All the irritating rumble and jounce of the gravel route out of Sojourn, they happily leave behind. Rather than continue east to CRP airport at Corpus Christi, they take a hard left and head north, to the rural hamlet of Cinnabar Springs.

On the town's outskirts, they spot a Valero gas station, branded in yellow and blue, then a Sonic drive-in, bedecked in garish yellow, red and blue, with cars parked below its long awning. They see more boarded-up storefronts, buildings faced with hand-painted signs. A BBQ neon marquee features a joyful hog, clad in a sombrero, dancing back and forth over a flaming grill.

Melanie snorts. "Look!" she says, pointing. "Like Hitler doing his jig at Compiègne. Know that one?"

Linda shakes her head.

"Check it out on YouTube. You'll see…"

Then a bail bondsman's window, a taqueria, and a tattoo shop.

The sign reads INKS, INC.

"Well, whaddya know. A competitor. And plus, his place is open!" Mel exclaims.

She parks.

"My plan is," she tells Linda, "I go in that tat parlor to pull a ditzy blond act. Ask dumb questions in that way, nobody blinks. But… you walking in with me? Could make us too interesting. Know what I mean?"

Linda nods gravely. "America, this is country you know," she says. "You tell me how we do it in a best way."

"Right. So I'll manage the shop visit by myself, and meantime, you wander about. Chat up some of these people around here. See what you can find out."

"Of?"

"Well, ask about Sojourn. Pick up info about the game ranch, or the jail. Maybe find someone who works there?"

"Okay."

As they passed the Sonic drive-in Linda saw an older, Indian-looking man in a worn plaid shirt and a straw cowboy hat sitting placidly at a bus bench with his hands on his knees. Something about the man's stillness, and his easy watchfulness, had drawn her attention. She decides that, first, she'll walk back south and talk to that man.

∿

Melanie pushes open the door to the tattoo shop, a brass bell tinkles. A middle-aged man with long hair and goatee, wearing square reading glasses, looks up from a magazine he's paging through. He's on a brown-leather barber chair. Nearby is an antique cabinet that holds rows of jars with powdered dyes in sumptuous colors. The man swings his denim-clad legs to the floor, grabs an aluminum cane, and limps over to the counter. He slaps a tattered issue of *Outlaw Biker* down, and a bare-breasted woman straddling a Harley looks coyly back up at Mel.

"Help you?"

"Oh, I don't know…" Mel sighs. "I'm having such a wild time out here in Texas. And I guess I want a souvenir. My boyfriend sort of dared me…"

"What? To get a tat?" The man's voice is gruff, sounds as if it rumbles from a larynx damaged by smoking. "Easy 'nuff to give you a bit of Texas stuff. Bluebonnet, yellow rose, the star flag. Like that."

"Will it hurt?"

"Naw. Not much, 'specially we make it small. Can put it just about anywhere on you. Want to really surprise him?"

"He told me that I ought to drive out to a cool place in Sojourn to get it done. But then I saw your shop…"

"Sure." He shrugs. "Mark's a guy can do it, no question, that's what you want. Kind of a long ways to go. But dang, you're here, we can get 'er done, quick and simple. Make it a one-stop, know what I mean?"

"Well-l-l, anyhow, he did say to be careful around that Mark guy, too. Made me feel a bit nervous about going to him actually, you want to know the truth."

"Huh." The man looks down, and smiles into his beard. "Wise for a gal to take extry care in any strange town. That's just good streets."

"Well this Mark… I don't know… not weird or anything, is he?"

He looks up. "Man's got a history," he says. "But like I say, I can get you fixed. Want to see my binder of sample images? Some real showcases. 'Course, don't imagine that you're 'zackly in the hunt for full sleeves."

"History? What sort?"

His eyes are watery brown moons that slowly rise over the top rim of his glasses.

"Cons and guards, and folk like 'em, are Mark's preferred customers," he says. "What's 'at tell you? Need a snake crawling out of a laughing skull, he's your man. Ton of practice with stuff like that." He raises an index finger to tug at the outside corner of his eye. "Teardrops? Cobwebs? Good at those, too…"

He's gazing past her, out and down at the floor, his eyes focused on something else, something distant.

"So, you know Mark, then? Pretty well?"

His face shifts, he settles on her a look of appraisal.

"Not really in here for a tat, are you. Who are you really? A cop? Parole officer? What 'zackly are you fishin' for?"

Mel rolls her eyes. "Okay," she says softly. "Busted."

He nods.

"I'm a reporter."

He waits.

"A magazine, *Nation's Forum*, hired me for a feature story, on issues around solitary confinement. After research, I decided Tank Burnett, out at Sojourn's CCI max, might be a good subject. I mean his crimes are kind of lurid, and he must still be hard to deal with, since he's mostly been stuck in isolation for years. But once we got out there and saw him... well, lots of things about that prison seemed kind of 'off' to me. And I began to think, maybe there's a different story I should tell..."

"Tank Burnett." The man strokes his beard. "Good Lord. Shy ol' Tiny who turned himself into badass Tank. So if you went out to Sojourn to see *him*, how'd you end up taking any interest in Mark Nader?"

"Nader found me, he came straight onto me. At the Mexican restaurant, there in town. Just walked up and sat down like he owned the place."

"Well, lady, that he does. Owns the Tex-Mex dive, and everything else to boot. Like, the prison. That's his main business, any other stuff's only a sideline."

He lowers his head. Drums fingers slowly on the counter. Reaches a decision. Picks up his cane, stumps to the shop door, flips the dangling *Open* sign around to *Closed*, pulls a red curtain across the glass panel. Late afternoon sunshine glowers around its edges.

When he comes back to her, he thrusts out his hand. It's surprisingly slim, with perfectly manicured nails.

"I'm Dalton," he says. "You know, between the ones around here who've bought into Mark's shit, the folks blinded by fear, and those who just don't give a flyin' fuck, you won't find a whole lot of people ready to up and talk straight about Sojourn. So far as you're concerned, guess I'm it. Only reason *I'll* do it is because I had a friend who got himself killed, up there in that joint."

"How?"

"The KGB," he says.

"*What?* Here? And, uh, aren't they called something else now?"

"Not what you think." He lifts his eyebrows. "Insider joke. Means a particular squad of goons who always wear 'Kevlar Gloves, Black.' Term they use to order special mitts. Need 'em to safely grab away razor blades and shanks from the cons. You know, when they're preparin' to give 'em a beat-down.

"That happened to my friend Mick. Refused to do what KGB ordered, so they walled and beat and Tasered him so many times, when his body came home, looked like he'd been worked over with branding irons. Bruises and scorch marks all the hell over him."

"Oh. Awful. I'm sorry. Where... How can they find guards who will do such things?"

"Cherry-pick 'em from all over the country. Same way they find their prisoners. Ninety-nine percent of inmates in Sojourn are here from out-of-state. That way, the warden can say Texas officials don't need to inspect, seein' as they're *not* Texas prisoners. And the other states can't hardly send inspectors out here, 'cos it's way too far and costs too much, and they're understaffed and scrapin' bottom of the barrel back home. Why they need to farm out their baddest prisoners in the first place? Just like that, what with one thing and 'nother, Nader pretty much runs the Sojourn Max however the hell he wants."

"And... no one's ever tried to do a story about this before?"

"Not 'til you." He glances down, forehead corrugated by thought. He looks up. "Well, I'm not fully certain that I even want my own name in a story about Sojourn."

She nods. "Dalton, listen. A reporter can use named sources, or unnamed sources. Or for more protection I can take you off-the-record, or even have you speaking totally on-background. Want that? Okay, so let's say I put you just on-background. What then?"

He considers things a bit longer, shrugs.

"Had a bad crash on my putt last winter," he says. "My own tail is down a peg. Can't run fast as I used to. Nope, nor fight, neither." His smile hints at embarrassment. "Best I can do for myself now, is try extry hard to be smart."

"I understand."

He nods.

"So, doin' a 'background' deal sounds 'bout right to me. Git out your notebook or whatever, and grab a seat." He waves his cane at the leather barber chair. "Like a beer? Got us some Lone Stars, and Jester Kings."

~

The SUV hums down the highway, and its headlights slice cones of white out of brooding darkness.

"Yep, I'd say we're fully prepped for our chat with Dan and Carl now." Mel says. "Damn, they'll go nuts over all we've found out! Impressive, truly. You and me, girlfriend. We pulled it off."

Linda has already punched up Dan's number. But then she waves the lit screen of her smartphone at Melanie. "Yes," she complains, "only *now* when you finally let me call, I do not get a signal!"

"No biggie. Maybe pick one up as we close in on highway I-35. Try it then." Mel takes a deep breath. "Sorry," she says, and shakes her head. "Bright side, it does give us time to review what we've learned.

Help us keep the story tight, in case we don't get much time to talk to them."

She takes a deep breath. "So. Ted James Burnett. Only child of the Cinnabar Springs funeral director. Big fat kid, so his first nickname is 'Tiny.' Awkward, so bullied and teased. Doesn't play sandlot baseball after school, comes home to help out dad in the mortuary. But he gets caught prying gold crowns out of the stiffs. Dad punishes him, he flips out. Whacks pop over the head with a crowbar, puts him in a coffin, then hammers a 20-penny nail through his heart. And pounds more spikes into a few other places on him, too... eyeballs... groin...

"So, he's mad at him. Nuts, too.

"Runs away, hides out. But calls his mom, and she tips off the cops. Ted's juvy, hard to charge as an adult, even in Texas. Claims he was only trying to stop all the sex abuse by the dad. They find evidence to support it, like secret video diaries. So they stash Tiny Ted in a youth camp, which is what prison was at Sojourn years ago — private site focused on rehab, experimenting with drug and cognitive therapy. Begun and owned by none other than the Naders. The founder had degrees in law, business and youth counseling. Sees private corrections as a coming thing. Damn, is he right! I'd still question the quality of his therapy. Under Nader guidance, Tiny starts to turn into Tank.

"Then he's back out on the street, an iron-pumping monster who's nobody's punk. Finds guys who beat him up at school, returns that in spades. Goes to Dallas and joins the skinheads. Starts a far-right splinter, the Axskins. Arrested for assaulting blacks, again he pleads self-defense. But it doesn't work, so he scores more pen-time. After that, goes to Houston and San Leon to play with the Bandidos, but finds out he doesn't like Latin guys much, either. Launches the Ostrogoths MC, but it's a tiny outfit, they get into a gun-and-knife war with the Bandidos, and soon his future looks dim.

"Next, he makes a real strange move. Rides to Cinnabar and

murders his mom, inflicting worse mutilations on her corpse than he did on dad. Oddly, he doesn't run. Hangs out till the neighbors get wind of it, due to the fact that he has her nailed up to a post on the front porch for a while in August.

"Finally, after question of his sanity gets settled, more or less, he's off to the slammer, zero chance of parole. He's at Sojourn again, run by Mark Nader, cousin of the founder. But the place is transformed. Nader names his corporation the Coahuila Corrections Institute, and the prison's been rebuilt as a private supermax to house the baddest, smartest and most dangerous criminals."

"Just a skinny guy who makes tattoos," Linda murmurs.

"A village oddball," Mel echoes, "who also owns CCI, the prison, most of the town, and serves as mayor. At election time, he's never opposed. Nice work if you can get it."

A vehicle approaching from the east flicks its high beams at them.

Melanie absently clicks the SUV's light lever to low beams.

"Our man Dalton gave me a lot, yet not all he knows. Not by a mile. There's an outfit long-timers call 'the Finishing School.' What's that do, what's it for? Dalton says, I'm a reporter worth my salt, I find out. Also, what's the stuff that old guy told you…"

"*El Pasillo Vacío*," Linda muses. "What he names land between the border and Sojourn. It means empty place. Old man say he must watch over, that's his job. I ask explain, he says it is not empty because it is empty, but it is cleaned of rivals, now is one boss. He must send messages to boss about stuff that he sees. His job is to talk to the *pollos*, the *polleros*, the *coyotes* and *mulas*. Migrants and guides and mules who sneak across the border with Mexico, y' know. This job lets him to support his family."

The oncoming vehicle's brights flare through their windshield.

"Dammit, I'm already *on* low!" Mel says, jiggling her own lever.

The vehicle sweeps by them. In a brief glimpse, its silhouette seems to resemble a huge tow truck.

"Okay. Maybe the old boy's a sentinel, like." A thought strikes her. "So, how interested was he in you? Think he wound up reporting to someone about us?"

"No-o-o," Linda says slowly. "He seems most friendly, like he loves somebody to talk. I call him *abuelito*, which means little grandfather, and he says I am *mija*, like a daughter to him. Serious!"

"Shit." Mel looks in the side mirror, then the rearview. The truck that passed them is making a u-turn. "What did I do, piss off a redneck? Just what we need."

She checks on her speed, shoves the accelerator down.

"Sorry. You were saying?"

"Old man seems he likes me, and so I have no worry…"

Light floods them from behind. Not only has the truck caught up to them easily, its high-beams are on again.

"Dude!" Mel says, glancing nervously back and forth between the mirrors, seeing a blinding white glare. "You need to back off!"

The road ahead of them is suddenly ablaze with a more intense glow, another truck comes, high-beams on, fog lights on, even a searchlight that sweeps and stops with dead-on aim into their windshield, saturating their cab with light.

They hear a grinding thump from the SUV's left quarter panel and are launched into a tire-screeching spin to the left, then take another hit and spin right. The vehicle rises from the pavement, seems to float for a second. There's a rapid series of impacts as the tires hit and the SUV rolls, bounces, hits, rolls again, slides — to sounds of crackling glass, shrieking metal. Next comes stillness. A drifting, choking fog of dust and smoke.

An automobile horn blows, and it keeps on blowing.

Chapter 10

"Ahoy, shipmates. Let's gather on our poop deck," Carl says. "Have us a council of war."

The ad hoc gang of fugitives from Ecuadorian law sit on the balcony of the waterfront condo overlooking Manta's beach. Wind direction has changed, and their lovely coastal vista is now streaked by bunker-oil smoke from the freighters moored at the commercial pier. A hint of dead fish reek also drifts in from the seafood packing plants, as another workday for the town gathers steam.

"Meaning, you'll finally give us the straight poop?" Dan asks.

Carl squints, and permits himself a Jack Nicholson moment. "You can't handle the poop," he says.

"Wrong!" Dan asserts. "We deserve it. Beyond that, we all have big decisions to make, which must be based on solid fact. Yes?"

They sit around a wrought-iron table on the balcony. Núwa sets down a platter of fresh quesadillas, and takes a seat. Aromas of hot jalapeños and melted cheese win a decisive victory over the town's industrial odors. Hands reach out to seize triangles of crispy flour tortilla.

"I mean, mainly, if we don't hightail it out of Manta soon," Dan says, "we're hosed, pretty much. True?"

Carl glances around the table, and rubs his jaw. "More'n likely," he concedes. "Every day that goes by without the local cops nailin' us will just make 'em that much more cranked."

"So?"

Carl chews thoughtfully on his quesadilla, swallows. "We're all in the same fix," he says, "though our stakes differ. That's what we must address."

"Begin with us," Dan says. "You 'n' me are operatives, from what's supposedly the globe's final superpower. Why not use that? Get our government to pluck us out? And since Bernardo and Núwa have assisted, they oughta come with us."

"Not that easy."

"Because?"

"Sets off a diplomatic ruckus. If we can figure a way to sneak out, that's better."

"How so?"

Carl looks around the table again. "Well, shit," he says. He drums his fingers on the table, then clasps his hands together. "Here it is. There's what you might call a 'shituation' back in the States. A certain pair of prosecutors from the security fraud division in the Justice Department recently switched sides. At five times their former salaries, they went to work for Daringer, Campion & Zane. That's a law firm based in DC that handles all legal matters for Tenemos, Limited. Name of that outfit ring any sort of a bell for you, Dan?"

"Does, kinda."

"As I believe I mentioned, that's the umbrella outfit for Leonid Andreyev's various enterprises."

"Hm. And these DOJ prosecutors who went over to the dark side were in the department how long?"

"Years. Long enough to build plenty of strong personal contacts in the SEC. And the IRS, CFTC, FTC."

"And the FBI, too?"

"'Fraid so."

"Y'know," Dan says, "every once in a while that ol' revolving door seems to spin 'round hard enough to smack the republic right in the ass."

"Uh-huh."

"Hey. Look at it from their perspective. They can score way sweeter benefit packages than they'd ever get as mere public servants."

"Not only. They can also give generously to their besties. Everything from crucial tip-offs to stacks of cash."

"Ah-h-h," Dan says. "I get it. You mean, their pals who *stay* in government." He curls his fingers into semicircles and places one hand atop the other. "Your investigation needs to stay tightly silo-ed within the agency. That makes you cagy about how you call for help. Might trigger alarms in sensitive spots."

Carl licks a fingertip and inscribes a slash in the air — as if to say, score one for Dan.

"Right. My team has to figure out what Andreyev & Co. is up to, build evidence, then bust up the ring and slap down indictments before the opposition can launch damage control. 'Cos they can really bring it. Including political pressure at, oh, about a thousand psi."

"So we must stay below radar, and not just in Ecuador."

Carl nods.

Dan glances around the table. Núwa sits with her legs crossed, fingers laced around one gracefully raised knee. She does not look surprised. Instead — and he now sees it for the first time — a dark cloud of *tristesse* is afloat in her eyes. He realizes the sensitive matter Carl has just described is something she's seen before. Probably, way too often. Her looks says, "Oh, so that's how it works in your country too."

Bernardo's elbows are on the tabletop and his chin is pressed down against his folded fists. He frowns and his eyes flick from side to side.

The young man probably feels like he's poised on the lip of an abyss. As a satirist of Ecuadorian politics in Ecuador, he's already trodden a risky line. Suddenly he finds himself booted across it. A day ago, the worst thing that could be said of Bernardo was he'd published drawings that made fun of *el presidente*. Now, he can be accused of collaborating with American spies who are tussling with some sort of criminal cabal. His career could be ruined and his status as a target for prosecution enhanced, while his relationship with his father gets demolished. As a cartoonist, he's tried to transform major issues into laughing matters. But no one seems inclined to laugh now — he, least of all.

"I have a plan," Carl says. "Each of you must decide whether to go along with it. For any who opt out, I'll try to dream up a different move." His gray, gunfighter eyes sweep the table and he rests a brief gaze of assessment on each of them.

Dan, Núwa and Bernardo all respond by glancing at one another.

"Here it is." He points at Bernardo. "Our young man here says the dockmaster down there has spare ignition keys for the boats, for use in case of emergency, all held in the yacht club safe. That's attractive. Also, needlessly complex."

Dan blinks. "Any way to deploy a KISS rule?"

"'Zackly. Tonight, let's kick open a dashboard and hot-wire one of those boats. Got my eye on a Prowler Havana. No point in grabbin' anythin' larger, and it's certainly fast enough, with a long range. I say in the wee hours, at 0200 or so, ol' Cow-bell here and I swim out and cut that target loose. See if we can get 'er runnin'. If we do, we motor along shore to the north. That's where you two come in."

"Yes? And we do this, how?" One of Núwa's slim eyebrows arches in inquiry.

"You squirted with a big wad of cash in your bail-bag, yes? Cool. So, this afternoon, please go out to a hardware store and buy us six waterproof LED penlights and three foldin' knives with serrated blades. Then, this evenin', I want you to go on down to the harbor and buy you guys a skiff and trailer, and pickup to haul it. Only slightly used. Somethin' with a motor that sounds awful damn good, and real easy to start. Get me?"

"Bernardo?"

The curly-haired youth's head jerks, as if he'd just felt a policeman's hard palm smack down on his shoulder from behind.

"Still have a charge on your cell phone?"

He looks puzzled, then shrugs.

"Half, maybe…"

"Enough. Don't plug it in to recharge, and don't turn it on. Have you ever made any calls from offshore? If so, what's the longest distance you've reached?"

"Yes. From my father's boat. Five kilometers, *mas o menos…*"

"Great," Carl says. He rubs his hands together. "That means my plan has a slim chance of workin'." He smiles at them. "Two percent at the very least."

Dan makes a face. "And at most, what?"

Carl hesitates. "Three?"

"Hilarious."

"Here's the crux. Once we're offshore, we need to get our sorry asses picked up by a crew with some major oomph, and goddam pronto."

"Picked up?"

"C'mon… think anybody could conn a lil' tub like a Prowler all the way to San Diego? That'd be totally nuts."

"'Kay. Which tow service you ordering?"

"The ol' boys in blueberries." Carl is referring to U.S. Navy sailors in their new-style camo fatigues.

"What if they can't make it?"

"Then we *will* have to sail that dinghy to San Diego."

"Good thing we *are* nuts, then."

"A very good thing."

~

Carl and Dan wade slowly into the surf under a blanket of humid darkness. Silver curls top black waves that surge and tug at their knees. Further out, bright bars of color flung out by town lights and the pier's streetlamps tremble across the flat surface of the bay. They both wear dark slacks and dark shirts culled from the closet of Bernado's father. Carl leans forward and slips into the water without making any splash or noise. First he's visible, then not. Dan follows.

The water is blood-warm. Dan's head pops up for a breath at the end of a breast-stroke, and he sees a pair of security guards strolling on the pier. But they don't glance out at the bay; they focus entirely on their gossip and their cigarettes.

Carl and Dan swim up to their targeted boat without being spotted. Slack mooring lines loop down to the dark water, and they grip one as they listen, wait and watch for the guards on the pier. They pass. Carl and Dan both swim to the boat's stern dive platform, clamber onto it and then go up over the transom, slithering aboard to inspect their prize.

"Untie her stern," Carl whispers. "I'll drop over the bow, use one line to haul her from the slip. We'll let offshore breeze move us out a ways, 'fore we crank up."

"Tow us out, how? By you, swimming?"

"Uh-huh."

"Dude, what a total frogman! You amazing studmuffin, you."

"Hey, if Jack LaLanne can do it..."

"I knew Jack LaLanne. Jack LaLanne was a friend of mine. And you, sir, are no Jack..."

"Oh, shut up."

Dan smashes a door on the main console. He finds a small pouch of tools within its cubby that includes a Leatherman, and employs its pliers and screwdrivers to open up the boat's control panel. He studies it for a second, then points to wires on the engine ignition switches, and gives a thumbs-up to Carl. Carl nods and lets himself slip back down over the gunwale. After the guards pass by again, Carl starts to gently tug the boat from its slip.

Twenty minutes later, shoved along by a faint breeze, they are a hundred yards out into the bay. Dan tapes together wires he's stripped of their insulation, and the boat's diesels come to muttering life. Carl climbs back aboard.

"Good news is," Dan says, surveying the gauges, "her tanks are full. The other news is… well, how far do we have to go to reach the Colombian border, again?"

"Two hundred klicks. Very makeable. And only about thirty more to that bay at Caraquez, where we're 'sposed to pick up Núwa and Bernie."

"Hope they're still cool."

"Absolutely. We need that guy and his phone."

"Why didn't you ask him if we could take it?"

"He had a better chance of keeping it dry."

"We care about them escaping too, right?"

"'Course."

In the fan of dim green light flung up by the console, Carl's grin looks feral and toothy.

"That phone's major. Boat radio's a poor second choice. Any transmission is really a broadcast, so everybody gets to listen in real time. Rather not release a come-hither scent like that to the Ecuadorian Navy, at this point. Next time we're grabbed, the friskin' won't be so gentle. And it only goes downhill from there, I promise you."

"So, as to ringing up our savior. How does one order a deep-sea limo? Who ya gonna call?"

"Bill Murray."

"Joker."

Chapter 11

Linda, recovering from the shock of their wreck, shoves fabric of the airbag away from her face, struggles to breathe, abruptly understands that's she's upside down, with the belt cutting into her hips. There's a faint glow from the dashboard lights. She sees Melanie, eyes closed, blood from her pale face dripping slowly along strands of blond hair to fall on the overturned SUV's crushed roof.

"Melanie, Melanie!"

No response.

She manages to find and push the belt's release button, feels herself drop heavily onto her neck and shoulder at the same time she hears a sharp *whack* and the crinkled side door groans open.

A rough hand grips her by the upper arm, drags her out through the crumpled door frame. Anger and rage and fear surge together and boil up inside her like magma, and erupt in a jet of action. She gets her legs under her and launches her body. She flies away from the car and drives a shoulder into the midriff of the man who tugs on her, knocking him over. Flashlight beams scissor all about her. Another man reaches out, she bashes him in the face with the cast on her arm. The next one, she kicks viciously in the groin and he falls over backward. A further apparition is dispatched with one of her newest tricks, a thrust-kick into the side of his knee.

"Whoa, whoa, whoa!" a man yells. "Grab her!"

She tries to run, falls. Her ankle catches on wire. She realizes their tumbling SUV broke through a ranch fence. She wrenches free, runs. Hears pounding footsteps, a pneumatic hiss passes, she smells something bad, holds her breath. She runs. A thing stings her shoulder, like a wasp. She runs. Plants and brush slap at her thighs and the muscles burn. She disregards all of it to run. She desperately pants over and over, air sobs through her throat, and she runs and runs.

Back at the wreck, a man holding a flashlight yells, "You limpdick sons-a-bitches! Lettin' her get away like that!"

Another man says, "Calm down, Brody. Our main gal's still here, so we're squared away. T'other gal just ran out into a hunnert square miles holdin' not a dang thing but cactus and brush. Can't get far. Not all that much, nohow. Let's call Frank, tell him to truck out his hounds."

~

Linda runs, stumbles, and runs. Only if forced to cross steep draws and gulches does she walk. Just once she indulges herself by sitting down, cross-legged on the uneven and rocky soil, where she places her elbows on her knees and drops her face in her hands, to think forlornly about Melanie. And yearn for the comforts of Dan, his steady mind as well as his strong and protective arms.

How bad is Mel hurt? Does she yet live? And if alive, what are those bad men doing to her now? Who are they? Why cause the wreck, why attack us this way? How do we draw them in upon us?

She has to link this attack to their prison visit. What else of any significance had they done in Texas? And those men, the ring of them around the crumpled SUV, their arrogant manner, the brutal way they hauled her from the car, not caring a bit about how badly she could be hurt! She's met thugs like that in Honduras. They did seem to her like rough men from a prison. But whether they'd been inmates or guards, she could not tell...

All I can do, the only thing, is keep on, get all the way away from them! Finally, maybe find a person who can help me get a message through to Dan...

She rises, totters on stiff legs. The front of her thighs and calves feel seared from a sting of cactus spines driven through the thin fabric of her slacks by collisions with the arms of jumping *cholla* and the paddle leaves of prickly pear. Muscles in her jaw tighten as she sets her teeth against those pangs and her deep weariness. Again, she moves blindly through the night.

Finally a ribbon of dull orange unfurls and the horizon begins to catch fire with the first hint of sunup. She sees rumpled gray earth over which she moves, can take each footstep with more care. This brings her a measure of hope. But then she raises her eyes and sees the way a terrain furred in mesquite recedes into the far distance. This had seemed a vast, featureless land as she and Mel speedily drove through it on the highway. After a hard night lost and afoot, she sees it now as an implacable foe, omnipotent and enveloping. Linda despairs. Which direction should she head? What difference could it make?

A faint *creak*. And it comes again, a groan of metal on metal. Something pokes high up from the brush, it rotates slowly, making rhythmic complaint about being forced to turn, a wheel of suffering thrust into the dawn's pastel gloaming.

Almost imperceptible movement of the morning air forces a windmill's gears to ratchet. She goes to it. Sees a trough standing at its base, a large, galvanized metal tank, blotched with rust. The torment of thirst assaults her anew. Her tongue feels like a dusty rag, rolled up and crammed into her mouth. Her pace increases to an uneven jog. She sees gold, russet, and peach of sunrise reflected on a lozenge of still, dark water. She reaches it, leans over to suck up a gulp. Instead, her weary body just flops over and slides into the trough's cool depths.

The tops of her shoes scrape across the rolled steel edge as her feet drop in last. Facedown, she drifts low as a sweet coolness penetrates her skin. Her nose touches a mucky bottom. She flips over abruptly and comes up into air, sputtering. She unknots the silk scarf around her neck, uses it to mop her face. For a long time she just sits, her head and shoulders jutting up from the water, occasionally tilting her head down to take a drink.

Then she sighs, shakes her head, put her hands on the rim, shoves herself upright. Standing, she looks out at the expanse of cactus and mesquite, and the scruff of her own footprints coming out of it. The only sound is the windmill's grind of complaint. No sign of her pursuers yet.

They say about using dogs, I hear this talk as I run off. And so I should keep on the move now! But... to where?

On the metal tub's windward side, a mound of dust and loose plant fibers lies heaped up in a blob of shade. The ragged pile of debris looks soft and comfortable to her. A decent spot to finally take some sort of rest...

Only a moment. I take off my pants, try to pull out the needles. Relax, think about which way to go. That is how Dan does things, it is what he would like me to do. Just have some method when you think, he always says. Be clear. Next make a decision...

Some of the cactus spines wrench loose from her skin as she gingerly tugs down her slacks. Especially painful ones sticking more deeply into her, she hunts down and plucks out with her fingernails. She throws her pants into the water, imagining that might soften all the fine, hair-like glochids from the *cholla* that remain caught in the fabric. Wearing only her underwear, a brassiere and blouse, Linda sinks down into the cool dust and lies on her side, pillowing her head on a bent arm. She drapes her folded scarf over her eyes.

Just for a moment.

Chapter 12

Tiny white sparks of light blip out from shore. A sequence is repeated three times: long flash, short one. It's an "N" in Morse Code... and it stands for Núwa.

The fishing boat's diesel engines mumble on idle as it rocks in the coastal swell.

"Her," Dan says.

"Well? Copy."

Dan ruminates on the code for a moment, then deploys his flashlight to send back the dahs-and-dits for "D" and "C."

"Y'know, sunup is in one hour," Carl says. "Let's make this snappy."

Barely visible but purring their way is an outboard skiff that bears the shape of two hunched figures. It gets quite close before Dan can make out Núwa sitting at its stern, her hand on the motor's tiller. Then he realizes that the forward shape is not Bernardo, it's a duffle propped up on one of the skiff's bench seats.

"One to come aboard," Dan says.

"*What?*" A scowling Carl peers into the darkness.

Thump at the dive platform. Dan grabs the skiff's painter and makes it fast to a stern cleat. He snatches her duffle, heaves it over the transom rail into the boat cockpit, then grabs Núwa's arm to guide her on as well.

"Welcome aboard," he says. Then he asks, "Cast it loose?"

"Nope," Carl replies. "Put the skiff under tow. Less evidence drifts ashore. Plus, we get the outboard motor for our auxiliary."

"How far out do you plan to go?"

Carl's grin flashes above green console lights.

"Quite a ways! Aim this sucker at 270 magnetic and just run."

Carl spins the wheel and pushes the throttles forward. "All ahead flank," he intones with mock pomposity, as though he sits in a chair on the bridge of a ship, with a commander's scrambled eggs on his cap visor. He shoves the throttle levers forward. They feel the deck begin to quiver below their feet. He turns his gaze to Núwa.

"So! What happened to Bernardo?"

"He makes a hard choice," she says. "Feels that, if he leaves this country in such a way, might never see his father again. Also, he feels like he's still got a big role at *El Satirico*. He is a voice for so many of those worried for Ecuador's future…"

"So no phone?" Carl gripes. "Cut to the chase, goddammit."

"Let me finish! Number three, he will throw the authorities off our course. He'll tell them you kidnapped him, then forced him to help you steal a boat. You departed the harbor, turned it south and pitched him overboard, to swim in to a beach. When he arrives in Manta, he'll come from the south, and that's what he will say."

Carl rubs his jaw and gives a grudging nod. "Well, not bad," he admits. He sighs. "Okay, if you've got the phone, where is it?"

She slides a hand far down into the neckline of the dark blue sweatshirt she wears, plucks a cell phone out of her sports bra, gives it to Carl.

"Aww. And you warmed it up, too!" he says. "Thoughtful, Núwa. Truly 'preciate it."

Holding the phone in his fingertips, he puts his nose on it as if to inhale her scent.

She inclines her head, smiles.

"So? Who you going to call?" Dan asks. "Don't say, Bill. Or Rick Moranis."

"How about Sigourney Weaver?"

"How about that Global Response Staff from the state department? You know, the outfit you thought might ride to our rescue that time we were up to our eyebrows in the Honduras shit?"

"Um, no."

"Special missions unit from SOCOM, then, like the Joint Personnel Recovery agents?"

"No."

"*Well?!*"

"You get three guesses."

"I'd prefer three wishes. All of 'em would be for you to perform an anatomic impossibility on yourself."

"Okay," Carl relents. "Look, we don't have any time to screw around."

"Duh."

"Which is why I'll go straight to the brotherhood."

"But how?"

"Call up Admiral Pete McBride at SOCOM. I've scraped his bacon off the grill a ton. He owes me a solid."

"He's at McDill, up in Tampa? What makes you think you can get through?"

"Know the number for his personal dark phone. It'll bounce through a satellite. *No hay problema*, as the locals say."

"What do you think he'll do?"

"Hey, y'know the way an admiral looks in his dress whites? Even if he's got a trident along with everything else on his chest, still resembles a doorman at the Waldorf? Well, I'm gonna ask him to call us a cab."

"I assume you mean a water taxi. How will it find us?"

"Dead reckoning first, my man. Tell them we're running magnetic West from Bahia de Caraquez at 20 knots. After they work up a solution for that, they can dial us in by deploying their PFM mast." (The letters stand for Pure Fucking Magic.) "And if worst comes to worst," he holds up the phone, "I'll turn us around and keep buggin' McBride. Guaranteed, he won't sleep till we're out of the shit."

"Okay. But how about Bernardo? Won't he catch hell if they pick up a signal from his phone in the north, after he tells 'em that we are heading south?"

"Good point. But why on earth would we *not* lie to Bernardo as we drop him off? We'd never want him to know 'zackly where we're headed."

"Another good point."

"Thank you. Núwa?" Carl snaps his fingers. "Now, can I have the battery, please?"

She slips a hand down her neckline again, gropes about for a moment, then a pair of her fingers emerge from her top pinching a silvery rectangle that she extends to him with a flourish. Carl bows, and takes it.

"Not leavin' you out, by the way, Núwa," Dan says. "You make good points, also."

"You *crazy?*" Carl says. "Núwa has fabulous points."

Chapter 13

Rock 'n' roll guitar riff, then pounding drums. The sounds jolt Linda awake. Riff, then drums. Riff, drums.

She opens her eyes. For a moment, she can't fathom where on earth she might be. But when she rolls and sits up, she bangs her head against the side of the metal water trough and then looks up at rays of sunlight that flicker through blades of the windmill.

The whole sad puzzle of her situation rushes back into her awareness.

Riff, drums.

She stares at the windmill, trying to figure out how its rough squeak could have changed into music. But then she also hears the roar of a truck engine, and leaps to her feet.

A big pickup truck that trails a billow of dust and sends out a blast of CD music rushes toward her.

She spins, leans over and reaches into the trough, groping frantically for her pants. She hears knobby tires grind to a halt, and she turns back, clutching wet slacks to her chest and tugging one leg like a dripping curtain across her bare thighs.

Dust billows around the truck as it stops, and a young man in wraparound sunglasses peers at her through the driver's side window. On his head is a crumpled straw cowboy hat, and he wears a faded shirt of blue plaid with both sleeves and collar scissored off. A thin beard of curly blond hair tumbles onto his chest.

For seconds, neither speaks. Music thumps out of the truck's speakers, complicated by an off-beat grumble from the truck's holed muffler. The driver turns down the volume and gives her a long, appreciative wolf-whistle.

That message translates globally. As does Linda's response, when she angrily brandishes a middle finger. She then sits on the tank's rim to slide her feet into her slacks and quickly tug them up her legs.

The man opens his door, gets out. "Well now," he says. "How's a purty gal like you git so fricken' far out in the brush?"

Another door creaks and slams on the truck's far side. A second man comes around the robust front bumper. He looks like an elder version of the first, and his beard, threaded with gray, falls much further down his chest. His shirt is red plaid, with sleeves rolled up to the elbow. His hat's a worn fedora with its brim entirely turned down. Both men wear footgear with camo Cordura uppers that reach their knees — snake-proof boots.

"Happen to speak any English?" the second man asks. "Ma'am?" he adds, but the word has a tinge of sarcasm. He suspects that she's an undocumented border-jumper, separated from her guide and group, and now just wandering lost.

Linda knows she needs help, but doubts these rough-looking men will provide any. Worse, she senses they might pose a new form of danger.

"I am good," she says. "Leave me alone, and let me go where I need to go."

The men glance at one another, shake their heads simultaneously.

"Ain't gonna happen. Just toss that idea away, and set your mind at ease," the older one says. "So, you speak English purty good. You in the U.S. legal-like, or no? Where in heck're you from? Some idiot *coyotero* just bug out 'n' turn you loose after you come over the border?"

The young one asks, "Anybody else stuck out here with you?" He scans around the clearing, fixes his gaze on her solitary line of footprints straggling off into the brush.

"Yes! I am legal, okay?" Linda is indignant. "A visa for a tourist to America, that is what I have."

"Haw!" The young man slaps his thigh and a faint puff of dust spurts from its sheath of denim. "'Splains it all, hey? Give me idee for a tour. 'Come Out 'n' Git Your Sorry Ass Lost in Cactus Country!' Whatcha think we kin charge for that?"

The older man scratches his beard and grins. "Not charge much to come," he allows. "Prob'ly, though, yer tourists'd pay a heckuva lot to git back home."

Linda searches their faces. Her eyes drift to their truck, hunting for more clues about who these men could be. She's unsure what to make of their vehicle — it's a battered Dodge Power Wagon jacked-up high above worn lug tires. It has a Smittybilt bumper and Warn winch out front, with a jack and shovel lashed over it. A tiny flag dangles from a bent antenna that tilts across the truck's crumpled fender, reminding her of a banner she saw hoisted along the highway route the previous morning. However, she has no idea what a Confederate battle flag signifies. Her survey of the truck ends at its windowless camper shell with roof and walls made of splintery, sun-bleached plywood.

She decides to offer a scrap of real information, see how that plays.

"I come here from your road," she says, pointing to the north. "Walk all the night. Serious!"

"The road? Which road?"

"A long, smooth one. You say that is a highway to Corpus Christi, yes?"

"Naw," the young one scoffs. "Lady, you shittin' us? That's like twenny mile away, over real bad ground. Tellin' me you did this all in the dark? I'm most amazed you can even stand up."

"What hair poked up your butt, make you want to take such a wild-ass jaunt in the first place?" the other asks.

Linda bites her lip. If they won't trust her when she says something true, why say anything more?

"Oooh-kay-y," the young one says. "Reckon you'll tell us when you're ready."

"Or you can give answers to the Turco County sheriff, whether you're ready or not." the older man says. "Go on ahead and get in our truck there, and we'll take you to town."

"No thank you," Linda says.

"Not askin', I'm tellin'. Get in! 'Cos we're not even close to leavin' you out here. 'Sides, you're actually trespassin', know that? This ranch here's private prop'ty."

Linda slips on her torn and scratched canvas shoes and bends to tie the laces.

The men trade a glance and step closer to her.

Linda straightens up, glares at them, fakes a quick dash to the left but then bolts right. The older man makes a swift leap, snatches her by a wrist, uses her own momentum to spin her around and yank her against his chest. He grabs her flailing other arm and holds her tightly with her arms crossed over her stomach. His hands are hard and callused, his grip powerful. She's immobilized. All she can do is kick her heels at his shins, and when the other man moves in front, to kick even harder up at him. But he catches her legs. They lower her to the ground, flip her onto her stomach, then both men sprawl their bodies on top of her, pinning her down. Their voices mingle in guffaws and curses.

She feels like she's being smothered by their combined weight, as well as a malodorous fog of male sweat, tobacco juice, gingivitis, desert dust, stale beer and diesel-soaked clothes. She screams, tries to wriggle free, immediately realizes it's hopeless, and makes herself go limp instead. Linda understands she needs to retain every scrap of energy left to her. She must get these bearded strangers either off balance or off guard before she makes another effort to flee. She tries to empty her mind of fear and be patient. And she also tries not to dwell on what this odd pair might have in mind for her if she doesn't escape from them, and soon.

Chapter 14

"What's that I'm seeing, way over there?"

"Uh, it's either a whale's fin… or a hood ornament on our water taxi."

Carl swings the wheel, cuts the throttles.

"Shit, you were able to call in a two-billion-dollar ride?" Dan asks.

"Yep, and she does have amazin' fins, just like a '59 Caddy."

A slim wedge of dark steel rises like a carbon blade to slice the water. It glides to a halt, and a white foam vee that marked its progress subsides. Below the black sail, they now can see a dark line of a submarine's upper hull emerge on the surface, a navigable metal island somewhat longer than a football field. A hatch swings open and a man emerges who wears an olive-drab drysuit and a life jacket. He waves an arm at them.

"Wonder what the heck *he* wants?" Dan says.

"Dunno," Carl responds. "Let's go over and ask."

"Sure." Dan shrugs. "Ya feel like it…"

"Only to be polite."

Núwa, who also stands at the console, bows her lips in a smile.

Carl idles their fishing boat over to the Idaho, a Virginia Class fast-attack nuclear submarine commissioned for the U.S. Navy at the Electric Boat Yard in Groton in 2011. He brings her alongside gently,

Dan heaves a bow line to the man clad in the olive drysuit, who draws their boat's curved prow snugly against the hull and makes the line fast to a cleat inset on the submarine's deck. He's wearing sunglasses and a fatigue cap, but he still shades his eyes with his hand as he peers into their boat. His gaze settles on Carl.

"Are you Jar-dar Blackadar?"

"Maybe. Who's askin'?"

"Outstanding. Hoped to meet you someday. I'm Muley Caves, of Class 274."

"Cool."

Carl measures and times his leap from the gently rocking boat's prow over to the sub's deck, and he sticks the landing. He and the man shake hands by slapping palms and curling their upraised thumbs together.

"Any more team guys on your sub?"

"Chief Bo Watson."

"Christ. Too bad you deployed with that mangy ol' dog-dicker."

Caves — whose broad shoulders, short legs and barrel chest do indeed suggest the shape of a draft animal, a correspondence advanced by his prominently bucked teeth — awards them a grin.

"Bo speaks poorly of you too, sir. Said he'd've come topside to welcome you aboard, however, there's 'bout a million things he'd rather do."

"Let me guess. He's in the rack with both hands clamped around his patrol sock. Never mind. Let me introduce you to my companions here…"

Dan makes his own jump to the sub. He turns to catch Núwa, but she needs nary a scrap of help, landing on the non-skid coating of the sub deck as lightly as a ballerina polishing off a grand jeté.

"Now, this here's Daniel Cowell, who almost won a brown shirt with my class, but rang out in Hell Week. Next, he tried a few things to redeem himself — but the guy's still a major wuss, so I want you to show him nothing but disrespect. And Núwa Robles, who's been downrange doing this 'n' that for years. She come along, mainly 'cos we promised her a submarine ride."

Muley claps Dan on the shoulder, offers a paw to Núwa. "Pleasure," he says.

"Interestin' you mention it. Often the first thing she makes guys think about," Carl says.

Muley displays his impressive choppers, then bends his neck to speak into a small mic on the shoulder of his vest.

"Zulu Five Oscar," he says. This code indicates an intruder has been detected aboard a Navy vessel — though it's usually a commando tasked with testing the ship's security.

Dan snickers. "Why don't you just say, 'The ego has landed'…?"

Muley holds up a finger, and they understand that he's listening to a response on an earpiece. "I copy," he says. "So, ask Weps what he's got in the way of contacts…. Uh-huh… Copy that, too!"

Muley looks up at Carl. "No skimmers in range. But we have a bogey inbound at five angels, closing at an estimated hundred knots. ETA, about fifteen mikes."

"Military helo?"

"More'n likely."

"Probably should clear the deck, then."

"Right. It's a blow-and-go."

Muley has a drab canvas satchel on his back, it hangs from a strap over his shoulder. He now tugs it around into view and gives it a pat. "Far as your boat, I've got us a mooring solution right here."

"And the skiff?"

"How about, we just let it get dragged to the same dock down in Davy Jones's locker."

~

Carl descends through the hatch, followed by Núwa, then Dan. They pass through a compartment to reach the sub's control room. A pair of pilots sit before controls that resemble aircraft joysticks, at a station bracketed by nearly a dozen screens laced with glowing status graphics. A young man with short, sandy blond hair paces behind the pilots, his hands clasped at the small of his back. They all wear blue coveralls with a vee of white t-shirt showing beneath — standard-issue "poopysuits" — but the blond man has a lieutenant commander's oak leaves pinned on his collar.

The sound of a dive klaxon already reverberates out of the sub's 1MC boat-wide intercom. The officer allows their approach, but holds up a hand to command their silence.

"Pressure in the boat, aye," the pilots tell him. "I have a green board."

As a navy vet from the previous decade, Dan is amazed when he sees that one pilot is a woman, with brunette hair coiled and pinned in a tidy bun at the back of her head.

"Ahead one third," the OOD — officer of the deck — says. "Steer two-five-four."

"Ahead one third, aye. Course two-five-four, aye."

"Vent main ballast tanks."

"Venting MBT, aye."

"Three degree down bubble."

"Three degrees down, aye."

Muley has joined them, and is unzipping his life vest. "Sir?" he addresses the OOD. "Might want to alert your ping jockeys, and tell 'em to turn up the squelch." He glances at his watch. "In about two minutes, there will be a very loud noise."

"Two?" The OOD checks him with a glance.

Muley nods a confirmation. "Given the charge, range will likely be adequate. Still, some insurance never hurts. Right, sir?"

The deck officer smiles slightly. "Never a bad day for a good drill," he says. The pilots sit up straight, both of them anticipate something that departs from the ordinary. They're not disappointed. "Emergency deep!" the OOD says loudly.

In seconds, the deck begins to tilt under their feet.

The officer now has a moment to spare. "So you're Blackadar..." he says, and thrusts out a hand. "... the spook of legend and song. I'm Jenson, XO of this sewer pipe." He briefly looks Núwa and Dan up-and-down, but his facial expression says: *I don't feel as if I need to know who these other people are, and it might be best if I don't.*

"Skipper's ready to meet you down in the wardroom," he says. "Too bad we didn't hook up yesterday, that was halfway night. Cooks served up surf-and-turf. Don't imagine there's much in the way of leftovers, but our 'cuisine specialists' should still be able to locate some choice mid-rats for you. Welcome aboard."

Muley unzips the front of his dry suit, pulls the rubber collar over his head, and ties its now loose arms together over his belly, to keep the suit held on at his waist. He beckons, leading them to another hatch.

Awaiting his own turn to clamber down, Dan looks around. He'd been on a Seawolf-class sub once, when he was still in the navy, but this sleek Virginia Class fast attack boat seems a creature of a far different order — roomier, more technically evolved, like something built for an oceangoing starfleet. Militating against that air of sophistication is an odd mélange of smells, the same as on all modern subs: a blend of machine oil, warm plastic, a chemical reek of amines from CO_2 scrubbers, plus the only slightly muted odors from the boat's full complement of eleven dozen human bodies. A submariner shower delivers only a bit more water than a sponge bath, and is at best only moderately effective. Another portion of the sub ambiance is a constant hum — something that does vary between boats. Each vessel has its own sound signature, a mingling of vibrations from fans, turbines and servos, punctuated by announcements on the intercoms as well as echoes of anything spoken by anyone, and any object that's dropped by the sailors.

It's almost like being within a living organism, Dan thinks. *We're Jonahs, swallowed by a cybernetic whale. Except, of course, it's one that responds to human commands. Well, probably, mostly.*

As he makes his way down the ladder — presumably to discover what Carl and the captain jointly think their next move should be — he overhears a last bit of the ongoing litany between the OOD and the Idaho's pilots.

"Make our depth five-five-zero. After we level off, we'll go hard left rudder and all ahead flank."

"Depth five-five-zero, aye…"

Chapter 15

Melanie Olson awakens. White acoustical tiles hover above her like a broad expanse of square clouds. She feels a sticky film around her eyes, tries to bring a hand up to wipe it away, but something clinks, her forearm catches and halts, her hand won't move any farther.

A bronze face above a white uniform appears, then vanishes.

Another face. Topped with a hat and fringed by brown, stringy hair. It wears a sardonic leer. Melanie's startled. *What the hell is Mark Nader doing in my dream? I don't want him here!* She closes her eyes, opens them. He's still there, wearing a smile that displays his crooked front teeth.

"Hi. Welcome to our humble abode. Whether or not being here bodes well, well, that's up to you. So, hum me no bull."

Gibberish. She needs something simpler, to help gain her bearings. "Where am I?"

"Great question. Before I address it, answer mine. Who are you?"

"You know."

"No, really."

His irritating presence speeds her return to full awareness. "Dammit," she snaps, "you already bragged that you backgrounded me!"

She puzzles over what she did wrong, to leave her trapped in a room with this asshat. The last thing she recalls is driving at night with Linda, heading for Corpus Christi. *There were those huge bright headlights that came up so fast behind us…*

"Sure. But the time is ripe to dig a skoch deeper. C'mon, spill. Who're you with?"

"I'm with Linda! Who else? And… where is Linda?"

Mel attempts to sit up, but she lurches and falls backward, and realizes both wrists are cuffed to the gurney by padded leather restraints linked to cables.

"Not your big-booby pal. What agency? Who sent you?"

"*Nation's Forum* magazine! I…"

"Now, that's a book I really *do* judge as a cover. And under which is what? Who're you really in bed with?"

"Won't answer *any* question until I see Linda."

Mark Nader clicks his tongue, wags his head. "Let me clarify the obvious. Your power is now zip. Nil, nada."

Mel clenches her jaw and gives him a hard stare.

"The ol' gamin gambit?" Nader chuckles. "Gotta take a look on my own hook, see what you've got to hide…"

A hand goes to a back pocket of his black jeans, tugs out a clasp knife. He snicks its blade open with a thumb.

She's wearing a pale green cotton hospital gown. As he grasps its hem between his fingers, Mel involuntary tries to jerk her knees together but finds she can't — her ankles are shackled, too.

Nader slices upward with the knife. The gown's thin fabric sighs apart, renders a faint pop as he snaps the blade up through the seam at her neckline, and then the fabric falls away.

She's naked now, folds of the gown loosely bunched to either side of her body.

"My my, what sweet lil' boobs you got. What they call

'champagne-glass.' But as the good ol' boys say, 'anythin' more'n a mouthful's a waste,' right?"

Nader drags the blade's tip down her bare torso, scratching her skin. She stiffens with fear, all bravado has fled for the moment. She swallows hard and squeezes both eyes shut.

The knife incises a line of pain all the way down to Mel's feathery patch of pubes. At a corner of her blond triangle is a tattoo of a morning glory. Across her *mons veneris*, on her right thigh is the tattoo of a bumblebee. Nader pokes both images with his blade. She flinches and her eyes snap open.

"Bee and bloom! Fine work there. But lots of blank space left on you. Be happy to complete your canvas. It'll be like earning your third degree at Needle U." He sniggers. "Might find work at a carnival after, but only in a freak show. Ya feel me?"

He stares at her, the vacuum of his gaze baleful and hypnotic, and she's unable to turn her own eyes away. She understands then that Mark Nader *wants* her to see into him, to sense the high intellect and bent will, to feel an amused cruelty that writhes through his every thought.

She suddenly fears that he will get what he wants from her, break her down over a long march with some steps hurried, most lingering…

"Really squeezin' your phone now, and Linda's too," he says. His voice is almost wistful. "My techs can pull every last secret. So I'll be back soon, with more questions and a lot less patience."

Unexpectedly, he rams his knife down into the padding of the gurney, grazing her ribs, and she flinches in terror. He chuckles, tugs the knife free and snicks it shut again. He slides its clip over the rim of a coat pocket, turns and walks off. Despite herself, she strains her eyes, peering over her cheekbones to watch him depart. She sees him twiddle a dial on a small brown box on the wall by the door.

"'Where the bee sucks, there suck I,'" Nader says, haphazardly quoting from Shakespeare's *The Tempest*. His teeth flash in a yellow smile. "'On a bat's back do I fly…'"

He leaves, the door sighs closed. Cold air puffs into the room. She shivers.

Chapter 16

Linda Parker sits, her back pressed against the galvanized water tank. Her legs are bound together with a length of hemp twine just below her knees, more twine binds her wrists. The young man squats nearby, the other kneels to offer her a strip of pepper jerky.

"Y'know," he says, "kinda feel like we got off on the wrong foot, here. Mebbe, you can see that too. Howsabout, we start over? Wanna give that a shot?"

Linda's face stays bunched in a furious scowl. If her energy had not been depleted by her night trek — and, of course, were she not tied up — her expression leaves little doubt her first choice would be to resume physical combat. But since she's both exhausted and immobile, taking in a bite of food seems better than further rebellion in the face of impossible odds. She raises her bound hands, takes the dried meat, pushes it between lips already damp with saliva, and chews.

"That 'ere's homemade jerky. From a whitetail buck we got 'bout a month back. Like it?"

"He's kiddin' ya," the younger one says. "It's armadillo... roadkill, y'know? Hank just run over it with the truck. Some hunter, eh? Happen to come on some deer hogtied, he couldn't hit it in the butt with a banjo."

"Shadup," the kneeling one says pleasantly. He takes his sunglasses off and stashes them up on the brim of his fedora, tucking the earpieces into its snakeskin hatband.

"I'm Hank Purdy, and there's Larry, who has the 'markable good fortune to be my nephew and work 'longside me on our ranch just now. Trainin' him up, but it's a giant chore. Me hirin' him was a bit like losin' two good men. But I got forced to take him on, 'cos his ma was fixin' to send him off to a military school in Georgia, see if he'd straighten out that-a-way. So, that's us."

He spreads his hands. "Honey, why not give us your handle. Tell us somethin' 'bout you."

Linda swallows. Her frown eases, but she looks confused.

"What he's sayin' is, he'd like to know your name," Larry interprets.

She takes another bite of the venison jerky, and chews thoughtfully for a moment. "I am Linda," she mumbles.

"There now. Not so hard, huh? Look here, Linda, I need to offer you a 'pology 'bout all this rude treatment. But our job is overseein' th' ranch you're on, plus a few more, and it's a heap of ground. Cain't leave anyone wanderin' around out here, no way. Seems like you don't much cotton to the notion of meetin' our sheriff, and I don't really like the guy myself. Howsomever, we *do* need to take you someplace, get me? Now we been chargin' all over hell, tendin' to our chores 'n' whatnot 'bout three days, and we were just runnin' for our home ranch when we spotted you. My figger is, we can still go back home, and you can visit with us for a lil' while. But you need to think 'bout where you hope to wind up. And if there's any stuff you want to let on to us... we can maybe help you with mullin' that over, hm?"

"T'other hand, best you keep quiet," Larry says. "Once Hank commences bestowin' his advice, awful hard to get him to quit."

"Many folks, like my nephew here, are *sore* afflicted by lack of ability to see good sense. Stubborn and foolish, cain't be persuaded by nothin' but a rawhide whip."

"Why I like crankin' up the stereo," Larry confides. "Drown this ol' boy out. Well, mostly. Nothing gets it fully done. A nuk'lar bomb might do it, but only if a big 'un."

"Linda, ignore the ign'runt. Right there, my advice for a more pleasin' life." Hank places his fingers lightly on the bands of twine lashed around her knees. "Lemme ask you a 'nother thing. Now you've calmed down, and I take this off, what is it that you guess you're gonna want to do?"

Her eyes shift back and forth between them. "All right," she says, resigned. "I ride in the truck with you."

"Hey, great. That works."

Hank then glances over at Larry, who gives back a subtle nod. Hank unties her knees, next her wrists. He stands, offers a hand, helps her up.

Linda totters toward the truck. Hank catches up, and she takes his arm. She aims herself at the camper shell.

"Maybe I now can sleep more in the back, as you drive?"

"Whoa, whoa, not such a hot idea."

"Why?"

"Lessee. Number one? We've a big live-box jam-full of rattlers back there we just caught. Can't hardly say they're domesticated... Number two, there's the pump and fuel we use to drive 'em up from holes 'n' catch 'em so it's kind of fumey..."

"Rattles?"

"Snakes. Y'know, kind have all thet pizen?" Hank droops two fingers over his open mouth, to indicate fangs. "We catch 'em up, so the game ranch don't have to worry about 'em bitin' on their ol' ibex or whatever. One of our chores."

"Ibex, Kleenex and Windex, Rolodex and Rolex. Just some of the weird critters they keep out there," Larry puts in.

"'Sides, know we're getting' to be friends 'n' all, but trust is somethin' you develop over time. I'd suspect you of jumping out the back and running off again, after we get goin'. Hm? So you'd best ride in the cab. It's got just a couple bucket seats, but we can fold a blanket up on the console, should be all right."

"Ma'am?" Larry asks. "Not to get personal. But I kin see you don't wear no kind of a ring on your hand 'er nothin'. Got yourself a man around? Someone who hopes to take care of you? 'Cos if so, ain't doin' none too good at it, in my 'pinion. Lettin' you wander off out here all by your lone self! Know what I mean? It's just plain luck that you found us, and we come 'round to perfect you."

Chapter 17

Carl steers a purring BMW 435i coupe past the FBI field office on Second Avenue in Miami Beach — a building that manages to convey an aura of menace by dint of sheer architectural blandness, with its blank white sides gouged by narrow black windows that strongly resemble big gun embrasures.

"You're not turning in?"

"Not where we'll meet our honcho." Carl points out through the tinted windshield. "Picked an ocean pier for that. Walls can't have ears if there's no walls, right?" He looks at Dan. "Sides, man, it's Miami Beach! Don't object to a dose of salty breeze, and cute gals stretched out on a beach in their bikinis, do you?"

"Not hardly," Dan says. "Guy's your boss, huh?"

Carl's mouth twitches. "Well, I reckon he'd lay claim to that. Reality's a tad different." He looks at Dan. "Speaking of gals, such as ours for example, you pickin' up anythin' on 'em yet? Any hit on Linda?"

"No pickup, and never a word of text in reply to ours. For calls, just get a few rings of response, then it goes straight off to voicemail."

"Crap. Still?"

"Tell me about it."

"Dammit, we have enough to worry about, without them —"

"Stuff it, huh? I plan to worry about Linda all I want."

Carl's lean face jerks in a faint smile that's almost a grimace. It's been three days since the American fast attack submarine picked them up, and two days since the USS *Idaho* surfaced again, this time to rendezvous with a vessel from Panama's maritime force, SENAN — the *Servicio Nacional Aeronaval.*

Performing an off-the-books favor at behest of the U.S. Navy, Panama's Point Class cutter then sailed them to a pier of the former Rodman Naval Station at the port of Balboa. A ministry of public security jeep whisked them to the Pacifico airport. There, they boarded a U.S. Navy C-40 that flew them to Key West.

On the Keys, Carl rented the Beemer from a Wheel Dreams — his favorite, high-end auto-leasing outlet — and then, on the FBI's dime, they drove north to Miami.

Núwa had to stay at the Naval Air Station on Boca Chica. Her employer asked her to hang out until one of "the company" operators could fly down to discuss a new Latin American assignment for her. Carl and Dan both wished Nuwa an affectionate farewell. Mainly, Carl did so, amid a fleeting moment of privacy.

Before they left the Keys, Dan and Carl bought new cell phones, and used their lengthy drive up highway A1A to try to ring up Melanie or Linda, with altogether vexing results. They took turns at the wheel, alternately signed on to e-mail accounts, only to find no message from either woman in any inbox. *What in hell are our women up to?*

Now they tease each other, marveling about how rapidly and thoroughly they'd been dumped, wondering who their gals' new boyfriends might be. Brad Pitt? Mitt Romney? A mash-up, somebody who's not only young and handsome but also famous, rich and powerful, maybe he's going by the handle of Mitt Pitt?

Carl continues to drive eastward along Sunny Isles Boulevard to Collins Avenue. He parks in a metered space near the Newport Hotel, and they stroll toward the entrance gate by the pier.

Jade-green Atlantic waves shuffle languidly onto a slope of beige sand. A seagull wheels, shrieks, then dives avidly on an abandoned French fry.

Carl points a finger at Dan. "Now's a good time for you get lost, okay?" he suggests.

"How lost?"

"Not so far, you can't keep an eye on that pier. You see me gettin' bopped on the head and shoved into the water, come help out."

"Meaning, come and help you out. Not the assailant."

"Yeah."

"Copy that."

Dan pokes his sunglasses up onto his forehead, and squints across the sand. The only beach-goers in view are an elderly couple in droopy shorts walking hand-in-hand while a spaniel scampers along in front of them, dragging a furrow in the sand with its leash.

"Hey, you promised me babes in bikinis." He points. "What the hell?"

"Guess you just have to use your imagination."

"*Again?*"

Carl drops a two-buck entry fee into the hand of a pimply teenager with a mis-buttoned green uniform shirt, then strolls out along the pier to a square patio enclosed by a pipe railing where seagulls perch and flutter. The onshore breeze feels stiffer out here, and frosts the warm Atlantic with a meringue of whitecaps. Minutes later, a thin and tall older man wearing a blue suit and a white straw hat flaps toward him. A companion, in a blue windbreaker and wraparound sunglasses, but with no hat and a bristle of short red hair, peels away and leans casually against the railing, hands in pockets, staying just out of earshot.

"Hey Sam," Carl says to the tall, thin man.

Under the straw hat is a bland, oval face. It's Sam Lundts, a unit chief for International Operations Division at FBIHQ in Washington. His body is almost skeletal, but his face is a smooth, fleshy oval fringed by dark hair and graying sideburns. His eyelids hover just above half-mast, conveying not so much drowsiness as a calculating remoteness.

"Hello, U-C fifty-five ninety-nine."

"*D*," Carl emphasizes. "D-U-C." He gestures with a hand. "I'm your deep undercover operative. That's why we're meeting out here, right?"

"Of course."

Lundts moves up to stand beside Carl, folds his hands and props them on the rail. He looks out to sea, and gently tugs the brim of his straw fedora down on his forehead, so it's less likely to blow off.

"Got a major thing or two to discuss," Lundts says. "But let's start off easy. Clear up one item I find most puzzling. Amuse me. How in hell did you ever get out of Ecuador, then up here so fast?"

"Caught a ride." Carl offers a sharp-toothed grin.

"With whom?"

"To be shared in my full report."

"Tell me now."

"Can't."

The egg-like face rotates toward him.

"And you will file it, when?"

"At the very first second it can no longer harm an investigation. Right now, maybe, a few too many eyes on it."

Lundts sighs. "You know, fifty-five… can I use your first name?" His lips purse. "You display a level of independence… and stubbornness… that's distressing to find in a Bureau employee. I've noted it showing up all too frequently, though our time together has been short."

"Not your employee, sorry," Carl informs him. "On loan, only. As you know. From the Federal Protective Service."

"Right. In the National Protection and Programs Directorate, under the aegis of our Department of Homeland Security. Supposedly."

"It's my story and I'm stickin' to it. Makes me your guest, one might say."

"All the more reason to adhere to protocol in an agency willing to host you."

"Just rate me on initiative. Who's gotten further into Andreyev and the 'Y's' guys than I have, hmm?"

"Further isn't always better."

"Since when?"

"Pace of this operation is my call. Since it's my show."

"Nossir! It is the Bureau's show. You happen to get hit by a beer truck — God forbid — we'll struggle on. Somehow."

"Until or unless that happens, you ignore my direction at your peril. Powers-that-be have stated their concerns, and I'm making a judgment that we'll back-burner this for a bit. Let it cool. Make them think we've lost the scent."

"Uh-uh. We're *this* close to a breakthrough on Andreyev's ties inside the U.S., I can almost see it. That's exactly why they tried to take us out in Ecuador. If we don't make it happen now, we might lose the chance, and who knows when the hell we'll get another one?"

"There are other considerations. Priorities must align."

"Christ, Sam! When did you stop being a cop, and turn into a Head Shed clerk?"

"The moment when I saw debits of a project swamp its benefits."

"Horsepuckey. Can't know that 'til there's a bust. And you should know, I intend to make one."

"Not without my say-so."

"Let you know before it comes down. Or, just after. I promise."

"Per-haps…" Lundts cocks his oval head. "… you never were the best operator we might've picked for this job."

"Way-y too late to second-guess it now." Carl bares his teeth. "We *will* get IDs on the people Andreyev picked up in Key West, sooner or later. And figure out the boats they transferred onto, one way or another. Once we have that, we'll hold the string to the seam — to use a country metaphor — and should be able to unzip the whole sack. I look forward to seeing what sort of rancid swill comes pourin' out. Be awesome, don't you think?"

"Consider it from the Bureau's point of view," Lundts says. "We've been severely overtasked. Nearly half our agents are devoted to counter-terror. Criminal investigations, particularly the international variety, stay important, yes. But we need to move like a free safety on an NFL team. Run to a spot of highest priority, depending on the play we face, see? And right now, Andreyev, well, he's not it."

"What tops your list?"

"Other stuff."

"Ah."

"Aside from that, there are, well, complications. Including, I'm sad to say, some that are probably quite personal for you. Sorry to break it to you on the fly like this. But once I tell you what's come down, you'll probably want to take a break from the investigation, anyhow... You'll have lots else to think about."

"Yes?"

Carl looks almost bored, while Lundts gamely attempts to wear a look of solicitude.

"We've had no way to contact you the last few days. Sorry, or I would've let you know sooner. Your girlfriend, that's the right term? Melanie, the former Mrs. Symes, has disappeared, I'm afraid. Along with that other lady, common-law wife of your associate, Dan Cowell. Her name's Linda Parker, correct? Seems rather an odd moniker for a Honduran national. Assumed name? Anyway, she's gone missing, too."

Carl's bony face stiffens. "Missing?" he hisses. "How?"

"You mean, how it looks? Assaulted by human traffickers. Border smugglers. Apparently kidnapped, but no one knows why. Happened out in rural West Texas, their car was rammed, and they were taken. Have any idea what they were doing, way out there?"

Carl takes a deep breath. Then another. His body is tense, his face surly. "Do you?" he demands.

"No. Did she ever mention to you they might want to travel there? Or did she go out there to undertake some sort of chore or task for you?"

Carl shakes his head.

"Ah. Then, it was a kind of vacation, perhaps."

"Sure," Carl snarls. "Go and party hearty out in West Texas brushland! A jetsetter's dream. It's like Tahoe, right?"

"Anyway. The bureau will help as much as we can. If it's a true kidnapping, of course, it falls under our purview. I can tell you that we have picked up signals from their phones in Matamoros, Mexico. Right across the Río Grande...."

"I *know* where it is, dammit. Where am I from?"

Lundts lifts his eyebrows a notch.

"Austin. I was born and raised in Austin. I know where Matamoros is. And Nuevo Laredo. And even Ciudad-fuckin'-Acuña, all right?"

Lundts says nothing.

Carl breathes. "Ransom demand? Any signal from the snatchers?"

"No. But we do have a SOG" — meaning, special operations group — "detailed to take a look over the border. A task force is forming also, to assist the sheriff in Turco County, where the grab went down. For now, appears as though their rental car might've been run off the road in an empty area. Apparently, they were on their way back to the airport in Corpus Christi...."

"I'm goin' in," Carl announces.

Lundts' eyelids fall and rise in a reptile's slow blink.

"Thought you might wish to." He shakes his head in gentle negation. "But even you must admit, this cuts much too close to home. Most I can allow is, to let you observe from the sidelines, perhaps with the SOG going to Matamoros. Where the women most likely have been taken, anyhow. So after they get sprung, you'll get first hugs."

Carl squints but says nothing.

"Perhaps you imagine that's not enough," Lundts says. "However as soon as I get anything solid, I'll bring it over to Critical Incident Response Group, okay? They're pros, the tops. Look. Yes, Melanie Symes acted like a total pill, and got herself kicked out of Quantico. But that doesn't mean we don't give a damn. She's an American citizen, and happens to also be a somewhat famous ex-journalist. Also, a congressman's former wife. Anything about all that even *begin* to sound like, 'fuggedaboutit'? Carl, you and I don't see cye-to-eye on everything, but it doesn't mean I'm trying to blow you off. We'll do all we can to get her safely released, okay?

"Just saying, let's leave the Andreyev project alone for a while, till we get this and a few other matters figured out."

～

Dan straightens up from his slouch against a seawall when he sees the two blue-clad figures who met with Carl come off the end of the pier. He watches them clamber into a black SUV with tinted windows and drive off. But when Carl appears, there's fury in his stride, a barely-contained energy, as if his legs were mighty pistons on some low setting, yet ready to provide bouncy, ten-yard strides at the flick of a mental switch. After he draws close enough to see the icy calm in his metal-gray eyes, he understands that Carl's actually well past lit up — his friend is now ready to kill someone. Or a couple someones.

"Got some bad news, and I've got some worse news," Carl announces flatly.

Holy Christ. What's the worst I can imagine? Is it that bad?

"Which might I want to hear first?" Dan wonders aloud.

"Trust me. Not a speck of it."

Dan flinches.

"Linda and Mel are in big trouble. Huge."

"How so?"

"What I'm told, they both got 'emselves nabbed by smugglers out near the Mex border, in west Texas. After some kind of road-rage incident, maybe."

For a second, Dan can't even speak. Then his face swiftly contorts through expressions that hit marks of astonishment, curiosity, dread, and fury... as if he were a runner, tagging three emotional bases, before finally sliding into home plate.

"And what the fuck were they doing way out there?!" He yells.

"Indeed. That's question *numero uno*, ain't it? But my putative boss, ol' dickhead Sam Lundts, seems to attempt to suggest they went out there because of something you and I arranged. Like we might've put 'em up to something."

"How? Not even possible! We had no contact with them for days, I mean *shit!* We were on the lam from both cops and crooks in Ecuador. Last we knew, they were lovin' life and trying to behave themselves in DC."

"Exactly. So, who or what could make them head out to West Texas, for godsakes? I mean, do they jump out there on their own, or are they lured or pushed? And *is* there any possible link to what we've been doing?"

"You're saying, like, either the motive for them going out there, or the reason they got snatched, might connect to the case we've been working on?"

"Even if it wasn't hooked up before, now it is."

"What? How?"

"Lundts just told me he reckons it's a fine idea for us to back away from the Andreyev probe for a bit. And a huge side benefit of that is, then you and I can make a primary goal just seein' that our gals get safely back home."

Dan's face contorts into deeper rage as he hears this. He jabs an index finger at Carl. "You! Come clean! Right now, goddammit!" he demands. "Other than your supposed boss, who the hell *is* this fucking asswipe?"

"Truthfully?" Carl sighs, glances away, again levels those gunfighter eyes at Dan. The gaze remains merciless, yet at this moment also holds a smidge of regret. "Sam Lundts is my other main target. I've been investigatin' both Andreyev and him. As well as their links."

Dan startles again, this time it's almost a shudder, as he gets it. "Ay-yi-yi…"

"Right." Carl is grim. "My top goal in this meetin' was to rattle him. Make Sam feel like he's lost control of our operation, and so force him into an unplanned move. Yet as it turns out, he's way ahead of me on that, and what really pisses me off is that I don't know how in hell he got there."

"Yeah?" Dan scowls. "Know what blows *my* mind? You turned Linda and Melanie into pawns — captured pawns, now! — and you didn't warn 'em they might get shoved out into play!"

"No."

Dan grabs Carl by his shirtfront, twists the fabric into a knot with his fist, and hauls him in so close that their chins are barely an inch apart.

"Never told me this crap was so deep in-house." The words spurt out past a clenched jaw. Dan looks like he's ready to tear Carl's face off with his teeth and spit it out onto the beach.

"Wrong! On the balcony in Manta? I told you about those DOJ lawyers that went over to the dark side. 'Member them?"

Carl raises his own hand to sink a thumb and a forefinger into pressure points on Dan's wrist. Dan feels his grip on Carl's shirt growing numb, but sends a surge of will into his fist, to keep it strong. Eyes locked, they engage in a brief yet ardent duel of minds and bodies — a conflict that would be nearly imperceptible to someone standing even a few yards away.

"Think, godssakes," Carl urges, his tone almost contemptuous. "Linda got shot in her arm, *why?*"

The question finally makes Dan slacken his grip. Carl brushes his hand away as if removing lint, then tugs the hem of his shirt down to straighten it. He takes a step back.

"Because in Key West, one man decided he was gonna be a hero when he didn't need to be," Carl says. "But see, by that very act... other stuff did happen. Including me, arrivin' on your scene. So who really shoved Linda out onto the board? The one who did that, well, it'd be you. Big hero!" He scoffs, shaking his head.

Dan blinks. "You would've acted exactly the same way, that day on that bridge," he growls.

"Not sayin' I wouldn't've. All I'm sayin' is, want to *stop* bein' a hero? Now's *not* the best time! By a long shot. Need to make you some follow-through, dude. Tryin' to blame me for trouble you jumped into is a pure waste of our time. Which — I should not have to point this out — we ain't 'zackly got."

∼

A half-hour on, they still wrangle, though the topic under debate has shifted. Dan no longer accuses Carl of failure to reveal his investigation's true depth, target and scope. Now they fight over what they should do next.

Dan urges that they immediately charge out to Texas to start kicking ass and taking names. Carl argues that first they should gather more and better intel, which can permit them to come up with a smarter and more productive plan. On the drive to Miami International Airport they debate hotly about which city they should fly to. Dan says their destination needs to be Corpus Christi, but Carl insists on Washington, DC.

Only by resolute stubbornness does Carl achieve victory. They end up flying north instead of west, buckled into a pair of first-class seats — the last ones left on the plane. Dan continues to seethe and gnaw on his knuckles as he stares out the window.

"'Nother thing. If we go straight into Texas now, we'd be followin' leads that are likely distorted for our benefit, too," Carl says.

"I'm sitting right here, right now, doing it your way," Dan snaps, barely turning his head. "Am I not? Show some fucking 'preciation."

A flight attendant comes by to serve little paper cups full of hot mixed nuts, and plastic flutes that glow with amber fluid and champagne froth. Dan drains his glass at a gulp, and immediately holds it up to be refreshed.

He finally looks directly at Carl. "Okay, all right, distorted, by who?" he says. "Sam Lundts?"

Carl nods. "And friends," he adds.

"Who at this point, could apparently be anyone."

"Right."

"So, what's our next move, Jar-dar? After we dive to your Gungan city?"

Carl ignores this snide use of his Navy SEAL nickname, as well as the ref to his former habit of dropping lines from old Star Wars movies at odd moments — a tic he abandoned after a network TV show began to turn it into an overused script motif.

"First off, it's important that we do something Lundts expects. So, we pick over Mel's condo for any clues as to what prompted her and

Linda to light out for Texas. Even if we don't find anything, at least it makes him feel that he can predict our movement. Number two, it also gives us a chance to sneak off and do something I hope Lundts does *not* anticipate — which is, rendezvous with my real boss."

"Boss Nass?" Dan suggests nastily.

"No. I mean, a manager of the show *behind* the show. After some palaver with him, we can head out to Texas or across the border or wherever it is we really need to go. But we'll have a bunch of ass behind us. You know, support. Good guys."

"Yeah? Seen many?"

Carl pinches a nut out of the cup, pops it in his mouth, and crunches it.

"You've got to have hope, dope," he says. "Cool folk are out there. I mean otherwise, why bother? Might as well pack it in."

"Yeah? You mean, quit? What sort of job could you *ever* hope to do, other than this kind of crap?"

Carl mulls it over. "Talent scout for Hooters," he says finally.

Chapter 18

The old Dodge Power Wagon lurches, jolts, yaws, and bounds over rutted roads that are barely more than rough tracks wandering over the landscape as Larry and Hank — each taking a spin at the wheel — steer back toward the narrow swath of what remains to them of the ancestral Purdy ranch. Linda sits balanced on the center console with a folded blanket under her ample butt, both hands braced against the dusty felt of the cab roof to keep her head from hanging up into it.

Since the Purdy men removed her bonds after her vow to behave, in return she's forced them to promise not to crank up the ZZ Top CDs. So now they have Waylon Jennings's classic *Honky Tonk Heroes* playing at a modest level. Consequently, *en route*, they're able to converse.

"How you git thet-aire cast on yer arm?" Larry asks.

Linda considers, then answers. "A woman be shootin' at my husban', Dan," she says. "I fight to make this stop quick, 'nah mean. But then so a bullet hits me."

The men glance at each other, then Larry nods. "Wull now, that makes sense," he says.

"So real bad folk was comin' after you, huh?" Hank asks. "Think they maybe still have some int'rest in that?"

"To me it seems as though, yes, it can be so. Many, in Florida and here too…" She pauses. "But I do not know who, or why. It's a perfeck ponder."

"Like them guys made you wanna run off into the sticks, here?"

"Yes. It is at the road where I run from, last night. Men come up on us, hit our car with another car, and it makes a big accident, a terrible mess. And they try to grab us. So I run away!"

"Us?" Hank raises his bushy eyebrows, "Y'mean, you 'n' this here Dan feller you're hooked up with?"

"No. Melanie, who is my good friend, and almost like a sister to me, y' know. She is hurt, and I see they want to hurt me, so I go. I am sorry to have to leave her, because I feel so scared! I hope, somehow, Melanie is okay. But I do not think she is."

The men exchange a glance.

Hank's voice turns a notch less gruff. "So, you cain't imagine nothin' you did, what made them bozos come after you?"

"No, we are not here long, and we are nice to everyone the whole time. Our last thing is, we are in the Cinnebar town, speaking to people. And before this in the Sojourn town, up at the big jail in there. That is where Melanie talks to a prisoner, because she is like a big magazine reporter, a *periodista*."

The men hold eye contact with each other a bit longer.

"Shit," Larry breathes. "I'm surprised they let you in there."

"Even more surprised they let you out," Hank says.

"And why you say this?"

"Them people like to keep ever'thin' buttoned up all tight, over there. Like, they're control-freaks to the *max*."

"Know us a few of 'em run that joint," Larry adds. "A bit o' work we do is on Xanadu Park, a big game ranch those same people also got. Tell you straight up, ma'am, they ain't 'zackly our fav'rite bunch. Not by a mile!"

Seeing her expression grow more fretful, Hank reaches out to bestow a tentative pat on her knee. "Now, doncha worry none. You'll keep right safe with us for the time bein'. An' we'll put a lil' bit of time and effort into tryin' to suss this out."

Linda shifts a look of evaluation back and forth. "Thank you," she says, eventually. She's beginning to relax with them, seeing them less as a threat and more as men of the land, perhaps like *hombres de campo* in her own country.

The Purdy home ranch is a narrow swath of cleared earth where a sun awning of rusty tin roofing has been nailed onto a post-and-beam frame erected over a venerable double-wide trailer. Other features include a crooked outhouse that appears to be a relic from an earlier century, a pump shed on a concrete slab, and a barn made of plank walls and roof shingles so weathered and sere that sunlight shows through gaps at every seam.

Large dark lumps of something-or-other dangle from wires slung over the beams that hold up the awning over the trailer. As the truck's knobby tires grind to a halt, Linda realizes that these blackened objects are the salted limbs of large animals, hung up to dry and cure in the wind.

Larry points with pride at the row of dangling shoulders and haunches. "Them there's wild hog parts. Keeping that swarm of varmints down is a huge piece've our work. Get 'em good with these ol' Chinese semi-auto SKS rifles we just bought, recent. Interestin' guns, 'cos they still got bayonets. See? Right here, on the rack behind the seats."

"C'mon, let's go see what we can rustle up for chow," Hank says, as he exits the Power Wagon's jacked-up cab, then offers Linda a hand down.

They walk past yet another Confederate flag, this one lifting and flapping from a lodgepole pine that had its bark peeled off with a drawknife. The long, thin mast is set in a hole and braced upright by a pyramid of rocks.

Outside of the trailer stand ramshackle tables sagging under a clutter of rusty tools, bolts and nails in jam jars. The inside of the trailer is a musty den of battered furniture sprouting tufts of stuffing through rips in upholstery. A mélange of tattered jackets and hats droops from pegs, and ancient posters for Western films cling languidly to the walls.

"Lessee," says Hank, as he leans into the small fridge. "Got us 'bout a dozen cans of Shiner left, 'nuff to get through the night." He lifts the lid of a plastic bowl. "Last week's beans. Hm. Kinda on the edge, yet not over it. I say we nuke 'em with an onion, a tomato, and a lil' pepper jack 'n' call that good."

Linda peers over his shoulder. "I see you have *ajo*, jalepeños. Do you have a lime, a blender? Get me, and I will make you good soup, Honduras style."

"So, that's what country you're from, huh?"

"C'mon!" Linda claps her hands. "You get me what I ask, then stay out from my way, and I turn this into food. Serious." She unties her scarf, slides it off her neck, drapes it on a bar that runs across the top of their oven door.

~

They sit outside the trailer, on a bench that's no more than a thick plank nailed over a pair of stumps. They each hold a metal bowl full of savory black bean soup with chunks of wild hog meat, and each wields a GI messkit spoon, while open cans of Shiner Bock sweat on the ground between their feet.

Linda aims her spoon at the flagpole. "What is that, your flag thing? Three times now, I see it."

"Oh, well, y'know America had a civil war, way back when. Ever hear 'bout it?" Hank responds.

She shakes her head. "Just some, that you have one. And we have ours, too."

"Sure. What goes 'round, comes 'round." Hank sets his bowl on the bench beside him, wipes his lips, crosses his legs, then clears his throat.

"Uh-oh," Larry says. If he reads all Hank's signs aright, his uncle is preparing to launch an oration.

"Guess I should more 'r less catch you up from the beginnin'..." Hank says.

"Hank! Please, c'mon, don't need to do that."

"See, before that war, 'long both sides most the rivers, there was a bunch of cotton farms out here, and the settlers brung in black slaves to work 'em. One a' them farmers was my great grand-daddy, Eustace Purdy. Well now, it's the year 1860, and there's an assembly, calls in delegates from ever'whar, 'cludin' Turco County here, to figger out whar Texas is gonna come down on secession, y'know. I mean, our state'll def' support the Confederacy, but the question is how hard? Both feet, or hedge yer bets? Ther's the figger. Puts ol' Eustace in a bind, 'cos he believes in the Union, but he don't think he can make a nickel on his land without his slaves, followin' me, here?"

Linda nods vaguely.

"So he's one of the few who votes agin' secession, but it passes anyhow by a big, huge margin. And next he has to choose his path of honor, and decides what it is is, he's got to join up and fight with Hood's Texas Brigade anyhow, which he does, as an officer in the Fifth Infantry. Well, they have battles all the way to hell and back; Eustace was with John Bell Hood when he got his left arm tore up at Gettysburg and then lost his right leg at Chickamauga. Went on fightin' though, and Eustace sticks with him. Finally got the holy crap whaled outta 'em at Knoxville, and they retreated to Tupelo. By the time the South surrendered at Appomattox in '65, the Texas Brigade was down to 'bout a third of what it was. And Eustace got hisself shot up some, but all his bandages wouldn't make a patch for what was wrapped on Hood. Still with me?"

Linda nods.

Larry stands, upends his can of Shiner to pour its final shimmering thread of suds down into a gap in his sparse blond whiskers, then gives a long and resonant belch.

"Larry?" Hank says menancingly. "Din't nobody teach you no better manners? You need to 'pologize to the lady!"

"Sor-r-r-ry." Larry pronounces the word through one more prolonged burp. He smiles. "I'ma check on our snakes, back of the truck. Think I hears 'em callin' me. Don't 'speck they're feelin' none too comfy."

"Hey, if that box looks jammed up, dump 'bout half of 'em in a 'nother box. Pull one outta the barn," Hank says. "Got two deliveries to make next week, anyhow."

"These snakes, you deliver them, sell them?" Linda asks.

"You bet, live, to restaurants in Dallas. They barbecue 'em, make stew, canapés and what not. Freeze the skins, give us those back, which we cure and sell to folks to make belts and hatbands, boots and vests even."

"A-n-d bikinis, too!" Larry puts in. "Y'know, for club dancers. Bet you'd look absolutely terrific wearin' one a' them, ma'am. Can prob'ly get you one at discount, mebbe half off..."

"Lar-ry!" Hank growls.

Larry, about to say something else, stops, flushes slightly, turns and walks to the truck.

"Hard to fix thet kid's major lack o' home trainin'." Hank shakes his head. "Man can only do so much."

Linda shrugs and smiles. "Not to bother. He is a boy."

"Anyhow. Back to the story I was on. War's done, and John Bell

Hood and Eustace, who've grown into bein' purty tight pals by that point, head on down to New Orleans, where they find work in a business they know a ton about, which is brokerin' cotton. They do good, then the old general gets hitched and has him a passel o' kids, 'bout a dozen or so. Eustace marries also, but his situation is a tad more complex, which I'll 'splain in a minute. But yellow fever hits the city, so Eustace skedaddles with his sweet bride way back out here to the home ranch.

"But things don't look so great 'round here either, 'cos the former slaves have run off all the plantations to start their own lives, plus there's a bunch of other settlers now squattin' on big hunks of Purdy land. Show you how much got took, that town of Sojourn, where you visited? Well that was the west side of the old home ranch, and this here lil' sliver where we are? It's the east part. Biggest land grabber of 'em all was another Civil War vet, name of Jubal Nader. Eustace took 'im to court, and lost, took 'im to another court, and lost there too.

"How come? Well now, some say, it was all due to his wife." Hank gives Linda a long and appraising look. "Why's that? Kinda interestin'. A freed woman, what they call a quadroon, Eustace met her at a fancy party in the French Quarter. If they'd stayed in New Orleans, would've been fine, but out here in West Texas my great grandmomma was just seen as an uppity nigger, though she was only a breed, so that got ol' Eustace tarred as a nigger-lover too, and he couldn't win no respect from the law or anyone else. Fact that he was a gen-u-wine war hero of the Texas Brigade din't make no never-mind. By then his soldier dander was up, and he figgered he was not about to let himself get driven out. If he could not beat 'em, he'd damn sure outlast 'em. And so, here we are."

Hank points at the flag. "We fly that ol' rag now, for all kinds of reasons. But our best one is what you might call ironic. It's sort of an in-your-face to all the good folk of Turco County."

After he has checked on the snakes, Larry detours over to the trailer, then strolls back to the bench holding more ice-cold cans of Shiner as a quasi peace offering. He arrives just in time to hear the conclusion to Hank's peroration on Purdy family history.

"Wull, thar' ya go," Larry says. "Now you know more'n 'nuff 'bout our deal. Only just a story Hank's laid on *me* one hunnert-jillion times." He hands Linda a beer, then offers Hank one — but only lets him take it after pretending to draw it back out of reach. "Bet you're up for some cool refreshments after swallerin' so much hot air, huh?"

He pops his own can open.

"Y'all set?" He raises an arm. "Then let's hoist up a toast to all we black folk."

Chapter 19

A surveillance van sits parked at the Arlington National Cemetery visitors' center. The up-armored Ford XLT has a raised roof, windows tinted so darkly that they blend in with glossy black sides of the vehicle. On its rear door panels — incongruously — is stuck a motley collection of faded vinyl badges that indicate its owner has toured more than two dozen state and national parks. One sticker reveals that he likes to shop at Sam's Club.

Carl raps sharply with a knuckle five times on the van's side door. It clicks, hums and slides open. The interior is aglow with soft, indirect lighting. A short and slender man wearing a faded blue T-shirt and jeans beckons them to enter. He sits in a padded swivel chair in front of an electronics panel with several flat screens that he's just switched to generic wallpaper. He points at two metal chairs, which Dan and Carl unfold and sit on. The door hums, slides closed, and its locks snick again.

"Dan? Like you to meet Bob Smith," Carl says. "Otherwise, known to the DOJ's *cognoscenti* as Master BS." As he usually does when he deploys a fifty-cent word, Carl drawls out the Latin with the full force of his Texas twang.

Dan and BS shake briefly. Carl and BS grip hands longer, like good friends, or perhaps like long-term colleagues who simply have respect for each other.

"Damned sorry about your ladies," BS says. "Right up front, let me say I've no idea how they got in this fix. And thus far, no grasp of what the Lone Star point-of-origin for their problem really means."

Master BS has a pallid face outlined by limp and longish black hair as well as eyes of a startling shade — a powdery blue. As Dan peers at BS, trying to make sense of the eye color, he comes to realize it's produced by a pair of tinted contact lenses. He's an operator who wants nobody to know what his irises actually look like.

"As far as involvement by any parties the Bureau's been tracking in any other case, we have no evidence of that, either." BS holds up a monitory index finger. "However, lack of evidence sometimes only indicates the presence of skill."

"What about the local law, Turco County sheriff? Right now, he a potential asset, or liability?" Carl asks.

"Sheriff Jack Baxter has handled it all by the book. Deputies secured the site where their car got run off the road, then afterward seemed to cooperate fully with the Evidence Response team we sent. But." BS rubs the side of his nose as he gives Carl a look. "His department also has launched a whisper campaign inside state law enforcement. What it does, is suggest a scenario where *your* women stage this wreck themselves, then run off into Mexico of their own volition."

"Say wha'?" Carl's eyes bug slightly, and a few V's stack up between his eyebrows.

"They're selling a yarn that Mel's a rich 'n' wild playgirl, and Linda's a Central American with unknown connections, maybe to cartels. Who knows what they're up to?"

"That's a crock."

"Anything to muddy the waters, right?"

"Hold it!"

Dan's eyes shift back and forth and he thrusts up a palm. "Can we start with a foundation of fact? Something you *do* fucking know?" he yells. "Like who *you* really are, and your actual job?" His patience is at an end.

"Chill now, *compadre*," Carl says.

BS waves a hand, leans forward. "S'all right. In your place, I'd feel the same." He looks at Carl. "What's his clearance?"

"Squat."

"Screw it!" Dan bangs a fist on the narrow counter below the electronics panel, making them both jump. He levels a finger at Carl. "Dammit! You sucked me into this mess to help you make an ID for cops south of the border. Instead, we're busted for murder in Ecuador, need to make a jailbreak, then flee and have to get our sorry asses back home by one of the most cockamamie methods a body's ever heard of! Once here, we find out our women are now screwed up in ways we can't begin to grasp. Plus, a federal agency we'd ordinarily look to for help is corrupt or useless? Christ on a crutch! I either get straight talk from you jokers this very goddam minute, or I swear, I'm going to bolt and freelance until I know for sure that Linda's finally safe and sound!"

Dan pauses. "So, what'll it be?"

BS and Carl shoot a glance at each other. They say nothing, but thoughts that flicker midair between them seem nearly visible. *Tell him? Sure. It's either that, or we have to let this goddam bull gallop straight into the china shop...!*

BS looks at Dan. "Far as my real name, sorry friend, we just can't go there," he says gently. "As for a job description, officially, I'm analyst for a task force assigned to Carl's investigation by the Bureau's International Operations Division."

"An *analyst*? Oh, for shit's sake..." Evidently, Dan knows enough about the FBI to envision his proper slot on the status pole.

"Just his cover inside the Bureau," Carl adds. "Actually, I can tell you this man's a new type of investigator at the Office of Professional Responsibility in the DOJ. Know of it? You might describe OPR as Justice's department of Internal Affairs. With BS, here, they've created an agent who can go anywhere and do any damn thing. And pretend to be just about anyone as he does it."

Dan settles down. His eyes go back and forth between them.

"And he's investigating…?" he asks.

"That pair of DOJ attorneys that jumped ship, like I told you. Any involvement by their good buddy Sam Lundts. As well as all links, obvious or hidden, with Andreyev's global enterprises."

Dan absorbs this. "Casting a huge net," he says, at length.

"Big as it gets," Carl replies.

"You guys absolutely need a tight ship. Loose lips, all that…"

Both of the other men nod.

"So." Carl checks Dan. "Might we move on?" He looks at BS. "Dan and me went to Mel's condo right as we reached DC Somebody had tossed it, and whoever did that was careful. Even raked all the carpets to remove their footprints. Upshot is, if Linda or Mel left any kind of note or message for me and Dan, it's, like, down the rabbit hole."

"Black-bag job by TacOps," BS says.

"Ordered by who?"

"Lundts. Who else?"

"I took a hair, pasted it with a dab of Vaseline across my laptop cover, which was in her safe," Carl says. "But it got shook off. So, looks like they squeezed my 'puter, too."

BS appears sympathetic. "What was on it?"

"Well, a ton. Anythin' else you can tell me about the job? You happen to have a mole along for the ride?"

BS considers for a moment, decides to tell the truth by omission. "Hard part was trying to disable Melanie's security."

"Yeah?"

"You knew her system was state-of-the-art, right? Motion detectors and mini-cams absolutely every-goddam-where. Backups to backups. Probably..." he pauses.

"What?"

"Probably due to when Congressman Symes lived there with her. Way more paranoid than your average bear. Disconnecting that system, then scrubbing all memory was certainly a trick. The operators didn't even bother to lay in false records, would've taken too long." BS squints at him. "But you knew about the system, right?"

Carl glumly shakes his head. "Understand why they did the search, if her going out to Texas happened to trip some sort of wire with Lundts. What I don't get at all, is why she went out originally. Plus, what's their tripwire? It's all so sketchy." He sighs. "Well, we *do* have those ten pieces of laundry off Andreyev's boat, which we sent up from Ecuador. Get anything in the way of DNA hits?"

"Not a thing, according to NucleoLab's last report. The Bureau took that stuff back in-house, to double-check the results."

"Fuck me. Haven't heard a peep from our shop. That's likely a blind alley too."

"Wait. Did you say ten?" BS, looking thoughtful, swings his chair around, taps a button, and a screen lights up. He looks back over his shoulder. "Ten, right?"

"Uh-huh."

Clickety-clack from his keyboard. A pause. BS swings his chair back.

"Found a receipt for nine articles forwarded from NucleoLab to our CODIS."

Carl's head jerks up.

"You affirm it was ten?" BS asks.

"Does the pope wear funny hats?"

"Ah-h-h." BS steeples his fingers. "If Nucleo only sent nine on, won't admit to receiving ten in the first place. Never! Their Bureau contracts get cancelled in a heartbeat."

"Buy an item at Target, toss it on the pile to make up for the missing one?"

"Hey. Dipshits make zero mistakes? We'd never catch 'em."

"So, one item falls through a crack?" Dan hazards. "Or was it disappeared?"

"'Zackly," Carl says. "But you know, amigos, my deal with that lab was that I should get preliminary notification of *any* hits, instanter, by e-mail."

"You checked your in-boxes?"

"Of course, on the drive up to Miami, hunting for messages from Mel. But I saw nothing from Nucleo, either."

"You wouldn't, if Lundts had some tech pros hack. They disappear stuff."

"True." A grin starts to appear above Carl's sharp jaw. "But you know, in this here cyber age, a man needs to back up if he wants to stay ahead, right?"

Dan and BS catch his drift and look at him expectantly.

"Gear in this van is fully encrypted? I mean like, OPR-eyes-only?"

BS nods.

"Well, I've installed a system, refers every one of my incoming messages to a secret backup stash in the Cloud."

BS nods several times in a row, and begins to smile, too. He spins his chair around, puts his hands on the keyboard and looks back over his shoulder. "Host, user, and password?" he inquires.

Minutes pass. Then he whistles. "Lookie there," he says. "NucleoLab to ChuckBlack. Should I open it?"

"We're all pals here, right?"

They pull their chairs nearer, and BS points at the screen. "Well, right there's your DNA hit off the mysteriously missing laundry. Let me check the book on this guy now... okay... he is one Ted James Burnett, currently a long-term guest of a highly secure unit at the Sojourn prison of Coahuila Corrections Institute. About as far out in the sticks as you can get in West Texas."

"How in *hell* does a convict jailed way out there spill his scum on a bed in a Russian yacht cruisin' off the coast of Ecuador?" Carl muses. "Two thousand miles away, and the furthest I've ever been able to shoot, is like, a foot."

The keyboard clacks with a flurry of keystrikes, then a mug shot and rap sheet post on the screen. Dan leaps to his feet, simultaneously bumping the top of his head against the van's ceiling and knocking his chair over backwards.

"It's him!" he yelps. "That gorilla who jumped us on the bridge in Key West!"

Silence reigns for a second in the van, as they grapple with implications.

"Allow as to how that does solve one mystery," Carl eventually drawls. "But poses a question big as any it answers. How in God's name, Mel and Linda find out 'bout this guy?"

"For a follow-up, I'd raise this," Dan says. "Why'd Mel decide she had to even *try* to go spelunking on Burnett, and drag Linda into the shit 'long with her?"

"You don't think Linda instigated?"

"Come on. Got Mel written all over it. Linda'd leave a message to say where she was going. She didn't, 'cos Mel probably talked her out of it."

"Well, that pair did team up to go rogue in Honduras. Remember?"

Dan folds arms on his chest, shakes his head. "Not this time. She and I had an agreement to lay low."

"That what *you* did?"

Anger leaps in Dan's eyes. "No! And whose fault is that?"

"Already had this discussion."

"Ain't over."

"Apparently not," Carl says. "But let's postpone it. Let's figure out why Mel might launch both of them into this mess. I'd say, 'cos she hopes to prove the Bureau is wrong. Mel handles criticism or rejection poorly, as you know. She's out there showing the Bureau, me, you, God and everybody what a kick-butt investigator she is. Make 'em regret they showed her the door."

"A plan so-o-o working out." Dan's expression is sour.

"Gentlemen?" BS forms a football official's "T" gesture with his hands to signal a time-out. "Our issue isn't how any individual fell into this swamp, but how we all might wade out. In short, I'm now ready to entertain any creative proposal on strategy and tactics, going forward."

Carl rubs his jaw. "Well, Lundts probably expects us to bite on his idea of going into Mexico with a team, supposedly to find the women. But he'd only let us be observers."

"He can bite himself," Dan grumps.

"Second that motion," BS says. "Don't sign onto any game plan from Lundts. Might be bad for your health."

"Set him up for a head-fake?" Carl suggests. "Like we agree to his plan, sure, and fly to Corpus Christi. Make like we'll drive into Mexico with him. Instead, we fall off his screen to start diggin' 'round in Texas."

"What brings us to Linda and Melanie the quickest? Far as I'm concerned, that's the key."

BS and Carl look at each other, then back at Dan.

"Maybe yes, maybe no," BS says. "However, if Lundts said they're in Mexico, I'd guarantee, it's not the right place."

"Okay, so, assumin' we do Texas, what's a point of attack?" Carl says. "I'm thinkin', got to be one of the deputies the Turco sheriff put

on the crash site. Twist his balls, until he lets us know what's goin'
on. We work our way up the chain. See if we can ID any boss-type
person who knows a bunch more. Then we twist *his* balls."

BS shuts his periwinkle eyes. For a moment, he hums tunelessly. "I
concur," he says, and his eyes flick open. "I'll work up HUMINT on
which individual you target."

"Good," Carl says. "What do you propose for step two?"

"See what you get," BS says. "I'll move in overwatch, I can detail
SSG's to the San Antonio field office. I mean, they'll appear as
regular support, with an assignment that looks both local and logical.
Actually, they'll be a squad of door-kickers able to scramble at a
second's notice."

"Okay," Carl says. "And where's your own savvy self?"

"Need to mull that over. Plus, run stuff past some muckety-mucks
on Mahogany Row. They're guaranteed to have an opinion."

"Sorta put your lips to God's ear."

"More like that than you'd ever want to know."

"But not a single one who'd ever tip off Lundts."

"Naturally."

Carl turns to Dan. "Hey. Hope you can see, this mess was not
my doin'. I mean, openin' moves, sure, after I came to the Keys. But
pullin' off a visual ID was the sole involvement I thought you'd have.
And Linda gettin' her tail dragged back into the shit came outta left
field. Feel bad about that. But I'll move heaven and earth — hell too,
if that's what it takes — to make sure you get Linda back. Mel, too.
Though, if it's her fault both of them got in this, I'll spank her within
an inch of her life."

"Right," Dan says. "And you get that chance, don't worry 'bout your
nuts. I'll be the one holding her down."

During this exchange, BS spins in his swivel chair to click away
on a keyboard, making images whizz across all three lit screens of his

console as if DVD players are running on fast-forward. It's difficult to make sense of all images as they flicker past, but they seem to be screen-grabs from TV news shows and stills of newsprint pages. Abruptly, one image shudders to a halt on the center screen. It's unclear if it does so in response to a search algorithm he's entered, or if BS actually boasts a preternatural ability to make sense of visual information that whips by in a near-blur and pluck out an item in midstream.

"Hey, check this."

It's a scan of the front page of *Comanchero*, a rural Texas weekly.

"See what's happening, downrange, there?" he asks. "You ain't exactly heading into Mister Rogers' Neighborhood."

The color photo shows the upper half of a man's nude and bloody corpse sagging from a barbed wire fence, its spread arms lashed to the upper strand as though he's been crucified.

The headline reads, "Tattoo Artist Found Slain Near Cinnabar Springs."

"Some local assholes gave this Dalton Post guy a worse deal than even poor ol' Matt Shepard up in Wyoming got," BS says, as he speed-reads through the copy below. "Dragged him down a gravel road behind a pickup, then strung him up that way. Cut 'FAG' into his chest with a knife."

Carl stares at the image. His jaw works.

"Tough time, hackin' out that 'G,'" he says in an icy monotone. "Looks like some jerkwad really fumbled 'round at it."

Chapter 20

Melanie slumps in a wheelchair that a short, copper faced nurse pushes down a dark hallway. Mel wears a fresh hospital gown, a dark blindfold crosses her pale face, her ears are cupped by large headphones. The nurse waddles as she pushes, and her rubber-soled shoes make tiny sucking noises as they pop from the floor tiles.

They enter a room that is amply furnished, but in a bland and tasteless fashion, like a suite in a two-star hotel. Wheels clatter across a tiled section of floor, and Mark Nader turns. The top hat is off, his fringe of stringy brown hair hangs to his shoulders. He still has on a frock coat. He's standing before a spacious row of plate glass windows. Outside, a rosy sunset hovers above the sprawling terrain of the Xanadu game park.

He holds up a palm, the nurse stops. Nader then waggles his fingertips to wave her away, and — her sullen face blank as an earthenware mask — the nurse flips the brake levers on the wheelchair, turns, and exits.

Nader approaches Melanie. She sits loose-bodied and heedless. In addition to the blindfold across her eyes and headphones on her ears, a strip of gaffer's tape covers her mouth. Swaths of that same tape wrap her arms and ankles against the frame of the chair.

Nader stands in front, almost straddling her lap, leans, cocks his arm back, then whacks an open palm across her cheek and mouth.

Mel's head stays canted from that blow, her cheek reddening as Nader pinches a corner of the tape sealing her lips and tears it off with a swift, brutal yank. Mel gasps, arches her back. A thread of blood winds down from a split in her lower lip and drips off the end of her chin.

Nader smiles, bends over, brings his face down in front of hers. Positions his hands below her blindfold. He shoves it up — and she's looking straight into his eyes.

"Boo!" he exclaims.

She needs a split-second to get her bearings, another to recognize him. As she does she gasps again and swiftly recoils, jolting against the chair back.

Nader leans over her, completes the removal of the blindfold and the headphones, flings them casually onto cushions of a black leather sofa.

"*Willkommen*, back to reality, honey pot." he says.

Melanie blinks, her mouth and jaw tighten. She struggles to regain control over herself.

"Like you'd know it," she snarls.

"I own it," he says calmly.

She tries to stare him down. "Bull fucking shit, asshole."

Nader wags an admonitory index finger at her. "*Au contraire*. And, I can demonstrate. Let's say I'm God, and we'll call this your judgment day. Show great judgment, and maybe you'll do well enough to get to purgatory."

"Where am I?" she demands.

He holds out his left hand, and taps a finger in the center of that palm. "Right here."

"People will be searching for me." She lifts her chin. "People that you really don't want to meet."

"Hah!" He smiles broadly. "Are you psychic? *Exactly* what I want to chat with you about. So, who are they? These… searchers, hmm?"

Melanie starts to answer, then abruptly decides that she won't. Her eyes harden.

"Okay, just nod. Confirm my vision. See, I have psychic powers too. You and me, it's like we're in the same coven!" He closes his eyes, raises both hands to his temples. "Now, I'm seeing a guy… some cop-like guy… very agro. The type that tries way too hard to compensate for an eentsy dick, I'd guess. He's your boyfriend, so you'd know, right? Now I'm picking up a name. Chuck. Chuck Hole? No… Charles… no, Carl. That's it! Carl Blackadar, a-k-a Charles Black, former lieutenant commander with the SEAL teams."

He opens one eye. "How'm I doin'? Sorta awesome, huh?" He shuts the eye, and frowns as if concentrating. "Pickin' up more vibes… even more vibes… After time in the Navy, Carl works as a chief for the CIA in Honduras, and next he's supposedly on loan to the Criminal Division of the FBI."

Nader opens both eyes and grins. "Have I impressed you yet?"

Melanie struggles to keep her face blank.

"Still coy, huh?" He squats down beside the chair. "Or, is it shy? C'mon, which is it, witch?" He reaches out, pinches her nose, gently shakes her head from side to side. "I hope it's not resistance. That'd be stupid."

He stands. "But oddly enough, right after he gets to the FBI, our guy gets his sorry ass called up on bribery charges, is disgraced, and then promptly dismissed. A sad tale. But to me? One that — again! — reeks of bogus cover story."

A hand dips into his frock coat's big right pocket and emerges holding a red-and-white pack of Marlboros as well as an old Zippo lighter with some of the chrome worn off its brass. He plucks out a cigarette, taps it on the pack, inserts it below his wispy mustache. Flips the Zippo's lid, thumbs its wheel, lights up, and inhales.

"Sort of reminds me of your own crappy cover yarn," he drawls, blue fumes drifting from his mouth along with the words. "Magazine writer, huh?" He ruefully shakes his head, then holds out and meditatively regards his cigarette. "Don't know why I need *this*. You folks've already blown way-y too much smoke up my ass."

He gazes down at her. "Confirm everything I just said. Then, we can move on."

She does not move. Her mouth remains a firm line.

His eyes narrow. He takes a deep drag off his cigarette, bends over and blows a thick cloud of smoke out with his lips three inches from her face. She tries to jerk her head back, squints and coughs.

He straightens up and cocks his head. "What? Couldn't quite get it. Was that a yes, a no, or a maybe?"

Her eyes watering, Melanie croaks out a faint, "No... way... I'll say a thing to help you."

"Dammit! Think I'm fooling? Think again!"

His own eyes harden. He shoots out an arm and grinds the end of his lit cigarette into the back of her bound right hand. She shrieks, her eyes bulge as she looks at the tiny black-and-red pyramid sending up a wisp of vapor from her burning skin. She desperately jitters and shakes the entire wheelchair and flaps her wrist below the bonds of tape, trying to get the coal off. It falls to the floor. She stares at the dark, suppurating crater in her skin. Her fingers tremble.

"See? Pain hurts. You need to admit that."

Nader walks away to put the crumpled cigarette in an ashtray, returns. She looks at the floor, refuses to meet his eyes. Her breathing is rapid and shallow. He shoves a hand under her chin, turns her face up.

"Look." He tries a kindly tone. "You *will* tell me everything I want to know. That's settled. Only part we're exploring right now is how messed up you'll be before you squawk. Remarkably, that's in your control. Can you believe it? Truly. You can jump out of the fix you're in, right this very instant." He snaps his fingers. "Go take a warm bath, pull a cork on some great wine, have a fine meal, and snooze in a nice, comfy bed. Want that?"

Her look is frozen. She's receded into herself as deeply as she can.

"No more latitude for attitude, doll. Go verbal. Tell me. Was Carl's dismissal an act? And assuming that's so, who's he really working for now? And I mean, give me a name."

She just looks at him, as if not seeing him.

"Eh? What?" Nader lights up another Marlboro. He steps closer, kneels at her side, takes a few puffs, brandishes the cigarette again, blows ash off its tip, and admires the glowing coal at the end. "Now, I could put this 'un out in your other hand. Or on your face, like right on the end of that cute nose…"

Now he gets a reaction. She cranes her head back, eyes rolling.

"Or even, right in one of those gorgeous blue eyeballs. How about *that*?"

He laughs, stands up, puffs.

"'Kay, is it just a bad time for any questions about Carl? Well, let's put 'em aside for a moment. Answer a few I've got for *you*. What's your role in all of this? And, why'd you come here to talk to Burnett? How do you know about him?"

She pants. "I… I'm a magazine journalist, I'm here to work on a story about…"

Nader throws his head back and shrieks, "Knock that shit off!"

As he looks down at her again, his eyes are hot anthracite. He releases the wheelchair's brakes and shoves the chair toward the suite's kitchen, bashing its sides into the walls as he goes. At the granite-slab counter he stops, grabs a wooden block filled with knives and spills it across the polished surface and floor. He jerks a knob on the gas range, igniting a burner. He lays the largest knife across a ring of blue flame. He looks at her.

"What does it take to get your undivided attention?"

He yanks open the stainless refrigerator.

"Let's see." Glances back at her. "Lamb shank!" He brandishes a paper-wrapped package.

He goes to the rear of the wheelchair and pulls a roll of gaffer tape from a pouch that hangs from the backrest, shows it to her. It's the same tape she's bound with. He rips off a length and winds it rapidly around the package of meat. He plunges the wrapped lamb shank down into the kitchen sink, and he switches on the garbage disposal. A clatter and chomp and grind and roar come from the disposal as the bone end jumps and jerks in his hand.

He grins at her. He pulls the package out of the grumbling appliance, holds it up. It's now a mess of torn flesh and shreds of tape and splinters of bone. Pale red fluid streams out of the shank and down his wrist and into his coat sleeve, but he doesn't appear to notice or care.

"Here," he says, and tosses it into her lap. "Get used to how that looks. Don't give me what I want? Your hands will end up about that mangled, little lady, and damn pronto."

Nader snatches up the heated knife, which now glows a dull red.

"Which one should get munched up first? How 'bout your right?"

He touches her arm with the hot knife and Mel shrieks. Then he uses it to slice away the tape that binds her right wrist to the chair arm, making smoke rise as he burns the tape and scorches her skin. He pulls her loose arm high and reaches for the roll of tape.

"No no no no no!" Melanie has come alive with terror, she thrashes against her remaining bonds, tries to pull her arm back from him, makes the wheelchair tilt and nearly fall over.

But he's too strong and fast. He swaths her forearm in tape until it looks exactly like the shank. The disposal is still making a metallic, gobbling sound, but it's a bit hollow now, as if the machine is eager and waiting to be fed. He drags her and the chair over to the sink. He hauls her arm over the rim and aims it at the drain hole, shoves it downward. She desperately jerks it, makes her bound fist catch and stop on the side.

"Carl! He works for the FBI! I found out about Burnett myself, I snooped on Carl's laptop!" she blurts out, almost jabbering. "He's still in Ecuador! He doesn't know I'm here!"

Nader lets her go, and the chair flops back on its wheels and settles.

"More," he says calmly.

"The e-mail," she sobs, so riddled with fear that she can hardly speak. "It was about Burnett. That it was his DNA on the sheet. That he sent up."

"Uh-huh. And the e-mail was from?"

"A contract lab. Does work for the Bureau."

"Why did Carl send it there, not straight to the FBI lab?"

"I don't know." She sniffs. Mucus runs freely from her nose, tears spill from her eyes.

Nader squints at her. She tries to hide the tape-wrapped arm from him, putting it under the chair seat, then sticking it behind her back. He smiles and reaches out to switch off the garbage disposal, which clatters to a stop.

"And who is it that you work for? FBI, too?" he asks gently.

"No." Sniff. "I… wanted to. But I flunked out. I wanted to come here… to investigate… on my own…"

"Why? To prove you could?"

She doesn't answer. Nader snickers.

"Okay. This guy, Dan Cowell, the one your pal Linda tried to call a few times before my team picked you up. Who's he?"

"Just… our friend. From Honduras."

"Some kind of a partner for Carl on this?"

"Yes."

"There. Not so damn hard after all, eh?" Nader pats her on the head. "Think we still might be able to be buddies, you and me. Intimate, even. In some ways, you're my type of gal. I mean, insofar as I could be said to have a type of gal. Know what I mean?"

Melanie shudders. He plucks a cell phone from his other coat pocket. He taps its screen. "Yo." He says. "Come on over and pick up the silly bitch." He puts it back in his pocket. "No offense," he says to Melanie.

He turns off the stove burners, turns and leans against the counter, arms crossed.

"Before you go, please help me guess who Carl's boss is," he suggests.

"Lundts," she says in a low voice. "At CrimDiv in the Bureau."

Nader barks out a laugh. "What you apparently want to sell me is that Carl thinks Lundts thinks that Carl thinks that Lundts is his boss. But Carl doesn't actually think that. Neither does Lundts. Now, that's a matter I happen to know more'n a little about…"

Melanie's head hangs. Her terror has receded, but she feels barren. She begins to see that she's bought herself only a tiny period of safety at an extremely high price.

Chapter 21

Carl and Dan fly to CCIA, the airport at Corpus Christi, on an American Airlines Boeing 757. Lundts offered to put them on a Bureau turboprop ferrying a few of his minions westward, but Carl refused this without explanation. They now sit in a largely empty first-class compartment. The man sitting across the aisle from them has his eyeshade on, earplugs in, and seat reclined.

"I'd say, first rule for a lion tamer is, you choose if and when you'll put your head in its jaws," Carl says quietly. "The lion doesn't get to pick."

"Right," Dan agrees. "But when does the big pussy discover we're not going anywhere near its cage?"

"Told Sam that after we land, we'll grab a cab and go meet him at the Bureau's office on North Shoreline."

"But nix on that, eh?"

"Then's when we hop the fence. Set up with a sweet ride from Wheel Dreams. Y'know, I win a ton of perks from that outfit by being such a steady customer. It's a Dodge Challenger SRT8 with a 6.4-liter HEMI, and 500 horses under the hood, plus cop suspension, brakes and a few other mods. Originally, it was a special order for the Texas Highway Patrol, but they cancelled. Their loss, our gain."

"Sounds, uh, inconspicuous."

"Hey, it *looks* vanilla. Just a white car. Yet, stompin' on it should feel like slingin' a Tomcat off a flattop. Anybody wants to rumble with us on the road? We'll bring major game. Anyhow, once we're on those wheels you can wave bye-bye to Lundts. We write our own ticket."

"I'm so down with that."

Dan points to a folder lying on Carl's tray table. "Can I check out the Master BS dispatch?" Carl nods, Dan picks up the file and leafs through it.

"All general stuff? Background?" he asks.

"Yep. What we got, at this point. But hey, don't dis' analysts. Like my man Sun Tzu says, you always need to puzzle out the terrain."

"Hm," Dan says, as he peruses the first page, a summary of findings. "Okay, the supermax in Sojourn is not all that unique. The great Lone Star state's been a leader in privatizing prisons since the 1990s."

"Yeah, well, it really began a century or more earlier. Let me toss in some gen'rally ignored stuff 'bout my home state. Slave-holdin' powered it up. Texan independence, I mean. Reason why the Texians chose to revolt from Mexico was 'cos Mexico was fixin' to ban slavery, and the farm owners here just wouldn't have it. Somehow, that part never makes it into the story of the Alamo! When the Civil War got goin', most private money was being made on cotton plantations and ranches worked by slaves. Heavy industry began at the prison in Huntsville, north of Houston. Had mills and looms for both cotton and wool, and convict labor to work them... many uniforms the Confederates wore came outta there.

"Anyways, followin' the war, some rebel vets figured out how to keep chunks of the old system goin'. They paid the state to use convict labor on their farms. That way, the state didn't have to house inmates, the prisoners were kept out of sight and out of trouble, and a few farmers got to make about as big a pile as they did under slavery. It's what happened on Sugar Land outside of Houston, cane farmin' under Colonel Cunnin'ham, 'bout 20K acres."

"So, the only ones stuck with a lousy deal were…"

"Right, cons assigned to do hard labor under heavy guard, while they made other people money. Not much different from how it was 'fore the Civil War. You know, the state capitol in Austin was originally built by slave labor. That burned down in the 1880s, then the tall domed building you see there now was built by convict labor. But basically, stayed a monument to the same kind of economy."

"All right," Dan says, peering at the file. "Modern times. Private prisons, late twentieth century, the second wave. Says here, stock in some of the corporations doing it shot up three hundred percent in just a few years. And some of the companies rake in more than half a billion, annually? For real?"

"Yeah. Think of what was going on in the U.S. at the same time. War on drugs, mandatory sentencing, three strikes, tough-on-crime political campaigns. Big sentences for pot, even bigger for crack. Better than printing license plates, this was like a license to print money. All you had to do was keep your warehouse packed about ninety percent or better with inventory."

"Okay, got it." Dan closes the folder and pitches it back to Carl. "Inventory, meaning cons. Their stock-in-trade. You already read this thing, so just tell me. Where does Sojourn fit in?"

"Began in the 1980s as a juvy rehab ranch run by a local landowner, name of Nader. He stuck a finger in the wind, saw how it was blowin', got financin', built his facility up into a private prison. After scorin' a taste, saw real big money might lie in a modern supermax, and led that charge. Not just lock up jerks, but specialize in warehousin' the most dangerous jerks. Ten years go by, Coahuila Corrections Institute is a huge success, and his logical move would have been to ramp up and open more facilities, yet instead he does somethin' curious, he keeps just that one prison goin', and becomes a specialist in transport instead. The outfit's wedge of the pie is now movin' badasses securely around the country and across borders, both in aircraft — *Con Air* if you will — and highway vans, what they call chain-buses."

"What's his full name, this landowner?"

"Original guy, the founder, was Cyril Nader. Apparently, a cranky and confirmed bachelor. He croaks, and has nobody to will his whole shebang to, except for a young cousin named Mark Nader. Now, he's the dude."

"Privately held?"

"*In toto.*"

"Maybe that's why he didn't grow more facilities, back when," Dan mused. "Would've needed to bring too many other foxes into the coop."

"Could be."

"All right. Mark Nader's *required* to keep monsters like Ted James Burnett under lock and key. Instead, he lets him out to run around. In which case, I kinda doubt Burnett's the only Sojourn con who ever scored a hall pass. It was a big, rough crew that day on the bridge at Key West, I'm tellin' ya…"

"Okay, but the development impressin' the holy hell outta me, is how Andreyev and his crew tie in. That joker has links to a huge set of prisons and correction companies across Europe and Asia."

Dan whistles softly. "What was it someone said about hard-core porn? You can't define it, but you know it when you see it?"

"Yeah. A judge said that. Maybe one of the Supremes."

"Diana Ross?"

"Sure." Carl snickers.

"Anyway. Can't really tell what we're looking at here, but for sure it feels hard core."

"Yeah. Hard core, but foggy outline. Even so, I can still tell you right now that something really doesn't fit."

"What?"

"Your part."

"*Mine?*"

"What happened to you and Linda on that bridge," Carl explains. "The Nader outfit has kept its ops all-pro and low-key for years. God only knows ol' Andreyev has never been caught with a fist in the cookie jar. Or if so, he's been able to bribe his way out of it, quick. Your scene that day on the bridge, it's harsh. Even worse — from a manager's perspective — it's obvious. Same thing with the murder precedin' it, up in West Palm."

"Meaning what?"

"The sort of screw-up that's *not* 'sposed to happen."

"Ahh. You mean, out of control…"

Carl nods. "Draws attention they absolutely don't need."

"Right. It did put you on the scent."

"Uh-huh. There's a weak link. Tank Burnett makes a hell of an intimidatin' enforcer, sure. But can he be managed?"

"How I'd do it? Tongs. V-e-r-y long ones."

"Exactly. After he's on the loose, he can hook up with other scumbags, then run totally amuck."

"Why even keep him on the squad?"

"Don't know he still *is*, huh?" Carl cautions. "Might take his boss a day or two to discover the snafu. Tank won't rat himself out, right? 'Hey boss, I just screwed up twice in Florida.' The guy's a con, so an unforced plea just ain't in his playbook. Once they find out, maybe they boot him off the team. Wrap him up in an anchor chain, and roll him over the side."

"Speaking of their team, the OpFor…" — Dan uses military slang for an opposing force — "…must include a big chunk of the Turco County sheriff's department, don't you think? An operation like that needs locals on board."

Carl taps the file with a forefinger. "That's the last page in our brief from ol' BS. The county sheriff, Jack Baxter, like most of his department brass, got a start in law enforcement working as a corrections officer in, where? You guess."

"Sojourn."

"And the man wins a kewpie doll!"

"Okay. So who's the guy on Baxter's force we hope to turn?"

"One of the deputies who did *not* start out like that. Came in from Utah. A guy just keepin' his head down, who goes along to get along. With us, he finds out there's a new game in town, and there's mucho grief in store if he doesn't cooperate. Make that work, gives us a chance to score a line on the real whereabouts of Melanie and Linda without sendin' up the whole yellowjacket nest."

"When do we call in the cavalry?"

"Soon as we figure out how to make a precision bust. Like that line, 'When you strike a king, you must kill him?' Our moves have to be smart, fast, and precise. Otherwise, Nader, or Andreyev, or Lundts will slip out of our grasp. They all must go down at once, or some might get away. Maybe they all do."

Dan nods. Frowns. "Thoreau said it, right? That king bit?"

"Have no idea. Like how it sounds, though, has that thump of truth."

"Perhaps it was Emerson. Been years since I read 'em."

"Never have. Didn't have the time."

"Or any interest?"

Carl shrugs.

~

The Boeing's long hull dips and tilts. Dan looks out a side window to see the cloudy brown expanse of Nueces Bay glide past, the ragged green oval of Corpus Christi Bay, then the dark slot of the bay's entry channel at Port Aransas, flanked by commercial wharves and yacht harbors. The aircraft circles out above the Gulf to approach CCIA from the south.

Dan wonders if any of the vessels moored down there could be the *Dean Swift*. After their battle with Andreyev via the proxy of Ecuadorian cops, Dan knows he'll always look at huge yachts and the people on them differently. Certain thoughts will nag, such as, *Who is that really? How'd they make so much dough?* and, *What sort of bizarre shit might they really be up to?*

The plane cruises inland over barrier islands, then blocks of urban buildings and streets flash by. A dull thump comes from the landing gear, the engines roar, and they roll smoothly toward the terminal.

Dan gestures out the window to the vista of sprawling plain visible on the opposite side of the runway. "Damn. That's a bunch of level ground."

"My granddaddy used to say, after the days of Creation, God had way too much flat stuff left," Carl says. "So, South Texas is where he pitched it."

As they make their way from the boarding gate, they see a ring of limo drivers and personal assistants holding up squares of cardboard and small dry-erase boards — and, in one case, even an iPad — with names written across them.

Dan nudges Carl and points. "You?" he asks. He indicates a small shirtboard that reads, BLACK.

"Right."

The man holding it is short and bulky, with a bright smile and dark sunglasses, a pair of classic Wayfarers. "Mister Black?" He peers at the ID Carl flashes him, his white smile incandesces a bit more, then reaches into a pocket of a gray leather vest he wears, and tugs out a set of keys. "Your custom ride from Wheel Dreams is parked in a special area, out just beyond the rental fleet."

"Excellent." Carl tips him with a twenty.

They follow the signage, go through baggage claim, out past the Hertz and Avis lots, and reach a stretch of access road where two vehicles are parked a hundred yards apart. One is an idling flatbed tow truck with its driver standing outside his cab, apparently on a break, sipping from a Styrofoam cup. Carl assesses him, guessing he's the delivery guy for Wheel Dreams.

And there sits the Challenger, a gleaming, hulking, streamlined wedge crouched over its mag wheels and short sidewall race tires like a mechanical tiger, only waiting for a twist of the key to bring it to purring life.

Dan and Carl sling their bags in the trunk, jump inside, and sink into the firm embrace of the bucket seats.

"Wow. X-harnesses," Dan observes.

"Better believe it," Carl says. "Might want to buckle up before I even turn this baby on."

"How? Gonna tell her what a pretty lil' ride she is?"

Carl smirks and turns the key. The body heaves and rotates a bit, and a deep-throated rumble bleeds into the passenger compartment.

"Lordy," Carl observes. "'Nuff power to light a town."

The door locks click. Carl dismisses this as an automatic safety feature. But then he hears a soft, percussive "*whump!*" and the car instantly fills with a gray fog. Astonishment makes them both suck in a breath — and they are done for. Dan only manages to touch a finger to a lock button, Carl to thump his fist ineffectually against window glass. Then they slump down in their seats, heads lolling forward.

The short man who handed Carl the car keys at the terminal approaches. He peers at their limp bodies, raps with a knuckle on window glass, gets no response. He waves an arm, signaling the tow-truck driver. The driver dumps the dregs of his coffee on the asphalt, clambers into his cab, switches on his yellow light bar, and slowly backs his rig up to the Challenger. Meanwhile, the short man paces back and forth, as if he's a driver in distress.

The truck stops, its bed tilts, and the driver jumps out to hook up the Challenger and drag it aboard. He glances into the car. "Huh," he grunts. "Gas works okay, I guess." He looks at the short man. "But, no risk to us?"

The short man shakes his head. "Nuh-uh, all sealed off."

"Kinda stuff is it?"

The short man looks irritated by the question, then decides to answer it. "A knock-out gas called isoflurane. Not used much on people. Have a large-animal vet we get it from. Mixes it up with nitrous. Yeah, does great."

"Nitrous, huh." The driver grunts again, and starts his winch to pull the car up. "Wouldn't mind getting my hands on a tank a' that. Makes a great party."

"K," the short man says, and grins. "Done deal. Be your bonus." He glances at his watch. "Let's hit the road. Xanadu's a long way."

The driver gestures. "What if those guys come to?"

"No way. Gas flow is on an auto feed so they keep getting dosed. Kind of an air sensor and metering thingy on it, so the level don't rise too high. Like they've just been laid out on a hospital operatin' table somewheres."

Chapter 22

Melanie slouches against a bathroom sink. She keeps both eyes squeezed shut so that she won't see herself in the mirror.

She wears a green wool blanket draped over her shoulders. A locked leather cuff around one ankle has a thin cable leading back to the bedroom, where it's looped around a steel bedframe that's bolted down to the floor.

She came in here because she had to pee. And after, she washes hands and face, more from habit than any thought of improving her appearance. So far, she's managed to avoid a glance into the mirror. But then she can't help it, her eyes do pop open for a second. She quickly averts her gaze.

That blond head she sees in the glass no longer resembles the Mel of three days before. The skin is too shockingly pale, the eyes too blank. It's as though she sees her own ghost peering up from a black abyss. She knows that place, dreads it, has not visited it for decades. It's a pit she's fled for her entire life. Now she feels herself falling back into its depths slowly but unstoppably, with the chill of its shadow seeping into her bones. The jaunty, proud, confident Mel, a complex creature she'd artistically assembled over all the years since her troubled childhood, the professional woman who could boost

Washington figures with deft public praise or cut them down to size with a stinging remark, the gorgeous media star who could draw men with a single glance from half-lidded blue eyes… that persona lies in tatters… flimsy shreds flapping and spinning around her as she drifts and falls.

She'd spent a long time describing herself to herself as person no longer vulnerable, more than the world's match, a woman who could never again be dominated or broken. She sees now —all that was self-delusion. A faltering whistle past the graveyard of her dreams.

"I don't want you to come." That whisper slides past her clenched teeth.

She's not talking about Mark Nader, who invaded this suite again last night, eyes gleaming, mumbling crazy talk as he again sliced her clothing away with his knife. She did not respond to any command or request, but went limp, removed herself from what he was doing, let him flip and flop her body in whatever way he desired, not adding a grain of cooperation or resistance. He still seemed to please himself, but she strove not to care, one way or the other. She was absent.

The abyss had yawned open at her feet when Nader had threatened to torture and maim her in the kitchen of the suite, and she tumbled into it at the very moment he broke her will and made her babble out her words of betrayal. That night he had come to savor his victory, to sink his crooked teeth into her again, to gnaw rat-like upon her spirit. That was when she had launched herself out and down into that cool dark vastness she'd once conjured as a child whenever bad stuff started to happen. And all things she had known for sure about herself as an adult began to fragment, slough off as she fell… back, back there again…

"I don't want you to see me."

Melanie is talking about Carl Blackadar.

She began to fantasize about Carl riding to her rescue when she first lay bound on the gurney with her hospital gown cut open. She imagined hearing a scuffle in the hall, and Mark Nader being shoved in backwards through the door, stumbling from a fist in his face, a sword at his throat, or no, some kind of big hook through his chest and then Carl entering, holding up a bright light and running over to unlock her shackles... and next he would wrap her in his arms and lift her... bearing her away, telling her over and over she would be protected and safe...

Then again, when Nader dragged her into the kitchen to sheathe her arm in tape and his eyes gleamed as he switched on the garbage disposal and she realized he's going to do it, he's actually capable of totally doing it, shoving her arm right in there and grinding her hand down to a mangled stump, and she abruptly lurched into telling Nader everything she imagined he wanted to hear... even then, she thought she might hear the *thump!* of a sudden gunshot, see a zero magically appear in the exact center of Nader's forehead, observe that black hole pulse blood and gray gel and she could watch him slump over in death, his eyes already beginning to glaze... and she would turn and find it's Carl standing there, arm outstretched, pointing a long steel finger from which lifts a wisp of smoke, and above that his lean face looking calm and fierce and intent, like an angel of vengeance...

"Shouldn't even let myself think of you."

Carl is the main one she failed with her treachery. Worse, she's shown herself to be unfathomably weak. So, so unworthy. Not only of love, perhaps even undeserving of life. It's obvious she's not what she's always pretended to be, which must mean that she's also a liar, into the devil's bargain. Worthless. Evil, perhaps. Unwittingly, but so what? Does that mean she's stupid, too? Certainly, thoroughly dangerous to anyone who might ever want to get close to her.

Also, she's guilty of betraying Linda. *Don't forget!* Coaxed her friend to come along on a stupid, blithe and heedless ride straight into this hell. *How dumb was that?* And then she'd practically coerced Linda, manipulated her, prevented her from calling Dan to tell him what was going on, didn't even let her try until it was entirely too late…

So, what's any possible reason for me to even try to keep on? Has there ever been anyone who I've not let totally down?

Summer.

So yes, finally I can truly let myself think of Summer. My sister. The only one who ever understood what it was like, back when we were young. Our stepfather, and all that utter evil he did to us. At least I did not let Summer down! I always tried to be there for her. Even after she got hooked on Oxies. Even when she ran off to Honduras with that scumbag dealer. Because I was ready to come there, I told her I was ready to pay whatever was demanded, I'd bring her back home and give her some help again, as much as she ever might need. And after she got killed, I went down there, trying so hard even then to show my love to her bones…

A vision of Summer alive arises within her. Summer stands on a tropic beach, wind whips her hair, and a look of joy suffuses her face, although it's still a bit wounded, an expression that seems to acknowledge the shared pain of their childhood, yet it's also sober and wise and hopeful, and she points up toward the core of a giant cylinder of misty light bordered by rotating clouds, and there's flocks of birds up there, scads of them, floating cruciform and sailing along like angels in the vast eye of the hurricane, and Summer holds out her other hand, beckons to her sister, asks her to come join her in a flight up into this enchanted realm where bad people can never find them, not ever again, where there is only transcendent peace and soft, drifting light…

Pounding at a door.

"Rapunzel! Time to let your hair down," a voice calls.

Mel shudders. She hears the snick of an electronic lock, then the grind of a key and a deadbolt. Door to the suite flings opens. A fist smacks a wall and lights flick on.

"Hon-eee, I'm home!" Nader uses an overcooked, Ricky Ricardo accent.

Melanie's eyes roll up, eyelids flutter down. She collapses like a marionette with cut strings, and slumps onto the bathroom's tiled floor. Her white face pokes out from rumpled folds of the green blanket.

Chapter 23

The alto whine of a dirt bike ululates on the breeze as the machine approaches the Purdy home ranch. First they hear it, then they don't, then they do again. This time, they can tell it's a lot closer. Larry and Hank glance at each other.

"'Spectin' anyone?" Larry asks.

"Oh heck yeah," Hank says. "Hotshot model, Kate whatshername Upton? Always rides out here on Tuesdays to give me a foot rub."

Larry snaps his fingers. "Right, I forgot."

Hank looks at Linda. "Might want to stick yourself in the trailer, hon'. 'Til we find who this is, and 'zackly what they're after."

Linda nods, gets up, walks off.

A red and white Honda dirt bike comes up the drive, trailing a long feather of ocher dust. The man riding it wears a visored helmet, padded gauntlets, high boots — and a deputy's uniform. He waves a gloved hand at Larry and Hank, then shuts off the bike and leans it on the kickstand near the back of the ranch truck. He takes off the helmet and hangs it from one end of the handlebars, and he stares for a long moment at the tires on the old Power Wagon as he does so.

"Tread pattern," Hank mutters to Larry. "Shit."

The rider is young and fit, has a full head of dark brown hair, a freckled, slightly sunburnt face. He pulls off his gloves as he walks toward them.

"Larry, Hank," he says, by way of greeting.

"Cousin Robbie!" Larry replies. "Nice to see ya. What brings ya out here?"

The rider whacks the gloves against his leg and dust wafts away. "Not joy of the drive," he says. "Can tell you that! Ever plan to get your road bladed?"

"Like it how it is," Hank says. "Keeps the riff-raff out."

"Or in," Robbie says. He looks down, sees the six cans of Shiner, three of them empties that lie on their sides.

"Just takin' a break, tryin' to relax after a few days out in the sticks," Larry says. "Get a brewski for you?"

"Thanks, but no thanks. I'm on duty."

"Smart," Hank says. "Your boss prob'ly watchin' you work from his helicopter, even as we speak."

Robbie smiles thinly. "Truth is, that's what brings me out here."

"Huh. Thought it was your motorcycle."

"No, no. My job. See, we happen to be lookin' for somebody, who run off. Might'a come this way."

Hank snorts. "Don't see why anyone would do that. Not if'n they had any choice in the matter."

"It's a black gal. In her twenties, or so."

"Larry?" Hank looks at him. "How many black gals we seen while we was out tourin' the ranches?"

Larry ponders. "Least two hunnert 'r so. Mebbe three…"

"Yep, y'see, this time of year? Them gals just be swarmin' round like jackrabbits out there." Hank gazes at Robbie. "So, can you say what makes that 'un you want stand out from the herd? You know, anythin' diff'runt?"

"Hank, can you just please cut the crap for one single second? I'm serious."

"Uh-huh. Can see that." He gestures. "From the way you've got your hands on your belt. Makes you look all official and important. Kinda."

"Did you see anyone out there? Or even come across human footprints?"

Hank slowly shakes his head while his long beard follows suit, its waggle a half a beat behind the end of his jaw. "Nuh-uh. Only scapegrace in my view whole time we were out was this partickler rascal, right here." He jabs a thumb at Larry. Then he turns his head, smoothes the hairs away from his lips with a finger and spits on the ground. "Now, howsabout that beer? Got 'em all good 'n' cold."

"Well, dogs got her tracked as far as the well on the Carson place," Robbie persists. "But next, her sign just sort of vanishes. Same place we saw from tire marks that you'd drove, not so long ago, right? Sure you didn't see nothin'?"

"Hell yes, we saw nothin'. 'Bout all a guy can see, out that way."

Robbie stares at him and Hank stares right back. It's not a hostile contest, but it is a mute battle of wills. Larry pokes at the ground with the toe of his boot and sips from his beer.

"Tell me, what's this gal done, makes you so eager to slap cuffs on her?" Hank finally asks.

"Had a big crash on the highway. Reckless drivin', you know. Then, fleeing the scene…"

"How do you ever cause a wreck, if you're wreckless?" Larry puts in.

Robbie ignores him. "And we have good reason to believe she might be involved with drug smuggling. Maybe even human trafficking. We're still sorting through evidence and leads. Drugs *were* found in her car."

"See what you mean," Hank says thoughtfully. "Makes her unusual. Nobody tries to pull that kinda shit 'round here, ever." He looks up at the deputy. "Anybody with her?"

The deputy's eyes narrow. "Why do you ask?"

"Just wonder if we're only 'sposed to be on the lookout for just one," Hank says.

"She's the one we're looking for," Robbie answers flatly.

"Okay, tell you what. We can cruise back thataway tomorrow. See if we turn up anythin'. But hey, the Carson trough and windmill's down at the end of a ridge. After that, soil turns rocky. This lady knows her bidness, she could hide her track, easy. Mebbe why you din't see it. Even if she's not that smart, she could luck-out on where she goes. Find anythin', we'll call you on your cell. How's that?"

"Fine. 'Preciate it," Robbie says. He looks at the trailer. "Hey, I need to take a leak. Can I use your bathroom?"

Hank guffaws. "What, you turn into a city slicker? Hose down a rock!"

"Misspoke. I mean, I need to take a dump."

"C'mon, cuz, I'll show you where it is," Larry rises to his feet.

"Hey, I can find it. A trailer's not that big."

"Need to grab me a fresh brew, anyhow."

Larry rises, leads the way toward the ramshackle trailer at a brisk pace. Shaking his head, Robbie follows. On the top step, Larry trips, thumping his shoulder loudly into the front door.

"Oops!" he says.

"Maybe you don't need another beer," Robbie says coldly.

"Bird can't fly on just one wing…"

"Or four," Robbie says.

Larry fumbles at the knob, wrenches the door open, enters. "Bathroom's down that way," he says loudly, and points.

Robbie nods, and goes that way, looking over the trailer carefully as he goes. After he passes the oven, Larry sees Linda's colorful silk scarf is still draped over its door handle. As soon as he hears the bathroom door shut, he yanks that scarf off and crams it deeply into his pocket. He opens the fridge, pulls out more cans of beer, and pushes one against his forehead. He closes his eyes, and slowly rolls the cool metal cylinder back and forth with a palm.

Chapter 24

Dan watches a glob of mingled colors shimmer and twist. Slowly the swirl resolves into a precise and stable matrix. He feels both surprised and gratified, since he's been hoping that damn blur would evolve into a view that begins to make sense. Finally, he understands that he's looking down at the patterns in a hand-loomed Persian carpet.

His body lies flopped over the arm of a large chair. His muscles are limp, his head holds a neural thunderstorm, a dark mist fitfully lit by throbs of lightning.

He tries to raise his hands to his temples, to rub away that aching, nausea-making cloud, but his arms bump to a halt before he can even touch his head. Shaking them, he hears a clink and a rattle. *Ah!* Padded leather cuffs are on his wrists, a cable clipped to them runs down to a padded leather belt locked about his waist. He feels the weight of a cable snaking along one thigh, guesses it continues on to ankle restraints, perhaps an eyebolt set in the floor.

Something white swings in front of him. *Bedsheet? Curtain? Towel? No, no... it's the hem of a skirt.* He tilts his head up to see a short, thick woman in a white dress who stands at a rolling table of stainless steel. He watches the woman put a syringe into a biohazard waste container.

"*Spasibo, sidelka.*"

The words come in a baritone voice that's suave and resonant. Doesn't really seem to fit the woman in white. Plus, her lips did not move. Dan concludes it wasn't her speaking. He applauds himself for this train of logic and insight. His heavily sedated brain is gradually lurching back to life...

The woman departs from his field of view, and another face enters at close range. It's an older man's head, creased and lined, hooded eyes below thick white brows, a strong nose. Almost recognizable. No, wait, he does know it! A face he's glimpsed before... he recalls now... that Russian guy in Carl's sheaf of photos. Back in Ecuador.

"Leonid... Andreyev?" Dan wonders.

The head bows, grins, deep dimples forming on each side of the broad, loose mouth.

Damn, I've dropped way-y-y down the rabbit hole on this one! Dan thinks. *Seriously. What in hell was I drinking? And how much of the stuff did I guzzle? Got to quit with the hootch! Totally...*

The old man extends a hand to give Dan a gentle pat on the head. "And hello to you, *droog muy*," he says.

Wait. Not drinking. The very last thing I did was get into that car at the Corpus Christi airport with Carl. Then came that hiss of gas...

"Where am I?" Dan's words are slurred. It feels like another person's tongue has been sewn into his mouth, an unwieldy organ that requires far too much effort to operate.

Looking around as best he can, Dan sees he's been placed in an overstuffed wingback chair. He straightens up. The chair is situated in a well-appointed private library or den. On a nearby wall hangs a painted icon of a sad-eyed saint clad in armor, with a gold-leaf nimbus radiating out around his head. This saint holds a Russian cross up in one hand, cradles a spear with the other. There's also a gilt carving of a double-headed eagle behind a man crucified on a large X.

Weird... Dan thinks.

A round walnut table holding crystal glasses and Wedgwood plates is just behind Andreyev. Beyond that table is a wall lined with bookcases and a gallery of black-and-white photographs.

The old Russian general cocks his head. "You are in my *academiya*," he says. "Where you face simple test."

"What've you done with Carl?"

He ignores the question. "You wish to refresh yourself?" He gestures with a sweep of his hand at the table. "I order servants here to bring us pickles, good black bread, tea. Country food, it gives strength worthy of a man. So please, you eat now."

Dan eyes the food, but raises his shackled arms and shakes them.

"Oh, but you can stand," Andreyev says. "Try! Do not falter."

The leg restraints are indeed not fastened to the floor. Dan stands up, staggers a bit, waddles toward the table, his ankles linked so tightly he can't take a proper step. He's not hungry, he feels numbness more than anything. But he figures if he does eat, it might push the haze from his brain. At the table, he grabs a heel of black bread and munches. With his other hand he pours hot tea from a ceramic pot into a delicate cup.

"Good, good," Andreyev encourages. "Here, eat with Beluga, genuine!"

He demonstrates, scooping up a heap of the moist and glistening black pearls of caviar with a bread slice, then tearing away that heaping morsel with a snap of his white, even teeth.

Dan nods, but just keeps chewing his bare crust. He surveys the room warily as he chases the bread with a gulp of tea. He sees that all the images on the photo wall are from an American figure, the early 20th century journalist and author, Jack London.

Here's one of Jack straddling a horse, a broadly grinning Jack at the wheel of a sailboat, Jack booted and striding through urban rubble after the great San Francisco earthquake of '06.

The largest frame holds the words of a London quote, scrawled in stark black calligraphy on creamy parchment: *"They were potent. They were iron. They were perceivers, willers, and doers. They were as of another species compared with the sailors under them."* — *Mutiny of the Elsinore*

Dan turns from the bookshelf to Andreyev.

"Academy? Yours?" he asks, puzzled. "To study… Jack London?"

The Russian, smiling warmly, nods. "If man can have things in this vale of tears," he says. "I make this place. Do you know your London?"

"Yeah, sure," Dan says carefully. "Um. *Call of the Wild.* And… *White Fang…*"

"*Bezobidnyy,*" he scoffs, and flips a hand. "Mere children's books! But, *Sea Wolf, Iron Heel, Martin Eden,* and best Alaska story, *Love of Life.*" He raised a hand to kiss his fingertips in accolade. "You starve, you freeze, your enemy is savage, it is impossible! That's where man finds his core."

"Right. Sure," Dan mumbles.

Dan pours more tea, sips from his cup. His brain still seems woefully clogged. *A room this big and fancy couldn't be on the Russian's yacht… or could it?*

"Why bring me here?" Talking still demands great effort.

"Life. Eternal struggle for supremacy, yes?" the Russian says. "Cosmic war in worldly battle. Hear me? Understand my meaning?"

"No," Dan says.

"Come. Sit. We talk."

He gestures back toward the wingback chair. Dan now sees another chair is beside it. Andreyev twists those heavy chairs around so that they face each other. He appears to have retained great physical vigor, for all his apparent age.

Dan sinks onto the ruby velour upholstery, cradling his tea. Finally, he's starting to feel a bit sharper.

"Two women disappeared in Texas," he says. "Not many days ago.

Their names are Linda Parker and Melanie Olson. Do you know where they are?"

The hooded eyes regard him steadily. "I do," Andreyev says.

Dan nods slowly, sips, tries to conceal his eagerness. "Anything you want from me, that I can swap for that info?"

Andreyev crosses his legs, leans on an armrest. "This, we can perhaps discuss. But a more important thing must settle, first." He raises a magisterial finger. His tawny eyes hold an amused gleam.

"Mr. Cowell, it seems you wish to be enemy of me, hm? No, no, do not trouble to deny. But, do you fully grasp result of this view?"

"Tell me."

"Well, well." The general chuckles. "Big one is, I must defeat you."

Dan considers this. He upholds his shackled arms. "You're off to a good start."

Andreyev grins and slaps his knee. "True!" He points the finger at Dan. "Now, I have two routes to victory. First, I crush you. Not difficult, given your present condition. But second, more interesting path, I convert you. Bring you to my side and make you loyal to me. What say you to this?"

"Hard to imagine," Dan says. "How would it occur?"

"Beliefs that are yours now, don't keep. Throw all out, like rubbish! Gain new belief. Awaken to realities that are most basic. To stark facts of life and death, to existence, and to mastery. Do you agree?"

"Any alternative?" Dan inquires.

"You might say right now, old Andreyev, you are so full of crap! My thinking is already correct, and you are big criminal bastard who should be knocked low. Say this with confidence and with pride, and I shall respect it. Soon after, you will be dead, of course, but I let you die on your feet like man."

"And if I agree to join you?" Dan asks.

"Still, this only means you gain chance to live. To seize it, you must fight, just as in Manta. I feel impressed by outcomes there. Soon you can impress me even more. Part of your education at this academy, shall we say.

"Ask the question — are you man of superior quality, or mere caricature of man? Only deep inside yourself do you find answer."

Dan notices movement in a shadowy corner of the room. Someone's been quietly observing, and now that person approaches. He's middle aged yet remarkably trim and fit, with broad shoulders and a V-shaped torso. As he gets nearer, Dan sees that he's clad in a black silk T-shirt, black gym pants, and black running shoes. His exposed forearms and neck are knotted with tattooed muscle, and his blocky face is crowned by a gelled thatch of gray hair.

"Well, Viktor," the general says. "How do you estimate our guest?"

"Worth an effort," he says. "Questions and his answers, all seem okay to me…"

"There, see?" Andreyev says. "You pass first test. I must warn, though, others not so easy!"

"Who's this mug?" Dan wonders.

"This man is Viktor Mandić, my *dukhovnik*," the Russian tells Dan, "which means, spiritual advisor. Every leader should have."

Viktor and Leonid look at each other with an expression of mirth.

"My big advice to you," Viktor says. "Never annoy God with small sins. Choose grand sins, so He can reveal almighty power of His forgiveness!"

"*Russkiy mozhet greskit, no on ne mozhet byt' bezbozhnym,*" Andreyev replies.

"What in hell's all that?" Dan asks.

"Oh. I explain. Viktor try to make his joke about crazy monk in old film," Andreyev says. "I top him easily with the great Dostoyevsky." The general kisses a fingertip salute to the geniuses of a bygone age. "I say, 'A Russian may sin, but he cannot be Godless.'" He looks at Dan.

"Is possible, you understand that?"

"My mom used to say, we all fall short of the glory of God," Dan ventures.

Andreyev nods. "True, and close. Glory can be chased, or earned. But best is to have glory by simple birthright, eh?" He leans forward. "To uncover this, that is main quest. Do well, and maybe you become squire to *rytsar' Svyatogo Andreya komandir*, a knight of Saint Andrew the Commander."

"Whatever..."

"Do not dismiss it!" Andreyev scolds. "Is no small thing! Do no insult with American sarcasm."

Dan perceives that if the ground he's just trespassed upon is not sacred, it's at least shaky.

"Sorry. I do apologize, sir."

"That's better." The general raises his hoary eyebrows, his eyes widen expectantly. "So, to your second test. Tell me of your companion."

"Carl? Sure, yeah, maybe, if you tell me how he is. Linda too!"

"*Droog moy*, you are in no place where you bargain. Answer question. If you please me, then perhaps I answer yours."

Dan considers. "What do you want to know?"

"We have idea, already. Carl Blackadar is in job with your government. Also, we know you have work there. But I want to understand Blackadar better. You are also his friend. So, you now tell me. What sort of man is he?"

"Huh?" Dan doesn't get what the general wants. *Do they know Carl's job is deep undercover work for the FBI...?*

"Does your Mister Blackadar have signs of..." the general looks up at Viktor, says, "*Neobychnoye blagorodstvo?*" The muscle guy bends over to whisper. Andreyev looks back at Dan. "Extraordinary nobility?" he asks.

Dan feels both puzzled and relieved. If all they want is bullpuckey, well, he can shovel that with the best.

"Sure, of course, Carl's like the original white knight," he replies, glancing up again at the icons looming over him. "Galahad in a stained-glass window. Gleaming armor and spotless virtue, and handy with a spear. Need somebody to slay a dragon and rescue a maiden? He's your boy. Can't bribe him, and you can't distract him. Assign him a mission and he'll stay on it until it's all like, 'target destroyed.'"

Andreyev and Viktor glance at each other and whisper some more.

"Good," the general says. "Okay, more question. Who is Carl's boss man? Who leads him on present operation, if you please?"

Involuntarily, Dan visualizes Bob Smith in the surveillance van at Arlington. But immediately he realizes he should not for a second think of that. A look on his face, even his body language, might surrender a tell that lets his interrogators sense he knows more than he admits.

"Truly? I have no idea," Dan says. He lifts and drops his shoulders in a helpless shrug. "I mean, a guy like Carl? Big-time Dudley Do-Right? Come on! Think he'd ever leak a big secret to some merc fuckin' civilian like me? Not hardly. If there's any rules, Carl follows 'em, to a 'T'. Or an 'R,' I guess. Anyway, never has talked to me about who he might report to…"

Andreyev and Viktor confer.

"*Otlichno!*" The general beams at Dan. "Good. He is noble, loyal, discreet. For now, you and we are done."

Chapter 25

"Robbie ain't so much of an idiot as he looks," Hank asserts.

"For true?" Larry says. "Cos to me, he's always seemed way-y dumber. Even so, they could be gettin' onto us."

"Well, let's review. Got our tire tracks by the Carson well, sure. But nothin' puts us out there same time as Linda."

Larry ticks off more items on his fingers. "He did prob'ly notice they was too many cans of beer out, even for us. And plus, in the trailer, he saw Linda's scarf, which she left hangin' on the oven door. Which I know, 'cos I saw him check for it again when he came out of the bathroom. By then, though, I had it already hid in my pocket."

Hank's black eyebrows jitter toward each other like agitated centipedes. "Larry, Larry... Jayzus! Now, why'd you go and pull a damn fool stunt like that?"

"What?"

"You snatched it, so he knows you was tryin' to hide it! Leave it there, he mentions it, you just say, maybe, it's from one of our dates."

"Our what?"

"Dates!"

"Oh. Like, Kate Upton?"

"Any woman!" Hank glares. "Not necessarily that'un gives me foot rubs. T'others, too."

Larry mulls it over. "Guess you'll be seein' me as stupider than Cousin Robbie, now."

"You're a goldang pinhead. I've always said that."

He sighs. "So, what we gonna do? They come back here and try to grab Linda?"

Hank inserts fingers of one hand into his beard, tugs at its formidable tangles while he looks at the ground. "Hey first, howsabout, you go see what you got comin' in over the scanner?" he says. "Maybe he'll radio back to the department, soon as he gets 'round a bend in our road."

"Which scanner is that?"

"Your goldang fricken cop radio scanner!"

"Oh. Y'mean the one you tol' me to unplug and stick away? Since all the chatter comin' out of it was such an aggravation? Now, I'm sposed to pull it out and hook it back up? Okay. Check with me in 'bout a half-hour."

"Ne'mind." Hank scowls at the earth. "'Kay," he says then, looking up. "Might's well hit the Carson place, since that's what I said we'd do. But then we keep goin', back up the ridge. Know that lil' cave below the hogback, it overlooks Xanadu? We let Linda jump out there'n hide, but we keep on drivin'."

"That's a plan? Stick her in a cave, an' we jes' go off?"

"Want to stay right up there with her, provide her some comp'ny?"

"Hey, fine idea..."

"Gal's got a husband, you ninny! Anyhow, stashin' her in a hideaway's just a short-term plan."

"Uh-huh. Next?"

"Pullin' me out a jug a' rye after we pitch camp. Sip 'n' ruminate. Need us to figger on all this a bunch more."

"Cool."

"Glad you see it so. Since you'll be settin' thar right next to me. Don Juan."

~

The cell Dan inhabits is stark, barren. A concrete shelf bears a foam pad sheathed in vinyl to sleep on, there's a steel toilet, a steel sink, a steel door with a thick rectangle of wired glass in its center and a steel tray with a shutter that can be raised from outside. Four white walls. That's it. Well, he's also got a baggy yellow suit with drawstring pants and a long-sleeved shirt. And an LED bulb in a wire cage that dims occasionally, yet remains lit perpetually.

Plus, he sees a glossy black dot high up in one corner that could be a camera lens.

He's on his side, using a bent arm for a pillow as he seeks to puzzle out which moves, what words he might deploy to best shape coming events.

How can I fix this? How do I make them tell me where Linda is? Does anyone have even a scrap of influence over Andreyev? What've they done to Carl, and why's the general so keen to know such wacky crapola about him? Who the hell is Viktor, really? Looks like some iron-assed uber-commando... Spiritual advisor? Shit. C'mon!

While evaluating scant options for dealing with his captors, Dan hears a sequence of soft noises.

Slither, bop, scrape-scrape.

He looks down at the slot of light where his cell door almost meets the floor.

Slither, bop, scrape-scrape.

And.

Slither...

A square of white vinyl with a length of yellow thread tied on whips into his cell, sliding through a narrow slot under the door. He leaps from his hard bed to snatch it up. The slick front is blank, so he turns it over. On the fabric backing, scrawled in brown fluid, is a word and a question mark:

Dan?

The cord has been woven of strips torn out of a cotton-poly shirt like the one Dan wears. He gently pulls on the string until it grows taut… and then feels a slight, answering tug.

Okay! Damn. He tries again to recall sequences for letters in Morse Code. He takes a deep breath and composes a note: Four short tugs, one short tug, short-long-short, short… *HERE*, he thinks he has said.

Then a message comes back. *C… A… R… L…*

Chapter 26

A meeting gets underway at a walnut table in Andreyev's study. Along one wall, brocade curtains have been drawn back to reveal undulating plains of the Xanadu game ranch. A herd of tawny animals with spiky horns can be seen grazing in the distance.

Seated around the table are: Leonid Andreyev, decked out in a starched white shirt and quilted red robe; Mark Nader, for once not clad in his steampunk costume, but in pressed khakis the Sojourn guards use; and Sam Lundts, in the somber blue suit he wore to meet Carl on the pier in Miami. Close by, her gray hair pinned up in a bun, a slender woman in a nondescript black dress sits on a folding chair at an end table, staring through bifocals at a stenotype machine, her fingertips poised on its keys. Near it lies a printed meeting schedule.

"Debt purchase and collection," Andreyev says.

Nader consults an iPad at his elbow. "Up 20 percent over last fiscal year, net. We have located three fresh sources for bad paper, and are purchasing tranches at one-to-four cents on the dollar. With new staff and training in the OCCA, we're clearing at least a fifth…"

Lundts tilts his head. "OCCA?" he asks.

"Outbound call center. Our 'boiler room' at Sojourn, if you will. Quite the show, you ever want to go down and listen in. Nobody bullies deadbeats into paying up faster than our cons, I'm telling you. Works like black magic."

"And, just on phone," Andreyev muses. "Imagine, assign *znakomikh* to show up in person on doorsteps… as we do in Europe and Latin America."

"Well-l-l, could do it here, too, but that requires care," Mark Nader says. "Can go south awful fast, as the screw up in Florida showed." Nader knows the Tank Burnett fiasco in West Palm and the Keys shall be discussed. He put it on the agenda himself. Yet he hopes to bleed heat from the topic early on — as well as distance himself from the mess. He knows where he wants the blame to fall: not on him.

"Agree. Direct action must be precise, targeted, under control. That is key to success," Andreyev says. "But your new politics here can open up new chance. For example, when you sell protection? It is best to demonstrate first what happens to client who fails to buy your product."

Nader squints. Is that it, then? Do they accept that Burnett just ran into some bad luck and was forced to improvise? Really, it could've happened to anyone.

"Well, no shit, that Burnett deal went totally sour!" Lundts grouses. "It put Blackadar and his pal right on our tails. And I want to know what measures…"

Andreyev holds up a hand. "Excuse me, Samuel? That matter must be with Unfinished Business, right before New Business. Can we maintain proper order here, please? Mark, continue."

"Okay, so an extra boost comes from hacking our competitors' accounts. We have an insider planted with our main supplier of consolidated debt, who's willing to say where else they're making sales." Nader's rendition sounds a bit rushed, even to himself. He needs to slow down to convey utter competence. A partnership with Andreyev hangs in the balance. He must act the part of a worthy collaborator. "We hack that customer, grab his debtor info, and then begin to collect without even actually owning the debt. Zero overhead!

"Plus, I've an idea to start building our own tranche of debt from the get-go, by launching a chain of payday lenders, but I'll save that pitch for when we move on to New Business." He smiles.

Andreyev nods approvingly.

"Now, a looming threat is that do-gooder from Vermont..." Nader strokes his iPad to scroll to a name "... our scuttlebutt is that Senator Ron Briggs plans to re-introduce his bill for a national debt registry, which would assign each loan a ULIN..." he looks at Lundts "... meaning, universal loan identification number. That would give officials a way to track each debt, who owns it, and who's got a right to collect. Obviously, that can do serious damage to our operation."

"Well, then," Lundts drawls. "You ought to put a top DC lobby on it, no? Use the regular formula, it'd likely work... government overreach, would invent a big new bureaucracy that spends taxpayer money just to hamper the economy, our industry should be allowed to self-regulate first, *etcetera, etcetera*?"

"Why not," Nader says. "Who do you have in mind?"

"Let's draw on our in-house talent, Daringer, Campion & Zane, to start. If they can't manage it, they'll know someone who knows someone."

"Good. And we should ask for updates on progress. And vote counting, if it should even get so far."

"God forbid," Andreyev says.

"Can we involve a player that high up? I'll inquire." Nader chuckles, combs his wispy mustache with a fingernail. "Our tech shop is becoming quite the profit center, too. Got a ton of guys with time on their hands, eager to learn new tricks. Most of our income there derives from encrypting data on servers and computers, then holding it hostage — pay up, or it's lost forever. Called 'ransomware,' and our beta works like a charm, so we're ready to go full throttle. A sideline has been posting mugshots from public arrest records on proprietary urban sites and making embarrassed citizens pay to take them down. We're also mulling a scheme to distribute kiddie porn and then blackmail the shit out of the idiots who download, but the Feebs…" he gives a nod to Lundts "… take a dim view of any activity in that area, and I'm not a hundred percent convinced we can keep our distribution secure. Until we can, I'm not inclined to go there, lucrative as it might be. Industrial espionage remains a possibility, but since that's where so many of the big boys go to rumble, I'd just as soon not draw the attention."

"Yes, that's right," Andreyev agrees.

"As far as transport of hard goods, I think we'll stick with smuggling ammo and weapons into Mexico. It's got low risk, high numbers, reliable clients — the trifecta. Working the other way, on imports into the U.S., that I'm not so wild for. It comes with a huge competition factor, and again, there's rough outfits already duking it out. Why try to play on their turf, when we already do so well our own? Importers can pay our roll if they use our corridor, otherwise, I say, leave it alone.

"And then, when we come to direct acquisitions, we do stick to a policy like your 'precisely targeted and carefully controlled' formula…" Nader nods at Andreyev "… we cherry-pick a squad, let 'em run out of Sojourn for the heist, bring 'em back into the barn, and reward them with a rasty bout of recreation. Man, you should see our boys settle in to party! It'd make the ol' Marquis de Sade squirt in his bloomers, for sure.

"Top projects in the snatch-and-scram category are…" he consults his iPad "…jewel thefts at airports on both coasts, high-end home burglaries where we can nick insider information from servants and cleaners and dog-walkers and the like, as well as the occasional armored truck job. But you have to be selective on those, each score must look different. Show an M.O., and you get the wrong folks way too interested." He looks at Lundts again. "Am I right?"

Lundts offers in return only a bland and faint smile.

"Do you consider to boost Arab princes on holiday?" Andreyev asks.

"Wow, right, you heard about that? Went down last week, in Naples." Nader's grin sends his thin mustache aloft. "What's the score from grabbing a raghead's satchel of play loot out of his limo, a cool half-million, for just ten minutes of work?"

"Twice that on the money, and yet it only needs half that time," Andreyev says.

"Wham, bam, thank you, ma'am!" Nader exclaims. "Hey, hold it. You know details like that, musta been one of yours..."

Andreyev smiles.

Lundts clears his throat, tilts the blank egg of his head.

"Next?" Andreyev asks.

The woman peers down at her meeting schedule. "Unfinished."

"Might's well tackle the difficult subject first," Nader volunteers. "The Florida blowup. Burnett's now on ice in the D-Seg at Sojourn, pending my decision on how to reintegrate him into our operation."

"Blackadar and his lil' buddy?" Lundts asks.

"Stashed 'em there too, as we discussed."

Andreyev folds his large and knobby hands over his belly. "Let us go over event," he says. "Collection effort by your staff seems to turn badly. I say this, your report's headline. Now please to fill in detail."

"Yes." Nader nods. "Our target was a handler of bad paper named David Carleton, out of West Palm, specializing in credit card debt. He double-sold to us, which we found out when we made contact and found the deadbeats had already been tapped. We demanded a full refund, plus a penalty, and Carleton laughed us off. We sent Burnett with a backup team of two other enforcers to convince that idiot he'd taken an unstable position."

"Then it grows a mess," Andreyev prods.

"Part of that... complication... was, right about then, you asked us to supply some top-end motorcycles that you could present to your... ah, associates, in Colombia," Nader explains. He wants to maintain his composure, but this exchange works on his nerves.

"So you mix up these missions," Andreyev says.

"Well, why not? I didn't know that..."

"Burnett might get all wound up or confused? And just wing it?" Lundts says, a look of incredulity on his face. "An unstable psycho? With no top manager in the field to ride herd on him?"

"He's never mucked up an assignment before." Nader is defensive. "There were extenuating circumstances. I told you our target displayed a weapon, had a..."

"Nevertheless. Burnett *fails* to bring target to comply and secure payment, right?" Andreyev's inquiry is genteel, yet his eyes are as hard as polished topaz. "Instead, Burnett slays him, in daylight, in public! Then, to fix, after mission goes to hell? He contacts, not you, but members of gang?"

"The Ostrogoths, his old motorcycle gang, yes," Nader admits.

"And upshot?" The Russian doesn't wait for an answer, he gives one. "Not few good machines, there is dozen, in convoy to Key West. Your people ride them, plus random outlaws who are not vetted by anyone. They arrive to rendezvous at port with me, and *all* of them expect to board *Dean Swift*, together with all their rolling booty. Picture my surprise."

Nader spreads his hands. "Still might've been contained."

"Except that Burnett, who's now completely full of himself — is that right expression? — gets into 'beef' on highway bridge, with man who happens to be good friend with highly skilled agent in law enforcement brigade of U.S. government."

"No one could have..."

Andreyev lifts an imperial hand, and Nader falls quiet. Lundts leans back in his chair, a faint smile flickering on his lips.

"Blackadar's skill is so, that he tracks me, and defeats my countermeasure in Ecuador," the general continues. "He comes to Texas, then, to put damage on my enterprise and yours too. It's only due to fast and creative action by this associate…" he inclines his hoary head to Lundts "… that we have slim chance to control. We have possibility, yet no plan.

"Samuel? What are your thoughts?"

Lundts leans forward, puts his elbows on the table, and taps the ends of his index fingers together. "This matter has worsened to a degree that eliminating the agents alone will not eliminate our problem," he says.

"Agree." Andreyev nods.

"We need to reach further."

"And?" Andreyev prompts.

"If making them expendable doesn't solve our problem, perhaps we should consider making them useful, as a better alternative."

"And it means?"

"Turn them. One, or both. We don't yet know for sure who directs their activity, but Blackadar does, maybe Cowell too. A solid conversion means we can send one or both of them after their own boss. Whack that leader, then we'd be in fairly good shape. The op is tightly siloed in the Bureau. We blow up the silo. Whether or not we retain their services afterward is immaterial. Doesn't need to be decided now."

Andreyev sighs. He turns his craggy face to Nader. "There, you see?" He taps his forehead. "Great minds. Good manager does not waste talent, he repurposes. I made start on Cowell. Clearly, this Blackadar is — what is saying? — tough nut to crack. Yet maybe of great value at end."

Lundts nods. "Not even a walnut, more like a Brazil nut," he suggests.

"Not to brag, but conversion's sort of my specialty," Nader says. *High time I took control of this!*

"Truly?" the Russian's snowy eyebrows rise.

"Psych was most of my education, when Sojourn transitioned from juvy ranch to supermax, and my older cousin groomed me to take over," Nader assures them. "After I did, few can match my record for developing skilled personnel."

"He's telling us, he's the shit," Lundts translates for Andreyev.

"I get that." The old general smiles.

"Blackadar's woman, Melanie Olson, is now pretty damn well tenderized," Nader affirms, riding what he perceives as momentum. "I say, we trot out the sight of her deterioration to rock Blackadar, use their emotional connection as bait, and her survival as payment. That way, I think we pull him in."

"Not enough," Lundts says, shaking his head.

Nader turns toward him, eyes widening in challenge.

"Agree," Andreyev says.

Nader gives the general a hard look too, then realizes he can't allow himself to appear angered. He dials it down, tries to look thoughtful instead.

"That first shock, it needs to be stronger," Lundts interjects. "Much."

Andreyev nods. "Life or death," he says, "for him!"

Nader frowns. He's losing control. Again. Now he doesn't know where to look, so he studies his fingernails. He notes he's almost due for his next French mani.

"And let's imagine, we do shock Blackadar yet we're not able to turn him," Lundts continues. "He'll see what we're after. He'll think a smart move is, he *pretends* to turn. To perfect that, he acts like he does plan a hit. Instead, he moves to warn and inform our target. But we carefully follow. After he leads us in, we finish the job. So it ends to our advantage no matter what. We leave both him and his boss kacked at the site. A riddle the Bureau must seek to unravel."

"Perfect," Andreyev says.

Nader raises his head, scans back and forth between them, and he notes Lundts' smugness. They've cooked this scheme up in advance. Not only that, but the early part of their meeting, where Andreyev appeared to bully Lundts, it had to be a charade. Meaning his two ostensible partners are in far deeper cahoots than he's foreseen. A big annoyance, and it poses a challenge. Can he steer outcome of this present crisis — and indeed, their overall business plan — in a direction that he wills?

"So we begin with a fight to the end," Andreyev adds. "Irony, yes? And Blackadar's big shock."

"Here's the fight card," Lundts says. "A three-way between Blackadar, Cowell and Burnett."

Nader feels stunned anew. By stashing his long-time confederate Ted James Burnett in D-Seg, he thought he'd also pushed him out of harm's way. Surely, a few days in the hole would be adequate reproof for a mild transgression like whacking a non-complying associate.

"I…I don't see… why…" Nader sputters.

"Well, we obviously need to get rid of Tank Burnett. I mean, he's just a loose…" Andreyev turns a look of inquiry to Lundts.

"End? Cannon?" Lundts guesses.

"Right, either. Now, you have him confined. But I say, eliminate him. Clean that slate."

"But how do you know…"

"Of three, two will win," Andreyev predicts serenely. "Next, of those two, one wins. Great enjoyment to think of way to set Cowell and Blackadar against each other. But if champion is Burnett…" he shrugs. "Bad luck. He still must lose. He's surplus, and he's trouble."

Nader's face drains, becomes an ecru palette of gray and yellow. "You... you just told me you hoped to use Blackadar to go after his boss," he falters.

"Well, yeah," Lundts interjects. "But see, that's only if he wins. First we have to show him the stakes, then motivate him. If he can't win, guess we just have to think of something else. If he loses? Can't even send him crawling back to his boss like a whipped cur, 'cos he'll be dead, probably."

"And, Mister Tank Burnett? Come on. Why care about what occurs on this loose end?" Andreyev inquires, squinting at Nader. "Useful as enforcer, sure. But do you have special attachment?'"

Nader swallows hard, but tries to conceal it by tilting his head down again, and making a faint cough. "No," he mutters, and looks up, his eyes bright but his face impassive. "He's not among my top personnel. So all right, whatever."

"Good. Then it's settled. Let's mount their fight soonest," Lundts says. "We can watch it on a video feed, from a spot where you've got a lot of cameras. Bound to be able to learn a great deal, about the strength and weaknesses of each individual. Useful for showing us how we'll need to handle our survivor. If we get one."

Andreyev swivels his head to the stenographer. "More items, in Unfinished?"

The woman checks her printout. "Linda Parker," she says. "Cowell's woman. On the run from security teams, but they're certain she's still present in our region. Sheriff Baxter says it shouldn't be long before they can nab her and haul her in."

Chapter 27

Larry Purdy spins tumblers on a long brass lock that secures a back entry to the Xanadu game ranch. He swings wide the green pipe gate, Hank guns their old Power Wagon through, Larry secures the gate and clambers up into the vehicle.

Larry lost a coin toss on this leg of their drive. And as a dire consequence, the album playing on the truck stereo is, "Saturday Satan Sunday Saint," by Ernest Tubb, the Texas Troubadour. Larry winces as he lowers himself onto the seat, slams the door, and takes a direct hit of the singer's twangy croon backed by a chug-a-lug bass guitar. It blasts out of custom speakers set in the door panels.

"Hey," Hank says, nodding at the stereo controls. "Mind crankin' that up?"

Larry glares. Hank chuckles. He lets out the clutch and the Power Wagon lurches ahead. They've jolted barely a half-mile onto the Xanadu grounds when a two-way radio handset bouncing in one of the cab's cup holders emits a beep.

"For you," Larry asserts, and smiles as he seizes this opportunity to turn the CD player volume knob to zero.

Hank plucks the radio out of the holder, stabs its transmission button with a thumb. "Yep," he says.

The radio crackles and a tinny voice says. "Stop right where ya are."

"Huh. Why?"

"I'm comin' over to ya. Out."

Hank sighs, and shuts off the engine. The V-8 clunks for a couple of beats, shudders, and quits. "Might's well injoy some music, 'til the rent-a-cop shows." He gestures. "Turn it back up."

"And poke burnin' matches under my fingernails, too?" Larry responds. "*You* turn it up. I won't cause my own torment."

Hank cranks the volume knob, props an elbow on the window frame, and gazes moodily out over the mesquite-sheathed plain. Then, in a low voice, he begins to sing along with the CD.

Larry rolls his eyes up to the sky. "Lord, I ask you to please gather me into your peaceable kingdom right now, today," he beseeches. "In the name of a merciful Father, amen."

They don't have long to wait for the man who asked them to stop. A moving dot at the end of a dust plume resolves into someone riding an ATV. This all-terrain vehicle vanishes then reappears as it crests each rise in the landscape, and soon slews to a halt in front of their Power Wagon

The ATV rider wears a white cowboy hat secured by a horsehair stampede string, a gray jumpsuit with a radio mic that hangs from an epaulet, and a black nylon duty belt with a snap-top holster that holds a big Glock pistol. He swings his leg off the saddle, adjusts his sunglasses, and walks to the driver's side window. As he does, Hank shuts off the CD player.

"Hank," he says, and nods at Larry.

"Hey, Lew," Hank says.

"What're you doin', comin' out onto Xanadu today?"

"Only here 'cos it's a visit we got right here on our schedule. Wanna see?"

Lew shakes his head. "Don't matter. Got us some real bigwigs on the premises. Y'all hafta vamoose 'til they leave."

"Nobody tol' us 'bout it."

"Also don't matter."

"Y'know, Lew, we sell these snakes by the hundredweight, right? Well, we're runnin' a few pounds short. Why not just let us have a coupla hours to top off our load here, then we'll git outta yer hair."

Lew stridulates an edge of his thumb across the tip of his forefinger. "See this?" he says. "It's the world's smallest fiddle, playin' 'My Heart Bleeds for You.'"

"Aw-w." Hank turns to Larry. "Tol' you Lew was our pal." He looks back. "So just one hour of gatherin', then, okay?"

In the shade of the hat, Lew's face reddens. He yanks off his sunglasses and glares. "No! Now turn this raggedy junker truck of yours around and drive on outta here."

"All right, all right, we're goin'." Hank starts up the engine. It backfires once then settles into a low burble. "So, who're these big shots you've got visitin'?"

"I tell you and it gets out, my ass is grass and my job is history."

"Well-l-l, can you just say how big a party it is? Did you have to pack in a buncha them exotic dancers from Dallas, like last time?"

"Oh boy, strippers!" Larry chimes in.

"No, no, nothin' like that."

"Bummer," Larry sympathizes.

"Look," Lew pleads, draping sunglasses back over his ears and nose. "Y'know they got cameras and motion detectors all the hell over, right? In the secur'ty office, already see you're here 'n' want you gone. Not just the ranch, neither, the Russian brought in his own guards, and those dudes're some highly unreasonable *hombres*."

"Russian?" Hank inquires.

"Goddammit!" Lew yanks his sunglasses off again and kicks the truck door. He points back to the fence. "You! The fuck outta here now, Hank!"

"Jeez, okay… uh… Say, anyone else we need to worry about?"

Lew unsnaps his holster flap and rests a hand on the butt of his pistol.

"Me," he says. "You nosy old buzzard."

"Well, *adios* then," Hank says amiably. He puts the truck in gear. "See ya."

"Not in less'n a week!"

"Got it."

The truck swings in a wide circle and jolts back out the gate. Its driver and its passenger exchange a mute look. After a minute of travel, Hank switches on the stereo, and Tubb's baritone, sounding like something marinated in a bowl of barbecue sauce, mule piss, and cheap whisky, begins again to blare from the speakers. Larry heaves a sigh, leans forward and punches the 'eject' button. He grabs the shiny disc as it emerges and scales it out of the passenger window like a tiny Frisbee. With his left hand, he makes a pistol shape and aims it after the whirling chromium dot.

"POW!" he exclaims.

"Damn." Hank chuckles. "Oh well, never did like ol' Ernie Tubb all that much, anyhow. Bought it by mistake. Was lookin' for some Tennessee Ernie Ford."

"How could you even make a mistake that dumb?"

"Oh, usual way. I was totally hammered."

Larry scowls. "Mean to say, that phony cowpoke bullshit was what you played just to annoy the holy fuck outta me?"

Hank feigns shock. "Oh, I'd never do that. Never." Then he frowns. "And you watch 'at potty mouth there, young feller. Or I'll phone up your ma, and next time you get home you'll be due for a birchin'!"

Larry almost sprains his eyeballs, he rolls them so far.

～

Linda watches the sun sink toward hills in Mexico's Coahuila State

on the west side of the Río Bravo del Norte, a Mexican name for the
Río Grande. She turns her head and looks back into a sandstone cave
— its shadowed interior mottled by rosy beams of sunset light. On
its sloping stone floor Hank and Larry have left her a tattered canvas
bedroll, an LED headlamp, a small foam pad, four gallons of water
in old milk jugs, an enameled steel cup, a box of Lipton teabags, and
a stash of food that includes a cured haunch of wild pig, as well as a
tiny Coleman stove and a fuel jug of white gas.

Plus, the huge temptation of Larry's cell phone.

She tries *extremely* hard not to think about it. They made her swear
to turn the phone on rarely, and if she did, only to use it to ring
Hank's mobile number — and that just in a case of extreme need.

She plucks a dry twig of mesquite and inserts it to scratch an itch
deep inside the cast on her arm. She pulls the stick out, and it reeks of
sweat and rancid skin oil. She wrinkles her nose as she flings it away.

She worries about Mel, and hopes she's alive and all right. Linda
feels guilty because she's not only still free, but has been fed and rested
and even befriended by strangers. A big improvement over last night,
when she stumbled out into the black desert as she fled the horror of
the wreck. Yet she's beginning to chafe under the burden of inaction.
To make no effort to solve any problem is alien to Linda's nature, it
frustrates and revolts her, since it can lead to her most loathed feeling
— a sense of helplessness.

And her eyes stray back to the phone.

Maybe she ought to switch it on, just to see if it gets a signal up
here? *Now, that would be smart. At very least, do that!* She presses
down the small green button at its corner, and the tiny screen flashes,
blinks, and comes to life. She has three bars. *Not bad, okay!*

Dan. Her eyes blink away sudden tears and she feels an ache in
back of her throat. *If he knows all the trouble we are in, he would be
here, right now, to help!* She considers. *But what if he himself is in awful*

trouble? Because, look how suddenly it comes upon Mel and me? And why...? It all started with that absurd day on the bridge, the savage onslaught by that monster biker — *the shaved ape!* — and then the still more bizarre attack by that fake postwoman.

Mel and Linda's effort to track down that biker on their own had led them to the prison, then the attack on that dark country highway had just exploded in their faces. *Evil ones may watch us, looking for a chance to attack. Since we don't know who they really are, we can't watch back. Which means a new threat can erupt in that same way for Dan, no warning...*

That thought nearly freezes her with dread. She can't help herself. She taps the phone's screen and a numbered grid is displayed.

Why should Larry and Hank say not to do this? What if I only ring Dan? I know his voice so well, just as he knows mine. If it is not him, I hang up right away, before only a second passes. So surely, no harm. And I don't let it ring for long, two times only, and if he does not pick up, very well, okay, I know it might not be good. But... if I do hear him... I can warn, put him on his guard... and say where I am...

Her index finger moves toward the screen then pounces on it, taps out his number in a flurry and thumbs the CALL button before any other thought can intervene. An anxious second of silence, then she hears his number ring once. Twice. A surge of panic follows a presentiment of danger. She shoves down the red button with her thumb to stop the call. She wipes a bead of sweat off her forehead with the back of a wrist.

Why am I being so silly?!

Around her evening sky shifts from blue to black while shadows deepen in the cave. The phone's screen continues to glow companionably. Invitingly. Then it starts to fade. She taps and its backlight renews. She punches in the first two digits of his number, whereupon the whole sequence pops up.

Just a few rings, and if Dan does not answer, then I stop.
She thumbs CALL.

~

Soaring high and tall over the roof of Sojourn supermax prison, the steel skeleton of a microwave tower blinks steadily with an array of red and white lights staggered up its 300-foot length to warn aircraft away from risk of a catastrophic collision.

Far below, on a computer screen in the jail's security control office, dubbed SecCon by its staffers, a screen icon brightens and then a line of text blinks. A tan-clad guard who leans back in a swivel chair with his legs crossed while he yacks with another guard notices it, stops talking, and leans forward. He types on his keyboard, something else appears, so he turns and beckons to his supervisor.

"Hey, got a hit."

"What?"

"Dan Cowell's phone."

"Where, who's on it?"

"Uh, both Cowell's and Blackadar's units were sent down to our tech hub in Matamoros. Parker's and Olson's as well. And, um, Faustino is handling the case, I believe."

"He's a good man, tell him to…"

"Oops. It's gone."

"All right. If it rings again, tell Faustino to answer. Any signal on who's trying to phone Cowell?"

"Nope. But that'll come, more'n likely in a minute or two."

"Good. Stay with it. And keep me posted."

Chapter 28

Mark Nader slaps a magnetic badge against a door lock at the prison SecCon and a thick slab of painted steel whisks back into a slot in the wall with a pneumatic sigh.

Inside, the room is a broad, low, dim, hushed chamber, where the upper walls are lined with color flat-screen TVs and the counters below hold laptop computers linked by a maze of cables. Before the computers sit men in tan uniforms, who poke fingers at keyboards, swipe screens and slide mouses on pads. Behind those men and their swivel chairs walk two more men in crisp khakis, supervisors, who pause momentarily to lean over shoulders and hold quiet discourse with those seated. So much is usual.

What's highly unusual for this chamber is the big man at its far end, the one wearing a black silk T-shirt, who glares and shakes a fist in the faces of both Warden Sanders and the SecCon's senior watch officer while he yells at them.

Observing this, Nader grimaces. *That fuckin' Russian and his obno crew, growin' soo-oo burnt out on 'em this past few days,"* he thinks. *Their default mode is to swagger and bully. Even the general. 'Course, they can scheme, too! But it's like they want everybody in range to just jump back whenever they happen to go anywhere... even if it ain't their own goddam country...*

A line supervisor appears at his elbow. "Sir? Want to let you know, we got a hit on that Cowell guy's phone. And we're a second away from getting an ID on source of the call."

"Mm, excellent." Nader says. It's an interesting development, however, much more of his attention is on the guy in the muscle shirt, the Serbian head of Andreyev's security detail.

And over what ridiculous shit might Viktor be pitching a hissy fit, now? What'll it take to maneuver him back to neutral?

He glances at the supe. "Tell me if you get any more on that, huh?" He starts walking across the room. Viktor sees him coming, shoves the warden and watch officer away from him with a sweep of his arms then shakes a finger at Nader.

"What's all this fuss about, Vicky?" Nader asks. Viktor hates to have his name chopped into a female nickname, he feels that it's weird and condescending. So naturally, that's what Nader always does.

"You have intruder!" he says. He raises the finger, and his dark eyes bulge. "Yet I am not told?"

Nader looks at the warden. "Tom?" he asks.

Sanders shoves his tortoise-shell glasses back up onto the bridge of his nose. The hushed atmosphere of the security control center is crisp with conditioned air, yet even in here the warden sweats.

"Ah hell, Mark," Sanders says. "Just the goddam Purdys, out to do one a' their snake patrols over at the ranch. Picked 'em up on a gate camera. Ol' Lew was already out on an ATV, so I sent him over to just turn 'em around."

"This is unacceptable. Your perimeter, I see is like Swiss holecheese!"

Nader makes a slight downward gesture with a palm, as if to say, 'chill out.'

"'K. Purdys scheduled to be there?" he asks Sanders.

"Uh-huh, yep. But they didn't get far in, either. When Lew told 'em to go, they left."

Nader turns toward Viktor. "See? No problem. Just some local groundskeepers that we bring in from time to time."

Viktor's lower lip protrudes belligerently. "This is *not* keeping up in agreements you make, so that the General Andreyev comes here for visit," he scolds.

"Um, no, your actual stipulation was, correct me if I'm wrong, is that we'd guarantee zero intrusions over the course of your visit, just as we've always done. And that's *exactly* what's happened. Intruders? Zero. Regular guests? Zero. Plenty of staff? On leave. What we've got, instead, is new prisoners. Not every single capture we'd hoped for, sure, but that's currently being fixed."

"Yes?" The Serb's black eyebrows migrate toward his gelled crewcut as he hears this specious parsing of the situation. "And two prisoners are what, FBI, that you bring on yourself? Another one is a reporter, and she might be FBI, also? And you still have one totally on loose and running around, escapee woman?"

"You've been briefed, Vicky. She ran off into the desert, all right? Twenty miles from the closest paved road, last place she was tracked to, still scootin' like a bat out of hell. No supplies, no phone, cold at night and tarantulas and rattlesnakes and scorpions all the livelong day. That lady's out in nowheresville, and the county sheriff who's tracking her soon will bring her in. Guaranteed. Unless she's already croaked out there. Which is, of course, a distinct possibility."

The earnest line supervisor abruptly reappears at his elbow. "Sir?" he says. "We've nailed it. The calls made to Cowell's cell both came from one Lawrence Purdy's cell, and that's a local man, sir, right from —"

Nader rounds on him. "Don't!" he growls, his jaw clenched.

"But sir, you asked —"

"That's *no way* to give me classified info."

The supervisor blanches to see hot anger spark in the eyes of Nader, the top boss at Sojourn, nods, and spins on his heel to retreat. But Viktor closes a paw around one of the man's wrists and snatches him back.

"You said Purdy?" he demands.

The supervisor switches his gaze rapidly to Nader, back again to Viktor. How should he answer?

"He did." Nader answers for him.

"So! This Purdy. Same man's name, the one enters your ranch back gate?"

Viktor relinquishes his grip on the line supe, who staggers, spins, then does an impressively fast job of rendering himself scarce.

Nader flicks a glance at Sanders, and he nods confirmation.

"This FBI friend your jail has, his number this Purdy has, and makes the call to him." Viktor again shakes an angry, accusatory finger. "How shall you explain?"

"I can't," Nader struggles to keep his voice calm. "Not yet. But I will. Obviously, the Purdy boys need to be roped in here for a little chat."

"We go and get them!" Viktor proclaims. "Right now, this exact instant!"

"No. That's dumb. Sheriff Baxter's already got plenty of his force out there looking for the woman, he can just gather up the Purdys along the way."

"I and my men go now to sheriff and make sure this all happens in correct way."

"Shut up, Vicky!" Mark Nader snaps. "Whose turf do you think you're on? While you're on my place — exactly like before and after you arrived — everything here gets run the way *I* say! Got it?"

Viktor crosses arms over his broad chest, flexes corded forearms. Says nothing, but offers an icy glare.

"Complete badass, right?" Nader sneers. "Lord knows you work at it overtime. Still, let's check the basic math. Your whole team is five guys, including you and your general. Now, we admire and like the general. That's why we're trying a major deal with him. But you, Vicky, are merely a giant pain in the ass. So, back to the numbers. Two hundred staff help me run this joint. Fifty are the toughest sonsabitches anyone could imagine. Plus, I've got select inmate squads even tougher, just 'cos they're twice as nuts, whom I can call upon at need.

"You might think you'd like to pick a fight with my guys? Maybe you would, for a second. After that, you'd look like a cow patty getting steamrollered. Flattened into a shit pancake, you following me here?"

"Threat from you? No concern to me," Viktor responds in a gruff monotone.

"Right." Nader turns to Sanders. "Tom, hey. How many KGB available right now, in their romper room?"

"Squad of a dozen kept on duty," he says. "Twenny-four-seven."

"Great. Send 'em up to SecCon in full hats-and-bats. Say, I've got a guy here needs some major sorting out."

"KGB?" Viktor looks contemptuous.

"Our all-pro goons," Nader explains. "They wear black Kevlar gloves. Each glove has a little bag of lead birdshot sewn in just above the knuckles. Can you guess why?"

"Ha," Viktor sneers, as if laughing. He doesn't actually look amused.

"So, why not toddle back to your general's suite and offer him a report on the recent happenings? Also, tell him I've not been trying to hide a goddam thing from him. That'd be a good use of your time."

Viktor thinks it over, uncrosses his arms, offers a mock bow to Nader.

"*Ya vernus,*" he says in Russian, and he accents it a bit like Schwarzenegger in the first Terminator movie. "I'll be back."

"*Mene vse ravno,*" Nader scoffs. Meaning, "I don't care."

Viktor stalks to the steel door, slaps a wall plate, it slides open for him, and he exits.

Sanders puffs his cheeks, and makes a silent *whew!* breathing out.

"That asshole doesn't enter SecCon again," Nader grates. "Never." His face is knotted with anger. "Are we clear?"

"Okay," Sanders says, and "Yes sir," the watch officers say. They speak simultaneously.

"How'd he even get in here, in the first place?"

"We'll make sure it doesn't happen again," Sanders assures, glancing nervously at the watch captain. "Ever."

Nader swings a dead-eyed stare back and forth between them.

"All right. Now, here's something else. We need D-Seg to go dark, for just thirty minutes, starting 'bout now."

"Say what?" the captain blurts. It's a highly unusual request.

"For real."

"'S all right," Sanders says. "What you need, chief?"

"Lights out, camera and sound cut-off."

"Of course, sir," the watch captain says, as he regains his footing.

"Neither of you guys asked why, which reassures me, sort of. But I'll tell you. We have a major gladiator bout scheduled for tomorrow. I need to head down there and do a lil' bit of prep."

"You got it."

"And the other thing, this call to Cowell's phone, from Purdy?" Nader takes a deep breath. "Bothers me. I want an explanation for that, instanter. Tom? Get ahold of Jack Baxter and brief him. Tell him to find the Purdys as fast as he can, then immobilize 'em. Then say to ferry the county helicopter over to Xanadu, first thing in the a.m., and await my further orders."

"Yessir."

Chapter 29

Nader walks down a bare prison hallway that looks as if it ends at a blank wall. Then his full-access card key triggers the D-Seg main door. A steel panel sighs as it whips up into the ceiling, while one beyond it vanishes into a slot in the polished concrete floor. The broad corridor revealed has a whitewashed expanse broken by rectangular lines of eight white doors per side, set flush into the walls. The center of each cell door has a small and thick window of wired glass, and below each window is a steel tray equipped with a sliding shutter.

With all of its lights shut down, the D-Seg is a dim, gray space, lit only by reflected beams from the outer hall, a pearly radiance that seeps in around Nader to cast his long shadow all the way to the end of the corridor.

This backlit effect distorts Nader's shadow as he walks up to the last door on the right. A metallic grind of its steel shutter echoes for an instant as he draws it back.

"Hey. It's me."

"Fuck you!"

Nader can hear Tank Burnett's harsh breath through the slot of the shutter. Which means he's by the door. Nader chooses to wait him out.

"You *said* it was gonna be one, two days, max," Burnett mutters finally.

"Sorry. Got complicated."

"Yeah? Like what."

"Well, lately, people linked with the FBI have cropped up."

"*Linked?*"

"We're still sorting it out."

"Speakin' of 'out,' it's high time I was. Goddammit!"

"Can't. Not yet."

"Why?"

"It's impolitic to let Andreyev and Lundts know… who you really are."

Burnett snorts derisively. "Who in this joint doesn't know?"

"I mean, to me."

Only Burnett's noisy breath can be heard.

"Miss you, too," he ultimately grunts.

"Good."

More breathing.

"Keep eyes on the prize." Nader advises. "We make common cause with the General, that means loot on a scale that's off the charts. Set up so all it can do is grow. I'm talking a global power beyond the reach or control of any nation. Now, both of us have a chance to sign on and benefit. But you've gotta get over a hurdle, first."

"Like what?"

"Gladiator fight."

"Huh?! Crap's for friggin' plebes, man! Not a guy already through the Finishin' School."

"You might dig it."

"Right."

"Even volunteer, after I tell you."

"Sure."

"Fight is with two dudes we consider high-level Feebs. Feds of some stripe, anyhow."

Breath, breath, then, "More," Burnett mumbles.

"Might not be a romp. Guys are smaller than you — who ain't? — but trained. It goes down tomorrow right here in D-Seg, after sunup. You must win."

"Always my plan."

"Smart money's going the other way. The Russkies hope you'll crash and burn."

"Why?"

"Let me finish on the who. One's ex-mil, totally serious, like, decorated to the max. So, you're lookin' at a skill-set."

"And the other?"

"Hard to believe, but it's a guy you smacked around on the bridge into Key West, coupla weeks ago, then pitched into the drink."

"That citizen? The hero?"

"Uh-huh."

"Here?! Now? Why?"

"Well… simplest way to put it, he's a friend of the law guy."

"No shit."

"So. The General wants you to lose this match, 'cos he wants you out of the picture. And Lundts does, too."

"Bull. What'd I ever do to them?"

"They totally hate the way you did that guy in West Palm."

"Dude was strapped, Mark! How many times I got to say it? He was bending down to snatch a forty-four derringer out of his boot. Right then's when I had to cap him. What would you have done? Or mister general high-and-mighty dickhead Andreyev?"

"And then?"

"Oh, c'mon. Huge mess. I needed cover, backup, and alibis, double-quick. So, called in some buds."

"Because your loyalty was… where?"

"How shoulda it gone? Who was the closest?"

"Right. Then your gang-bangers say, hey, let's double-, triple-down, on the ride to Key West?"

Silence.

"Okay, so now that created another mess, that 'un on the bridge, which brought in the feds. And so what you have to deal with now is spillover."

Breathing.

"That's why you need to win. It will eliminate some of the problem. Show your worth. Then I can make a case for you."

"A case for me for what?"

"To stay. At the level where I want to see you. Right by my side."

"Otherwise?"

"You end up someplace else."

"So, you're willing to dump me off." Burnett sounds glum, even hurt.

"Looking at the wrong end of it, as usual. Why am I here?" Nader demands.

"Why *are* you here?"

"Think your opponents get any prep?"

"Oh, a hedzup. Gee, thanks." Burnett is caustic.

"Not all. Brought you a tool." Nader tugs out from his waistband a thin plastic bar carved out of a nylon kitchen board. It's been filed into a sharp spike. "If you happen to need an edge, use this." He drops it into the tray.

He hears Burnett's big fingers scrape it out.

"Decent shank," Burnett mutters. "But why not something with more heft?"

"Has to be what you could supply yourself. If it looks like I stick my thumb on the scales, your victory won't take us where we need to go."

"Marky knows best, just like always, right?"

"Get it done, and I think you'll like how things end up."

Breathing.

"Hey, I brought tape for the shank. Stick it up and inside of your slider? Then you'll be able to grab it, even from outside, whenever you want."

"Don't need no tape. Cram it up into the crack. See? It stays."

"Whatever."

"Marky."

"Yeah, I'm here."

In the gloam of the corridor, Nader sees pale ends of Burnett's thick fingers poke out past the open slider and into the tray. He's adopting the position he would if he were being cuffed before being removed from the cell. Nader reaches out and clasps Burnett's groping hands in both of his own.

"I'll watch you win."

"Yeah."

"We get through this, it's a different world. We can be together, in a whole new way. Far more open. No one'll even be able to say boo."

"Can't wait for it."

Up in the SecCon room, the watch officer stands leaned back against the back wall's only blank section with both hands cupped over headphones that are wirelessly linked to the D-Seg camera mic feeds. He gets an uneasy feeling that someone in SecCon is looking at him and his eyes snap open to see a line supervisor's obvious smirk. He frowns and steps forward, and sees the line supe has widened a security camera's aperture and fully zoomed in on the door of the last cell in D-Seg. Even in the shadows, they can see Nader and Burnett holding hands.

So, the line supe has a good idea what the watch officer might be listening to on the headphones. The watch grins, makes a tight circle of his left thumb and forefinger, and plunges his right index finger in and out of that small circle. The line supe clears his throat to conceal an involuntary bray of laughter, then rotates his head back to the screen holding a dim image of Nader and Burnett.

Chapter 30

A thunk echoes down the hall of D-Seg Unit as steel bolts slide back to release three doors. A sigh of hydraulic hinges comes next, and three doors yawn wide.

Halogen bulbs on the ceiling flare, the corridor boils with stark light.

Dan moves to his cell's open door, tries to shield his eyes from the glare with a hand held to his eyebrows. He peers around the frame and down the hall.

A shirtless Carl comes out of his cell door, using clasped hands to make Eskimo snow goggles to protect his own eyes. He looks through his splayed fingers and spots Dan, who waves back at him.

"Hey," Dan calls out. "You okay…?"

Before Carl can answer, there's a rush of heavy footsteps. Tank Burnett charges from the last open door and smashes Dan with a huge, tattooed forearm. Carl sees Dan fly backward into his cell.

What?! A goddam cage match! Carl realizes.

Burnett runs at Carl, shovel-sized hands reaching for Carl's neck.

Shit! No way in hell do I grapple with that!

Carl half-turns, as if to sprint away. But instead he dives forward and rolls, lashing out with a kick at Burnett's left ankle as he slides by on the slick concrete floor. He uses his last momentum to roll again and snap to his feet. He glances into Dan's cell and sees him groggily trying to rise, a hand braced against the cell's rear wall.

C'mon c'mon, Dan-man, need you IN this thing!

Burnett spins about and glares. He's mad, not just because his ankle hurts, but also because Carl eluded his grasp. That cute dive, roll and slither tactic won't work again. He charges. Carl feints a dive to the opposite side, drops flat on his back instead, and kicks up at Tank's left kneecap and lands a solid hit. Tank tries to reach down and grab Carl but instead he staggers and falls, crashing into the corner between wall and floor. In an instant Carl's back up and leaping to the corridor's far end.

His eyes sweep for any object that could be a weapon. While in his cell he made one device — a long garrote braided out of the cotton-poly fabric of his T-shirt — but it's not yet the right moment to unwind it from his waist. The corridor is empty of everything but its own steel walls, an ammonia-reeking floor drain, and a piercing light that's banished any hint of shadow.

As he passes other D-Seg doors, he sees a couple of faces pressed against tiny panels of wired glass. Some faces bristle with hair and beard, others look fat and distorted as they push on the glass. Somehow, the unit's other inmates know a fight is on.

At the end of the hall, he spins. Burnett lurches to his feet, glistening with sweat, his face reddened by rage.

Got nothin'. Carl thinks. *Square up? Suicide! Might have to anyhow...*

He sees Dan emerge from his cell door behind Burnett.

～

The general's suite has all window curtains drawn closed. Images on a large flat-screen TV glow brightly amid the room's soft, indirect lighting. This screen is split into quadrants, each square offers a different view of the D-Seg corridor. Andreyev and Lundts lounge comfortably in the overstuffed wingback chairs. However, Nader perches on the arm of his chair, and keeps a booted foot on the floor while jiggling the tip of his other boot rapidly.

"Victory does not seem to come quickly for your boy Tank," Lundts observes.

Nader says nothing. Andreyev swivels his head, looks at him. Nader shrugs. The toe of his boot continues to bounce.

On the screen, they see Dan limp out of his cell door. At the opposite end of the corridor, Burnett closes in on Carl. Dan runs down the corridor toward them, launches himself, turns a bit in midair, then drives heels of both feet into the big man's back just below his kidneys.

Dan drops to the floor, Burnett puts a hand on the wall and sags. Carl tries to leap past him, but Burnett still manages to grab Carl by his throat with a free hand as he goes by. Still on the floor, Dan manages a kick that glances off Burnett's inner thigh and lands right in the balls. Burnett grunts, shakes Carl like a kitten, punches his face, then hurls him away. He bends down, reaching for Dan with murder in his eyes.

"Advantage, Mister Burnett," Andreyev intones in a nasal, flat voice, like an announcer at Wimbleton. "The big man can certainly absorb punishment, yes?"

～

Dan looks up to see Burnett's narrow white eyes. Bulging tattooed arms and fat fingers bent like butcher hooks extend toward him. Once more he gets a close-up of a black "Y" glyph inscribed on the end of the middle fingers, but he now can also see these merely form the tongues of serpents… and flat, triangular heads of pythons are printed on the backs of his hands, and scaled reptilian bodies of dusky green coil around the thick forearms and biceps… He has no time to wonder how that thug from the Florida bridge went all the way from Andreyev's yacht, way back here, to a jail corridor in West Texas. He only knows he must fight with everything he's got to survive.

Carl rises, jumps back into the fray, and delivers a stout thrust kick into Burnett's left hip. Dan barely avoids the meaty, grasping hands. He rolls to one side, getting out from under Burnett's massive body before it whacks onto the floor.

Enough dicking with these slippery punks, Burnett thinks. *I'ma just grab my blade and shiv 'em...*

He stands and lumbers down the corridor to his cell's open door.

Carl extends a hand, Dan grabs it and is hauled to his feet. Carl's face is a mess, a smashed nose sends a delta of blood over his mouth and jaw. His eyes are fierce, glittering slits.

"Bang him into hard stuff," Carl hisses, "shove him into walls, doors, the floor. And work that left leg! That's what I'm on. Get him down, we can stomp him!"

Dan nods. They see Burnett groping inside the steel tray on his cell door. Dan takes off, his gait more of a stumble than a run, but he builds up speed and jumps, aiming to use his whole body again as a ram. Burnett turns at the last instant, shoves out a white object with a straight arm. Dan suddenly finds himself impaled, a nylon spike has been driven into his upper chest, ripping into the pectoral muscle above his heart, glancing off a rib, then sliding up under his collarbone. He gasps as Burnett pivots around to drive him into the wall. Burnett pins him there with his feet off the floor, and twists and grinds the shiv into flesh and bone, holding his face a few inches in front of Dan's, the narrow white eyes shining with glee as he savors the torment he causes.

Carl pounces on Burnett's wide back and swings the yellow garrote he's fashioned over the thick, greasy dome of Burnett's skull, then swiftly embeds it in the flesh of his neck and hauls it tight with every bit of strength he owns.

Burnett's eyes bulge as he grasps the awful mistake he made by turning his back on Carl, and realizes the danger he's in now. He squeezes Dan by the back of the skull with his free hand and smashes Dan's forehead into the edge of the steel door. Simultaneously, he tries to yank out the blade, but it's wedged tightly in flesh and bone and as Dan's body goes limp and drops, his dead weight hauls the handle — now slick with blood — out of Burnett's grip.

The garrote Carl made from strips of his shirt bites deep. Carl knows that he can't wait for this giant to strangle from lack of air, he's got to bear down hard enough to cut off the blood supply to his brain. If he doesn't, the big man might still have enough energy to take counter-measures.

One of Burnett's coal-scuttle hands rises to shove a finger under the garrote and pull, while the other forms a fist and tries to land a punch on Carl's face. But Carl ducks his head down between Burnett's shoulder blades, yanks his feet up off the floor so that his suspended body weight adds to the force exerted by his arms. Burnett spins around and thrusts back with tree-trunk legs, crushing Carl against the unyielding wall. Carl feels more than hears a gristly interior crackle, he fears major things might be giving way in his spine, and he almost loses his hold on the garrote.

But only almost. He's wrapped both ends of the braided cord around his fists. Not only that, but he made his device *a la loupe*, French Foreign Legion style, so it dropped over the neck of his target in two coils. Which means, as Burnett tugs mightily to loosen the top strand, he manages only to increase the tightness of the lower. And thus he assists in his own strangulation.

His pale eyes turn entirely white as they roll up into his skull, and the nearly lashless eyelids flutter and twitch. Still he manages to fall forward, going prone with a hand that stretches out toward Dan's crumpled body. He seeks one last time to grab for the shank.

Carl drives a knee between Burnett's shoulder blades and leans back to haul the cord even tighter. The massive body trembles, the toes of Tank's shoes beat a spastic drum solo on the concrete slab, finally he droops. All the big muscles turn gelatinous. A shiver. He's gone.

Carl doesn't unwrap the garrote. He just lets go, and crawls on all fours to the body of his friend. He examines Dan's slack face, looks at the bloody nylon spike that protrudes from his upper chest, then grabs a wrist, tries to find a pulse. Does not get one, goes to his neck. Finds a loose, soft, thready beat. Sees a gash with weeping edges in his forehead, where Burnett drove his skull into the edge of the cell door. Touches it. That area of Dan's skull still feels firm, though there's only a thin scrap of tissue left over the bone. He checks an eye, can't tell if the pupil is contracting, but it's sluggish.

Carl stands with difficulty, clutching hard onto the door to rise. After he's finally vertical, his eyes wander until he spots the blank obsidian orbs of camera lenses, four of them, one placed at each upper corner of the hall. He glares up into the nearest lens, and jabs a finger emphatically toward Dan.

"Bring my man Cowell emergency med care, *stat*," he says. "Or you'll get doodly squat from me. Stabilize him, maybe I talk to you. If I do, I can tell you lots of things you need to know."

Chapter 31

Beaming from his chair in the suite, Andreyev applauds. His palms touch lightly and make no sound. He nods several times. "And so, nature issues her ruling," he says.

Lundts is impassive, except for a hint of a smile. They both look at Nader.

His eyes are still locked on the screen, where the huge lump that was once Ted James Burnett lies inert on the D-Seg floor. Nader feels them looking at him, and turns to answer with his own gaze, struggling to keep it steady and direct. He knows they search for any sign of weakness. He suspects they know about his relations with Burnett. There've been whispers for years among the Sojourn staffers… someone could've easily been bribed to leak that info. Were he in their position, he'd contrive to gain intel in precisely the same way.

Nader gives a slight, world-weary smile, turns his hands up and slowly lifts his frock-coated shoulders in a shrug. He couldn't — he mutely indicates — care less.

Andreyev shifts his gaze to Lundts. "So, we have a pair of winners. Or one and a half! How to answer Blackadar's request? Should Mister Cowell remain with the living?"

Lundts considers. "For now," he says. "But only if we can use him as a lever." He looks at Nader. "Mark? Want to bury Cowell with Burnett, or keep him in the mix?"

Nader clears his throat. He seems in command of his feelings, yet the truth is he's numb, nearly in shock. Tonelessly he says, "Since you both sound like you're in favor, I'll go with the majority."

"All right."

"Give him first aid at the prison, then stash him here in the clinic at Xanadu," Lundts says. "That way, we can keep closer tabs."

"So moved, and seconded, and the ayes have it," Andreyev says. "But Mark, another matter we need to deal with promptly. Viktor tells me that Dan Cowell's phone had two recent calls, from local man, by name of Purdy? Is there explanation?"

Nader shakes his head, blinks. "We can't say yet."

"Who is this man? One of your groundskeepers? How does he have Cowell's number? Two calls in a row, this is not a mistake."

"We're triangulating the location of those calls with data we're seeking from other cell towers," Nader offers.

"Purdy is one thing. But Purdy's phone we should consider as another," Lundts puts in. "Calls can be made by a different person."

"Who might know Cowell's number well, and wish badly to call it?" Andreyev muses. "Well, his woman, right?"

Nader's irritated that they seem to be on the verge of figuring this out. He wanted to fix the problem, and present the solution as a *fait accompli*.

"Well. Hoped to be sure of it first, but I'll say what we think. We know Linda Parker is wandering out in brush country to the east. Let's say the Purdys come across her, she cons them with a story and they take her in. She gets her hands on one of their phones, and tries to contact Cowell. Our man in Matamoros says he heard a word or two from a female voice before the call was cut off. That was recorded, naturally, and now he's trying to match it to see if it's Parker's. See, he's got her phone too, so he can compare it to the outgoing on her voicemail."

"Ah-h," the general winks as he wags a reproving finger. "Mark, you are sly one! You know more than you let on. But that is okay. Sometimes we do that too, right, Samuel?"

Lundts nods.

"Whether it's Parker or another woman, we'll soon have the call location, and we've been steadily tracking the Purdys," Nader says. "I've got the sheriff coming here with the county helicopter. We'll go out and pick 'em all up. All right?"

"Good," Lundts says.

~

Andreyev paces at Nader's side. They walk out to the helipad at Xanadu's airstrip, where a Bell 206L-4 Long Ranger with the Turco County sheriff's star and logo displayed on its hull sits on landing skids. Through the cockpit bubble of the aircraft, they see the potbellied, stoop-shouldered bulk of Sheriff Jack Baxter, who offers a laconic wave of greeting.

"This is correct and timely move, of which I approve," the general says. "There's saying we have, *Iskru tushi do pozhara, bedu otvodi do udara*. It means, 'To quench spark before house burns.'"

"Sure, once we have Linda Parker and the Purdys in the fold, one area of trouble is firewalled," Nader says. "The Washington end of things is more complex. I wonder if Lundts is really able to get that all handled."

"That will be his true test, for certain," Andreyev says mildly. "One I watch in keen interest."

"Interest!" Nader exclaims. "That's all?" And then he gets it. The general has steadily maneuvered so that he's not been forced to put skin in the game to the extent that he or Lundts have. If this whole project blows up in their faces, Andreyev can simply fly back to his yacht and sail off, while he and Lundts will be forced to face music guaranteed to be painfully loud, discordant, and prolonged.

"You imply that after we've gone so far together, you're starting to get cold feet?"

"No, no, no," the general soothes. "My feet feel quite warm to me as I walk here now, right beside you, Mark! If these matters work out properly, then you and Lundts shall indeed prove yourself worthy partners for my Upsilon Group."

"Uh-huh."

"But if not, then I'd have to describe you as something else. A rival or a competitor, perhaps." He grins. "That is, of course, a joke."

~

Nader clambers into the helicopter and sits next to Sheriff Baxter who has moved to rear seats of the cockpit. A deputy armed and in full battle-rattle has gone up forward, next to the pilot.

"Jack," he says.

"Mark." Baxter nods. He has a balding, spherical head garlanded with an omega of black hair and a walrus mustache.

"Your guys find the Purdys?"

"Yep, pretty close. Findley Ridge, not far from east side of your place. Damn rough country." Shakes his boulder of a head. "Can't believe some places those boys stick that ol' truck of theirs. I put a coupla ground units near 'em, and now we can go straight in with this." He pats the chopper's fuselage.

"Good investment, then, me buying it for you," Nader says.

"We're grateful, for sure," Baxter responds.

A shrill whine as the double-bladed rotor begins to strobe through the air.

"Everything else okay?"

"Oh yeah, for now, I guess," Baxter says. "FBI guys, them as pokin' around the gals' car wreck, seem to have changed focus. Started yackin' a shitload now about doin's in Matamoros. Not heard much else from 'em in the last day or so…"

Nader, who boarded the aircraft with his face still seamed by frustration and anger, now relaxes and appears more pleased. "Ah, good ol' Faustino," he says. "Man's the best! Must be workin' the holy hell out of all four of those phones. Like, he's feedin' 'em a radio play, or something. And Feebs are chewing on his bait, which is excellent."

The airframe vibrates, the turbines shriek, the rotor whaps out a harsh staccato as it twirls above their heads. Baxter points at the headphones draped over the armrests of their seats. Nader nods, and they both put them on as the Bell levitates from the tarmac.

～

Melanie is flat on her back on the floor of Nader's suite. She won't use the bed, she hates the bed. Her eyes are closed, she's pulled a pillow down to tuck beneath her head, and a blanket to drape over her nude body. Her breathing is deep and slow, she has now chosen her abyss and takes refuge there, willing herself to drop deeper, and deeper still… She dimly hears the door to the room open, which gives her impetus to dive further, faster…

Then comes a gruff voice, not Mark Nader's. Tinged with a foreign accent. Something European. That voice converses with another voice that seems to whine, it's so high, tight and nervous.

"I tell you, you are to be not concern for this act, yes?" the voice says. "Why we pay you! So you will shut up or be giving me back all the money. Right now. All."

"Sir, I'm sorry, I'm trying to help as much as I can, but we have definite orders that no one is to enter this unit or…"

"Silence! Or I cut tongue from your mouth. That will be ultimate definite order. Now go."

The conversation is so strange, Mel feels she must venture closer to awareness to see what it means. The room lights switch on just as she parts her eyelids a millimeter. A man in a black, skintight shirt comes around the bed to look down at her. Her eyes stay slitted as the man kneels beside her, and she makes no move, barely breathes, yet somehow the guy knows that she's present and awake.

Behind the man in black stands a thin, quivering individual clad in a gray Xanadu staff uniform.

"You are Melanie Olson," the man says gruffly. "I am Viktor Mandić. Tell me of your condition. How okay are you?"

"I…" her mouth is dry. "I…"

She feels a hard hand slip between her head and the pillow, another gently turn her face from side to side, and her eyelids slowly lift all the way. She sees a square, rough-hewn face topped by a steel-gray crewcut, a face that looks neither kind nor compassionate, yet does show curiosity. She can tell that he's reading her bruises, perhaps from a professional standpoint, as he tries to assess the degree of her damage.

"What things he does to you?" he asks.

"Kicked, bit, punched me," she hears a voice murmur. It sounds somewhat like her own. "Rapes, many of them…"

"Can you walk?"

"Why…? Are you…"

"You, I take to medical care, immediate," he asserts.

"Mister Mandić!" the Xanadu staffer protests. "I put my job at risk, just telling you about her! I can't…"

Viktor leaps up, grabs him by the throat. In a second his blunt fingers are rammed *into* that throat, gripping the larynx. The staffer utters a strangled gurgle and his eyes bulge.

"Keys," Viktor says flatly.

The man frantically searches his pocket, hooks a keyring with a finger and hauls it out. Viktor snatches the bunch of keys, bounces it in his hand, shuts his fist around it, then lands a straight punch on the center of the staffer's forehead. He performs a credible backflip, tumbles across the floor, hits a wall, and lies in a heap.

Viktor unlocks the leather cuff and cable around Mel's ankle and pulls her up so that she's sitting on the bed. He walks over, grabs the unconscious man by one leg, and drags him back to the cuff, locks it on him. Viktor then rips a strip of fabric off a sheet and binds his hands behind his back. For good measure, he tears another and stuffs it in the unconscious man's mouth.

Viktor pulls Melanie's arm up across his shoulders, hugs her body wrapped in the blanket to his side with the other arm, and helps her stand.

"Come with," he says. "And do not be in fear."

Chapter 32

Examined and treated by a nurse, all her burns and cuts and bruises salved, some bandaged, Melanie drifts in a vague bardo somewhere between the surface of physical reality and the deep refuge of her personal abyss. A few milligrams of sodium-thiopental help keep her adrift there. She feels a languid buoyancy, like a liferaft that bobs upon swells of a gleaming sea.

Then words summon her. She hears, "… Linda Parker…"

Linda?!

"She… she… she's alive?"

Sudden hope wrenches her so fiercely, it feels like a spasm of pain.

"Parker is that woman you travel with, yes?"

Her vision twirls into focus and it's him again, she stares up at that gray-haired, muscular Euro guy in the black T. Involuntarily, she reaches, wants to touch him… then finds her arms jerked to a stop once more by leather cuffs and cables. A sigh that's nearly a groan escapes her.

"I am sorry. I apologize. If I don't make you be secure, I cannot still help you." The words sound friendly, but his eyes are cold.

She realizes he doesn't care a bit about her, personally. Perhaps he does feel some sort of moral objection to how terribly she's been mistreated. But far and away his top priority is performing a task of some sort. Which, in this instance, seems to mean getting her to answer more questions. All right, by now she's used to spilling beans. But perhaps she can exact a small payment. She realizes there is indeed something she still hopes for.

"If I give you all you want, can that be bad for him?"

His eyes narrow as he calculates her meaning. He gets it.

"Who, Nader? Yes, bad for him. But I do need to know more. More than him."

"You don't work for Nader?"

"No, absolute."

"I'll say all I can. Only ask."

Viktor nods "Yes, my questions. You are FBI?"

Mel shakes her head. "I tried to join the Bureau, but they rejected me."

"And your man or husband, he is Carl Blackadar?"

"I... We... Well, it's complicated... Okay, sure."

"And this Daniel Cowell, FBI also? I must verify."

"I don't think so. But he is Carl's friend. They are both veterans. They met in the navy, years ago. They wound up in this together nearly by accident. Dan was just trying to help him."

"What is this Blackadar's official status?"

"I don't know. Truly. But... it's high. He was Navy, then CIA, then FBI. Now? Somebody special... a kind of covert mister fix-it. He moves around inside the government, and he gets borrowed by different agencies."

"Good. I understand. And now, the Linda Parker. She is a government something?"

"Definitely not."

"And she is tall woman, looks black?"

"No. Well, yes. That's her color. But she's Indian, a Moskitu, they call the tribe. She comes from Honduras. On the coast, an island,

Cárcelita. It is beautiful…"

Viktor waves an impatient hand. "And she works for you?"

"She came to help me."

"So, your servant?"

"No, my friend."

"If she escapes, if they do not catch her, what do you think she does?"

"Linda is smart. She will try to get the strongest help she can. And of course, she will try to reach Dan and Carl, get them involved."

"And come for you?"

She feels a surge of nausea. "No… I don't think so. She will be very angry with me. Them, too. Because… I pulled her straight into this mess. I screwed up everything."

Viktor nods.

"Okay. Tell me if you know. How does government investigation proceed? They start where, go to what?"

"Well first, it was Tank Burnett running into Dan on the Keys, where they had a fight. And next, they found out Burnett was with a Russian guy who owns a big yacht, I don't know how. But then they started to figure out a connection to Mark Nader and the prison at Sojourn. It was because of Burnett's DNA, they got that off laundry from the yacht. And that led to a criminal database, which led to the jail. I found out about that because I snooped on Carl's laptop… while he was away…"

A wave of sadness washes over her. She sniffles.

"Good. I understand," Viktor says. "And so, this turns into big troubles for everyone." He stands up, stares down at her. "For you, though, don't worry so much. I think the General, he makes a big dislike for Mister Nader. And so, things shall change here. Definite."

"The General?" She's puzzled.

"Never mind. Last question. If there is an FBI man, top guy, who wants to stop investigation, can he?"

She ponders this, shakes her head. "No, I don't think so. Even an assistant director might try, but the agency isn't entirely authoritarian, not in that way. All he might do in the end is just set off some warning bells."

"All right." Viktor nods twice, then pats her on the head.

"I go now. For you, I would only say, you must fight to live."

He turns and stalks off.

Chapter 33

Hank and Larry are squatting on mesquite stumps by a fire ring made of stacked rock. They watch an aluminum pan full of a black substance simmer atop a pile of glowing twigs.

"Now, don't let it bile," Hank warns.

"You mind?" Larry gives him an irritated glance.

"Hey, that's the tail end of the soup Linda made for us. I just hope to Christ you ain't gonna ruin it."

"And I hope you drop dead of a brain-injure-rhythm," Larry says. "But are my prayers ever answered? No!"

"A *what*?"

"It'll be hot soon. Meantime, shut up."

"Don't sass your elders, boy. And what's 'at you hope I die from?"

"A brain-injure-rhythm," Larry mutters. "What got ol' Bob McDougal. Out on his porch, and just fell over. Didn't even get his hands off his suspenders."

Hank snorts. "That's a brain *aneurysm*, junior."

"Whatever. It's fast, see? I don't want you to suffer."

"You'll suffer plenty after you see what my will says."

"Yeah? Like you're leavin' me everything? My plan is to burn you and all your crap piled up in the truck, just like a Viking funeral."

"I'm leavin' everythin' to the bank, 'cos they mostly own it already.

I'm leaving *you* to the bank, too. Was keepin' that as a surprise, but you provoked me."

Hank leans forward, sniffs the air over the pot. "I say it's ready."

"I'd say the guy what does the cookin' decides."

"Want some meat with it?"

"Like what?"

"Snake."

Larry screws up his face. "Purely sick of that."

"Well, you insist on havin' it the same way every time. You're actually sick of fryin'. We stew it, makes for a more delicate flavor."

"Need pig's what we need. Should've took salt ham with us. Oh well. Let's sneak onto Xanadu tonight and poach us a zebra or some such."

Hank chortles. "Right! Fun to leave ol' Lew a gut-pile to find in the mornin'. On a hunka zebra hide. With a note, thankin' him for the free hunt. He'd 'bout stomp his hat through to China."

Larry takes the pot off the coals and pours Honduran black bean soup into a pair of wooden bowls. He looks wistful as a curl of vapor spirals up past his nose. "Y'know, what we really oughta do is bring Linda down here, have her make us some more grub."

Hank rubs his face and drags the skin over his cheekbones, pulling down his lower eyelids. He peers at Larry with distended eyeballs. "'Pears to me, the boy's got it bad, doctor.' 'Yes, yes indeed.' 'What do you recommend?' 'Cold shower.' 'How long?' 'Bout a month should do it, mebbe. That don't work, make him go sit on a big block a' ice.'"

Larry starts to blush, but fights it down. "We could at least call her, make sure she's okay." He hands his uncle a bowl of soup.

"But we tol' her, only use your phone for emergencies," Hank says before he slurps up a spoonful.

"That was 'bout her callin' us. Not we callin' her up. See, it's different…"

"Ever thought of becomin' a jailhouse lawyer?"

Over their conversation, a background noise has gradually risen in volume. It now can be identified as the rabid throb of an approaching helicopter. The aircraft lifts into view above a notch in the low hills and its noise intensifies. They stop talking for a moment to study its path.

"Comin' straight for us," Larry observes.

"No lie."

They see that the aircraft wears the seal of Turco County's sheriff. It circles their campsite and sets down on the far side of the clearing, rattling the tarp that roofs their lean-to sleeping area. It flaps lustily several times, yanks up its stakes, then collapses. Larry unbuttons his shirt and holds the front tail of it over his bowl to shield it from dust. Hank just goes right on spooning food past the slot in his beard.

The aircraft bobbles, settles on its skids, winds down. A deputy exits a front door. He wears a Kevlar helmet and a flak vest, and holds a Ruger Mini 30 automatic rifle across his chest, his right index finger poised dutifully across the trigger guard. Sheriff Jack Baxter heaves his similarly flack-jacketed, rotund body out of the back, followed on the other side by Mark Nader, who has on his black frock coat.

Hank tilts his bowl up to his lips and drains it. He puts it down and wipes his mouth with the back of his sleeve. "See?" he tells Larry. "Good thing we don't have more soup. Did, might have to offer these sumbitches a bowl."

Baxter and Nader approach the campfire, while the armed deputy moves off to one side, giving himself a clearer field of fire.

"Hi boys!" Baxter doffs his hat, waves it, puts it back on.

"Bring a fifth of single-malt, like we tole you?" Hank asks.

"What?" the sheriff's grin is vague while he processes Hank's gibe.

Hands in the pockets of his coat, Nader swivels a bleak look back and forth between the Purdys.

"Mean, you ain't delivery boys from BevMo?"

Baxter scowls. "Oh, quit," he says.

"You, you're Larry," Nader grates out, with no preliminary. He pokes a corner of his coat pocket toward the nephew. "And your cell phone rang up Dan Cowell last night. Why?"

Larry glances quickly at Hank, then looks back at Nader. "Hell I did," he says. He sets down his bowl. "Never heard of the guy."

Nader pulls his right hand out of the pocket, and it's holding a black, snub-nosed automatic pistol. He pinches the slide, tugs it back just far enough to see brass in the chamber, lets it snap shut, thumbs off the safety, steps forward, and aims the sights at a spot between Larry's eyes.

"Hey!" Hank shouts. "No need for that…"

He starts to rise from his crouch but the sheriff slips his service sidearm out from its holster and waves him back to his seat with the barrel.

"Not one more shred of bullcrap," Nader warns. "Not out of either one a' you hick bastards. So, where's Linda Parker?" his eyes rove around their camp. Scattered evidence suggests the Purdy's have been in this spot for a few days. "Got her back of the truck?" he sneers. "Usin' her for entertainment?"

Larry's cheeks flame, his back straightens. "You'll shut your filthy mouth," he says.

"Oho! So you *are*! Tell me, she any good? Her gal-pal was great, I'm tellin' ya…"

Things happen fast after that. Larry's hand lashes out as he springs to his feet and he grips Nader's gun hand by the wrist with his left as he tries to wrench the pistol loose with his right. The weapon disappears into a jumbled ball of fists and fingers as the two men wrestle for control of it.

Hank leaps up but finds the sheriff's nine-millimeter auto is pointing straight at his chest. The men glower into each other's eyes. Hank sees his next move could definitely be his last, so he freezes.

There's the abrupt *crack* of a gunshot and Larry falls back, a hand rising to his throat as he stumbles, and a mist of blood dyes the air. Baxter turns his head slightly at the sound of the shot, Hank swats the sheriff's gun hand downward, there's a dense *boom* — as the sheriff pulls the trigger at precisely the wrong instant and fires a bullet straight through his own foot. Before he fully registers the shock, as his eyeballs bulge and rotate down, Hank has already grabbed control of the weapon, both his powerful hands wrapped around the sheriff's now-limp one, and he raises it and takes an instinctive shot at Nader, who still gapes at Larry as the youth's falling body hits the earth, tumbles and slides... and Hank's bullet hits Nader's gun hand, skates over the wrist, tunnels up his forearm and exits after it shatters his elbow. The little automatic spins free and whirls off into the brush.

Nader — traumatized beyond measure — gasps and begins to scream as Hank pivots with the pistol toward the deputy holding the Ruger. Hank struggles to keep Baxter upright so he can use him as a shield, and as he does so he manages to swing the sights around and yanks the trigger as fast as he can and the gun bucks as it churns through everything left in its magazine.

The deputy on guard and supposedly ready for action had been stunned into brief paralysis. He's finally able to level the Mini 30 and fire back at the same instant Hank starts to blaze away with the pistol. The deputy's aim is good but his judgment is off, and his round whacks into the sheriff's bullet-proof vest, merely knocking him and Hank backwards. Of Hank's more random shots, one grazes the inside of the deputy's ballistic helmet and the bullet tracks the inside curve of the Kevlar orb around the deputy's skull, practically scalping him, and as the deputy falls backward, Hank's next shot goes up his thigh and spins into the femoral artery, ripping it open to launch a dark geyser of blood from his groin.

The helicopter pilot sits frozen in his aircraft as — in mere seconds — he watches Larry go down, sees Nader run off holding his shattered arm over his head and shrieking, then sees the deputy tumble with blood gushing from his helmet and ripped trousers. He watches as Hank drops a half-fainting Sheriff Baxter and spins to aim the nine-millimeter pistol straight at the aircraft cockpit. The pilot violently flinches, and finds himself possessed by a mighty urge to flee. He accelerates the rotor for take-off.

Hank squeezes the trigger, nothing happens, looks down and sees the slide is locked open as the pistol awaits a fresh clip, drops the thing, turns and runs for the cab of the truck. When he reaches it, he yanks open the jammed and screeching door, pulls one of the SKS rifles off the gun rack behind the seat, turns back while pulling the bolt to charge the chamber, releases it, snaps down the curved safety lever, and raises the weapon to sight it on the chopper.

Then he pauses for a second, amazed, at the sight of Baxter hobbling at high speed, reaching the helicopter just before it rises, hopping onto the left skid. Baxter's upper body flops into the cockpit and the machine lifts off as he flails, trying to claw himself further in.

Hank swings iron sights, tracks the aircraft as it rises, and fires a round that creases Sheriff Jack Baxter across his pulpy butt. Then he works through the rest of the magazine, sending FMJ 7.62 bullets flying at the chopper as it turns, its turbines scream, then it hurtles west toward Xanadu. He lowers the empty gun, stands and pants heavily for a second. Then he runs for the fallen Larry.

Larry's on his back with a hand clamped on his throat, blood gushes around his fingers, his eyes stare up beseechingly. Hank falls to his knees, his first thought is to put a tourniquet on him, then understands, *a tourniquet around his neck, shit, that's ridiculous*, and he reaches in his pocket for a folded bandana, it's got food smears and snot and various dribbles and lord knows what else in it, but he shoves the wad of fabric and his own hand under Larry's hand, and then he feels the pulse, the spurting, high pressure of blood welling up under his palm and he realizes *I can't stop it hole's too big it's too late the kid's bleeding out* and he lets go and leaps up in horror...

Just in time to see Nader run back into the clearing. His smashed right arm is still above his head, he clasps it below the elbow with his left, he's out of breath and emitting tiny shrieks now, almost bleats, and his eyes are wide and crazed.

Hank jumps at him, grabs him by the collar of his coat, flings him down violently on the ground beside Larry. "You shot him, so you fix him," he growls. "Do it! 'Cos if he dies, you die."

Nader sits up, cradles his arm and moans, strives to grasp what's happening. As he does so, Larry spasms. "Han-k-k..." he breathes out a gasp that trails off into a sigh. His eyes go still and flat, his hand flops limply away from his throat. Grief and rage erupt in Hank as he sees his nephew surrender his life.

The pupils of Hank's eyes are hard black beads as he glares at Nader with consummate loathing. He'd shoot, but his rifle is out of bullets. And shooting's too good for the son-of-a-bitch anyhow. He reaches to the forestock, pinches the bayonet by the blood gutter, pulls it to him, swings the blade up, and lets the internal spring snap it erect on the end of the barrel.

"Up," he snarls.

"I... I..." Nader sputters. He feebly brandishes his shattered hand and forearm. His coat sleeve is wreathed like a maypole by dark ribbons of blood. "I need..."

"Up," Hank repeats. He stabs the bayonet's tip an inch into Nader's chest and pulls it up, ripping the flesh.

Nader gasps. He kneels, he scrambles to his feet.

"Listen to me, Purdy," he says. "Listen! Total accident. Didn't mean to shoot your kid. Did not aim to. Very sorry. I have lots of money. A ton. I can…"

"Shut up."

Hank jabs him with the bayonet, makes him take rapid, tottering steps as he herds him toward the rear of the truck. Once there, Hank unlatches the door of the plywood hutch mounted on the bed, flops out a set of steps. He holds the SKS with one hand wrapped around the receiver and stock, and he pokes the keen point of the blade into the small of Nader's back and keeps it there, forcing him up the stairs and into the structure.

He comes up after him. On the right side of the bed, there's a long plywood box with airholes drilled in its cover. Hank unlatches it, pulls up the lid. The interior of the box is shadowed, but it breathes out a musty reptilian funk, and there's a dim view of thick, patterned, cylindrical shapes inside, woven together in a large, loose knot. There's the languid shake of a warning rattle as the tip of one of the many tails vibrates slightly.

"In," Hank says.

Nader's eyes widen. "No!" he shouts, his voice shrill and desperate. "You can't! It's not… It's full of…"

Hank puts the tip of the bayonet under Nader's chin.

"In."

Nader tries to grab the end of the rifle with his good hand and shove the bayonet away, but Hank is too quick, he reverses the weapon and clouts Nader with the butt on the side of his head, knocking him over and into the plywood box, and in the next split second he slams the lid down and latches it.

The body inside thumps against the cover, kicks against the sides, screams, groans in horror, thrashes, screams again… a long despairing ululation… and then there is silence.

Chapter 34

Hank lightly drags his fingers on Larry's face to shut the eyes that still seem to hold a glimmer of surprise and dismay. He sits, just plops his dungaree-clad butt down on the dirt, reaches to hold Larry's hand, then closes his own eyes.

"Shouldn't've oughta tried it, nephew," he whispers. "Grab for a jerk's pistol that-a-way? Fuckin' stupid, Larry. Ain't nothin' hardly so dangerous as a coward with a gun, dint I always tell you that? And now, here we are."

Hank doesn't sob audibly, but his shoulders heave. A tear breaks loose from the outside end of his closed left eye and launches a complicated journey across ravines of his weathered face. It reaches his beard, escapes from view.

His eyes half open and gleam.

"Got to tell your ma, now. Ain't lookin' forward to that much."

A new sound breaks upon the scene, the buzz of an ATV in compound low, climbing up to the end of the ridge.

"God*dam*mit! You *freakin'* assholes!" Hank exclaims.

He leaps up onto his feet, grabs his rifle, runs at the truck to get more ammo. En route, he spots the deputy he shot, spread-eagled in his own patch of maroon-stained dust, with the dropped Ruger carbine lying at the rim of the broad splotch. He flings away his

SKS and runs over there, snatches up the Ruger. The corpse wears a canvas rack of fresh 20-round magazines on the front of his flak vest, so Hank rips up Velcro tabs, takes four clips, drops the partially used one out of the gun, and slaps a fresh mag home. Checks settings, see's it's on semi-auto but actually can go full-auto.

He smiles grimly, switches to auto, racks the bolt. Walks toward the sound of the approaching ATV. It's coming up the rough steep track they had driven to get the Power Wagon up here. He sees it crest at the rim of a draw, puts the crosshairs on a spot just in front of its wheels and holds down the trigger.

Dust and rock fragments spurt from the road and then chunks fly away from the vehicle's right fender. The driver stops, turns, and frantically drives off in the opposite direction.

Hank thinks about giving its driver another burst right in the spine before he vanishes, decides not to.

"Hell, you're just another bonehead depitty," he mutters. "You all now best steer clear of my path, you know what's any damn good for you…"

The cell phone in his hip pocket astonishes him when it bumps and buzzes. He's not often in a spot that receives a signal, and there's never many people who try to call him. He nestles the Ruger in the crook of his left arm and tugs out the phone with his free hand. Peers at the screen. Larry is calling. He can't help himself, his head rotates and he takes in his nephew, lying supine with a slack face turned up to the bright noonday sky. But after a second, he knows who's really on the phone.

His jaw works as he lets it ring a few more times before he thumbs a button and grunts, "Yep."

"I hear some guns shoot, so I think, maybe it's the emergency that you say," Linda says, "and I should call."

"Ain't no damn 'maybes' about it," is Hank's gruff response.

"So it is all right I call? What happens?"

"Yeah, *this* time."

There is silence on the other end.

"Did you use Larry's phone before?" Hank demands. "Last night? Tryin' to reach this guy named Dan Cowell?"

Long pause. "Yes, I confess, I am afraid I do that. I am sorry."

"Uh-huh, well guess what? Your call might just be what blew our whole deal up into a giant fuckin' mess."

"I am so sorry, it is a bad mistake that I do not totally keep my promise. But see, I think that I need to warn him, Dan…"

He brusquely cuts her off. "Larry's dead."

"What?"

"Larry… is… dead."

Pause. "Oh." Her voice goes small, registers dread and horror.

"Plus, so are a coupla more bastards, 'cluding the one that kilt Larry. Which'll rip the string off the shit-sack. Gonna be a total poop-storm 'round here in a bit." He pauses. "So, you might wanna award yourself a big dose of the credit for that."

Chapter 35

He'll miss this place, Leonid Andreyev confesses to himself. Oh, he owns access to a cluster of superlative play spots all around the globe, but he's always had a special feeling for Xanadu. It could be the sprawling vistas and wildness of the place, or the rustic period style of the lodge that bestows an air of the Old West — though he knows well that this decor is derived from movieland myth, not the tawdry historic truth.

He peers through large Leica binocs screwed to a tripod to admire a band of springbok, grazing on a dry, beige meadow about a half-mile out from the lodge balcony where he stands. As he watches, two bucks begin to "pronk" — as Afrikaners would call it — leaping high up and bending their backs as they make their white rump patches bristle. He imagines that it's an antelope signal of something or other.

Andreyev sighs. Not so long ago, he would've summoned a jeep and driver, then charged off in pursuit of those elegant beasts, standing in the bed of the jouncing vehicle, bracing a rifle on the roll bar, and snapping shots at a buck with the tallest set of lyre-shaped horns as he levitated across the landscape.

Excellent diversion while it lasted, he reflects. *But there will be many other places, more hunts. Besides, time has ripened, and I must focus single-minded on my goals. An hour is near to hand when we shall be strong enough, wealthy enough, to take down all pretenders and mere apparachiks in order to consolidate our power. We shall rule through our proxies, yet stand close behind them, unseen in the shadows, where we can remain unknown, untouched...*

A glass sliding door whispers open behind him. He turns to see Viktor escort a blindfolded Carl Blackadar out onto the balcony. As a sign of his newly enhanced status, Carl has been permitted to swap his yellow prison garb for a set of navy blue sweats. He's still a prisoner, though. He wears handcuffs that are cabled to a thick leather belt.

"Ah! You arrive for visit." The general beams. "Viktor?" He points to Carl's eyes and snaps his fingers.

Viktor tugs off Carl's blindfold. Carl blinks and looks at the general, who stands before him, clad in a white safari vest and khakis.

"My sincere praise for your recent triumph," Andreyev says.

"Thank you."

Carl knows immediately who the general is from all the files and photo surveillance he's seen. He turns his head to take in Viktor. The Serb commando's tight muscle shirt now is accessorized with a black leather shoulder harness. Under his left armpit dangles a Sig Sauer P250 Compact in a plastic fast-draw holster; under his right is a pouch holding spare clips. A flesh-colored wire drops from an earpiece down to a small radio transmitter Velcroed to the back of the harness.

Viktor's square face remains stern and vigilant, yet he seems to accord Carl a measure of respect.

Andreyev smiles cheerily. "Shall we sit?" He swings his hand toward a long table of slotted teak boards that's flanked by benches of the same construction. At the table's far end stands a stainless steel barbecue and tiled serving counter.

Carl's broken nose has been reset by an expert — himself — but not bandaged. Lacking any materials for that, he's jammed fat twists of toilet paper up both nostrils. He's wiped all blood away, but flesh around his eyes remains puffy and discolored. Breathing through his mouth, he nods at Andreyev.

"Thought you and I would meet up soon," Carl says. "Once I spotted your yacht down in Ecuador, figured I was closin' in."

"Man's fate meets him even on path he selects to avoid fate," the general says.

"Well, *you* might've planned to avoid me," Carl objects, "but I sure wasn't thinkin' along any similar line."

The general chuckles as he sits down on the far side. "Well," he says. "You finally win your great wish."

Carl lets Viktor guide him by an elbow and seat him across from the general.

Viktor takes up a stance right behind Carl, with his knotty arms folded across his chest.

"Ah, I praise you again on fight at Sojourn jail," Andreyev says. "How artful, to avoid grip of strong opponent." He mimes a reaching fist. "I see you do work to weaken him, on his left side. I think this strategy might have prevail. But then you win more quick, due to foolish bravado from Mister Cowell. Distracted, giant Mister Burnett falls victim to mere loop of cloth! I bet you'd win, ultimate. You bear fine legacy, true mind of conqueror."

"Uh, sure like to think so," Carl responds. "By the way, speakin' of Dan, where'd they take him?"

"Of Mister Cowell, I stay curious," the Andreyev says. "Your first thinking, after the blood of your victory, is to see to his care, immediate! Why does Cowell hold this much value?"

"No big mystery there — he's my friend."

"Not more?"

"Well he's sorta my partner, too. Once upon a time, we were brothers-in-arms. Navy."

"And now?" the general asks. "Do you not work same place?"

"Can't you just say what you're drivin' at, General?"

"Oh, yes. In due course."

"So where is Dan?"

"In the clinic, right here at Xanadu. Medical doctor introduces — is that proper word? — a coma. With narcotic. But Cowell needs better treatment, surgery, maybe. Does he get? We shall see. You recall, yes, you promise me good intelligence, trade for his well-being."

Carl nods.

"You know word, 'triage'?"

"I understand it," Carl affirms.

"Good. Cut losses, hm? Well, I find triage I must do today."

"How come? Things not going according to plan?" Carl asks.

The general smiles.

"Or, perhaps they are?"

Andreyev's smile broadens. He throws back his head, emits a laugh.

"Men say crisis means opportunity," the general says. "Well, true only when opening is taken. You see, that is genius in men like Alexander, Caesar, Napoleon, Lee, Zhukov, Rommel and Patton. Where other commanders stick to old plan, they shift on spur of moment.

"I first arrive," he tells Carl, "years ago, to Mister Nader's Xanadu to hunt. Like others. Yet I come for most exotic game. Or to say it different, I chase most exotic game… opening to let me to extend my business through the United States."

"Because you're hoping to…?" Carl asks.

"I tell of my goals only after I bring you in confidence. Let me just say, I feel disappoint. Mister Nader meets not my hopes, not my expectations. He and I must sadly part our ways."

"Mark know it yet?"

"Perhaps, he suspects."

"Interestin'," Carl says. "On the surface, you guys seem a great fit."

"Yes," Andreyev agrees. "But!" — he raises an admonitory forefinger — "Go deeper! And one finds Nader is traitor to his class, his blood. He becomes total unsuited."

"Now, what class is that?"

"Ruling class," the general says quietly.

Carl can't suppress a sardonic grin.

"Oh, I assure you, Mister Blackadar, I am in earnest." Andreyev puts both hands on the edge of the table and leans forward. With that flowing mane of combed white hair and classic profile, he'd look quite grandfatherly — except his light brown eyes don't twinkle at all, they're as intense as lasers of amber.

"Mark Nader boast true bloodline, he's of family that has noble past in East Prussia. I mean, five centuries ago, with Teutonic Order, before his ancestors are in America. And perhaps more further, to brave soldiers who fight with Saint Andrew Stratelates. But he proves to be not worthy of such heritage. He degrades himself with unholy lust, with lies, with foul behaving."

"Got an example?"

"You meet his big example before," the general says. "You fight and defeat him in the prison."

Carl takes this in. "Well… huh," he says.

The general holds up a palm. "Not to make only wrong. Carnal love between men, at times in history, that is artistic and for purpose. Ancient Greeks, tales of Achilles and Patroclus, Alexander and Hephaestion, three hundred Spartans — people forget, at gates of fire, these men battle next to lovers, eh? Even Templars, brother knights. I have sense Vatican is correct, the charge of inquisitor is no trump up.

"At time of hardship, a fraternity it turns inward, I accept this. Special relation among blood brothers. Even now, in my group, I agree.

"However! This degenerate, Mark Nader? He love Ted James Burnett, murderer, rapist, sadist? Idiot, no education, no culture, only criminal acts? Disgust. We obliged to handle such men, yet always we rule, not submit. Never! You understand me?

"Like with drugs. At times, money is needed badly, yes, drugs sold. As clever yellow fellow Mao did, early in revolution, with opium his 'special product.' But your people fall to tempt, be corrupt and use product?" Andreyev widens his eyes and slashes a finger across his neck. "Eliminate! Because they debase themselves. They depart ruling class, fall to lower orders. No longer to be trusted. Does not discipline go same way in your own warrior brotherhood?"

Carl clears his throat, nods. "Uh-huh," he says. "Yep, to a degree it does."

Andreyev inclines his head to demonstrate a regret that any such situation might ever occur among the knightly.

"And Burnett," he says, "profanes what he is not worthy to know."

"How?"

"He dares to call himself Ostrogoth."

"So? Just his old motorcycle gang."

Andreyev shakes his head emphatically.

"Genuine Ostrogoths still exist, *Ostgoty*, descended from ancient *Greuthungi*, whose kingdom goes from Black Sea to Baltic, from Volga to The West. We conquer Italy, take over from the Romans. In time, we blend with brothers known to you as Prussians, and Teutonic Order. And we preserve our ancient lore and way through the centuries."

"Yeah?"

Carl cranes his neck back to see how Viktor might be relating to all this twaddle. Viktor seems fascinated.

"Yes, Viktor is one of us," the general says serenely. "Special, with spiritual insight. Pure. It is easy to research bloodlines now, no matter how far one strays from motherland."

"No foolin'."

"Absolute. My staff can check, and in speed. Your Mister Cowell comes near ideal. Two degrees off. But *you*, Mister Blackadar, less than a single degree. And so it is day of great fortune, when your parents meet. Now *that* is fate!"

Carl looks thoughtful. "Huh," he says. "You know, from when I was small, I *always* felt that there was something unusual going on…"

"Call of true blood cannot deny," the general affirms.

"And now, you suggest a kind of special path may await."

"To rule!" Andreyev exclaims. "You are born to it. You walk into sunlight, like first time. After eyes adjust, you see colors as they are, your world is never the same."

"Tell me more."

Andreyev's smile goes almost ear to ear, and a king's ransom in dental implants gleams like a snowy ridge.

"Viktor?" he asks. "A toast is in order. Be so kind as you bring cold Stoli and glasses?"

"Why, don't you have any *slivovitsa*?" Carl asks casually.

The general claps his hands. "There, see, Viktor? This man has idea for proper thing, yes?"

"*Da!*"

Carl turns his head, sees the Serb too has broken into a smile — but his face is creased awkwardly, as if jovial expressions are unusual for him.

～

"Some men near Putin, they are rough bastards, Bortnikov and Zolotov, completely unworthy! Grand Russia, that is our common vision, but they are not ones to make dream of Ivan the Fearsome, of Peter the Great, come alive in world. Holy task must fall to others, of far more skill and finesse."

"Yeah? Like who?" Carl asks.

Andreyev does not answer. He smiles, his amber eyes shine, and he sips from his glass.

"Hey, I thought you and Putin were on the outs," Carl says.

"It's true I'm not at present very far 'in,' as one might say," Andreyev admits. "Not all great alliances or partnerships are clear at first. They become more obvious as they grow. Thus, even Putin might not yet grasp or acknowledge what I bring. But when I am ready, he shall indeed discover it. To his great joy, I assure you!"

Andreyev waves a hand expansively, slaps it down on the table. He curls his fingers around the crystal shot glass in front of him, raises it in a toast. "*Tvoye zdorovie,*" he says, clinks glasses with Carl and Viktor, tosses the tawny liquor to the back of his throat. Viktor follows suit.

"Ah!" Viktor growls. "*Pobeda!*"

Carl — who's had a single handcuff removed to make the drinking go easier — takes a tiny sip, then lowers his glass to covertly slop its contents out under the table.

"Men around Putin now, not so clever as they think." the general continues. "Say they wish to return pride in Grand Russia, and forge a new Soviet Union. *Govno!* This means bullshit. They undertake holy work in crass way. All hollow, Potemkin villages, like you say. They turn our ruble into rubble. Oppress and slay dissidents, not convert them. Money of smart people, it grows wings of geese now, flies out of Russia in big flocks. A hundred billion just last year, can you believe it? To where does it fly? Ver-rr-ry good question," he rumbles.

He snatches up the bottle of Bistra plum brandy — faintly beiged by cask aging — and pours more shots. He drains his glass, immediately refills it, plonks the bottle down.

"Not funds to be hidden and kept, but to give giant return! That means work with superior people. Best, most enduring power. Our tribe of knights, the *Ostgoty*! You ask, who has heard of them? Obvious answer. We take careful. Not to boast, not seek spotlight, this is stupid. Not to waste energy, time. To put correct measures and personnel in place, that is essence. Make noise only at need."

"Grand Russia must *not* be story, to keep patriots mesmerized. Project must be solid, deep, led by the wise. Ones who reach far, like roots of great tree. Ones who network, leap over border, slip past laws. Popular movement they use, yet they guide mob, never submit.

"Ours is ultimate network, we do it longer than anyone. Experts with no parallel! And elite, not just *Russkiye*, but many other countries, including yours too now, they swarm to us for security and for profit. 'Blind pool,' you know this term? Investment fund, discloses neither its assets nor its plans, yet stays highly attractive because it is reliable, and because its returns are spectacular.

"But we don't only protect and grow money. We also touch levers to guide politics and opinion. For example, now we have our staff positioned in what you might call far-right groups, some you hear of... *Front National* in France, *Golden Dawn* in Greece, the English Defense League in Britain..."

Andreyev looks to Viktor for assistance, and Viktor raises a paw to tick off more groups on his fingers. "*Jobbik* in Hungary, the *FPO* in Austria, *Frente Nacional* in Spain, *Fiamma Tricolore* in Italy."

"It is to defend pure blood," Andreyev says, "and slow — even if we cannot entirely prevent — pollution by barbarians, by servant class. Those of muddy ancestry formed by nature only to be ruled. Of course, as organization gain power, they can be of great use."

"So." Carl taps a finger against his shot glass. "Your outfit — which we called the 'Y's guys, like wiseguys, due to that letter 'Y' you seem to use as a symbol, is a global commercial enterprise, with the twin goals of creating a powerful underground economy, and a political infrastructure to control and sustain it? With an ultimate aim of putting the *Ostgoty* in charge — whether the general population gets to realize this, or not?"

"Well put," the general says.

"And some of your holy work involves use of the world's criminals, both inside and outside of prisons…"

"Think of us as great agrarians," the general says. "We milk cattle, slaughter hogs, shear sheep, herd goats. And foxes, rats, wolves? Yes, we use them also! Yet we must select. For example, this Ted James Burnett? Too foul, too degenerate, for effective use. And so eliminate."

"You can't, I don't know, evolve the guy?"

Andreyev shakes his head. "His blood is five degrees off. Impossible! And to say how degenerate, this gang, so-called Ostrogoths, he takes our symbol, how he hears of it, I do not know. But he imagined a snake's tongue? Not an idea more far from true!"

The general plucks a linen handkerchief from a pocket of his safari vest, and with a certain degree of ceremony, wipes flesh-colored makeup from the last joint of his third finger. He shows Carl the dark squiggle, the y-shaped rune that marks his skin.

"This is not 'Y,' or Cyrillic *che*. It is Upsilon, that Pythagoras himself says tells a fork in man's path. Glory fate takes one higher, or low road leaves one in mud of beasts and slaves."

"*Odanost, čast!*" Viktor exclaims. "Loyalty, honor!"

The general offers Viktor his handkerchief. Viktor wipes a finger to display his own Upsilon.

"Soon, this very day, we prepare you for your own mark," the general says. "And put our microbead under, next to bone."

"Ah. So I take it, you're invitin' me to join up?" Carl asks.

"No," Andreyev says.

Behind him, Carl hears Viktor emit a gruff chuckle.

"Incorrect. There's no 'inviting' stuff, for *Ostgoty*. We recognize man as worthy, and say he now belongs."

"And if that person happens to refuse?"

"Well, that shows degeneracy, does it not? To save for purity of blood, it is like he asks for his own elimination."

"I see. Well… then guess you'd better count me in."

"Good. To show loyalty, answer question. At United States Federal Bureau of Investigation, who is your boss?"

"Samuel Lundts," Carl promptly replies.

The general smiles. "I know Lundts is your named boss. Yet he is not real boss. Actual person is what I want."

"Why do you want him? What for?"

"It is not for you to question me!" Andreyev snaps. His air of good humor whisks off in a blink. Then the flash of anger melts into another brilliant smile. "However, I say. I wish to understand what he knows of my affairs, and why he sends you for me. Then I decide what to do about it."

Carl nods slowly. "All right, that makes sense." He sighs. "My real boss is Daniel Cowell."

Chapter 36

Hank has Larry's body bundled up in his sleeping bag. He is folding the lean-to tarp around it as a final cover, when he hears a sound of running footsteps. He jumps up, grabs the Ruger and whirls… to see Linda jog into the clearing. Holding the carbine at his hip, he trains it on her. Seeing the threat, she falters, slows, stops. They maintain a frozen stand-off. Then the end of the rifle droops.

"What the hell d'ya want?" Hank demands.

"I am sorry," Linda says. "I do… I did not want this."

"Mark Nader tole me he din't want it, too." Hank says. "Even so, the nasty fuck went and done it."

"Nader?" Linda is amazed. "Mister steampunk man?"

"'Zackly. And the prison boss, and the king of Sojourn, and the demon spawn of the scumbag clan that screwed us Purdy's out of our ranch, origin'ly. Guess that weren't enough trouble for Naders to make, so now they took up killin' us, too."

"He shoots Larry? Where is Nader now?"

"His soul's 'bout halfway to hell and speedin' on home," Hank says. "But his lousy corpse is over there, back of my truck. Left him where I done for him."

"I hear a helicopter fly, too, is that how he comes?"

"Uh-huh, him and the sheriff both. Skeedaddled out that way, too. Well, not all of 'em. Besides Nader, over yonder's a depitty won't be writin' anybody no tickets anymore. Tried just now to bring some more idiots up here in a quad, but I made 'em turn tail."

Linda briefly gnaws her lower lip. "Are you mad at me?" Her voice is unusually timid.

"Goddam right! What the fuck you think?"

She bows her head. Tears begin to stream down her cheeks.

"Can I see Larry?" Her voice has gone even quieter.

Hank snorts, shakes his head — whether he's negating her request or simply can't believe she has uttered it, at first is unclear. Then he goes to the folded tarp, lays down his rifle, raises a flap of the canvas, and beckons to her. Linda walks up, sinks to her knees. Larry's pale face has been washed of blood, and his curly blond hair combed. With his eyes closed and slack expression, he seems at peace. Yet nothing reduces the horror of seeing a young man so handsome and vital, with so many decades of life in store for him, now lying utterly immobile, wan, and drained of possibility.

Linda reaches out to lightly caress the pallid cheek. She puts both hands on his chest, leans her forehead down against him, and cries.

"I am sorry, I am sorry, I am so sorry…" she murmurs. "Terrible, terrible."

Hank coughs and looks away.

After a while she rises, and just stands to look down at Larry. Hank moves to stand beside her.

"You know, he was sorta in love with you," he says.

"Yes, he was so young," she says.

They gaze down at him. Then Hank bends over, folds the tarp back across his slack face.

"I beg of you to give me forgiveness. Please." Fresh tears stream down her cheeks. "Both of you."

Hank gives her a sharp look, says nothing.

"It is bad, a horrible mistake. I feel big fear for my husband Dan, and for one moment I can only think of calling to him. But I do not know *this* can happen..."

"Yeah, a mistake," Hank growls.

"I can not make up for it. But I pay for it in all the ways I can. Please."

"Oh, just shut up for a minute."

They stand side-by-side and stare down at the bundle that holds Larry.

"What will you do?" she asks, at length.

"Do?" He straightens. "You mean, next?" He scratches at his beard with his right hand.

"If we stay here, they come back, yes?" Linda says. "The ones who hunt for me? They now hunt for you, too. Serious!"

"Prob'ly right."

"So?"

"Have to think on that. Be a big insult to Larry's memory to let 'em do all their stuff 'zackly how they want, yeah." He scratches his beard on the other side. "But got to say, my first inclination is just to make a stand and blast 'em all to hell until I go total Winchester on ammo. Then I reckon Larry 'n' me can go chase animals about in the hereafter. You got any diff'runt ideas, lemme hear."

"I feel just awfully about Larry, too. And I own much guilt, which makes it a *very* bad feeling. I must do something. So I think we must revenge on them in a strongest possible way, because their blame is so much more."

"Okay..."

"They know who Dan is. Which makes my head spin! And they have his phone, which is how they catch my call. Do they also trap and have Dan? And Carl? Very, very bad, if this is so. I would say, we call your FBI in Washington, DC, but I bet they can now catch your call, too. So I think we must run out from here and go to law people in person, or at least go closer and call from a different place, where they cannot catch us."

"All right. But even far as we hightailin' outta here, gonna be tough. Got a bunch of undoubtedly pissed-off sheriff's depitties on this side, and a pretty tough private security force over on the Xanadu side. We're squoze in the jaws of a set of pliers, like."

Linda mulls this over. "When you kill Nader, in the truck? Do they know this? They see you?"

Hank shakes his head. "No, come to think of it, they din't. Saw me shoot at him, saw him run off, but that's 'bout it…"

"All right. They love cell phones. Does this Nader have a phone on him?"

"Don't know."

"Can you copy the way he sounds, do his voice?"

Hank's mouth bends into something that's not quite a smile. "Might could take kind of a shot at it," he says.

~

The back of the hutch is open, and Hank and Linda stand beside the chest that is full of snakes and the limp body of the ex-tyrant of Sojourn.

"Now, box side here is tall enough, the snakes can't strike high enough to flop out," Hank says. "Not most of 'em anyhow. Big 'un, maybe. So let's do it smooth 'n' quick." He brandishes the catch pole he holds, a thick staff with a noose on the end and a cord running down through eyelets along the handle.

"Plan is, I snag Nader's foot and pull it up. You grab on, hold it outside the box. I fish out a hand and I grab that. We both haul him out, give him a good shake, let him slide down onto the bed of the truck. Anything else come along, you jump out and let me deal, okay?"

Linda gives him a slow, serious nod.

"Right. Let's git 'er done."

He unlatches the box, raises the lid, lowers the pole and shifts it about. A sleepy rattle buzzes. A limp human foot wearing a black, zippered boot comes up, Linda snatches it as he shakes it out of the loop. Next, a hand that droops out of the cuff of a frock coat is hauled up. Hank grabs onto that, drops the pole. They both stand straight and pull. Now many rattles *whirr*, like a band composed wholly of maracas, playing fast and angry. Hank looks at Linda, they jointly give the corpse a jolt, then drag it over the rim of the box. Something slithers out of the other sleeve of the coat as the body rolls and drops — but it falls back into the box. Hank slams the lid.

"Drag him out in the sun."

Nader lies on his back on the rocky ground, slack-jawed, eyes wide, white and dull, his lean and lined face rictus in an expression of agony.

"Well," Hank says. "Lil' siesta the dude took sure din't do much for his looks."

"Ugly as sin," Linda agrees. She looks at Hank. "And if you don't wish to touch him anymore, I understand, and I'll do it," she says.

She kneels by his corpse and methodically pats it down. An inner breast pocket of his coat yields an iPhone in a black leather case, which she brandishes with a look of triumph and hands over to Hank. She continues, and comes up with a wallet, a wad of money in a silver clip, a notebook and two all-access card keys, one emblazoned with the Xanadu logo.

"Want these?"

"You can keep 'em."

"Your pockets are more."

"Okay." He stuffs the items into his jeans.

"Have you thought about what to say to them?"

"Uh-huh." Hank looks at Nader, mutters as if he is practicing the opening lines of a speech. He flips open the case, taps the Home button, and sees the image of a fingerprint pop onto the screen and the words, *try again.*

"Shit, it's locked!" he says. "Not a password, which is better I guess, but hell, friggin' thing already knows *my* finger's not right…"

He and Linda glance toward Nader's corpse simultaneously. "Must be a righty,'cos that's how he was shootin'," Hank mutters. "However, I did blast him in that hand." Linda pulls the limp hand straight out from the coat sleeve. Its shattered backside is clotted with gore, but when she turns it over, they can both see that all of the bloodstained fingers are perfectly intact.

She looks up at Hank. "How many tries, do you think?"

"Usually three, ain't it?"

"Does he need to be alive?"

"Maybe parts of him still are. Ain't been so long."

She studies the hand for a second, then spits on Nader's thumb and wipes it clean and dry on the dusty fabric of his frock coat. Hank holds the phone down to her, and she presses the ball of Nader's thumb against the Home button. The phone remains locked.

"One more try," she murmurs. She spits on the tip of the index finger, wipes that off.

"Whoa, one minute," Hank says. "This is Mark Nader we're talkin' 'bout, huh? So, why don't you try that 'ere middle finger?"

Linda looks dubious and hesitates, but complies. And when she touches the tip of the middle digit to the button, the phone opens up.

Hank grins. He checks the phone index under "favorites," under "recents," and goes back again. He sees SecXan and SecCon as his most likely targets — he's been around long enough to know those names signify the security centers, first at Xanadu, and then the main one at the prison — and he taps on the first. There's an instant answer.

"*Hey Mister Nader, great to hear from you, are you all right? We just had the county helo land with wounded. Apparently, the Purdys…"*

"Yeah. I got hit too, but it's superficial, and I've got my situation fully under control," Hank says. "Need you to send Lew and the active grounds patrol to the corner gate southeast, *de pronto*."

"Yessir. But is…"

"Just do it! The Purdys are heading that way, and I want them stopped. Don't be gentle about it. As soon as they are, have Lew come my way and pick me up. I'm at the south end of Findley Ridge."

"Sheriff's department made a report of recent gunfire…"

"That was me, giving the Purdys a send-off."

"…directed at them."

"That must've been the Purdys, shooting back at me. Had to be their stray rounds."

"We can send them up there now…"

"No. Listen, tell the sheriff's men to keep their distance. All they've done is fuck things up. I want to handle this totally with SecXan. And I'll call SecCon and tell them to stand by. Then I can send them right where they're needed."

"Yessir. Do you…"

"Shut up and listen. I'm heading over to a viewpoint now, and make sure the Purdys are still going south. If they turn off anywhere, I'll call back. Otherwise, I want this managed, good and quick and quiet. You hear me? Right. Out."

Hank ends that call, makes a similar one to SecCon at the Sojourn prison.

He looks at Linda. "'Kay," he says. "Our way's 'bout clear as we can hope for. Plan is, we sent their goons south while we go north, cut through the Xanadu fence, then bust out on their entrance road. What happens after? Be a pure lie to say I even know. Your guess is as good as mine! Hope we can reach some badge-holders ain't screwed up. Got an ol' buddy in the Texas Rangers, could try him, we don't reach some Feds. But 'fore we go for it? Arm ourselves best we can. Might need to put up buncha sparkle, we to make it out."

Linda holds up Nader's phone. "What about this? Do we keep it, or can they trace it, 'nah mean?"

Hank squints. "Best to lose it," he says. "And know what? I'm gettin' me an idea of just 'zackly how."

He goes to the truck and pulls out his catch pole. Then he grips a rope loop handle at the end of the snake box. "I'd back up, were I you," he says. "'Cos it's high time… to… free the vipers!"

With that, Hank drags the long plywood snake box out of the hutch and off the truck bed and lets it thump heavily on the ground. A chorus of tenor buzzing greets this particular move.

"Soundin' kinda agitated," he says. "Few more steps back, if ya please."

He unlatches the box, then dumps it over on its side. A reptilian tapestry rolls out, fat ropes of patterned skin woven into one another… yet speedily separating once the individual serpents feel real earth under their bellies, and they begin to writhe off in all directions.

Linda jumps back still further. Hank leans forward with the catch pole, and drops its noose just behind the broad, flat head of the largest snake. "Ah, and right *there* you are, my proud beauty…" he mutters. He tugs it closed, and the rattlesnake thrashes. He puts a boot on the snake's neck, pinning it to the ground.

He reaches into a battered crate just inside the truck bed and tugs out a roll of duct tape. He pulls off a foot or so of tape with his teeth, then gets a fresh purchase and rips the segment away from the roll. Holding the strip, he turns to Linda. "Phone?" he mutters. Amazed by observing his ease with the snakes, she hands it over. He lays the phone on the massive diamondback, then secures it by wrapping two loops of tape around the snake's body. He lifts his boot, then slips the pole's noose open to release the serpent.

"Now them lousy bastards can hunt it down to their heart's content," he says. "And I hope they find it!"

The snake wriggles enthusiastically away from the open air, the sunlight, and all its problematic interactions with humans.

He looks at Linda. "Help me put Larry up in the truck?" he asks. She nods. "Good. Got to bring that boy home to his mama... Then, after we get him loaded, let's scavenge up all we can find 'round here in the way of loose guns 'n' ammo. Remember, it's better to have it and not need it, than need it and not have it. Get me?"

Linda nods.

"As for him?" He points at Nader. "We'll leave his rasty ass out to get chewed up by the coyotes and buzzards. And just hope he don't gag 'em all."

Chapter 37

When Carl announces that Dan Cowell is his real boss, Viktor and Andreyev lock eyes for a moment — and their mid-air swap of thought is so clear and vivid that it's nearly visible.

Can that be true that Cowell's the one in charge? The woman Melanie Olson Symes did not think so. Yet, it may be possible.

We must have them confront each other, then, to see who is telling the truth.

"Make sure Dan stays alive," Carl says, "and maybe you end up gettin' two for the price of one."

"Ah," Andreyev responds. His tawny eyes crinkle at the corners. "But, two of what?"

"Ostrogoths," Carl says. "You know, Upsilon knights."

"We shall see. But, let me inquire. What say you to chance of three? At times, women of talent also prove good for our organization."

"Who'd you have in mind?"

"Young and clever one, your Melanie Olson Symes."

Carl blinks, tries to keep his voice steady. "Yeah? Where'd you find her?"

"Mark Nader holds and abuses her badly for a time. But we decide that period must end."

"Where's she now?"

"Safe. In clinic, right here, in this lodge. She is being treated."

"For?"

"Injury. From car wreck they make for her capture. And other activities, many of them quite unworthy."

"I want to see her."

"Thought you might. And I hope you can observe, we do take your major interests to heart, yes?"

"Is Linda Parker with Melanie?"

The general purses his lips. "Her companion? No. Perhaps soon. But we have asked into her, and I think Linda Parker does not qualify for any help from us," he says.

"Why not?"

"She must be at least thirty degrees off! A bloodline of minimal use."

"And what about Nader?"

"We think of him, we dismiss him." The general spreads his hands and smiles. "Let us say he's opted for early retirement."

"Proned out on a slab?"

"Crude, but close," Andreyev says. "However, we look for no blame. It will seem like choice on his part. The death of companion is big distress. He cannot handle. Too sad."

As they speak, the sound of a flying helicopter grows louder. Viktor abruptly cups a hand around his earpiece, stiffens and scowls. The general looks at him, eyes narrowing.

"What?" he barks.

"Gunfight…" Viktor says, trying to listen and talk at the same time. "Ambush… by Purdys… sheriff was shot… Nader wounded and left there… but he fights Purdys off… they flee from Nader and deputies… go south… pilot flies sheriff right to clinic now…"

"*Drisnya!*" the general exclaims. Then he lowers his eyes, rubs his chin for a moment. When he looks up, he's smiling. "Yet… all it really means is we speed up time of departure."

Viktor thinks that over, nods curtly.

Andreyev points at Carl. "Secure him."

"Hey, wait a minute. Aren't we brother knights now and all o' that?" Carl protests.

"Emergency plan must rule," the general soothes. "You professional, so you understand perfect. No concern! We shall return for you." He flicks a glance of command at Viktor.

Carl glances at him, too. Viktor is strong, trained, experienced and fit. Equipped with a weapon he likely can use quite well. Out in the open, with surprise on his side, Carl figures he might have a chance to take him. But with his left hand still cuffed to his waist and Viktor armed and keyed up by news of violence, he'd have about zero.

Therefore, Carl meekly holds both of his wrists out above the slotted teak table. "Okay, guess I can be cool with that," he says. "But please, let me stay out the deck here, so I can at least see what's goin' on. All right?"

Viktor cocks his head, evaluates this proposal. Andreyev nods an affirmative, so he unlocks Carl's other cuff, feeds both of them up through one of the slots at the center of the table, and locks them around Carl's wrists again. He checks the cable that leads from Carl's waist, makes sure it's secure as well. Carl now is thoroughly shackled to the center of the heavy table.

Dust and wind and leaf litter and engine noise rush over the balcony rail as the chopper lands on a grassy strip in front of the lodge. Xanadu staffers shove a rolling gurney along as they trot toward the aircraft and a woman jogs with them who swings a black medical bag from one hand. The rotor slows, and the pilot jumps from the cockpit, goes to the opposite door, swings it open. Sheriff Baxter kneels there, blood welling out of the seat of his pants and gushing down his legs.

Carl swivels his head to watch Viktor and Andreyev hustle off the balcony and exit the suite, then waits a full ten seconds. He carefully pushes the bottle of slivovitz back and clambers onto the table so he can lie down on it. His toes point toward the stainless steel barbecue. The cable won't move any farther, it's halted by a stout crossbeam. He stresses the cable and stretches his body, until he's able to reach the closed hood of the barbecue with a foot. He kicks the handle, and the hood glides up.

He strains to see past his own feet, spots a butane-fueled lighter. *Way better score than matches! Well, maybe...* He struggles to elongate himself another inch, and scrapes the lighter with the tip of a toe. Yet he's also jiggled the lighter farther out of reach. *Still near enough for one more try. Don't blow it...*

He closes his eyes, hauls against the cuffs until the steel bracelets jam into the backs of both hands and the leather belt is jerked up toward his breastbone. He bends both ankles to the maximum, gently moves the toes of his shoes toward one another. He feels it, he's pinching the thing. *Now, what? One swift move. Gradual won't cut it.*

Knees splaying, he yanks both feet up. The lighter flies out of the steel barbecue and skitters on the table. He can't believe his good luck, but then as his knee flops back down it knocks the lighter off.

Cursing, he wriggles back onto a bench until he's sitting, looks under the table and tries to reach the lighter again. He steps on the nozzle, slides his other foot under the trigger and reservoir handle and raises that shoe slowly. The lighter trembles and waggles, but stays balanced on his foot until he's able to dump it onto the bench. He gets back on the table, leans over the bench, grabs it with his teeth, picks it up and drops it on the table. He sits down again and scoots everything — himself included — down to the table's far end, where he pours the slivovitz on the two-inch-thick end beam at both corner joints. He thumbs the wheel of the lighter and sets the table on fire.

Teak is tough, dense wood, but this table is old, sun-bleached and dry. It burns readily, and he drops off the end of the bench to get away from the heat. Lying on the deck beneath the table, he can see its corners are reinforced by metal angles, so he reaches up and pours more of the high-proof liquor on these areas.

He pulls the cable taut and squats as far away from the flames as possible. As he waits impatiently for the table to weaken, Carl thinks. Andreyev said they had a plan to cut out, so they must've made preps. One aspect must've been setting up Nader to get whacked. Probably an inside job. Must mean the general's been offering bribes and turning staff when he's made his visits. Far from bringing Nader in as a partner, from the very start he figured he'd maneuver to take his operation over, and use it to get cranked up in the U.S. after making sure that Nader has set it up the way he likes.

But this fresh attack — *by the Purdy people, whoever the fuck they might be!* — isn't part of that plan, or Viktor wouldn't have gotten so lit up. *So. Purdy...rogue competitor? Traitor?*

Sam Lundts must be in this scheme up to his eyeballs. But, a Texas sheriff getting plugged, especially if he ends up dead, how's that going to play? Damn hard to explain. General says, speed up departure. Well, sure! Last thing they need is Rangers and-or Feds to hit Xanadu with a full-court press. *Lundts must be crappin' his skivvies right now.* Got a foot on the dock, and one on the boat. But his only real choice is leaping aboard with Andreyev. His career in DC is already toast... toast burnt black.

I'm gettin' loose. I'm takin' Lundts out. And I'm gonna find and rescue Mel!

Carl hears the roar of multiple vehicle engines. He stands up so he can see over the balcony rail — although the side of his body nearest to the burning table begins to feel scalded. He watches a quartet of jeeps and ATVs crowded with grayclad men holding guns speed away from the compound toward the south.

He glances at the fire, judges its damage as almost sufficient.

He squats, braces his feet against the lower table legs, grips the cable with both hands and gives a heave. The teak beam he wants to break offers a groan, and few sparks shower down. He doesn't bother to try to shake them off. He readjusts his hands, bends his back, and makes another mighty effort. The beam wrenches free and he's just able to turn his head in time to take a clout from it on his ear instead of directly on his broken nose. This time he does brush aside crumbs of the burning wood, leaps on his feet, and yanks the cable loose. Now he's free to move, though his hands are still cuffed together and cabled to his waist.

The hardwood table burns hot, it doesn't smoke. Thank heaven for small favors, he thinks. And now — let's score a weapon!

He runs into the general's suite, looks around. *C'mon you duke of the ancient Ostrogoth barony or whatever the hell, how come you don't even hang a friggin' sword on your wall?* He sees a brass poker in a stand of tools by the fireplace, goes and grabs it, then advances on the general's walnut desk. The side drawers open freely, but they only hold mail, office supplies, and files; the central drawer is locked. He rams the tip of the poker in at the top of that drawer and cracks it open. Slides it out. Sees a Beretta 950 with two loose clips, and snatches them up. Checks the top of the clip, sees the gun's chambered for .25 ACP.

Great. Fricken popgun. Good thing I've got a poker. It's more dangerous…

He slaps a clip into the automatic pistol, drops the gun and its spare clip into a pocket of his sweatpants.

On the desk is a dish of stout paperclips. He seizes one, bends it out into a prong, crimps it into a slight hook, and uses that to pick the locks on his handcuffs. Next he unlocks the belt, and almost removes it, but after thinking about it, leaves it on, coils the cable and tucks it and the cuffs under the leather.

He runs into the bedroom, sees a quartet of suitcases at the foot of the bed. He opens all four, dumps their contents, finds no weapon, but does see a zippered pouch full of 64-gig SD cards. He stuffs that into the front of his underpants. Checks the closet, finds nothing interesting.

He enters the den, looks at the intricate cabinetry on the bookshelves. He taps, pushes and pulls on things, trying to discover a latch to open any kind of hidden compartment. As he moves, he idly notices the array of photos of Jack London. He notes one framed shot of Jack in a white suit, tie, boots, and sombrero, leaning back against a stone wall. On its butt beside the author, also leaning on the wall, is a new rifle.

Beneath that picture is a tooled wood panel. He raps on it. Space behind it sounds hollow. He grabs, tugs and pounds on all parts of the woodwork, but nothing budges. Finally, he two-hands the poker like a Louisville Slugger and bashes the panel's center, splintering it. That impact also jolts and prompts a servo. The cracked wood panel tilts up and glides from view, while a big drawer upholstered in red felt slides out. On it are three guns, along with their cleaning kits and ammo boxes. Two are hunting rifles — a Dragunov sniper rifle with a black polymer stock, and a scoped Winchester .30-06 mounted on burled Circassian walnut. The third is more industrial and brutal-looking piece: a short SRM 1216 semi-automatic shotgun, with a sixteen-round rotating magazine and adjustable sling. Next to it are four boxes of 12-gauge rifled slugs and double-ought buckshot.

He chooses instantly. He grabs the shotgun, promptly stuffs two tubes of the four-barrel magazine with slugs, and the others with buckshot. He crams as many extra shells as he can into both pockets of his pants as well as the hand-warmer pouch on the belly of his sweatshirt.

He next goes into the suite kitchen and rummages through supplies under the sink, coming up with a can of oven cleaner, a pressurized can of furniture polish, and a can of wasp and hornet spray. The label on the wasp spray proclaims that it can squirt a dense stream of poison for twenty feet. From a block of knives on the counter, he selects a keen meat-carving knife with a nine-inch blade and slips that under his leather belt on his left side.

OK, loaded for bear. Let's go see if I can find one.

He peeks outside, sees that the burning table on the balcony has collapsed and begun to smolder the rubberized deck coating. He wonders how well that stuff will burn. That gives him an idea. He goes back to the kitchen, tosses the two cans of polish and oven cleaner into the microwave, sets it to operate on high for 20 minutes, and punches the ON button.

Chapter 38

The Power Wagon lurches across untracked terrain in compound low gear. Linda braces herself with one hand shoved against the cab roof while her other keeps a white-knuckled grip on the door handle.

"Now, Xanadu does a hecka job with their fences, 'cept in one spot," Hank says. "'Bout four years back, they tried a 'speriment with cape buffalo that din't work. Them big ol' critters love to wallow in mud, and it was a dry summer. So couple of buffs come up a draw to break out. Even stout wire has no chance 'gainst a bull weighs a ton. Two busted through. One met a pickup on the Nopales road that totaled the bull and the truck.

"T'other made it into Nopales and went apeshit. Tore up the village worse'n cowhands on a toot! Took rounds from every shootin' iron people could lay hands on to settle that bull's hash. Which is the word! They skun it out, butchered and wrapped it, and jammed freezers full left 'n' right. For a year the café in town had a special on buff' steaks 'n' burgers. And when they finished payin' off all the damage done, Xanadu decided they din't need nothin' that rasty on the ranch ever agin'. And din't have it. Least, not 'til now, with you'n'me showin' up…"

Linda looks at him, nods. She intuits that his now-relentless telling of barely relevant stories is a way Hank copes with stress — in particular, the calamity that's resulted in hauling his nephew's shrouded body along with them in the bed of the truck.

"Anyhow, a guy they hired to fix that big hole in their fence din't do such a great job," Hank says. "Which would be me. Oh, I hooked it up 'n' all, but kinda loose, so if I ever had to grab me a shortcut in or out in a hurry, there'd be a spot where I could do it. And, well… here it comes."

The truck's groaning suspension straddles a rocky trough as the knobby tires scratch for traction. Ahead, a net of wire looms before the dusty windshield. Hank doesn't slow down. Steel wire wraps the front bumper and hood, shrieks and snaps and falls away, and then they're over the crest and descending a steep and rumpled slope.

"Think more critters might escape through now?" Hank speculates. "Not my problem! Our big hurdle now is gettin' out past the airstrip, 'fore we hit the entrance road. A thing in our favor, though, I'd say, is total surprise. Ya think?"

～

The general's suite is huge, well-insulated, and Carl has run far enough down the hall that when the microwave oven explodes the pressurized cans, he just hears a dull *whumpf!* But he can well imagine a sheet of flaming shrapnel fanning out across the general's kitchen.

He reaches an intersecting hall, hears other people approaching, flattens himself against a wall. As they come around his corner, he has a split-second to look, judge, and act. He sees one young man in Xanadu gray pushing a laundry cart, and an older, more portly one wearing a duty belt hung with small black holsters — probably holding basic security gear like CS spray and a collapsible baton.

Carl nails them both with a jet of wasp spray. They stumble, clasp hands to their faces, sputter and choke. He jumps out, swings an arm and clips the fat one in the side of the neck — aiming his knife-hand strike below the jaw, at the carotid artery and vagus nerve. He drops like a felled ox. Carl kicks the younger one in the balls, grabs him by the front of his uniform and slams him down on the floor.

"Your med clinic, where is it?" he hisses.

"Agh," he gags. "Uh… it's back, one floor down, south side…"

"Keys?"

"He… he has…"

Carl sees a magnetic master badge on a retractor keychain clipped to the lapel of the older man, and snatches it off. He deploys it to enter the nearest suite door, grabs the kid by the scruff of the neck and hurls him inside.

"Find a sink, wash that crap out of your eyes," he orders. "Don't come out for ten minutes. Got it?"

"Y-yes…" The youth rises into a crouch, looks back at him through one bleary, half-closed eye. "Who are you?"

"Janitor," Carl says. "Fresh hire. Aim to put a real shine on this joint."

A fire alarm goes off, its clanging bell, instantly echoed by other alarms in Xanadu lodge. Carl sprints across the hall and into a stairwell, hurtles down the stairs, spins around the landing and meets someone running up the steps — gray crewcut, square face, and a bulging torso shrink-wrapped in black silk. Viktor halts, stares, reacts. He yanks his Sig Sauer out. Carl lowers and levels the semi-auto shotgun. They both trigger their weapons and the stairwell fills with thunder.

Carl feels a slap on his left cheek that twists his head. Since he's firing buckshot he's not too worried about his aim, just keeps tugging on his trigger. After four rounds the slide hangs open and he rotates the magazine to the tube of slugs.

Smoke and concrete dust churn lazily in the stairwell's abrupt stillness.

Carl inhales the acrid scent of burnt powder, a combat stink that jacks his nerves to a higher pitch.

No sign of Viktor. No blood spatters the steps. But he pats his own cheek, and his palm comes off smeared by crimson. *Cheekbone and teeth feel okay, though, so no biggie. Just a graze. But my oppo evades, knows I'm free, can come back on me with major ass. That, I need to counter...*

Carl bounds up the stairs, bursts into the hall, uses the access key on the nearest suite door, runs through it and out onto the balcony. A glance left reveals black gouts of smoke starting to billow from the general's rooms, and he smiles. A look down shows him a van backing up to the building. Its rear doors swing open and a gurney crew appears, shoving along a wheeled stretcher with sheet-draped body on it. Carl squints at the thickly bandaged head and face and shoulders, trying to make out the identity of the patient. He remembers Viktor saying a sheriff got shot, recalls the sight of the tall, pudgy guy with the bloody butt who clung to the helicopter seat. *Same guy? They taking him to a real hospital now? No, they'd have him lying face down...* Then he gets a better angle on the face and is shocked. *Fuck, it's Dan! They're taking him away!*

Andreyev, Lundts, and Viktor Mandić stride into view together. Viktor waves his arms and gesticulates wildly. Plumes of smoke and flame are spiraling out of the general's suite and they turn as one to gape at it. They also spot Carl and claw for their guns. Viktor's draw is swift and smooth, he's already aligning the sights as he brings the Sig up. The general also has a big pistol, a .45, but he catches its hammer on fabric as he tries to tug it out from under his safari vest and drops it. Lundts actually pats himself down, it's ludicrous, he apparently knows he's got a gun on him someplace but in the heat of the moment can't recall exactly where.

Carl only has time for one shot, and he doesn't hesitate. His runty shotgun *boom*s and jolts. A 12-gauge rifled slug drills Lundts dead-center through the sternum, launching him into low flight as ruptured body tissues fan out around him in a scarlet nimbus.

Viktor's shot *pings* off the balcony rail and whirrs past his ear. Carl doesn't wait to see if his aim improves. He ducks down and scrambles on hands and feet backward and to the right. Now the crack of Viktor's Sig is mixed with the bass thump of something with more heft — Carl guesses the general has involved his .45.

The shots abruptly stop. Carl hears the van engine roar and its tires squeak, then a clatter of gravel flung up against the side of the building. He peeks up over the railing and sees the van rapidly pull away. Also, he sees a pair of men wearing black, not SecXan gray, who peer through sights on automatic rifles as they scan back and forth across the balconies. One spots him, immediately fires. Bullets *whap* and *ring* and *buzz* as they stitch across the building and the second gunman joins the first in hammering away at Carl's balcony.

Carl drops, writhes on toes and elbows toward the door that opens onto the deck, moves up to hands and knees, then gets to his feet and sprints through that suite and across the hall — he hears shouting in the hall but sees nobody — slaps his key on a lock and enters a suite on the other side of the lodge.

This unit does seem to have a tenant — clothes and possessions are strewn about, a large-screen TV is on with its sound turned down — but he or she does not appear to be present. *Likely fled at the sound of the initial fire alarm.* He shoves curtains apart, yanks open a balcony door and rushes out to the railing.

He's on the north side of the lodge, and looks straight down into a small parking lot with a high fence and a gate secured by a padlocked chain. This lot holds a Jeep Grand Cherokee with a prominent Xanadu logo and an amber emergency light bar — and it also contains a hopped-up, sleek Dodge Challenger. It's the very same vehicle deployed to gas and abduct Dan and Carl at the Corpus Christi airport.

Well there you are, my sweet lil' kick-ass whip....

He goes back to the door into the suite, yanks both curtains off their tracks. Pulls the kitchen knife from the leather cuff belt, and uses it to slice off the top and bottom of each curtain, where the fabric is triple thickness and stitched. He ties these together with square knots, and then fastens one end to the balcony railing. He pulls it up between his legs, wraps it over one shoulder and drops it back past a hip so he can begin to rappel, when he hears a sharp hiss. He whirls, reaches for the trigger of the shotgun, but sees the suite's ceiling sprinklers have just begun to spray.

Fire must be starting to spread into this wing. Good.

He goes over the rail, lets fabric slip through his fists, can feel the skin on his palms tear a bit as the knots jolt by, doesn't care. It's two yards short, so he drops the last bit onto the asphalt of the lot. Runs to the Challenger. Keys are in the ignition.

Must rely on the locked gates for security.

At the gate, he pounds the lock with a slug from the shotgun and shatters it. Pulls down the chain.

Runs back to the Challenger. Cautiously opens the door. Pokes at the seat. Looks under it. Sees the screws and frame of a mount for the gas equipment, now empty, and a loose electrical wire with a plug. He sits, lays his weapon on the passenger seat, twists the key. A look that's both grim and satisfied crosses his face as the engine bellows to life.

He guns the big V-8 a few times, shifts into first, puts his foot down and blasts out through the gate, whacking its chain-link panels aside as if they were made of pasteboard.

Chapter 39

Hank has to focus on wrestling the Power Wagon down a trackless hill, so it's Linda who spots the thick cloud of black smoke first.

"Look!" she says. "That is the Xanadu? It is on fire!"

"Huh! 'Peers so." He sounds cheerful.

"No, it is not nothing!" Linda's brow is furrowed. "People there are in danger, okay."

"Sure. It's a fire."

"I mean, those I know!"

"Like who?"

"Melanie, my friend, who I am travel with? If they catch her, where do they take her? Maybe this place!"

"Hm. Yeah, okay, Nader and our sheriff were tight, and they were out huntin' you. Fair guess he'd want Melanie too. If he had her, wouldn't stick her someplace obvious, like Sojourn jail or Baxter's lock-up in the Springs. Xanadu *is* prob'ly where they'd bring her."

Linda snaps her fingers, points. "Then, we go," she asserts.

"Hold on. You mean, not get our own lil' curly tails outta the fryin' pan, but go jump onto that fire instead?"

"Yes."

"Rrrrr…" Hank growls, claws at his beard. "Okay. What about findin' some outside 'thor'ties we could trust? That's important, too! But… y'know… way Xanadu is puttin' up smoke, 'thor'ties'll come to us, mebbe a passel of fire trucks, minimum. Means good guys with good radios out the yin-yang." He shrugs. "So, sure, let's go try to find your pal. But there's guard staff down there too, kind of people don't cotton to intrusion. Regular security, and Russkies as well. So prep yourself for that!"

"You mean, we bring the sparkle?"

He grins. "'Zackly.' Cos I'm still feelin' ornery 'nuff to want to shoot somethin', and 'bout any a' them bozos down there'll do for a target."

~

Carl fishtails through a left turn on the lodge driveway and straightens the car up just in time to swerve past a man in a gray jumpsuit who runs toward him with both palms held up. Carl spins the wheel, stomps the brakes, the Challenger goes sideways, rocks, halts. He levels the shotgun out the driver's side window. The man blanches, dives across the curb and vanishes into a thatch of decorative shrubbery.

He spins the wheel, pushes the pedal, the Challenger's V-8 raps out a throaty bellow, he blasts down the road and screeches around a turn.

One of the black-clad men with an automatic rifle suddenly appears in the windshield, his jaw is dropping, he's wheeling around to aim at Carl who floors the accelerator and the guard takes the front bumper at his knees and does a bloody faceplant on the windshield, cobwebbing the glass, then his body thumps and clatters over the roof and drops behind the car. *Huh, looked like he held an M-4,* Carl thinks, *should I stop, and grab it? Naw, could be all busted up. And at least one more of 'em armed bastards I need to handle super-quick…*

He whips around another corner. Now he sees the parked Bell

helicopter, furrows ripped in the turf by tires of the fleeing van, and the limp body of Lundts, staring up past tangled tree branches at the bright sky, his face pale and blank, his blue suit darkened by blood. Then he hears a roaring truck engine, scattered gunshots. He stops, swivels his head, sees a battered truck with an old plywood camper shell that slews through zigzag turns down a hillside as it heads for the lodge. A woman with a mane of black hair is leaning out the passenger window and firing at the last remaining armed guard.

An enemy of my enemy must be a friend, is Carl's swift assessment, but he's surprised and puzzled by this development.

The guard flips onto his back as his own rifle looses a final burst at the sky.

Carl double-checks the shooter in the truck as it roars toward him, and is stunned. *Well screw me naked,* he thinks, *it's Linda.*

He flings his car door open, gets out, and raises both hands.

The truck slews and skids to a halt ten yards away, and bobbles on its suspension.

A door screeches as it's yanked open, Linda hops out, almost levels her rifle at him, gasps, then drops it. Carl's broken nose and gashed cheek — plus the fact that his presence at Xanadu is fully unexpected — made him hard to recognize at first. Now she runs toward him.

He runs too. They meet, their arms wind about each other, he smells female sweat and hints of coconut and ginger on her hair, suddenly understands he's always picked up notes of tropic aroma in her presence.

She pushes him back, they stare at one another, and the eyes of both cradle glistening tears.

"I should be surprise to see you, yet I feel no surprise," Linda says.

"Take it, you folks happen t'know one another," Hank says. He stands a few yards off, his bayonet-pointed SKS rifle droops from the crook of one arm.

"Yep!" Carl affirms, while Linda nods vigorously. They move apart.

"Melanie," he says. He points to a plate glass window on the lodge bottom floor that has a foot-high cross of red on it. "That must be their clinic. Told she's there. And basically okay, too, if these assholes been talkin' straight. Which maybe they haven't."

Her cheeks flush, and she raises her hands to them. "I so hope this is true," she murmurs. "For three days, I worry so bad for Mel. And Dan… Dan is where?"

"In a minute. Mel's up first. Let's get her."

"An armed and wounded sheriff might be inside, too," Hank says. "Flew here on that chopper. 'Cos I shot his ass up."

"Ah. So you must be one of the Purdys."

"Yep. I'm the one that's left."

"Did Linda bring you into this?"

"Might say that. She hadn't, we'd be way better off."

Carl sees that Linda looks distraught. Clearly it's a bigger story, yet there's no time to get into it. He grasps how badly she needs to hear about Dan.

"Look. Viktor and Andreyev just sped off in a van, my guess is they're heading for the Xanadu airstrip. They took Dan with 'em."

Linda is startled, then looks fierce. "Who? Why?" she demands.

"More details later, okay? Basically, it's my bad. Told 'em Dan was my boss. Seemed like a great idea at the time. Thought he'd get better care. However, now, the Russky general thinks Dan is one huge cache of high-value intel. We need to prevent 'em from takin' off. Or God only knows where they'll take him. And it could play badly once he finds out Dan ain't got the goods. So let's grab Mel if we can, then move on the airfield."

Carl looks at Hank. "Ever clear a room?"

Hank gives a shrug. "Back in the day," he says, "I trained up with the Rangers."

"Okay. I'm on point. To cover, Hank, stick right back of me. Linda, you're reinforcement. Grab up your rifle, let's roll."

∾

Carl fires a slug high through the plate glass window that bears a cross. Shattered glass still falls as he yanks open the door and rushes inside. He aims his shotgun at the first two people he sees, a plump nurse and a skinny orderly, who are kneeling behind a desk with their hands up.

"Don't shoot!" the orderly begs. The nurse wails like it's her final hour.

"The sheriff! Where's he?"

The orderly points toward a half-open door. The end of a white-sheeted bed is visible.

"Due to the fire… and all the shooting… we're getting patients prepped to evacuate…" the orderly says, his Adam's apple jerking nervously in his throat.

Carl runs at the door and kicks it wide, sees the bed is empty, then spots a man crouched behind it with a dark mass of metal in his hand, sees he doesn't even have enough time to aim his own gun and shoot. He drops and does a backward somersault back out the doorway at the same instant the sheriff's pistol fires and a bullet splinters the frame. Carl completes his roll and bounces to his feet, trains the shotgun.

Then come six ear-splitting thunderclaps. Hank has fired metal-jacketed bullets from his SKS right through the wall and into the room.

Carl edges back to the door, takes a furtive peek around the frame. He puffs out his cheeks and releases a breath.

"Okay, you got him. But shit, coulda been someone else in there too, you know? Just dumb luck there wasn't."

"Right," Hank says. "Sorry, felt a bit worked up. Thought he'd nailed you."

The orderly is still bug-eyed, his hands are up and his knees shaking. The nurse now lies prone on the floor, her back heaving, and she snivels into her cupped hands. Linda is in the doorway with the Ruger, sweeping its muzzle back-and-forth, seeing if there's any fresh target to acquire.

"Who else you got in here?" Carl demands.

The orderly points to another door, this one fully closed. "It's the woman…"

"Melanie?! Olson?"

As soon as his thin face jerks in a nod, Linda drops her weapon and leaps for that door.

"Wait!" Carl yells, but she ignores him and yanks the door open.

"Girl!" they hear her shout. She enters, Carl rushes in behind her.

Melanie lies on a bed in fetal position, curled around a pillow. Teary, red-rimmed eyes are tentatively raised to them, her mouth becomes an "O" of astonishment. Linda sits on the bed, tugs on the pillow. Mel lets the pillow go and wraps herself around Linda instead.

Mel sees Carl and he reaches for her, but she closes her eyes, shrinks away from him. With a faint cry she buries her face in Linda's soft curves. Carl is nonplussed and left staring down at her. His hands drop to his sides.

He taps Linda's shoulder. "Love it if we had more time to deal, but we don't. Get her in the car."

Linda nods, picks up a folded blanket at the foot of the bed, starts to drape it around Mel's shoulders like a shawl at the same time she seeks to get her to sit up, and then they see that one wrist is cuffed to the bed frame.

"Goddammit," Carl shouts. "Unlock her!"

The orderly enters the room and does so, then slinks away.

Bundled in the blanket, half-supported by Linda, Melanie is able to stagger outside all the way to the Challenger. She blinks in the sunlight, looks around herself with bleary eyes.

"Back seat," Carl says curtly. "Belt her in. You jump in front with me. Keep your rifle out." Even as he speaks, he stuffs fresh shells into the tubes of the shotgun's magazine, then snaps it into place.

"Where d'you want me?" Hank asks.

"Ride with us, you want to."

"D'ruther take my truck. Be slower, but my nephew's in the back. Can't leave him."

Carl observes Linda flinch, realizes there's an issue with that.

"Nephew?"

"He's gone."

Carl looks from one to the other. "Sorry," he says. "But okay, we've gotta rock 'n' roll."

He jumps in the driver's seat, fires up the Dodge. Spins its tires and fishtails away from the lodge, accelerating in the direction he saw the van take, presumably toward the airstrip.

Hank runs for his truck. As they leave Xanadu behind, black smoke continues to gout from the lodge. From the distant main gate of the resort comes a banshee wail of fire truck sirens.

Chapter 40

At the airstrip, several light aircraft are tied down on concrete pads out in front of small hangers. Andreyev's floatplane warms up on one apron. The white van is stopped beside it, all doors agape. Viktor sits in the pilot's spot, the general stands on one of the plane's pair of canoe-like floats, and is being helped up into the cockpit. Carl takes it all in with one sweeping glance as he steers the Dodge Challenger onto the airstrip. He aims at the general's plane and boots the accelerator. Just as he does so, the aircraft starts to move.

Linda, twisted around in her front seat, has a hand on Mel's upper chest, to keep her from sliding. Mel has both her hands clasped on top of Linda's. Her eyes are half-shut, her breathing is shallow and rapid.

"They're takin' off!" Carl yells. "Get ready!"

"For what?" Linda asks.

"I've no idea!"

Viktor sees them coming. He taxis the Pilatus Porter down to the runway's far end, its engine humming like a hornet, its three-blade propeller whirling in a blur. Carl knows a Pilatus has short take-off ability, but it's toting a load of at least four passengers. What he doesn't know is how much runway that demands.

"Don't want to crash it, so I guess we want to disable it," he shouts. "Dan's on it!"

Linda nods, checks the Ruger's chamber, clicks off the safety.

Carl aims the Challenger straight at the floatplane. Viktor swivels it for take-off, which also aims it straight at them. He cranks up his RPMs, the plane accelerates. And Viktor calls Carl's bluff in their game of chicken. Carl curses, twists the wheel, and throws the car into a slide as the plane whips past. All four tires screech across the tarmac in a bootleg turn, then blue smoke boils from the rear wheels as he straightens out to chase after the plane.

A turbo V-8 emits a throaty howl as the Challenger's turbos surge and its speedometer leaps. The tail of the plane is just beginning to lift as he catches up. Carl grabs the shotgun, he steers with his left hand and lays the barrel on the sill of his open window. Linda sees that he's going to shoot, and she pops her seatbelt and climbs into the back seat so she can fire out that side too. Mel shrinks back into a corner, her eyes wide and her face pale.

Blam! Blam! Blam! Blam! Carl puts four slugs through the plane's right float, ripping out chunks of metal. The aircraft lurches and slews slightly as the float's rear wheel droops and deflates. Not seeing a better place to shoot, Linda fires through the plane's vertical stabilizer.

But they're not the only ones shooting. A cockpit door cracks open on the plane and a hand pokes out holding a big automatic pistol. The first round blasts down through the roof between Carl and Linda. Carl stomps the brakes and the shooter's next three rounds drill into the car's hood. The Challenger's engine falters and quits at the same moment that the hood flies up to whap into the windshield and wrap over the roof, rendering the view ahead opaque.

Carl brings the car to a screeching, shuddering halt. He and Linda jump out to see the Pilatus now a hundred feet above the end of the runway, banking left and climbing. Linda tentatively raises her rifle, but Carl pushes the muzzle down and shakes his head. As the plane circles the airstrip, they can see Viktor leaning out of the open door and looking down, trying to assess the damage to the floats.

"Won't be so easy to land now," Carl says. "'Specially on water. Float might rip right off."

"What can they do?" Linda asks.

"Make some kind of a crash-landing on the ground, and hope it's gentle. We might be able take another whack. But setting down on water by the general's yacht? Out of the question."

They hear the roar of a truck engine and turn to see Hank charge across the tarmac.

Hank pulls up, sees the Challenger's wrecked engine and hood. "Sounded like hell's-a-poppin' out here," Hank says.

"Was," Carl says.

"What now?"

"Exactly."

They all look back up at the Pilatus, which completes a long circle and then begins to lose altitude.

"The fuck?" Carl says.

It's flying back toward the Xanadu lodge and dropping steadily.

"What *can* they be thinkin'?"

Carl and Hank look at each other. "The helo!" Carl cries, as Hank shouts, "The chopper!" at the same instant.

"Into the truck!" Carl orders.

Linda hesitates and points at Melanie, who peers out the window at them. "And her?"

"Okay, both of you stay."

Carl runs around the front of the truck and jumps in the passenger seat. Hank already has it moving before Carl shuts the door.

Linda watches them speed off, and goes to the Challenger. She opens the door to sit beside Melanie on the rear seat. She picks up her hand and strokes it. "My sister," she says. "Did they do very bad things to you?"

Melanie stiffens, hesitates, nods.

"I am so sorry." Linda puts an arm over Mel, hugs her. "But that badness is now ended. It drifts away behind you. Soon things are better for you again, okay."

"No," Mel says, her voice quiet and convicted.

"Why not? Of course it goes better."

"Don't you see? "This... all of this... what happened. My fault. Mine."

"You say nonsense. Yes, maybe a mistake is made. But I do, too! I have much hurt feelings too, about one that you don't even know. Because of me a beautiful young man is dead! It is not my intent, yet even so."

"I betrayed him. Carl. Twice! The first time, when I snooped on his laptop. Maybe, three times. Again, when I made you come out here with me, just to go one up on him. So stupid! And... and then, I gave all of you away. Everyone. I was so scared!"

Melanie's face crumples just before she buries it in the crook of an elbow and she begins to sob.

Linda rubs her gently on the back. She doesn't know anything else to do, or what she could say to make her feel better.

～

A distant clatter of rotors mingles with a faint whine of turbines, and the Bell Long Ranger rises above the Xanadu lodge, its white hull sharply outlined against the pall of dark smoke.

Linda pats Melanie, gets out of the car and gazes into the sky with one hand shading her eyes. The Turco County chopper whaps straight overhead, then churns off to the southeast. Its fading clatter is replaced by the roar of Hank's barely muffled truck. She turns back to see it charge onto the airstrip. The truck lurches to a stop by the

Challenger and Carl leaps out.

"That goddam Viktor! Can't believe he can fly a plane, *and* fly a helo. Guy's seriously pissin' me off."

He strides to the car and leans in. "Mel. How're you doin'? Melanie?"

She shrinks back, keeps her eyes closed. He touches her arm lightly.

"Look, you've had it tough, that's real clear. But we're in a bad jam. Got to find out if you can do somethin' for us."

Her eyes open to slits.

"We need to get another plane up, track that helo, and radio for an assist on pursuit. So how 'bout it?"

Her eyes widen a bit more, yet her face stays frozen.

"C'mon, Mel," he pleads. "You're a pilot! Maybe it was a while back, but you can still take one a' these crates up, right? Look, we can radio in now, say the last direction we saw them head, but the general and Viktor are crafty enough to give us a bum steer. Plus, they're holdin' Dan. Soon as they find out he's not what they want, he's expendable. So, need to get a pro force on 'em soonest."

"Yes!" Linda says. "Melanie, please!"

She looks from one of them to the other.

"I'm *not* tellin' you, just shake it off. But… can you shove it to one side for an hour? You can do that, right?"

Melanie clears her throat, lifts her chin.

"Okay." Her voice sounds firm, but faint.

"Outstandin'! C'mon, Hank, let's pick over the airfleet."

They cram everyone and the weapons into the truck cab and motor toward the hangars.

"Here, Mel, some info to help you choose." Carl says, talking rapidly — all business now that there's a way to further his mission. "That Bell helo can hit about 120 knots, more or less. We need something a bit faster, good at flyin' low. The helo already had a flight this mornin', she likely did not refuel. So, top range has got to be no more than

300 klicks, maybe half that. Viktor will be at cruisin' speed, hugging' ground and hopin' to conserve fuel. Where he's headed? My best guess is the general's yacht. It should be in Mexican waters. Either Sea of Cortez or in the Gulf somewhere off Matamoros."

"Stop," Melanie says, pointing out the window. Her voice is low, toneless. "There. That's a Citabria. Not real quick, but fast enough. Simple, basic. I can fly it."

"Great."

They pile out. The aircraft has high wings and perches on a pair of front wheels with nacelles and a "taildragger" rear wheel. It resembles the boxy old Cessna 180s that she trained in. Mel lets the blanket flop off her shoulders, walks to the cockpit wearing only her medical gown, and pops its door.

"No keys," she says.

"Shit. Where'd they be? Pilot's got 'em?" Carl asks.

"Yep," Hank drawls. "But this is a secure, private airstrip. Office could hold a lockbox for all the keys, too."

Carl squints at Melanie. Her face stays blank.

"You okay to fly?"

"Said I would."

"Right. I'll look for keys."

"I'll do a pre-flight." Her voice is dull and toneless.

She walks to the front of the plane and begins to minutely inspect the propeller for any flaw.

Hank goes to the back of the truck, rummages in a box, then walks over to Melanie with a faded brown canvas coat. He helps her shrug it on over her medical gown, then he pats her gingerly on the back.

The Citabria's apron and hanger is adjacent to a small clapboard building with a small, glass-sided booth jutting up from its flat roof. And beside that observation cupola is a pole that brandishes a fluttering orange windsock, faded by the Texas sun to near-yellow.

It seems logical to Carl to check that place first. Within, bolted into a wall behind a desk, he finds a steel flatbox that looks a bit like an armored medicine chest. It has a brass padlock dangling from its door, but one slug from the SRM shotgun soon renders that feature irrelevant.

When he returns to the apron, Mel has just finished peering down into the fuel-tank caps on each wing. Hank has the nylon tie-downs arranged in neat coils on the concrete — not a necessary move, but it keeps him busy and he wishes to be of help. Arms crossed below her breasts, Linda stands nearby, talking, but it does not appear as if Mel pays much attention. Her movements are purposeful, yet trancelike.

Carl jogs up brandishing a key with a small chrome tag that has the Citabria's N-number engraved on it.

"Victory!" he exclaims.

Mel takes it without comment, opens the cockpit, sits. She keys the panel, finds the master switch, gives it a twist, and when the instrument panel lights up, raises a fingertip and taps on the fuel gauges.

Linda peers in the door. "Just two seats!" She sounds accusatory.

"Sorry," Carl says.

"You will save Dan," she asserts.

"Give it my best."

"And here? For us left, what is there to do?"

He thinks for a second. "You have a phone?"

"Yes," Linda says.

"Well, two," Hank says.

"Got a signal?"

"Sure," Hank says. "But a prob' may be, we ain't the only folks what got it."

"Meanin'?"

"Tall microwave tower over there, pokes up atop the prison at

Sojourn? Lot's of suspicion 'round here on just how and just how much thet stick sees use."

Carl thinks. "Gimme one of your phones," he says. And when Hank tugs his out and passes it over, he says, "Cool, okay it's on. How do I reach you?"

Hank's gaze flicks briefly to one side. "Try 'n' call Larry's number," he says. "That's t'other."

"Okay. You need to get far enough away that you at least have a chance your call will go through a different mast. Then call this number..." he recites it "... and you tell a guy who answers, Master BS, or anybody who works for him, everything you know about everything that's happened so far. Short version first, then a long. But you open with us chasin' after Andreyev and Viktor."

Hank lifts a shaggy eyebrow. "Kiddin' me."

"Nope. But don't worry. I'll also try to contact BS once we're up."

"So, meanin' to ask. This Russian guy I heard 'bout, yesterday. Andreyev, that's him, and he's a general?"

"Yes. Was a general. Now, independent."

"Fascinatin'."

~

Mel puts on a set of headphones equipped with a small boom mic, and Carl follows suit. She revs up the engine and moves the Citabria to the end of the runway. She switches on the UHF radio, sees its frequency, assumes it's the last one used and that it contacts all local fields. The approach is clear, there's apparently no one else flying in the vicinity, but she can't help herself, she has to follow procedure.

She announces her plane's ID number, then says, "I'm going onto the active at Xanadu, one-eight."

On the seat right behind hers in the Citabria's narrow cockpit, Carl marvels to find that the pads on the seat he's buckling into belong to a packed parachute.

"I get a canopy? Both seats have 'em?"

"Yes," Mel says. "'Citabria' stands for 'airbatic,' spelled backward. That's short for aerobatics. Our chutes are for backup, if a wing happens to rip off during a barrel roll. Not that I will try one."

"Cool! But… why did you announce our take-off?"

She flicks him a sharp look. "Some plane comes in, tries to land on top of us? How does our flight go then?"

"Ah."

Carl smiles to himself. An acerbic, argumentative Mel, that's the gal he remembers, and admires. He had felt impressed right from the moment they met, at the U.S. embassy down in Honduras, over a year ago. Familiar acts, like flying this plane, and making snarky comments, might help snap her psyche back into place. He does not doubt that captivity under Mark Nader and the general's crew was a dreadful challenge, much worse for her than it had been for him and Dan. But he decides not to ask about it. There'll be time for a "hot wash" debrief on that later. In a more relaxed setting.

She spins the plane around at the terminus of the runway, gives the windsock on the pole atop the FOB building a fleeting glance, sets the brakes by pushing with her toes atop the rudder pedals, runs up the engine RPMs, releases the brakes. The plane thrums down the tarmac, she checks airspeed, pushes forward a tad on the stick to raise the tail, and as the aircraft gathers speed, she pulls gently back and they lift into the sky.

Chapter 41

"How many minutes would you say we're behind 'em?" Carl asks. He already has an opinion, but he wants to keep her involved.

"Fifteen," Mel says. "At least."

"Tough to make up, but here's how. Guy like Viktor's gonna jag and jink, it's a survival instinct for him. Bottom line, though, is they want to get over the border and fly low in Mexico. If U.S. radar picks 'em up, may keep an eye on 'em, but chance of pursuit is minimal. If they're heading for the yacht, their main options are Sea of Cortez or the Gulf. Me, I opt for the Gulf. Already know they're sweet on Matamoros, could have a land base there for an alternate LZ. That town's also on the Gulf. So I'd say, take a straight bearing. Three angels up, so we score a bit of perspective, and full throttle."

"Aye-aye," she affirms, but her tone is sarcastic, making Carl smile again. Maybe the Mel he knows and loves is on her way back.

"No matter what, we're still rollin' dice," he observes. "So if we don't catch 'em, it ain't your fault. We'll just give it our best shot, okay?"

∼

The Río Grande is a gleaming ribbon that winds through a camo-cloth landscape splotched in tawny and olive-drab hues as it divides south Texas from northern Mexico. Carl finds a pair of Polaroid sunglasses in a pouch under his seat and puts them on. As he scans through the side cockpit windows — and tries to look forward by peering over Mel's shoulder and through the front windscreen — he spots a whirling dot that crosses the glittering river then slides away between low hills.

"Eyes on target!" he exclaims, putting an arm over her shoulder and pointing. "Over there, right, near two o'clock."

She banks the plane that way.

"This crate got GPS?"

"No, the avionics are too basic. No IFR gear at all."

"What's the FAA emergency channel?"

"On this radio?" She checks. "Basic, too. It'll be 121.5 megaherz."

"Put 'em on!"

She complies.

"May-… uh, no, this is an emergency, I am…" Carl says into his mic.

"*This is Brownsville Approach. Please identify your aircraft and the nature of the emergency,*" a voice crackles into the headset.

Mel starts to give the plane's N-number, altitude, course and speed, but Carl instantly overrides her.

"Never mind that! I am a federal law enforcement officer in close pursuit of an armed and airborne suspect, and I want you to patch me through to…"

"*Sir, if you're not the pilot of the aircraft, I need you to…*"

"Shut up. Patch me through to Naval Air Station Corpus Christi, and I mean, right now!"

"*I want the pilot to identify the nature…*"

"Goddammit, I am FBI deep undercover operator fifty-five ninety-nine. I am pursuin' a hijacked Turco County sheriff's helicopter with an abducted U.S. citizen on board, it just went over the border into Mexican airspace, and if you don't put me through to Corpus Christi this second, I guaran-damn-tee you the Secretary of Homeland Security will personally show up in your office a day or so from now and snatch your balls for a bowtie!"

More radio static mingles with a jumble of noises on the far end of the conversation, and then a different voice emerges clearly on the headset. Carl soon is rattling off a stream of military jargon mingled with code words and numbers, and receiving a similar litany of response. Melanie finds it incomprehensible, so she just focuses on flying the plane. As he speaks into the mic, Carl again points over her shoulder at the distant whirling disc of the helicopter's main rotor, then flattens his hand and makes a downward patting motion, indicating that she should bleed off altitude.

"Stay on this frequency," Carl says into the mic. "Keep the link open for us. Try flight-followin'. We may drop under effective range, but let's resume comms after we get over the Gulf. Feeb-duck fifty-five ninety-nine out."

"Cool beans," he tells Melanie, and heaves a sigh. "Finally got some backup on this bear hunt. So o... see where he's goin'?"

"Yes. He's weaving through the canyons, south of the river. Bearing averages out around 135 magnetic."

"Good. Drop to the deck, but stay on his six. Don't want to lose him, but also hope he won't spot us. Also, don't want Mexican air power involved, not just yet, and maybe not ever. If he's flat-hattin' toward the Gulf, odds are he's aimin' for the *Dean Swift*. That's Andreyev's yacht."

"I know."

After a second, Carl scratches his chin. "How'd you know?"

"I... just do."

He sees a ripple of tension in the muscles on the back of her neck and decides the real answer to that question isn't important enough to press for it.

"Maintainin' visual, that's key," he says. 'Might imagine our boys can pick up any ship on primary radar, but not if it's way offshore. And these dudes have skill at counter-measures, electronic and other, so pingin' 'em may be no slam-dunk. Now that I think on it, angles of that boat's superstructure had a stealth quality to 'em, wasn't just fancy design. Coat all that with a bunch of radar-absorbin' gunk, and it could look *way* smaller to our guys..."

He's telling her more than she needs to know, but he aims to chat Mel up, to bring her fully into the present.

Their altitude is just about three hundred feet now, and the Citabria slaloms through beige hilltops furred with scraggly vegetation — rounded peaks that cast wide black shadows across the narrow canyon under them. These give way to flat brown plains, segmented by roads and fences into towns and fields.

"Only 'bout an hour of daylight left," Carl says.

"I see the Gulf," Melanie says.

Through the windscreen, a surf-frosted shoreline appears, and beyond that a broad blue expanse that recedes into an indefinite horizon. The dot of their quarry windmills straight out over the sea.

"Drop and follow," Carl says.

She responds by going out low over the beach and chasing the white dot of the chopper into the blue gauze of distance.

After 20 more minutes of flight, another shape starts to appear in the early evening murk. It's the stern of a large vessel, topped by sloping superstructure and a low smokestack.

"And thar' she blows," Carl says. "Keep back, far enough so they likely can't see us, and spiral up, say to five or six angels. While I phone home, try to get bearin's on two points. One will be the mouth of the Río — the reverse of our course out, natch'. The other, I don't know, see if you can spot something, lights comin' on? A coastal town in Texas? Anything to the north... Give me those bearin's, our boys can triangle our twenty."

He starts talking mil-speak rapidly into the mic again. But the headphones remain silent except for a light buzz of static. "Down on that squelch," he orders, "They're not comin' back."

He tries the radio again. "Shit. *Nada.*" On a sudden inspiration, he pulls out Hank's cell phone, thumbs it on and sees the bars that indicate a signal, but when he dials a number, nothing happens. He looks down at the distant lozenge shape of the *Dean Swift.* The helicopter has landed on the yacht's fantail — the flat rear deck where he and Dan had seen the floatplane stored down in Manta. Dark specks of human figures move in around the chopper as its rotor ceases to whirl.

"Dammit all to hell, that yacht must be jammin' us," he says, "if it's ECM capable. Might know we're here now, too. I mean, they've got their own radar, of course. Maybe even know we were trackin' 'em."

"What do we do?" she asks.

"Out here on our own?" Carl rubs his jaw. "Once Dan is below decks, he's a hostage. And after they find out he don't know squat, it's a toss-up whether they'll keep him."

"So?"

"I'm closer to bein' a guy they actually want. And it's my fuck-up that Dan's in the jam he's in. So…" He pats the parachute that forms his seat cushion. "We can't just fly off, leavin' him in their clutches. Team loyalty is *numero uno*, forever. I've not abandoned a brother before, and won't start now! So, guess I need to jump on down there and bargain for Dan's life."

Melanie leans to a side, swivels her head as far as she can in order to peer back at him. She looks stricken.

"No…" she says.

"See no other choice. Hell, the cavalry's searchin' for us, hard and fast as possible. Andreyev and company might want to scoot, but I'm tellin' ya, they won't make it. Basically, I just need to buy the good guys some time."

"They can hurt you too!" Her voice abruptly turns frantic.

"Gotten hurt more'n a few times," Carl soothes. "Afterward, I always got better."

"Please…"

"Mel, ain't your call. Want to help? You can stall and confuse 'em a bit. Circle around at the ship's bow, make 'em look your way. Keep far enough off to mess with their aim, say four hundred yards. But make a few moves to distract 'em while I try to land on their stern. We get lucky, maybe I can sneak around and disable some key gear on the ship as I'm tryin' to get to Dan.

"Anyhow, after you put on a show for 'em, set your course for Corpus Christi. Head northeast, and home in on the city lights, as they come up. You've a choice of airfields, and hopefully enough daylight left to land easy. By then, your radio should be workin'. I mean, if they need to talk you down. Oh, and after you meet our boys in blue, hand 'em this…" He works himself around in the tight cockpit and pulls the envelope with the SD cards out of his waistband, pases it over her shoulder. "Tell 'em it's a lil' present from me."

She distractedly stuffs it in a pocket of the farm coat Hank gave her.

"Okay. Ready to crack the door. Give me about a thousand more altitude for insurance, and when I say the word, throttle back."

~

A blank expression has returned to Mel's face, her mouth is a firm, straight line.

Carl has the chute released from the seat-frame and the cockpit door half-open. He's squeezing by Mel's seat and preparing to exit the aircraft when she turns her head to stare at him. Her pale face is lit by a blended glow of dim lights on the instrument panel and auburn rays from a setting sun that wash in through the windscreen. Her eyes are an incandescent blue. For a moment, she is all the Mels that Carl has ever known, the pushy, combative gal he'd first met in Honduras, the slinky, twirling houri from the resort on Roatán, and the tough and ambitious journalist, avid to be badged as an FBI agent so she could hammer the bad actors she could only embarrass before…

"I love you," she says.

"Hey. Love you too, babe," Carl responds. "Don't worry. Stay hopeful, and you won't miss a chance to make it all better. 'Bout this time tomorrow, we should be sittin' 'round a table, relaxin' on a beach somewhere. Okay?"

She nods jerkily, whereupon tears spill from those brilliant eyes and track down her smooth cheeks.

He gives her an encouraging smile, a thumbs-up, then crawls out the door. With his short shotgun slung over his chest, his Polaroid sunglasses on his face, and the bulky chute on his back, he looks like an Airborne Ranger from World War Two. Clutching the wingspar, bowing his head to the propwash, he manages to plant both feet on the step atop a wheel nacelle. He glances back over one shoulder to ascertain location and height of the plane's tail. Nods through the door window at her. She throttles back, he lets go of the spar. With his limbs curved up and back arched, he falls away into the indigo sky.

Chapter 42

Carl calculates how long to freefall, decides to pull his ripcord early before trying to spiral down to land on the yacht — that will provide time to calculate the ship's course and speed relative to his own glide ratio. But he whips through a few maneuvers first, it's a way to use the harsh winds of his drop to scrub off inner tension before he enters the coming confrontation. So he flat-spins left, then right, goes into a stiff straight dive, resumes the basic arch to brake, before he tugs on the D-ring, feels the canopy shudder out of the pack and receives a swift hard yank from the harness.

He looks up to see the rectangular parachute flare and its long shrouds straighten, reaches up to grab the toggles, gives the 'chute a steer to the left and right, then makes his body pendulum as he feels out its performance.

Carl focuses on the *Dean Swift*, sees that Mel has put the plane into a long, steep dive aimed straight for the yacht. *That's my girl*, he thinks. *Clever! She makes more noise that way, grab more of their attention, plus she'll mask my approach…*

He also observes the ship's wake begin to lengthen and narrow. *Uh-oh, the Swift's putting on knots! Will I even be able to make it to the pad on her back deck? What if I don't? Long effen swim back to shore, for damn sure. I'd best spill air and fly straight to her…*

As he resets his trajectory, he sees Melanie buzz over the yacht at low altitude, no more than a hundred feet above a low stack that sheds a thin plume of exhaust. *Too close!* he thinks. She scoots along on a line from stern to bow, shoots out ahead of the boat, then uses all her collected airspeed to soar up into the sky. The bright cruciform shape of the Citabria, climbs and climbs into the evening sky, slows, seems to stop, hang, twist, like a pendant slung on a chain…

A hammerhead stall, okay, that's a beautiful move, all eyes on that boat will be on you, Mel, and you alone!

… then her plane falls away from the stall in a dropping turn that levels out for another close pass over the *Dean Swift's* decks. Except this one is really low, too close and far too low, it almost seems as if she aims to fly the aircraft right into the yacht's main bridge.

And then she does exactly that. The plane is instantly engulfed by a giant yellow-red carnation laced with black that blooms across the ship's entire foredeck. The thud of a great concussion rolls out into the gentle pastel haze of the coming night.

~

Carl is aghast, numbed, unbelieving.

"Oh my God, oh holy crap, Mel…" he mumbles. "Why…?!"

But he's now closing in on the ship's fantail and must swallow the hot lump of his anguish, cram anything that does not have to do with mission success into its own compartment, slam a lid and bolt it down. He must shrink his focus to tactical matters at hand. Carl knows this warrior's trick all too well; it's a default response. Over his years of service it's become a defining aspect of his psyche.

Alarm sirens hoot on the deck of the *Dean Swift*, and small figures begin to run about furiously, a few silhouetted against flames on walkways to the yacht's main bridge. Back on the rear deck — full of rampant activity just a moment before — sits the now-still and silent Bell helicopter. A gurney holding a sheet-draped form is nearby, as well as two figures in crew uniforms who seem confused about where to go or what they should do next.

As he sails in to land, Carl notices a tangerine blob just under the center of the aft rail and uses that as a point to aim for. When he's a hundred feet away, he identifies the blob as a lifeboat, painted international orange. It's secured to a roller track embedded in a wide notch in the stern. He glides in just above the thing, flares his chute, hits the deck running and pulls the cutaway releases on his harness. The yacht is heading into the wind, the parachute collapses, billows, flops over the side.

The two crewmen gaze up at the mayhem unfolding on the yacht's bridge, but then sense something odd transpiring behind them and spin around. Carl shoots between them, winging them both with the same burst of buckshot. They whirl toward each other, stagger and collide in a brief minuet. They fall to the deck. He runs up, takes a moment to ensure that the bandaged person on the gurney indeed is Dan, then inspects the crewmen. Both are bloody but still writhing.

One crewman sees Carl loom above him and tugs a folding knife out of a nylon belt sheath. He has zero chance to even get the blade open — Carl blasts him in the throat with another shell at close range, nearly tearing his head off. Seeing this, the second man has the sense to throw his hands up over his own head while it's still attached.

"Guy on the stretcher," Carl snaps, "what's his condition?"

"He… he… the general wants him to talk… we hit him up with naloxone, atropine…"

"Stay just as you are," Carl warns, "and you live."

He goes to the gurney while letting the shotgun drop onto its sling, raises a hand to Dan's cheek and shoves up an eyelid with his thumb. On its own, Dan's other eyelid begins to flutter and rise.

Carl abruptly feels himself being yanked backward, somebody else has seized the shotgun, is twisting and yanking on it, the sling's digging into his neck and binding his right arm, then the stock comes around and bashes him in the face as he tumbles. He feels the gun rip free as he falls, and when he rolls and comes up, his face drenched in blood from his re-broken nose, he finds himself looking at Viktor.

"I hear shooting," Viktor says, "and immediate, I feel like the idiot. You and I are not so finished, huh? But, soon!"

The shotgun muzzle aims straight at him. Carl's body freezes as his mind races. Any option to counter seems nonexistent. Then corners of Viktor's mouth quirk as his eyes seem to glitter. He drapes the shotgun's sling over his own neck, and lets the short weapon swing around to nest against his spine. Then he fakes a calf kick, spins on his left foot when it lands, and bends over to deliver a back kick with his right foot to Carl's abdomen.

Carl barely has time to tense his stomach muscles, arch and roll away from the blow. *It's personal,* he thinks. *Vik wants hand-to-hand!"*

Carl comes up on his feet, adopts a fighting stance, two-steps toward Viktor, throws a crescent kick, then snaps a roll forward and performs a leg sweep to take him down. Viktor nimbly leaps over the move, dodging to one side. Carl rolls up to his feet, sees his antagonist coming at him with a flurry of punches, and immediately drops and rolls backward. Viktor tries to kick him, and Carl comes up under his leg with a kick of his own and Viktor flops hard onto his back.

Both come onto their feet and circle each other. Carl is still groggy from the blow with the gun butt, knows he can't take another smash to the face or he's done. Viktor tries a right jab followed by a left hook. Carl twists and closes as he ducks under the hook, delivers a left elbow to the ribs, a left hammer fist to the temple, and tries to land a cupped right hand to Viktor's ear but misses.

Viktor continues his evasive action by spinning around, and lands a heel strike on Carl's left kidney. Carl stumbles and sags as Viktor spins again and hits him with a roundhouse kick to the lower back that knocks him over on his side. Then two things happen simultaneously. Carl feels something bruise his thigh when he hits the deck and remembers what he's got stuffed deep down in his pants pocket — the general's little "popgun" auto pistol. And he hears a rumble and sees something long and white and flapping shoot across the deck to bash into Viktor's hips.

It's the gurney, and Dan is pushing it.

Viktor falls over from the impact, and Carl comes to one knee, drawing the pistol. He snaps the slide and as Viktor rolls and rises, shoots him in the left shoulder. Viktor claps one hand to the wound, whereupon Carl shoots him in the other shoulder and Viktor drops. Carl sees Dan lying near the overturned gurney, sees the living crewman running away from the melee. He stands up and steps over to Viktor — who glares up at him, eyes shining with fury.

He didn't blast me with the shotgun when he had the chance, Carl thinks. *He chose a stand-up brawl.*

"Pro courtesy backatcha, Viktor. So, here," Carl says. Then he kneecaps him.

He grabs the sling and yanks the shotgun away as Viktor shrieks dire Balkan curses. He goes over to Dan. Whatever deep reservoir Dan tapped to make his charge with the gurney now seems utterly drained. He lies on his back, breathing raggedly, his eyes rolling slowly in their sockets. Carl hauls him to a sitting position, squats, gets Dan's arm over his shoulders, sticks a hand between his thighs, and hoists him up into a fireman's carry.

At that moment, floodlights switch on, washing the vessel's rear deck in a blinding glare. There's several rapid pops of gunfire, and Carl unleashes two rounds of buckshot at those muzzle flashes. The shooting pauses, and he carries Dan in a crouching sprint toward the lifeboat. Once there, he lays Dan down, clicks the magazine to the next tube of buckshot, and unleashes more rounds at the floodlights, wiping them out.

He turns to open the lifeboat hatch, finds that Dan is already reaching up over his head to grasp it. Carl opens it for him, climbs over Dan, pulls him in afterward, slams and dogs the hatch. He doesn't bother to strap Dan into a seat, simply lays him on the floor, and jumps up into the control cupola. Bullets have begun to *whack* through the fiberglass, so he bends over in the captain's seat as he pumps a hydraulic lever for the release mechanism, and then the lifeboat is scooting down its track rails at a rapid clip.

As the boat plunges into the sea, Carl hears a yelp from Dan who takes some of the impact on his head and shoulders as he slides forward to jam against its front bulkhead, and all the windows go dark. The orange hull bobs to the surface, and the crack of splintering fiberglass resumes as gunmen on the yacht once again find their mark. Carl scans the control panel, figures out how to start up the boat's two-cylinder diesel, gets it going, and the lifeboat begins to putt away from the *Dean Swift* at its paltry top speed.

Their cabin's still getting smacked by rounds from the yacht, and Carl jumps down to lie beside Dan on the floor.

Dan turns bleary eyes toward him. "What happened to Tank?" he asks in a hoarse voice. "How the fuck we end up on a boat?"

"You've been gone a while, brother," Carl tells him. "Like the Good Book says, all will be revealed. For now, just pray those morons don't realize they should aim at our waterline, okay?"

"And… what happened to your face? Jeez… looks like someone belted you with a coal shovel…"

"Peace, dog. Chill. Rest yourself."

The *Dean Swift* has its bridge on fire, and law enforcement aircraft have started to close in on it from the mainland. Coming about to chase a lifeboat is not a top priority. It's not even a briefly considered option. Gunfire gradually dwindles, stops.

~

Carl tries to make Dan comfortable on an improvised mat of life jackets. He opens supply lockers, feeds them both with emergency rations and water. An hour passes before he dares to use more than a flashlight, and switch on the boat's interior and exterior lights. Even then, he waits until he hears the whoosh of jet aircraft and the clatter of helicopters passing over them in the black night sky before he switches on the emergency beacon and the boat's VHF radio, and attempts to contact elements of the U.S. armed forces.

Chapter 43

Dan walks down South Street in the ritzy Georgetown neighborhood of Washington, DC. He's wearing a black wool peacoat, has his left arm in a sling, a watchcap is tugged low over the band of gauze on his head. He checks the polished brass plates mounted on brick facades until he finds the number he's searching for, and looks up through skeletal tree branches to see a glass-walled penthouse that sits perched on a corner facing the Potomac. He goes up a set of granite steps to the entry, locates the intercom buttons, sees one next to the name MELANIE OLSON in ornate black calligraphy, and presses it. No response. After a minute, he presses it again.

"Yeah?" a voice grates from the speaker.

"It's me."

A lock on the front door clunks, he shoves open a heavy walnut portal lighted with crystal panels, enters. Walks a thick carpet runner to the elevator, takes a smooth and soundless ride up to the seventh floor.

Only two doors face this hallway, and one stands open. Dan walks in, looks around Melanie's luxury condo, tastefully done up in shades of cream and subtle off-whites, but doesn't see Carl, and then he does. Carl sits in a big Pietro Constantini lounge chair, turned to face the expanse of glass that gives a sweeping view of Roosevelt Island, as well as a fringe of shoreline where tree limbs still bear a few russet streaks of foliage.

Dan hears a clink of ice cubes, and walks around the chair.

"Hey."

"What's that?" Dan points.

"Dose of brain oil."

"Thought you didn't drink."

"Don't. However, I *do* find a vodka gimlet sometimes helps me to mind my own business. Care for one?"

Dan studies his friend. Carl's clothing is spotted and wrinkled, his hair is unkempt, his beard has grown out into a crop of ginger stubble spread across his cheeks and prominent jaw. Dark, baggy pouches lurk beneath his eyes, and these are underscored by a broad white plaster splayed across his face — much like the nose casts worn by Dan and Linda in Key West over a month ago.

Carl's appearance, even when casual, had always been tidy and well-considered, so this disturbs Dan. But what really bothers him is observing Carl's slack, dispirited posture. The vital tension, the aura of muscular vigor that has animated Carl during all the time that he's known him, seems to have evaporated.

"Sure. I'll take a drink," Dan says. *Better to join him than confront him right now. Get further inside his situation that way....*

"Over there."

Carl points an index finger from the hand clutching his glass. On the kitchen's white marble counter, Dan sees a half-empty fifth of Belvedere vodka and a pint of Rose's lime juice.

He fills a tumbler with cubes from a dispenser on the fridge door, gives himself a generous pour of booze, adds a splash of Rose's, and stirs his drink by rotating the ice cubes with a finger. He walks back to Carl, sees a hassock that matches the chair's upholstery, kicks it over to the front of the chair, and sits.

"So. What do you think?" Dan asks.

"'Bout what?"

"'Bout whatever the hell it is that you're thinking about, natch."

Carl gives a slight smirk, pauses. "Want a do-over," he finally says.

"Hey. Don't we all..."

"No, I mean, really. On this last go-round, seems like I made nothin' but bad calls from launch to landin'."

Dan shakes his head. "Hindsight," he says. "I know the urge to Monday-morning-quarterback. We all do the ol' if-I-knew-then-what-I-know-now, but that's basically impossible. Consequently, it's unproductive. Beat yourself up enough that way, makes it hard to get going again."

Carl takes a swallow from his glass. "Spoken like someone who got to live," he says.

Dan thinks that over and sighs. "You *didn't* kill her," he says.

Carl grants him only another icy smirk.

"Y'know, one thing was perfectly clear about the Olson sisters from the git-go, down in Honduras," Dan continues. "Both of 'em were damaged. Doesn't mean they didn't have a ton of wonderful qualities, in addition to looking like major babes. But they still were limping through life. Summer was a sweetie, but a goddam space-case too! Melanie seemed more able and dialed-in, but a ton of fragility lurked below her feisty side. Which is what made her so unpredictable, wouldn't you say? I recall one time you said that if Mel was a super-hero, she'd be Batty-Girl. Remember that?"

"Don't speak ill of the dead. And *you* should remember something. Mel went out with major force. Didn't act as she did, neither of us might be here right now, bozo."

"I acknowledge that. All true. But what I'm trying to do, is maybe help you cope."

Carl's smile is slight and sad, but this time it's genuine. He holds his glass between both palms and rotates it slowly. "It's a hard thing to lose somebody, and only then realize how much you loved her." His speech is only slightly slurred. "Got to say, I sure miss the hell out of Melanie."

Dan nods.

"And about her deeper vulnerability, sure. Dealing with her feistiness, yeah, she was hell on wheels some days. Arguing was how we spent most of our waking hours. But I also saw all the other stuff, which is what made me love her and want to protect her, even from herself." He drinks. "Made a botch of that job, huh?"

"Nothing occurs for just one reason," Dan says. "Like I say, it's easy to call any move a mistake afterward, then beat yourself up. But! Did you lure Mel into snooping on your laptop? Did you ask her to steal confidential intel and run to Texas to play ace reporter? No, on both counts. Those were Mel's calls. That was her, setting herself up for trouble on her own."

"Right," Carl responds. "But I did pretty much make her fly that plane out to the general's yacht."

"Not knowing what would happen."

"Uh-huh. However, I *did* know that she'd been in the grip of Mark Nader and the general's crew. I could see they'd hurt her and terrified her, bad. But I made her suck it up and..." He can't continue to speak. He takes one hand from his drink glass and presses its thumb and bunched fingers against his eyes.

"Carl, you were *both* on-mission. She became a casualty. But far from collateral, you know? Sad choice. But it was hers, and she made it. Don't dismiss the idea that she wanted to strike back at people that hurt her, score vengeance, and it was her only card to play. Yeah, but what a biggie. At one go, she stopped the yacht dead in the water, enabled a huge bust, and let you haul my sorry ass out of harm. Look at it one way, and it's a horrible suicide. Look at it another way, and she's a *kamikaze* warrior. Still crazy, but..."

"Right," Carl says, taking his hand away from his eyes. "I had to save somebody, and it turned out to be you. Because I do remember the guy who dove into an underwater knife fight off the coast of Honduras to rescue me, and it was payback time. Yeah, let's take a flyin' leap here and say this is all *your* fault. 'Cos if you didn't choose to do what you did back then, I wouldn't have to do what I just did. So, fuck you, asshole."

"Now you're talkin' like you make more sense."

Carl shakes his head, takes a deep breath. "Let's try to change the topic. Don't feel like goin' on 'bout it anymore. Move to somethin' else. Where's Linda? What's she up to?"

"Out in West Texas, spending her share of Mel's money. Linda's got her own cross to bear. Feels to her like it's her fault Hank's nephew Larry got shot. Says that she hopes to make some amends by funding a records search and a lawsuit, to help the rest of the Purdys get their whole ranch back. With the Nader family line ending up as a lil' splotch out in the cactus, they have a good chance. Texas Department of Criminal Justice says it hopes to take over Sojourn, so if the Purdys win, the state needs to buy the real estate off of them. Won't come cheap. Probably recoup all the costs of a title search, legal action, and then some."

Carl scratches at his stubbled chin. "'Nother incredible part of this whole deal. Melanie bequeathin' us each a cool million like that. Must've updated her will over the past year."

"Smart thing for any of us to do. Well, she had the dough to give. Her ex might not dig her passing around so much of what she won in their divorce, but he no longer has any say. She had all her i's dotted. You hear any news about our buddy, the general?"

"Feds have him jugged in the max brig at USP Lee. So far, he's keeping mum. E-records and codes I grabbed out of his room disappeared in a puff of smoke with Melanie, so they're seein' what can be rummaged out of computers left on the *Swift* and at Sojourn. One thing we don't need to worry about is diplomatic pressure from the Russians. Putin's tickled pink that we took Andreyev down. 'Sides, the general became a citizen of Malta. Wanna guess how much clout Malta's got in the hallowed halls of DC? Ever hear a moth fart?"

"Viktor?"

"Still haven't found him. 'Course, he could've acted like an honorable Roman soldier, slit his wrists and gone over the rail. But that's not his way. He's a guy who will *always* try to bounce back for another round. Sees a major defeat as only a minor setback. Tough customer."

"Ha, remind you of anyone you know?"

Carl grunts. "If we could scoot off in a lifeboat, he might've, too. Would only need a few loyal minions to drag his ass onto it. Come to think of it, their go-fast, they probably had it up on davits. Make one helluva great escape pod." He swills from his glass, drains it, raises it, looks at Dan. "'Nother?" he asks.

Dan looks at him. He's gotten Carl talking, and pulled him at least a millimeter out of his funk. But drinking at all — much less drinking the hard stuff to excess — is so strange that he has to worry about the slope Carl is on. *Or maybe even plunging down*, he thinks.

"At least we kludged a few bits of a happy ending out of the mess," Dan says.

Carl snorts. "Not an endin', only an outcome. Temporary, at best. This shit never cleans up to stay. Always more."

He absently tilts his glass and slurps. Only a loose clump of ice cubes slides down to tap against his open mouth.

THE END

Deadlines, Paul McHugh's first crime novel, won a best mystery prize from the National Indie Excellence Awards, and another from the Bay Area Independent Publishers Association. *The Blind Pool* draws from his years as an investigative journalist and outdoor sports editor at the *San Francisco Chronicle,* as well as his international travels. McHugh has reported on U.S. Navy SEALs, corporate malfeasance, and high-risk, outdoor adventure. He is a hunter, surfer, trail runner, poet, and husband. *The Blind Pool* is his third novel and sixth book. Find out more at **www.paulmchugh.net**